First published 2016
by Black & White Publishing Ltd
29 Ocean Drive, Edinburgh EH6 6JL

1 3 5 7 9 10 8 6 4 2   16 17 18 19

ISBN: 978 1 78530 011 0

A CIP catalogue record for this book is available from the British Library.

ALBA | CHRUTHACHAIL

Typeset by Iolaire Typesetting, Newtonmore
Printed and bound by Nørhaven, Denmark

THE DOLOCHER

CAROLINE BARRY

BLACK & WHITE PUBLISHING

THE DOLOCHER

For Neil. For everything.

*

Thank you to Emer Fallon and thank you to my editor
Karyn Millar.

Contents

1

Black Dog Prison, Dublin, 1756

'Well, is the bastard crying out for a priest yet?'

Martin Coffey sauntered down the crumbling steps into the cellar, flung his satchel down and leaned his gun against the dripping wall.

'Y'er late,' Boxty grumbled.

'Got delayed.'

'It's not on, Martin. I've been sitting here, freezing me balls off when I could have been down in the Cock and Hen this last hour.' Boxty's head craned forward, his chin jutting at an angle. Martin snorted and fidgeted in his coat pocket.

'Here, for your trouble, ye old codger,' he grinned, flinging a quart of whiskey into Boxty's skinny lap. 'You're such a woman. I'd a bit of business to do.' Martin flicked his hand towards the red door. 'And I'm not in a humour to listen to him whinging the night either.'

Boxty fumbled at the jar, unplugged the cork and smiled, holding the promise of whiskey at a tilt to his narrow lips.

'God bless yer black soul, Martin me darling.' He raised the jar a fraction making a toast to the inmate locked behind the red door. 'Here's to the devil.'

'Aye,' Martin chimed in, 'and his bastard crew.'

Boxty took a long deep slug, his Adam's apple bobbing in his scrawny neck. He didn't cough or wince at the tart malt sliding down his grizzled gullet; instead he took three deep gulps, sucked in a cold sharp breath and in one bony movement wiped his mouth and ran his hand through his thick grey hair. 'That's the cure,' he mumbled.

'Yer nerves at ya?' Martin snipped, tugging his satchel open to fetch a bunched-up handkerchief and a knife.

'It's him.' Boxty nodded towards the red door. 'He's not the usual.'

'Isn't he?' Martin wasn't interested.

Boxty's watery eyes widened in the grim torchlight; he was surrounded by damp shadows, his boots grimy from the mud floor, his skin a faintly bluish colour from the stagnant air. Martin glanced at the flaking red door. Above the thick lock and iron ring handle was a window space studded with bars. Behind the bars he could see the pale glow of a single candle flickering. Boxty took another swig and licked his lips, savouring the warm heat of the whiskey. His eyes flicked anxiously into the pale gloom of the cell. He leaned towards the back of Martin's head and hissed in a loud whisper.

'Quiet as a church mouse he's been. Sittin' in there just staring. Never seen the like.'

'Makes a change.' Martin stood up, wiping the knife blade in the folds of his dirty coat. 'Usually they're weeping for their mammies, all snots and remorse.'

Boxty shook his head. 'None of that. I tell you, Martin, it's unnerving. He hasn't moved a muscle. Hasn't said a thing. Giving me the shivers, so he is. There's something not right about it.'

Boxty gripped the butt of his gun so tight his knuckles gleamed white. Beneath his papery skin blue veins popped in his forehead. He watched Martin unwrap the balled hanky, his attention momentarily distracted.

'What's that?'

Sitting in the palm of Martin's hand, surrounded by an unwashed nose rag, was a fuzzy, russet globe.

'It's a peach,' Martin smirked, holding the fruit out so that it glowed in the dusky light. He winked at Boxty, cocking his head conspiratorially before striding to the red door and looking into the cell where Olocher was sitting, half his body hidden in black shadow.

'See this, Olocher?' Martin's blue eyes glinted, his huge jaw moving up and down over his tight smile as he lifted the peach towards the bars. 'You should have seen the sweet little thing that gave me this. Christ her titties were pert. Young little squirmer she was. Tasty.'

Martin sniffed the peach's soft perfumed skin before his thick tongue suggestively licked the dimple where the stalk would have been.

'You liked to diddle them young, didn't ye, Olocher? No more of that for you, eh?'

Olocher didn't flinch. He sat looking into the gloom, the pale candlelight picking out half the hollows in his face, his eye sockets, his temple, his cheek, the cleft in his chin. The fingers of his left hand spread over his left knee. Each finger long and slender and pale, delicately carved, imbued with a hint of precision, like perhaps they could do fine lacework. Martin's eyes glinted like a hook flashing on water. His upper lip curled, exposing the telltale black spots of gum disease.

'What I don't get is why you had to cut them open, slosh about in their entrails. You see, I don't get that.'

Olocher's left eyelid dropped a fraction, but his brow remained smooth, broad and unreadable.

'Never mind, eh?' Martin grinned now, his haphazard teeth glistening with yellow spittle. 'You'll swing for it tomorrow. Isn't that right, Boxty?'

Boxty pulled the jar swiftly from his mouth. 'Off bright and early to Stephen's Green. There's a gallows waiting for you there.'

Martin leaned against the red door, his elbow resting on the ledge where the bars ended. He slid the blade of the knife

3

through the peach's soft flesh, cutting a segment and gliding it into his mouth.

'You must have really upset the magistrate, Olocher,' he said, his lips wet with juice. 'Mustn't he have, Boxty?'

'Turned the magistrate's stomach, so he did.'

Martin cut another peach segment, flinging it into the dark wet pocket of his mouth.

'So the magistrate has the last laugh arranging to hang you of a Wednesday.'

'Rolling about in his wig and his cape laughin', so he is,' Boxty agreed.

'If it'd have been Tuesday, you'd have been fine. But Wednesday, eh, Boxty?'

'Should be a sight. Hard to know which way it will turn out.'

Martin pointed the blade, the peach juice dripping along his index finger and sliding into the thick crevices of his gnarled hands.

'You see,' he said, using the blade like a conductor's baton, 'you're to be hung by Fuck-it-up Farley. And if there's one man that can fuck up a hanging it's . . .'

'Farley,' Boxty cheered, raising his whiskey jar.

'Last week he cut the rope too short, took half an hour for the poor sod to die.' The blade danced in the candlelight, the coating of peach juice making it glint and gleam. 'All that spitting and choking and kicking of feet.'

Martin's eyes wrinkled at the edges as he gleefully related the details. Boxty chuckled as he drank.

'Poor bastard danced a full thirty minutes at the end of the rope. Talk about capering the Kilmainham minuet.'

'But the worst was two weeks ago. Wasn't it, Boxty?'

'Disaster.'

'Farley made the drop too long. There was a big burly lad due to be hung and Fuck-it-up Farley doesn't calculate the weight properly. He makes the rope too long.'

4

Martin cocked his head to one side, throwing Boxty a quick glance. Both men sniggered.

'Tell him what happened,' Boxty said.

'The hatch opens, down the prisoner drops, keeps going and snap . . . the head is ripped off him. His body splatters to the ground, twitching like an eel, spine poking about looking for the skull, blood everywhere and his head rolling under the ladies' skirts. I swear half the men watching threw up.'

Martin laughed, his enormous shoulders moving up and down. Suddenly a pale hand reached through the bars and grabbed the knife from Martin's peach-scented fingers. Martin bolted backwards, his eyes fixed on the half-lit prisoner moving away from him into the shadows. Boxty snapped to his feet, pulling his gun upright. The whiskey jar clanged to the floor and rolled noisily against the wall. Boxty stared at the back of Martin's skull, his watery eyes blinking, a tight whistling sound wheezing in his chest. For several seconds neither man spoke nor moved. The air in the cellar seemed to contract as the two men stood frozen, staring through the barred window into the poorly lit cell. The gun in Boxty's hands shook. He peered fearfully over Martin's huge shoulder and saw in the square of frail candlelight Olocher's taut face looking back at him. Motionless. Something altered in Martin's stance. His spine lengthened, his chest broadened. He was shaping up, measuring his own wit against Olocher's audacity. Boxty said nothing but he could see the taunt forming in Martin's frame before the words ever came out.

'Do it,' Martin whispered. The words snaked through the choking damp, through the stench of pitch and the noxious fumes emanating from the slop bucket standing in the corner. Still Olocher didn't move. One side of his face hidden by darkness, the other softened by the meagre candle flame. He stood, chiselled by the diffuse light into a sculptural being, something impenetrable in his eyes, his mouth softly separated, nothing resolute nor harsh nor panicked about him. No single bead of sweat slid from his hairline. No rush of blood to his cheeks, no pulse throbbed in the vein in his neck, no quick flick or darting expression, just a granite stillness, dark and magnetic as a deep hole staring out of the gloom.

'Go on. I dare ya,' Martin goaded, his tongue drily touching his lower lip. 'Go on, ya coward.'

Boxty couldn't move. His breath came in short stabs, wheezing in the suffocating damp. Martin was faltering. His voice grew louder, but his tone was tinged with fear.

'Do it,' he bellowed. And Olocher's hand snapped to his throat, smearing the pale candlelight in a sudden stream of crimson red.

'Jesus,' Boxty gasped. He stared at Olocher's face as it fell backwards, and the bursting gush of blood as it splattered on the prison wall.

2

The Apothecary Shop, Fishamble Street

'Here we are. Sorry for the delay.'

Merriment O'Grady emerged from the small anteroom, her long auburn hair flowing in thick tresses about her shoulders. She was a fine, handsome woman, almost forty, with keen blue eyes, pale skin and a spattering of freckles that ran across her nose giving her complexion the fragile quality of an eggshell. However, at first glance the most obviously striking thing about Merriment was that she was wearing men's clothes. She wore buttercup-coloured breeches, an ornate buttoned-up waistcoat dyed a deep sloe berry and her lace shirt was high-necked. She had turned up the cuffs of her sleeves, rolling them above her elbows so as not to damage the fine lace trim as she mixed, siphoned, boiled and chopped in her workshop. Long used to being gawped at, Merriment was oblivious to the fact that she stood out. She popped a small vial on the counter and watched as two young ladies came towards her, one carrying an ornate bulbous bottle filled with a hay-coloured liquid.

'Take two drops with every meal,' Merriment told the taller girl.

'Thank you,' the taller girl replied, holding up the engraved bottle she was carrying for Merriment to see. 'How much is this perfume?'

As she asked the question, the door to the shop opened and a tall man, wearing his cloak collar high, tapped his hat lower over his brow and wandered to the side counter pretending to be looking through the small cures packaged in the drawers there. Merriment checked out his profile. Aware that she was looking at him, the man turned his back and stepped up to a glass cabinet. Merriment smiled at the tall girl, her eyes filled with a curious kind of glee.

'You've smelled it?' she asked.

The tall girl nodded, glancing guiltily at her shorter friend.

'You've excellent taste,' Merriment said.

'That means it's expensive,' the short girl said.

'Five shillings.'

'Dear God! What's in it?'

The tall girl laughed with shock. Her friend opened the bottle and brought it to her nose, inhaling deeply, her eyelids closed.

'Smells about five shillings' worth,' she agreed.

'It's a rare nectar milked from the stamen of the rootless desert flower called the bud of Jericho.'

As Merriment spoke she was aware that the man pretending to be absorbed by the instruments in the glass cabinet kept shifting impatiently. He glanced anxiously out the window, then over at the counter, looking quickly away whenever Merriment tried to catch his eye.

The short girl gave the tall girl the bottle.

'Sniff it, Stella,' she said. 'And take comfort in the fact that you have a good nose. Come on, pay the lady. I'll put this back.'

Stella did as she was told. She watched her friend take the perfume away and resigned herself to having a small bar of rose soap and a vial of concentrated drops to help her digestive system.

'Thank you,' she said, sliding four pennies across the polished oak countertop.

'Not at all,' Merriment said, waiting patiently with her thumbs crooked into her slender waistcoat pockets for her next customer to turn around and stop skulking by the glass case. The man didn't move. He waited for the bell over the doorway to chime and the latch to click before he approached Merriment.

'Morning, sir.' Merriment kept her thumbs hooked into her waistcoat pockets, faintly amused by the man's keenness to shadow out his features and hide his face. She could tell he was aristocratic from the impatient way he strode towards her; that and the fact that his cloak was lined with silk, his walking stick was capped with a silver mermaid, and his cologne was made by an expensive Parisian perfumery and smelled of spiced lemon with an overnote of cucumber.

'Take me to see Mister O'Grady at once,' the man demanded.

'Certainly.'

Merriment came out from behind the counter and made for the front door, giving the man enough time to initially grimace at her breeches before becoming intrigued by her legs. Merriment flicked the *Open* sign, latched the door and pointed to the ante-room behind the counter.

'Go through, sir.'

The man snorted disapprovingly out of habit and marched into the crowded anteroom. It was filled to the brim with glass jars, pickled roots, hanging herbs and bubbling in a large copper retort on the fire was a thick greenish liquid that stank of sour, fermented offal. There were two tables and two simple chairs, both pressed against the wall. Merriment stepped in behind the man and shut the door.

'You're O'Grady!'

It wasn't a question, the man just couldn't help himself.

'Take off your breeches,' Merriment said, fetching a leather-bound ledger from an open drawer.

The man didn't move; instead he stared a long, harsh, accusatory stare, examining the frank, open expression on Merriment's face.

'I am sure you came here on a recommendation?' Merriment suppressed her amusement, observing the tinge of purple

9

colouration around the man's mouth and the high white crescents of his polished fingernails.

'You're a woman,' the man hissed, his disgust faltering beneath a wave of humiliation.

'I appreciate that this may be something of a sensitive issue.'

'Beresford never said . . .' The man's grey eyes looked pitifully about. A fine sheen glistened on his face.

'What is your name?' Merriment asked.

'Rochford.'

The word was out before the man could deny his identity. He tightened his lips, suddenly furious at his own indiscretion.

'I mean . . .' he fumbled, wishing to hell he had never listened to Beresford in the first place. Merriment lost interest in his discomfort. She placed the ledger on the free table and stood square before Rochford.

'I don't have time to cajole you into an examination,' she said. 'This is a confidential meeting, Mister Rochford.'

'Lord.'

'Lord Rochford. I run an apothecary shop and have private clientele. Now, if I want to have repeat business it behoves me to be discreet, to operate under the strictest code of confidentiality.'

'But a handy woman.' Lord Rochford rolled his eyes despairingly. 'A bloody handy woman.'

He flung off his cloak, jigged from foot to foot and pulled open his breeches, exposing a shrunken penis and swollen testes.

'It burns when I piss. Is it syphilis?' His face distorted with terror.

'Is there a discharge, greenish?'

Lord Rochford nodded miserably.

Merriment leaned towards his crotch, gingerly moving his flaccid member to one side.

'Worst case of gonorrhoea I've seen in a long time.'

'It has me demented. The whore that gave it to me was fresh from London, may she die thrice from a triple load of pox. Damn bitch robbed me. Is this going to kill me? Has she shortened my days?'

'You're not going to die. I'm going to make you a salve.'

Relieved, Lord Rochford sat down, his breeches about his knees. He removed his hat and mopped the beads of sweat sprouting on his forehead with a lavender hanky.

'I'm also going to give you this.' Merriment opened a press and produced a small box. She threw it towards Lord Rochford. It landed on his naked lap.

'It's called Misses Phillips' Engine,' Merriment said as she broke the seal on a ceramic jar and with a small wooden spoon began stirring the contents, adding in drops from various vials and watching the waxy mixture loosen. 'You need to use it.'

Lord Rochford opened the ornate tin and gingerly picked up a long strand of gut between his manicured forefinger and thumb.

'A condom.' He winced. 'A damn condom.'

'Better than the pox,' Merriment said flatly. 'It's a proven preventative. You can wash it out, reuse it. You fasten it to your pizzle with the velvet ribbon, should be in there.'

'Wash it.' Lord Rochford flung the sheep gut back into the box and snapped on the lid.

'Keep sleeping with whores and you will get syphilis, just a matter of time. Misses Phillips' Engine is your only way of avoiding it. Well, that or abstinence.'

Lord Rochford snorted. Even without gonorrhoea he was a bad-tempered man, always dissatisfied with the incompetence he had to endure, always certain of some slight, some oversight, some failing on the world's part that was guaranteed to annoy him. He was spoiled and indulged and that made him cruel. But he needed a cure so he bit his tongue and listened to Merriment lecture him on best practice when swiving.

'Here we are.' Merriment brought him an amber wax that

stank of camphor. 'Rub this on. It'll cause blistering before it soothes the inflammation.'

'What the hell is in it?'

Merriment laughed lightly, a soft bubbling laugh that made her suddenly seem very young.

'*Clematis erecta*,' she said, winking audaciously at Lord Rochford like he got the joke. Lord Rochford stared back blankly.

'*Clematis erecta*,' Merriment repeated. 'Upright Virgin's Bower. Ironic cure considering the ailment?'

Lord Rochford stubbed his clean index finger into the soft wax and began cautiously applying it to his swollen testes.

'Very droll,' he said. 'Beresford told me you had an odd sense of humour. Typical that he should remark on your wit and not on your sex.'

'We go back a long way,' Merriment commented, opening the ledger and fetching an ink and quill from under one of the retorts bubbling by the back door. She carefully noted Lord Rochford's ailment in one column and her proposed cure in another, working out a price.

'We met at sea, when he captained the *Redoubtable*. He was a fine sailor.' She scribbled a bit more. 'You may have to come back for a second dose.'

Lord Rochford nodded bleakly, staring down at his sore orange testes.

'That will be one and six.' Merriment finished up her accounts. 'And may I advise you keep away from the tarts, at least give your pizzle time to recover, and to eat plain food, nothing fermented.'

'No wine! For how long?'

'At least ten weeks.'

'Jesus Christ. No tipping, no drink for ten weeks. Bloody hell.'

Lord Rochford buttoned up his breeches and fumbled in his purse for coin. The world had failed him yet again. He handed Merriment the money and grabbed his hat.

'Come back in three weeks. And it will be three shillings for Misses Phillips' Engine.'

'I won't need it.'

'When the ten weeks are up and you're better, you'll need it.'

Lord Rochford looked scornfully at the ornate pink tin trimmed with fake lace and pinched his mouth shut. He silently handed over three shillings and Merriment wrapped the tin box in brown paper.

'Good day,' she smiled, handing Lord Rochford his mermaid-tipped cane.

There was a thump from the yard outside. Merriment glanced behind her despite the fact there was no window in the room. She turned back and smiled at Lord Rochford, waving him through to the shop and escorting him out the door. He mumbled a goodbye and stormed off disgruntled because life had let him down. Merriment re-latched the shop door and paced through the anteroom, pulling open the back door to see what had made the noise in the yard.

There, standing on a mound of rubbish, barefoot and bedraggled, was a little girl. She sifted through the rubbish with her hands, pulling out a gelatinous wad of sloppy bread and sniffing the grey mass like perhaps she might consider eating it. She found a chunk of metal and flung it into the bucket by her feet with a noisy clang.

'What are you doing?' Merriment asked.

The girl shot upright, flummoxed.

'Sorry, mister . . . I mean, miss. I didn't know you lived there. I'm scavenging, miss, cleaning scrap, collecting for the Aldermen, miss.'

The girl was about eight years old with the thin limbs and huge haunting eyes of a malnourished child. Her lips were cracked and her petticoat was so filthy and patched it looked like she was wearing a dress made of moss and earth, a used shroud, decomposing on a living creature. Her left arm was crudely bandaged

13

with loose rags that ran from her elbow and completely covered her left hand. That didn't stop her rooting. She used her left hand like a trowel, so the area around her bandaged fingers was black as soot and soaking wet.

'What happened to your hand?' Merriment asked.

The little girl didn't answer. She just glanced at her bandage and looked back at Merriment, more interested in inspecting a half woman, half man than explaining how she got her injury.

Merriment swept her fringe back before turning.

'Come in and let me take a look at that,' she said.

The little girl climbed down, delighted to be invited anywhere. She left her bucket teetering on a mound of stinking dead cabbage and used mollusc shells and marched into the kitchen like she'd been invited to take high tea with the queen of the fairy kingdom. The interior of the anteroom stopped her in her tracks. The little girl looked about, her large eyes drinking in the bizarre retorts and hanging herbs, the fire and the furniture, the dark walls, the foul smells, the soft candlelight. She watched Merriment come at her, observing her long leather boots polished a deep tan colour and her buttercup breeches. She took in Merriment's long hair and the bulge at the side of Merriment's waistcoat that hinted provocatively at a secret.

Merriment took the little girl's arm and began unwrapping the filthy cloth, slowly exposing a septic, blistering mass oozing little runnels of purplish puss.

'This is badly burnt.' Merriment kept her voice steady and calm. 'How did you do this?'

'Carelessness, miss.'

The little girl's head pivoted, more interested in her environment than her own sore hand.

'Are you a physic, miss?'

'An apothecary.'

'Janey Mack, is that a baby in a jar?'

14

The little girl pointed to a huge fibrous root preserved in a large glass jar on a faraway shelf.

'Of course it's not a baby.' Merriment turned the little girl's hand over. 'This is very pussy.'

The little girl nodded.

'I try to keep it clean, miss. But you know, scavenging is mucky work. I thought this place was closed down, otherwise I'd have knocked in and asked yer permission to scavenge. Used to be a Doctor Grimshaw lived here. He was cranky.'

'We need to get this cleaned up and sealed, otherwise it'll have to come off.'

'Janey Mack. Amputated, miss?'

Merriment filled a basin with fresh warm water and added a few drops of lavender oil.

'Come here till we bathe it.'

The little girl looked forlornly at her hand like she expected it to disappear once it was immersed. Merriment smiled.

'Don't worry, it won't have to be taken from you. Now, what's your name?'

The little girl hissed as her sore hand was submerged in the warm basin.

'It'll sting a little,' Merriment said.

'Stings a lot.'

'Are you all right?'

The little girl nodded, tears popping into her eyes and staying there.

'Your name?'

'Janey Mack, least that's what everyone calls me on account of me saying Janey Mack so often.'

Merriment very delicately swept a soft cloth over the young girl's hand. The water in the basin turned brown with flecks of yellow.

'I'm Merriment O'Grady.'

Janey Mack's head shot back. She forgot her hand.

'Merriment O'Grady who went to sea?'

'That's me.' Merriment's smile split open and she revealed a captivating gap between her two front teeth.

'The one the ballad's about?' Janey Mack's huge blue eyes blinked incredulously.

'I haven't heard any song.'

'It's a great tune. You dressed up like a lad in a pair of breeches and you put tar on your face.'

'Is that right?' Merriment gently removed Janey's hand and rested it on a towel. 'You can't run about on a ship in skirts and stays,' she said. 'I got into the habit of wearing breeches and knee-high boots wading through the gore in the sickbay.'

Janey Mack nodded, her whole face alive with an infectious earnestness.

'Is it true you shot your lover dead straight through the heart?'

'No, it's not true.'

'You shot him but didn't kill him?'

'I didn't shoot anyone.'

'But you've a pistol stuffed under your waistcoat. I can see the butt end of it pokin' out sure as I'm standing here. Song says you saw him "walking along with his lady gay and you drew out a brace of pistols that you had at your command" and you shot him . . . he annoyed you so. And then you were made a ship's commander.'

Merriment shook her head.

'I was made a ship's surgeon.'

'After you shot him?'

Merriment laughed, reaching for Janey Mack's head and tousling her hair.

'No. There was no shooting . . . at least . . .' She paused a moment and Janey Mack leaned forward, waiting for a full confession.

'We did shoot at the enemy. But I never shot a lover who betrayed me.'

'Oh.' Janey Mack's tiny frame released a little. She was deflated. Merriment wrung out the wet cloth and ran it swiftly over Janey Mack's tiny face quick enough to surprise the girl into stunned compliance.

'Now,' Merriment said, bringing the bowl to the back door and flinging the contents into the yard. 'These are the best cleaner-uppers in the land.'

Merriment fetched a dark wooden box from one of the shelves and laid it on the table. Janey Mack watched her unhook the latch and lift the lid releasing an acrid smell into the already odiferous room. The little girl rolled down her bottom lip uncertain about what she saw.

'Maggots,' she said, looking at the seething mass of white plump pupae wriggling over and back. They seemed hungry.

'I'll bandage them softly,' Merriment explained. 'Let them clean the wound.'

Janey Mack's eyebrows lifted a moment. She liked Merriment. She would oblige her by giving up her sore hand to be wrapped loosely. Merriment tipped a pile of maggots into a linen bandage and brought Janey Mack's burned hand towards them, slowly lifting the cure to the septic wound.

'This is very severe, how did you manage it?'

Janey Mack shrugged, trying not to pull her hand away.

'Absent-mindedness, miss, least that's what Hoppy John says.'

'Hoppy John?'

'You know him?' Janey Mack's eyes darted to Merriment's face, looking for something.

'No. I don't know him. How would I know him?'

'He was at sea too. I thought . . .' Janey Mack didn't finish her thought. 'He ran a race with a cannonball, miss. Cannonball won, took his right leg clean out from under him. I think it took half his wits as well. He's always telling me there's bees in me head, on account of I don't listen much and I like to sing and talk and that aggravates him.'

'You aggravate him?'

'On occasion, miss.'

'Enough for him to stick your hand in a fire?'

'What?' Janey Mack looked curiously at Merriment, her head tilted to one side. 'He says I'm a jinny-joe is all. Whistlin' and wheelin' and good for nothing but sifting rubbish.'

'What is Hoppy John to you that gives him the right to comment so much on your character?'

'He's me boss, miss.'

Merriment washed her hands and fetched a loaf of crusty bread from a deep ceramic jar stored behind the door that led out to the shop. She cut two thick slabs and began to butter them. Janey Mack's mouth watered.

'Actually, miss, now that I think of it, he'll explode in a passion if he finds out I've been sitting here on me arse letting maggots munch away on me hand instead of rootin' and collectin'.'

Merriment looked up sharply, her eyebrows rising with humorous disapproval.

'Is that so?' she enquired lightly. 'Well, you'll have a glass of milk and a slice of bread while I make up the day's prescriptions. Shop doesn't get busy till noon or so and you'll sit here until I say you're ready to go. He'll understand if I tell him you were only delayed by having your hand seen to properly.'

Merriment brought the bread over and lifted down a lace-covered jug to pour a generous glass of milk.

'Eat up.'

Janey Mack took a massive bite, barely chewing before swallowing it down. She swapped the bread for the glass and paused, looking sadly at the delicious white liquid gleaming in the half-light.

'That won't stop Hoppy John,' she said, suddenly taking a deep gulp.

'What won't?'

Janey Mack's enormous eyes blinked behind the rim of the glass.

'You, saying how I got delayed and all. Won't stop him from grabbing the nearest stray stick to wallop me with for skiving off.'

Merriment went about her business.

'Then I won't say anything. Sure, what he doesn't know won't hurt him.'

'He'll know. Course he'll know when I've nothing to show for me day's labour, only a clean bandage . . . oh, Janey Mack, they tickle, I can feel them wiggling. Oh, it's horrible, miss. Is that what it's going to be like when I'm dead? Maggots eating away me smile and I won't be able to move a muscle?'

Merriment stopped fetching her jars and piling them on the table to pause and look at the little girl with the huge eyes and the milk-stained mouth. She shook her head and wondered what she was going to do with the urchin leaning against the table before her.

'You have an over-heated imagination, Janey. God knows where those ideas come from. Eat up and drink your milk and don't think about being dead.'

'All right, miss. Thanks for this. I'm starvin'.'

'I'll cut you another slice.'

Merriment cut two more slices and left them by Janey Mack's resting hand.

'Now, I have a bit of work to do.'

'You go ahead,' Janey Mack said, her eyes fixed on the delicious thick butter spread over the soft bread.

Merriment pinched back a grin, rummaged through a sheaf of loose papers that had been stuffed into a drawer and one by one began reading them. She weighed powders and cut waxy sticks, adding leaves and berries to several bowls and wine and crystals to others. Janey Mack watched her for a while, munching on her crusty bread and sipping her creamy milk.

'Where do you live?' Merriment asked without looking up.

'Down the docks, miss. Why do you have a pistol, miss?'

Merriment paused, took in a breath and stood upright. 'I discovered it was a very good negotiating instrument. You don't have to discharge it to settle a dispute.'

She reached inside her waistcoat, pulled out a squat pistol and gave it to Janey Mack to hold.

'I call it the Answerer,' Merriment told her.

'That's dandy, so it is.'

'Looks pretty too.' Merriment tapped the ornate ivory butt plate. 'Don't let it fool you, the barrel is made from Damascus steel and I've engineered the interior myself, rifled it. Learned that from a soldier who fought in Silesia. Means the aim is sure and true. Mind you, I'm still trying to refine the flashpan, make it more consistent.'

Janey Mack's little hand wrapped around the butt, her finger reaching for the trigger.

'It'll be handy if the Ormond Street Boys come calling. This'll shut them up. Pity poor Jo-Jo Jacobs didn't have it when Olocher dragged her away.'

'Olocher?'

Janey Mack's eyes lit on Merriment's face.

'You don't know who Olocher is?'

'I presume a reprobate of some sort.'

'Janey Mack. He's a murderer, miss. Cut the girls open so he did. Chillin' man, miss. Black as the devil. His eyes cold as the grave. He killed six young girls, miss. It was two men lamping deer what caught him out. Found him slicing little Jo-Jo open. And the two of them kicked him down the mountain and brought him to the beadles and he never admitted to killing the others, but everyone knows it was him. I'd liked to have squared the Answerer between his eyes.'

Janey Mack held her arm out straight, pointing the pistol into thin air.

20

'Poor little Jo-Jo,' she said, lowering her hand and taking a long sip of milk. 'Olocher's to swing this morning.'

'I see.' Merriment stirred the row of brass pots cooking on the iron stand. 'Well, that sounds a fit ending for the man.'

Janey Mack nodded, pressing her index finger into a wedge of butter and spreading it towards the crust.

'I was going to watch him dancing on the gallows. But . . . I'm afraid of his eyes.'

'You're . . .' Merriment shook her head. 'Why?'

'I seen him once, miss. He was being led into the dock and he turned his head and I was deep in the crowd, way back, but somehow his eyes found me and he fixed me with a stare. It was like I was the only one there, with no one between me and him and his eyes rooted me to the spot, like he could cut me down by just looking at me. I thought I saw a trail of smoke.'

'From Olocher?'

'Out of his eyes, miss. A dark little shred of mist, coming out of his stare. Following me. I couldn't sleep for a week after that. Hoppy John said I was ravin'.'

Merriment smiled. 'I don't think anything came from his eyes and nothing has followed you. Now, have more bread and milk and give me back the Answerer. I'm going to give you something to take the heat out of your imagination. Meanwhile, we'll have a sup of camomile tea. I just need to get these out of the way first.'

She stuffed the pistol into its neat leather holder beneath her waistcoat and had turned to finish making her prescriptions when Janey Mack tugged on her breeches and stopped her in her tracks.

'I think I've misled you, miss.'

Merriment realised the orders were going to take longer than usual to fill out. She sighed, resigning herself to the situation and sat down on the edge of the table, her unfinished work behind

21

her. She folded her arms and nodded seriously, waiting for Janey Mack to explain herself.

'There's been a terrible assumption.'

'Has there?' Merriment was entertained. She kept her face keen and sombre. Janey Mack stood upright, her huge blue eyes bursting with a desperate sense of urgency. She had to clear things up.

'On account of I said I worked for the Aldermen, miss.'

'You don't work for the Aldermen?'

'No, I do, miss. It's just that, you're under the misapprehension that I have coin in my pocket to pay for your services and ointments and I'm skint to me back teeth. I earn three pennies a day for me apprenticeship and have to cook Hoppy John's supper and wash his clothes and blankets and polish his boots and give him back the three pennies I earned to purchase my pease pudding and herring. I have nothing to pay you with.'

Merriment pinched her lips together compressing a smile. She looked down at the floor.

'I see,' she said slowly, showing the little girl that she was considering the dilemma.

'I'm very sorry, miss. Should've said earlier.'

Merriment kept nodding, pretending to be ruminating over the problem.

'I wonder,' she said, 'if I could come to some arrangement with Hoppy John.'

Janey Mack's face lit up.

'You could sow his leg back on.'

Merriment snorted, swallowing back a huge laugh.

'I'm good,' she said. 'But not that good. Perhaps Hoppy John might consider a purchase.'

'Him!' Janey Mack howled. 'Buy my medicine. He'd sooner knock me over the head than shell out for maggot bandages and camomile tea. The cannonball made him very sour, miss.'

'Did it? Right.' Merriment paced up and down not only to

hide her desire to laugh but to let Janey Mack think that she was pondering over the matter, giving it its due weight.

'How do you think?' The idea flashed into Merriment's head and for the first time in almost twenty years she couldn't stop herself. She was filled with a bursting compulsion, an un-thought-out, underdeveloped idea. Her usual measured response sank beneath a weight of churning emotions. Suddenly she was hot, her whole body washed over by the conviction that she had no choice. The idea had magnetised her and all her logic, all her practicality drowned beneath a simple proposal that she would normally never have entertained.

'Do you think you could work here, Janey?' Merriment asked, breathless from the sudden rush of excitement.

Janey Mack looked quizzically into Merriment's face.

'In an apothecary shop, selling potions and powders? I wouldn't know where to start, miss. What if I poisoned someone?'

'You won't poison anyone. I won't let you. You'd be my apprentice. You'd start off by watching me and when you learn more you can mix, but that's a while away. First you watch and clean and maybe cook a little and run errands.'

Merriment could feel her hands shaking, her heart racing. What was she doing? Janey Mack's eyebrows zigzagged towards each other.

'Here?'

'Here.'

'With you? And I wouldn't have to be outside rootin' and sortin' and shovellin' muck? And I wouldn't have to . . .'

Janey Mack's whole body swayed and jittered, only her limp arm lying wrapped on the table held her down, like a soft anchor, preventing her from flying away. The little girl was luminous at the prospect of such an exotic possibility. But just as quickly as her thoughts flamed up, her face suddenly clouded, pitched grey by the bleak reality that there was no way she could work in an apothecary shop.

'Hoppy John won't have it,' she said flatly. 'He's very contrary. He won't want the annoyance of having to train another up. He'll froth at the mouth, he hates inconvenience, boils his blood, so it does.'

Merriment leaned forward.

'I'll pay him to terminate your apprenticeship.'

Janey Mack clacked her tongue. 'Are ye soft in the head? Part with money for me? Are you a bit innocent, miss?'

The matter-of-fact tone wrong-footed Merriment, the question echoed in her own conscience. *Are ye soft in the head?* She could hear her inner voice bawling, *Yes, yes, she is soft in the head.* But she answered differently.

'No, I'm not innocent, as you so eloquently put it.' She looked about the cluttered room, the dark interior necessarily poorly lit to keep her potions from being contaminated by natural light. She gazed at the stock of herbs and spices she had invested in and lied through her teeth at the little girl staring up at her, because suddenly and very unexpectedly her laboratory no longer seemed enough.

'I could do with an extra pair of hands and if I rent the room upstairs I'll need someone to set the fire and fix a chop for supper for the lodger. Everyone seems to want supper with the room. I think I lost a few prospective boarders when I told them I didn't cook. You can sleep here. I could get a settle bed.'

'Live here, with you? In this fine establishment?' Janey Mack leaned back against the table, overcome at the very idea of living in a house. 'Have I fallen out of me skeleton into heaven? Really truly, miss? No messing?'

Merriment's heart melted.

'Really truly, no messing.'

'But why, miss?'

But why? Merriment's conscience wanted to know too. And while her inner wisdom dished out the one certain, unassailable truth – *This arrangement changes everything* – Merriment didn't

24

falter. She'd dug herself into a hole and now she'd have to stay there. A little girl with huge pleading eyes was hanging onto her every word for dear life. So Merriment did what she always did best: she committed to the situation and decided there and then that no matter how foolish an old maid she was, she was going to turn this child's life around even if it meant her cherished solitude was circumscribed.

'I can see you're a hard worker,' she said. 'And I think you've got potential.'

'Well, I'm gobsmacked, so I am. Gobsmacked.'

Janey Mack couldn't take it in. She liked the idea, but she had enough street smarts to know that liking something and wishing it were always so didn't make it always so. The fact was she didn't trust that good things could happen. She glanced at her dwindling glass of milk and her half-eaten bread and for a few minutes she let herself make-believe that she had a fairy godmother.

'Good.' Merriment snapped up straight and tried to quash all the niggling eventualities that suddenly flooded her mind. What if Hoppy John won't release her? What if the business doesn't pick up? No one takes the room? Then there's no jumping on a ship to earn a wage. Now she would have a little girl in her charge and financial ruin would affect the both of them. *I could bring her to sea with me,* Merriment thought, but her stomach tightened.

'We have an agreement,' she said brightly, reaching for the camomile leaves. 'Excellent. I'll make us some tea.'

The tea was more for her own nerves than for the little girl's. Was she really this lonely?

She sipped on her cup. Janey Mack imitated her and took a sip on her cup, then winced, pulling a disgusted face.

'I have to work,' Merriment said, sifting through her prescriptions, keeping her thoughts in check by weighing out pounds and ounces. The first flurry of excitement had back flipped into a stiff retreat and in its place was a shaky nervousness. *You're going to hell if this doesn't transpire*, she told herself. *That child is uncertain and half-feral and you've poisoned her with hope. She expects you to put up a fight for her. You told her you would.*

Merriment's conscience scalded her, bitterly duelling with the one resolute dimension to her character: her sense of commitment.

Nothing you can do now, she told herself. *You can't unring the bell.*

She was so absorbed with this inner dialogue that she was oblivious to Janey Mack opening a narrow drawer and pulling out a tiny oval frame.

'Who's this lad?' Janey Mack asked, holding up a small pencil portrait.

'Where did you get that?'

'In the drawer here.' Janey Mack shook her head. 'Oh God, miss, sorry. I'm so used to rootin' and pokin' about. Y'er offended. I can tell by the shade of yer skin yer not one bit pleased and now y'er regrettin' yer offer and I'm going to have to go back to scavengin'.'

'Are you always this previous?' Merriment asked, pouring tinctures into a row of small amber bottles using specially crafted small funnels to do the trick.

'I think so, miss,' Janey Mack said forlornly. 'I've no idea what ye mean, but I'm sure yer right. And I have to say now that I've offended ye and y'er going to sack me anyway, that the tea is awful, I wouldn't give it to a dog, sure a dog would turn his nose up at it.'

The little girl pushed the cup away.

'Firstly . . .' Merriment put down the brass bowl she was pouring from. 'I'm not going to sack you.'

'Even though I've insulted yer horrible tea?'

'Even though you've insulted my tea. Now, calm down,

sip up and put the portrait back in the drawer where you found it.'

Janey Mack opened the drawer and pulled out a curl of golden hair tied with a slender silk ribbon.

'There's a lock of hair in here too,' she said, still holding onto the portrait. 'Does it belong to this fella? Is this the lad you went away to sea to find?'

Merriment didn't answer. She counted out ten dried pips and crushed them in a mortar.

Undaunted, Janey Mack kept talking.

'I can tell by the way yer lip quivered there, it's him all right. Handsome lad. Nose is a bit big. What do these ciphers here say?'

She pointed to four figures inscribed into the small frame and gilded with gold.

'Seventeen thirty-six.'

Janey Mack stared at the picture.

'That's long ago, miss. What's the calculation on that, miss, between then and now?'

'Twenty years.'

Janey Mack's tiny mouth hung open, twenty years seemed like a biblical span of ages to her.

'Twenty long years, miss. Ye've loved this lad fair and true, forsook yer skirt and stays to follow him over the billowing waves and still yer heart pines.'

Merriment began corking up the tiny bottles and slipping seeds and herbs into envelopes, marking each one with a brief description and piling the lot onto a tray.

'I'm not pining,' she said. 'Put him back in the drawer.'

Janey Mack didn't move.

'Ye can't bear to look at him for the longing and the loss he rises in yer spirit.'

'The loss.' A dart shot across Merriment's face. She scratched the bridge of her nose and swept her hair back, brushing away an old memory.

'It was long ago,' she said. 'Nothing to me today. I'd forgotten . . .' The sentence trailed away momentarily conjuring up a stormy day buried deep in the past.

'I'll stick him up here so.' Janey Mack moved around the table, careful with her bandaged hand, and stepping onto her tippy-toes placed the portrait on the lowest shelf.

'There now, handsome fellow, she doesn't give a rat's arse what y'er up to now. She has a shop and an assistant and the Answerer and a fine establishment on Fishamble Street and you're nothing but a picture in a frame to her now.'

Merriment watched the little girl talk to the portrait, the back of her head bobbing as she spoke, her lank brown hair falling in unkempt tendrils over her tiny shoulders, and Merriment's heart compressed under the sudden painful pressure of regret. The little girl could stir up her emotions with a few choice words. Merriment wanted to rush forward, pick the child up and hug her tight and close and never let her go. Instead she turned her back, reached for the roots in a jar labelled *Actea racemosa*, black bugbane, convinced that her unstable emotional condition was a prelude to the waning of her periods. She quickly chewed on the bitter rhizome while Janey Mack kept talking.

'If you don't draw out the poison it festers, doesn't it, miss?'

Merriment spat out a clump of fibrous root and took a quick sip of cordial to wash away the taste.

'That's right,' she said. 'Like your hand.'

'Like yer lad hidden in a drawer turning yer heart yellow with puss.'

Merriment bit her lower lip, a smile pinching the edges of her mouth.

'Your similes are very graphic,' she said.

'Are they, miss?' Janey Mack looked forlornly at her maggot bandage. 'Is that bad for me hand?'

Merriment laughed. 'No. Drink your tea. I'm going to turn the sign.'

Merriment picked up her full tray and carried it into the shop. She undid the latch to the door, quickly scanning the shelves, proud of all she had achieved, terrified that she had sunk all her money into a business venture that so far was slow to pick up. Beresford was doing his best sending clients her way, but most of the gentlemen he had advised to visit her turned about and walked away the minute they spotted that she was a woman. Others viewed her suspiciously and stayed for one visit, not returning for the repeat prescription. She had enough coin to pay one month's rent and if she kept her diet to a minimum she could feed herself for three weeks at least. She glanced up at the ceiling, wishing the woman she had interviewed yesterday would come back and take the room upstairs. What had happened, Merriment wondered. She had hit middle age and suddenly upended her life, left all she had known and taken Beresford's advice to settle on dry land.

Merriment remembered sitting in Beresford's cabin onboard the *Redoubtable*. She was weary, staring into the brandy glass clasped on her lap and thinking that maybe it would be nice to own a shop and have steady feet. She mentioned it to Beresford and, to her surprise, he encouraged her. He had talked her into choosing Dublin, convinced her that the city was thriving, that news of her incomparable skill would spread and she'd be swamped with eager clients willing to pay handsomely for her help.

'Sea's cruel to a woman's face,' Beresford had told her. 'This is a stalwart business venture, you can't lose. Trust me.'

Then he confided that he was retiring to his country house on the outskirts of Dublin, to focus on building a parliamentary career.

'And I don't want to be worrying about you, stuck on this leaky pitcher. The damn boat is waiting until we're far enough away to split on us and bring us down with her into the grimy blue.'

That's what happens when you let yourself be flattered, she thought. *You let the charming old man with his silver hair and gorgeous eyes talk you into a disaster because he wanted to keep you close.* She thought of Beresford's eyes and the night he had lost one in battle. How worried she had been that he would go blind. How hard she had worked to save his sight. Her heart squeezed a little recalling how well they worked together and how much she needed him back then . . . She caught herself and took a deep breath. *The reason you're here is because you're the only one who can effectively treat his gout. Damn self-serving, handsome . . . Well, he can write me a promissory note if I get strapped.* She sighed, imagining herself having to go to the bank to cash in on her friend's social position.

She was emptying the tray when Janey Mack appeared in the doorway, peeking in as she swallowed a chunk of bread, holding her bandaged hand to make sure no maggots fell out.

'This is lovely,' the little girl exclaimed, looking at the shining glass cabinets and the polished floor. 'The smartest shop I've ever seen.'

The sunlight streamed in through the large windows falling in rectangular patterns across the wall, making the glass cases gleam. Janey Mack looked filthy in the daylight. Her face was streaked where Merriment had run the cloth over it, her neck was black and her hair looked sticky. The haphazard shift she was wearing had so many patches and tears that Merriment wondered if she had a shirt she could whip onto the little girl. She frowned at Janey Mack's muddy feet. The girl would need proper shoes if she were to work here. The child interrupted her musings by pointing to a green door next to the cabinet holding herbal teas.

'Where's that go?' she asked.

'Upstairs.'

'Where you sleep?'

'That's right.'

'And where the room for rent is?'

'That's right.'

'And do you eat up there, miss?'

'Not usually.' Merriment couldn't afford to light the fire in her room so she usually ate in the anteroom, watching her potions and reading by the fire.

'But, I could do if I wanted,' she added, thinking that maybe tonight she might set a fire to console herself. Somehow the day had got away from her, somehow she felt confused, like she'd delivered a great hurt and needed a modicum of comfort to make her feel better.

What if Hoppy John wouldn't part with Janey?

3

The Lodger

The shop bell tinkled with a flurry of sweet notes, startling Merriment out of her ruminations on Janey Mack and whether Hoppy John would part with her. The door behind her opened and when she turned around she saw a grave man somewhere in his late twenties or early thirties. He had dusty blond hair tied back in a short ponytail, a longish face with high cheekbones, pale lips and flinty eyes. Despite the fact that at first glance he seemed dashing, his green nipped jacket was threadbare, worn at the cuffs and elbows and missing a button. His silk shirt was spotted with traces of ink and his buckled shoes were scuffed at the toes. Something in his expression was truculent but when he smiled his whole face shifted and the sun seemed to originate in his eyes. He nodded at Merriment and Janey Mack and placed the large leather bag he was carrying on the counter.

'Morning, ladies,' he chirruped, and Merriment saw in an instance that the man used his winning smile as a currency to make the world bend to his will. He was a charmer.

'Hello.' Merriment emptied the tray and went behind the counter. 'What can I do for you, sir?'

She resisted the mischievous gleam from his blue eyes, but felt a curious magnetic draw as he gazed along the shelves, scanning the bottles. There was a hint of intelligence in his brow and while he examined the shelves behind her, Merriment caught herself looking at his lips.

'I need shellac, roman black preferably.'

Merriment wanted to kick herself: she didn't have any. 'I'll have to make it up,' she said, certain the man would turn around and leave. 'It'll take a few minutes.'

'No worries. Have you nibs as well?'

'I do.'

'I'll take five.'

'Right so.' Merriment pulled open a drawer and with a neat carved trowel began loading dried insects into a mortar, crushing their dark glistening shells with a heavy pestle.

The man looked down at Janey Mack, his eyes flashing with quick curiosity.

'What happened to your hand?'

Janey Mack leaned forward and candidly told him, 'I was involved with a difference of opinion. The maggots are eating it away now.'

'I see.' The man moved to look at something that caught his eye in one of the glass cabinets.

'Are you a law man?' Janey Mack asked, stepping into the clean glare of the lemon sunlight. She looked more filthy and feral; the layers of grime stood out against her pale skin.

'I was a student of the law.' The man straightened up. 'But that's a while back now.'

'What's yer name?'

The man didn't seem to mind the young girl's bald questions.

'Solomon,' he said. 'Solomon Fish. My mother had high hopes for me when she christened me. Thought I'd be rich and wise as Solomon.'

'And are ye?' Janey Mack asked, making Merriment chuckle.

'God no. Far from it.' Solomon snorted, there was a brief pause, a flicker of resentment. His mother had set him up for a fall; the Bible had set him up for a fall. He had fallen. He looked out at the traffic passing the window. A fine bray was pulling a newly painted cart carrying a plump country girl and an old man.

33

Across the road two hawkers shouted at the people walking by, one was selling Bullrudderie cakes, the other hot pease pudding from the lidded wooden tub she was carrying.

Solomon walked to the window and craned his neck to one side.

'This is a fine part of the city,' he said. 'Very lively.'

He looked over the cobbled street, past the music shop and the printers, past the lines and lines of fishmongers stalls to the top of the road where the thick buttresses and grey steeple of Christ Church Cathedral pierced the blue sky.

'Great view of the cathedral,' he said, watching the throngs file under the heavy gateway to the side of the cathedral into the Christchurch market.

'The market is thriving,' he said.

'That's Hell, sir,' Janey Mack told him.

'Metaphorically speaking?' Solomon asked.

Janey Mack frowned; she spun round to look up at Merriment. 'What does he mean, miss?'

'The area around Christ Church Cathedral is called Hell,' Merriment told Solomon as she added water to the crushed insect shells.

'Did you not see the big statue of Lucifer standing looking down on everyone?' Janey Mack asked.

'A statue of the devil?' Solomon leaned against the window frame, the shutter rattling a little behind his back.

'He's seven foot tall.' Janey Mack stood on her tippy-toes, her right fingertips reaching for the ceiling. 'You want your eyes testing.'

Merriment interjected, 'I think Mister Fish is new to the city, Janey. My guess is that he hasn't been over to the market yet to see the statue.'

'Oh.' That satisfied the little girl. 'Are you new here?'

'I am, kind of. It's been ten years. Dublin has turned into a fine metropolis, heaving at the seams.'

34

'It's busy all right.' And without missing a beat Janey Mack asked, 'What brings you back to Dublin?'

'Adventure. A fresh start. A whole new market.' Solomon's face was luminous now, but beneath his roughish smile there was a hint of desperation. Janey Mack caught his off note.

'Do you owe someone money?

Solomon flinched.

'Janey.' Merriment swooped in. 'That is inappropriate.'

'Is it, miss? I'm very sorry. It's habit.'

That made Solomon laugh, a short unexpected burst that ended quickly.

'You're habitually inappropriate?' he said, walking towards the little girl, interested in her chatter.

'If you mean do I poke about, upturn things over and back, it's me training. Best way to scavenge is to take a good look. Leave nothing to chance. What's yer profession, Mister Fish?'

Solomon and Merriment exchanged an amused glance. She liked Solomon's willingness to answer all of Janey Mack's questions. He didn't dismiss the child and that marked him as an unusual man. Merriment liked his good humour and the way that he moved with a kind of ease that curiously exuded self-confidence and mild disinterest at the same time. She guessed from his relaxed gestures and the cocky way that he grinned and talked that Solomon Fish was the kind of man to take things in his stride and do his utmost to turn events to his advantage. His instinct for survival had manifested as easy good humour and there was no denying his manner, as well as his face, was very attractive.

Probably used to everything going his way, Merriment thought, smiling at Solomon as he arched his left brow and cleared his throat to answer Janey Mack.

'I'm a writer,' he said boldly, his fingers vanishing into his pockets again.

'Janey Mack, is that so? A writer of volumes and books?'

Solomon's proud stance shifted, his tone lowered. He had been found out. 'Broadsheets,' he confessed, checking to see if Merriment's face had altered with disapproval. Merriment was still smiling. She stayed mixing, but Janey Mack's voice rang out like she'd seen a kite for the first time.

'Penny broadsheets?' she said.

'The very thing.'

'Isn't that marvellous.'

Janey Mack's infectious enthusiasm made him smile and the sun burst through his eyes again.

'That's Merriment O'Grady, she's a broadsheet written about her and all. Well, a song. A penny broadsheet.'

'Yes.' Merriment stopped stirring. 'Mister Fish doesn't need to know my life story.'

'But yours is interesting, miss.' Without stopping to draw breath the little girl turned to Solomon, her huge eyes gleaming intensely. 'She murdered a lad.'

Merriment gasped, half laughing, half horrified. Solomon's brows crinkled but his eyes glittered with interest as he stood grinning before her, his hands in his pockets. The last thing she wanted was this stranger thinking she was a murderess.

'I did not.' She moved out from behind the counter to clear the situation up. Solomon's eyes never left her face to look down at her buttercup breeches. Instead he stared at her face, his brows faintly raised, his expression a cross between mock disapproval and goading glee.

Merriment stammered, 'Janey, we've established that the song is full of inaccuracies. I murdered no one, otherwise I'd be in jail instead of here making ink for Mister Fish.'

'Suppose.' Janey Mack shrugged, instantly convinced. She looked back up at Solomon to interrogate him some more. 'Are ye here to write about the execution? I'd say there's a great crowd up in Stephen's Green?'

'Olocher's execution?'

36

Merriment went back to her work, checking Solomon's face. His eyes followed her as she stooped over the pestle and mortar.

'Yes, Olocher's execution,' Janey Mack said. 'Makes my skin crawl.'

Solomon looked from left to right even though the shop was empty.

'Didn't you hear?' he asked seriously.

Janey Mack's scalp fizzled. She scratched her head, shaking it 'no', blinking furiously with breathless expectation.

'Did he escape?'

'That's what some people are calling it.' Solomon Fish nodded gravely. He paused long enough for Janey Mack to hold her breath, her complexion turning pink with anticipation.

'Killed himself.'

The air shot out of Janey Mack's mouth; her voice squeaked.

'Did he? Oh my, that is shockin', so it is.'

Solomon flicked his thumb outward. 'There's murder up on the Green, they've set the gallows on fire, the crowd is furious. They can't believe Olocher took matters into his own hands. They're calling for the keeper of the Black Dog Prison to be given fifty lashes for disgracing the justice system. They blame him for allowing Olocher to slice open his own throat instead of making sure he stayed alive to be killed by the rope. They're baying for blood, so they are.'

'Janey Mack. I'm glad I didn't go up now. There'll be a riot.'

'You did right to stay home and rest with Mammy.'

'She's not my daughter,' Merriment interjected. She looked down at the sting evident in Janey Mack's face and added, 'She's my assistant.'

'Very good.'

Solomon leaned onto the countertop watching Merriment work, paying close attention to her hands. Used to scrutiny, Merriment kept stirring, adding drops of water every few turns, but there was something about Solomon's gaze that made her spine tingle, something about the casual, confident way he moved that made her want to look at him. She resisted the temptation to smile and instead asked a question.

'How did this Olocher fellow get the opportunity to kill himself? Wasn't he guarded?'

'That man,' Janey Mack piped up, cutting across Solomon's answer, 'could draw an opportunity for murder out of thin air, miss. He was in cahoots, plain and simple, whispering to the devil, so he was, miss, whispering to the devil.'

Solomon stood upright, his interest piqued by the little girl's answer.

'Who told you that?'

'It's well known about him.'

'Oh.' Solomon relaxed.

'I seen him, once,' Janey Mack told him. 'He had peculiar hands. *Ladies' fingers*, all soft and pale. Horrible to think what those hands did.'

'What else do you remember about him?' Solomon tugged a tiny notebook and pencil from his coat pocket and began scribbling. Janey Mack shrugged.

'He was ordinary. Nothing much to look at. You wouldn't pick him out in a crowd. A short, stocky little man with piggy eyes.'

'Piggy eyes?'

'Little shiny eyes that glistened, and when he looked at you your heart would stop in your chest.'

Solomon's mouth clamped shut, his eyebrows squeezed towards an unasked question.

'She saw him going on trial,' Merriment explained. 'It upset her.'

'I see.' Solomon paused. 'That's what I keep hearing.'

'That he upset people?' Merriment asked.

'That he was ordinary, soft spoken, quiet, but . . .' Looking

38

down at Janey Mack's face, Solomon added, 'Out of the mouths of babes. Strange to think what those hands did.'

He shut his notebook on the words 'ladies' fingers' and gazed a moment deep in thought.

'Still,' he said, shaking himself, 'It is a fit ending for the man.'

'There's a crowd up on Stephen's Green think he got off light,' Merriment said.

Solomon smiled knowingly. 'They haven't seen what I've seen.'

'What did you see?' Janey Mack wanted to know. Merriment wanted to know.

'I saw a group of medical students over in the College of Surgeons hack out Olocher's liver with a penknife.'

'Janey Mack!'

'An autopsy?' Merriment was revolted and intrigued. She wished she could have witnessed seeing the exposed organs arranged in the cavity of the human torso, if uncertain whether violating a body after it died was cutting into the ancient ideal that 'all was sacred and worthy of respect'. 'An autopsy,' she repeated.

'That's right. The man's corpse has been sliced open and pulled asunder, unceremoniously diced and profanely dissected while the room clapped.' Solomon seemed certain that the right thing had happened and for a moment Merriment envied his confidence. 'Now that, I think, is a fit ending,' he grinned.

'Janey . . . Was inside him black? Did something slither from him?'

Solomon laughed, perplexed and intrigued at the same time.

'Slither from him?'

'Like a snake,' the little girl suggested.

'No.' Solomon shook his head, the loose curls over his temple sliding softly with the motion. 'He lay down on the table and didn't move. But he had got ladies' fingers, pretty soft hands, just like you said. I'll put that detail in my broadsheet.'

39

Janey Mack's tiny chest puffed up. She was to be quoted. She was having an excellent day.

'Here you are. That'll be three pennies.' Merriment passed a cubed bottle across the counter and a folded sheaf of brown paper containing five nibs.

'Thank you very much.' Solomon rooted out his purse and drew out three pennies. 'Am I near the Petty Chapmen's office here?'

Janey Mack looked up at him.

'What for?'

Merriment shook her head.

'Janey.'

'I need to get a hawking licence,' Solomon said.

'For the Christchurch market?'

Solomon didn't remotely mind Janey Mack's constant stream of questions.

'That's right,' he smiled good humouredly. 'A hawking licence for Hell. Seems poetically apt somehow.'

There was something in his tone that told Merriment he was ashamed.

'You don't rate your work then?' she asked.

Solomon grinned, masking his abhorrence.

'It's grubby work, but someone's got to do it.'

Janey Mack pointed with her good hand.

'It's down by the river, the Chapmen's office. If you go down Winetavern Street . . .'

Solomon peered in the direction of Janey Mack's index finger.

'Near Cooke Street?' he asked.

'Past it.'

'Excellent.' Solomon Fish slipped a penny into Janey Mack's hand. 'I can kill two birds with one stone, get a licence and interview one of the guards at the Black Dog, find out what really happened.'

'What's this for?' Janey Mack asked, showing him the dirty coin.

'For your excellent conversation and precise directions.'

Janey Mack looked at Merriment. She wanted to keep the coin but somehow, under the rules of the day, standing in the apothecary shop, she thought that perhaps she should give the coin back.

'I'm an assistant,' she announced, solemnly waiting for Merriment to dive in and tell her to give the coin back like a good girl.

'And I think your mistress there has an excellent student in you. Now put that away and don't spend it in one go.'

Merriment didn't interrupt and Janey Mack wasn't sure what to do next. Quickly she bargained on the best of both worlds and shoved the coin into her bandage since her pocket had a hole in it and without blinking asked Solomon Fish about his private life.

'Do you have a sweetheart?'

Now Merriment did dive in.

'Janey!'

'Several.' Solomon Fish winked.

'Well, they won't be allowed back,' Janey Mack said firmly.

Solomon's eyes flicked to Merriment. He frowned, a little confused.

'Sorry?' he said.

Merriment could feel her heart beating in her throat. Janey Mack rattled on.

'Here. They won't be allowed back here. Them's the rules, aren't they, miss?'

Merriment was too slow.

'No women back and curfew at eleven. But you'll get your supper, and have a nice fire set, I'll do that, and you'll have a lovely view overlooking Hell, which'll please you.'

'Janey.' Merriment understood the muddle too late. 'Remember how we discussed about being previous and galloping over the hill into the next county? I think you think

41

Mister Fish asked you about lodgings and in your head you had a conversation that didn't happen.'

'You have to strike when the iron's hot, miss.' Janey Mack wasn't put off. 'Sure, it's obvious: if he's new to the vicinity and about to set up stall across the way, makes sense that he should lodge nearby in an excellent establishment for a reasonable rent.'

Merriment flushed. How could such a little girl generate so much turbulence?

'If someone makes a query, then you can inform them—'

'Actually,' Solomon interrupted, 'it does make sense. I've been staying at the Cock and Hen over by Cooke Street, and this is a prime location.'

'There, see?' Janey Mack was satisfied.

'And there's a printers nearby,' Solomon nodded at the window.

'And the Italian Opera House,' Janey Mack pointed out. 'And if ever you get sick, sure Merriment will fix ya.'

Merriment held her breath. Could Janey Mack close the deal?

'How much is the rent?' Solomon asked.

Janey Mack shook her head and fixed her big eyes on Merriment's face, wondering what to answer.

'Three and six,' Merriment said calmly, hoping he wouldn't be put off by the price.

'That includes a chop for supper,' Janey Mack blurted, 'and a warm fire and good company should you choose it.'

Solomon smiled, a dimple popping in his right cheek. He turned to Merriment.

'You have to commend her eagerness.'

Merriment thought he was backing out.

'She's a great girl,' she said.

'You're a bit of a whirlwind, Janey, aren't you?' Solomon said. 'Things happen about you.'

Janey Mack nodded solemnly. 'Hoppy John says I'm cursed.'

Merriment came round the counter and tapped the little girl's shoulder protectively.

'I'll sort Hoppy John out, you don't mind him.'

'Are you taking the room?' Janey Mack had refuelled.

'I've a few things to do.'

Merriment supposed he was looking for a polite way to decline. Then he grabbed his large bag and jovially asked if he could see the room.

'Course ye can.' Janey Mack almost ran to the green door and with her good hand tried to turn the large handle. It slipped.

'Allow me.' Merriment opened the door and Janey Mack was gone. She wanted to see upstairs.

The stairwell was narrow and twisting. The papered walls bore a pattern of an intricate web of green ivy tendrils wrapped around brown birdcages containing little yellow canaries. There was an arched window on the first landing. Janey Mack glanced out it, looking through the small squares of hand-blown glass down into the street below. The horses clopped past, wobbled and distorted, the ladies and men swelled up and shrank as they passed beneath. Solomon Fish followed, his large bag brushing against the dark banisters. Merriment was last, wondering how her whole day was being tugged along by an eight-year-old little girl with a contagious personality.

The upper landing was painted bright grey. Janey Mack stood perplexed in the middle of the landing, her bare feet softly cushioned by an embroidered peacock. She looked at the three white doors, one on the right, one on the left, one straight ahead, then back at Merriment. Solomon Fish stood behind her.

'Well?' he said. 'Lead on, Macduff.'

Merriment pointed to the right and Janey Mack rushed forward, her bandaged hand held level with her lower ribs.

'Here we are.' She plunged into the brightly painted room, her mouth forming an approving 'O'.

The room was high ceilinged, painted a mellow green. The

bed had a dark headboard carved with egg-and-dart moulding and covered with an exotic throw that Merriment had picked up in India. There was a large, long window overlooking the street below, the mullions and shutters painted white. The fireplace was black and narrow, the floor bare and cleanly swept, and beside a washstand that held an ornate pink basin and matching jug was a huge chest with gold initials carved into the top.

'Isn't this lovely?' Janey Mack beamed, her huge eyes swivelling around the room, taking all the details in. 'Full of space and clean as a whistle, and the bed is lovely.'

Merriment leaned against the door frame, her arms folded, enjoying watching Janey Mack explore. Solomon Fish paced the room, looking where Janey Mack pointed. He nodded, agreeing with everything the little girl said. He tapped the edge of the bed head, his ink-stained cuffs gliding over the scallop shell motif carved into the dark wood. His eyes quickly inspected the bedcover, the gold lettering embossed on the sea chest, the washstand. There was something so fleeting and quick about his glance that made Merriment uncertain.

You're not going to take it, she thought.

'This is a chest.' Janey Mack lifted the lid because she wanted to see inside; maybe there was treasure there. 'It's empty,' she said quietly. 'You can put yer stuff in here.' She walked to the fireplace. 'And there's tiles in there on the edges.' She pointed at the small line of decorative tiles surrounding the inner segment of the cast-iron fireplace.

'Very nice,' Solomon agreed. He looked over at Merriment, his eyes glowing with warm amusement. 'Very nice indeed.'

He followed Janey Mack to the window. The little girl was on her tippy-toes, her face pressed to the glass as she craned her head to see over the wall into the Christchurch market.

'Here,' she called Solomon. 'Ye can see the tip of the devil's horns over there.'

Solomon shoved in behind her.

'See?' Janey Mack's nose pointed. 'Over the wall, them's the horns of Lucifer looking down on everyone. That's the statue.'

'Oh, yes,' Solomon lied. He turned to Merriment and shook his head. She liked the way he included her in his jokes.

Pity, she thought, convinced he was going to shrug and say 'unfortunately it's not suitable'. He would have been very nice to have about the place. She stood up tall and straight, preparing for the expected rejection, when he surprised her by moving to the centre of the room.

'Well, this is very good,' he said, tapping the side of his blond head. 'Very good indeed. I'll take it.'

Merriment's brows shot up a fraction. She quickly disguised her surprise, collected herself and nodded. Maybe he always spoke in earnest? Maybe his charm wasn't invented but real? Maybe he was genuinely interested in everything, in Janey Mack, in the room, in sharing a joke with her?

When Merriment smiled, Solomon noticed the gap between her two front teeth. He wondered how old she was. Janey Mack came up behind him and smacked his lower back, delighted.

'There's a deposit,' she said and Merriment wanted to pick the little girl up and swing her. Solomon's laugh was quick and short and stayed in his eyes.

'Is there, by God?' He looked at Merriment. 'You've trained her well.'

'She was born with those wits,' Merriment said, feeling her face colour a little.

'And what's the deposit?'

'Three shillings and six pence,' Janey Mack said, walking to stand by Merriment.

'And you won't let me out of here unless I cough up. Is that it?' Solomon asked, pointing out the fact that they were blocking the door. 'Now, come here.' Solomon crooked his finger calling

Janey Mack over. 'Come on, you're the landlady's agent, here you are, my full week's deposit.'

Janey Mack watched Solomon slowly count out the money, her eyes firmly focused on each cold coin that he placed into the palm of her little white hand.

'There now,' Solomon said. 'I believe you've wiped me clean.'

'How will you get your licence?' Janey Mack frowned, genuinely concerned.

'Well, all right, I've a little more money.'

'Very good.' Janey Mack closed her fingers around the coins. 'I wouldn't want to fleece ye.'

She proudly passed the coins to Merriment. 'What time will ye be back at, Mister Fish?'

'Please, call me Sol. It'll be late. I've to move the rest of my stuff from the Cock and Hen. I've to get a licence. Interview one of the guards at the Black Dog.'

'So I'll hold off putting on a bit of supper for ye. But the fire will be lit, the room will be cosy.'

'Sounds good.' Solomon tugged on the edges of his jacket. 'I'll leave my bag here, if you don't mind?'

Then he looked directly at Merriment and she knew he wanted to say something for her ears only.

'Right.' Solomon nodded. 'I'll head so.'

Janey Mack led the way downstairs, pausing to look at the yellow birds trapped in cages climbing up the wall. Merriment stopped Solomon on the top landing, her fingers lightly touching his elbow. She moved towards him asking quietly, 'Was there something bothering you?'

His eyes filled with a conspiratorial glint as he paused and checked below, watching the back of Janey Mack's head as she disappeared down into the shop.

'I might not be staying long. A month maybe. Depends on how the stall goes, if you don't mind a short-term lease.'

For some reason, Merriment couldn't help but feel a little

disappointed. She masked the emotion and shrugged her shoulders, smiling.

'Some rent is better than no rent,' she told him.

'Good.'

Solomon paced down the stairs and Merriment followed him, finding his light step and sweeping energy highly infectious.

It'll be nice, even for a short while, to have the company of a man again, she thought.

They caught Janey Mack opening a glass case and pulling out a silver pillbox to admire. She dropped the box and slammed the case shut.

'You off so?' she enquired.

'I feel light as a feather not having to haul that bag around with me. Well, it was good doing business with you, madam.' Solomon strode forward and shook Janey Mack's hand. Merriment watched them, bathed in warm sunshine, the worn seams of Solomon's jacket shiny across his slender back. He wasn't that tall, maybe five ten, but standing next to the little girl, he looked large and benevolent and mischievously provoking.

'Right then.' Solomon tipped a little bow. 'I'll see you later.'

'Bye.' Merriment bowed back and Janey Mack waved.

'See you, Sol.'

He opened the door onto Fishamble Street, a flurry of notes announcing his exit, and he strode off in the direction of the civic offices. He seemed to take the sunshine with him and Merriment folded her arms, curiously intrigued by her new tenant. Janey Mack bit her lower lip, proud of her morning's work, and cocked her head at the freshly closed door.

'He's on the run,' she announced, making Merriment stop in her tracks. 'Handsome though, isn't he? Would you kiss him?'

Merriment rested one hand on the counter and the other on her hip, wondering what she'd missed.

'What do you mean he's on the run?'

'I think it was the way he reacted when I asked him about

47

the law. And he travels light, which is a dead giveaway. He likes cards.'

'Go on, I'm intrigued. How did you pick that up?'

Janey Mack shrugged. 'Bit of a hungry look in his eyes, you know. He liked your breeches.'

'Is that so?' Merriment smoothed her palm over the crown of her head, patting down her thick hair. 'I'll tell you this much, Janey,' she said. 'You've excellent observation skills. Now I just have to work on the conclusion you come to once you've garnered the facts. You've the makings of a decent apothecary in you.'

'Do you think so, miss?'

'I do. Come on, I've to check the distillation.' Merriment waved Janey Mack into the anteroom, glancing a moment at the door Solomon had left through. Had he charmed her? Had his bright smile and easy manner with a poor child dazzled her? Had she missed something that Janey Mack had picked up? Hoping that this handsome lodger wouldn't bring too many problems into her life, Merriment looked at the empty shop, worried by the echoey silence. Would business ever improve?

She drew in a deep breath, brushed her cares away and stepped into the dark anteroom only to find Janey Mack standing on a chair she'd moved and stirring the green liquid over the fire.

4

The Bargain

Solomon Fish took his time strolling through Christchurch market, sussing out the best place for a stall. The market was hopping. Hawkers selling everything from buttermilk to children's toys bellowed and called and cajoled the passers-by. He saw the huge statue of Lucifer painted jet black and malevolently cloaked and he suppressed a self-deprecatory smile. *That's the spot,* he thought, staring directly at the feet of the devil. Where better to set up shop selling tawdry stories? The passing throng intrigued him. Dublin hadn't the population of London, but it looked prosperous; at least there was enough coin exchanging hands for him to experience a flash of hope. Maybe it was a new beginning? He remembered his quick exit from London, the hurried dash as he packed his bags and flung himself onto a clipper bound for Ireland, leaving Stanley Jordon and the notorious Black Pit gang behind him. Out of habit, Solomon scanned the crowd looking for one of Stanley's lackeys. Anyone skulking was not glaring directly at him. Solomon blew a quick snort of relief. It'd been nearly ten years since he had left Dublin.

'Here, young fella.' A large woman with huge wobbling breasts reddened by the cool autumn breeze waved him to her stall. Solomon obligingly stepped towards her.

'Ye look lost and forlorn there, handsome. Here ye are, have a pie on me.'

She handed Solomon a pea-and-potato pie and patted the stool beside her.

'The cost of that is for you to sit your tidy arse down on this and tell me yer name and let me admire yer handsome face.'

'You're very expensive,' Solomon grinned.

'Cheeky monkey.' The fat lady adjusted her bonnet and introduced herself, 'The name's Gloria.'

'Solomon.'

'Aren't ye a beauty, Solomon? Are ye married?'

'Are you asking?'

'Jaysus, I wouldn't kick ye out of bed on a cold morning.'

Solomon sat down, taking a big deep bite of the pie, suddenly realising he was starving.

'By God,' he said, 'you make great pies, Gloria.'

'Don't I?'

Gloria shouted out to the passing foot traffic. 'Hot pies, hot pies, tasty hot pies, a ha'penny a piece. Get yer hot pies here.' Then turning her plump face to Solomon, her blue eyes glittering with unbridled good humour, she asked, 'What's troublin' ye?'

Solomon leaned back and laughed.

'I don't know, Mammy, the wind's too cold, the sky's too blue, there's a lot wrong with the world.'

'Mammy!' Swiftly Gloria's hands scooped under her huge bosom before moving quickly to tap the brown curls bursting out wildly beneath her white cap. 'Sure there's hardly three years between us.' Then just as quickly as she'd invited Solomon to sit down, she dropped her jovial expression, her sunny face filling with unguarded concern.

'Thought ye looked like ye were plotting something. Ye were givin' the devil a good once-over. In my experience lads that stare at the devil tend to be filled with some kind of guilt. Guilt for what they've done or guilt for what they're about to do.'

Solomon kept eating. A handsome young girl with red hair came to look at Gloria's pies.

'How much are these?' she asked, looking directly at Solomon.

'They're two pence, love, got meat in them,' Gloria answered.

The girl looked quickly at Gloria but told Solomon she'd take one. She fiddled with her purse, her fingers burnt red raw from her work as a laundry girl. She handed Gloria the money and Gloria handed her the pie on a square of brown paper. When the girl left she glanced back at Solomon, her green shawl tugged tight at her waist, her long skirts blown for a moment against her body, outlining her legs.

'Who's the market manager here?' Solomon asked.

'Market manager.' Three more customers bought pies. 'That'd be Jody Maguire.' Gloria didn't ask but Solomon told her anyway.

'I want that to be my spot.' He indicated to the butt of the black statue, delighted there was a space directly in front of the devil.

'Well now, isn't life looking up.' Gloria whistled. 'I'll get to look across at yer handsome face every day. Jody's an ol' bollix though.'

Solomon swivelled on his stool, turning all his attention onto Gloria.

'Ye have to have yer paperwork in order,' she warned him. 'He'll try and shaft ye. Don't pay more than four and six a week for yer patch. He'll start the bid at five two. What you do there is laugh, and when he glares at ye, don't flinch. The man robbed his mother's own funeral money.'

Then Gloria leaned back, a look of mock horror washing over her apple dumpling face.

'Ye better not be selling pies, Solomon. Don't break me heart now and we only after meeting.'

'Would I do that to you, Gloria?'

'Begod, I don't know, but sure with those thighs I'd probably forgive ye.'

Solomon laughed his short laugh. 'Gloria, don't make me fall in love with you now. I'm only after landing in Dublin. I can't be having my heart broken.'

51

'But sure I'd mind ye, Solomon. I'd put yer head right here' – she pointed at her cleavage – 'and I'd rock ye for a bit o' comfort.'

'You're an awful woman.'

'That's why I'm in Hell, Solomon. That's why I'm in Hell.'

Gloria laughed a loud, raucous laugh and slapped Solomon's thigh hard. She sold four more pies and pointed to a stout man with a face like a shovel dressed in a dark russet coat and swinging a walking stick ready to use it like a cudgel should he need to.

'See that lump of lard over there?'

Solomon nodded.

'That's Jody. Have ye yer licence yet?'

'I was on my way to get it before you decided to use me as bait to get more business.'

'Don't know what yer talking about.' Gloria's fair eyebrows shot up. 'Mind you, most of my customers do seem to be pretty young maids this morning.' Gloria winked.

'The offices are that way, aren't they?' Solomon stood up, brushing away the flaky crumbs stuck to his breeches.

'I could watch you doing that all day,' Gloria chuckled. 'Here.' She stuffed another pie into his hand; this one had slivers of meat in it. 'That'll keep ye going until supper.'

'You've a heart of gold, Gloria.'

Solomon kissed her soft, spongy cheek and gave one of her breasts a quick squeeze, making Gloria whelp and roar laughing at the same time.

'Cheeky bugger,' she howled, watching Solomon dive into the crowd and give a quick wave back. He cut out the back entrance to the market and turned down Saint John's Lane, gazing at the familiar Four Courts where he had gone to lectures and taken up the habit of card playing ten years ago. He brushed off his once promising past and sauntered down Winetavern Street and out onto Essex Quay.

Here we are. He spotted the brass plaque with the words

Dublin City – Commissioners of Hawkers, Pedlars and Petty Chapmen
engraved in black. He patted his right breast, feeling the bulge of
ten shillings in his top pocket, then ran up the steps two at a time
and pushed open the large black door.

The reception desk was empty. Two women wearing their
Sunday best were sitting on a low bench. Each had a covered basket.

'He'll be back in a minute,' one piped up. 'Have a seat, love.'

Solomon sat down.

'Terrible about Olocher,' the woman with the hairy mole
said, grabbing Solomon's attention. 'They say the Keeper beat
him to death.'

Her friend nodded.

'Should be sacked, taking justice into his own hands,' the first
woman continued.

'I knew Jo-Jo,' the woman with the red bonnet announced.

'Did you?' asked Solomon. Turning to the two women, he
got to work, pulled out his little notebook and began jotting
some notes.

*

In the distance the bells of Christ Church Cathedral rang twelve
times. The door to Merriment's shop opened and her customers
came in dribs and drabs, looking for powders and prescriptions.
By four o'clock she had taken three shillings, along with Lord
Rochford's four and six and Solomon Fish's deposit. It hadn't
been a bad day. She looked at Janey Mack, who sat propped on a
high stool, her bandaged arm resting on the counter. How much
would she have to offer Hoppy John to buy out Janey Mack's
apprenticeship? She thought about the last of her savings. What
if he asked for three pounds? She couldn't afford to purchase the
little girl, not if she wanted to eat for the month. Merriment took
a deep breath, smoothing her hand over her brow. She opened
the pill cabinet and took three silver boxes from the top shelf.

'Where are ye going?' Janey Mack asked her.

'I'll be two minutes,' Merriment said, slipping the boxes into her breeches pocket. 'You mind the shop.'

'But what if we're robbed?'

'Two minutes.'

Merriment slipped out the door and quickly dashed round the corner past the school for higher mathematics and the tailor with the gold brocade coat hanging in the window. She squeezed past a group of men grumbling about the price of cranage and pushed open the door to William's pawnshop.

She was given one pound for the silver boxes, three times less than their value. She folded the huge wrinkled note and slipped it into the deep pocket sewn inside her waistcoat.

Better than nothing, she thought. Her conscience disagreed. *Now you're selling your stock for well under its market value and for what? To hand it over to a one-legged man so you can take his helper away and complicate your own life.*

On her way back, small specks of rain began to fall. A horse whinnied and skidded on the cobbles as the child who had startled it raced down Werburgh Street shouting profanities at the rider. A gust of wind picked up Merriment's hair, blowing back her fringe. For a moment she longed to be on the deck of the *Inscrutable*, looking at the white sails unfurling, billowing fat and full as they caught the wind, watching the clouds gather over the grey-blue ocean and the distant horizon gleam silver at the edge of the sky. She missed the uncomplicated routine of being a ship's surgeon. Dry land tied her down with a ferocity she hadn't expected. Suddenly she was looking at property rents, the cost of stock, the new regime of having to shop for food, having to cook it. No galley with meals prepared by the ship's cook, no fuel stores with ready chopped wood, no hammock, no king's pay, just a long line of bills and tasks tying her in knots with a devilish kind of trickery she was beginning to think she could not outwit. Life on land was not what she remembered.

She burst into the shop to find Janey Mack talking to the short girl who had been in this morning smelling perfume with Stella.

'Here she is,' Janey Mack grinned.

To pass the time earlier Merriment had washed the little girl's face again, cleaning it thoroughly and without brushing her hair had tied it back with a length of pink ribbon. Janey Mack kept saying over and over again it was the loveliest piece of ribbon she'd ever seen and was Merriment sure she could spare it? Spoiled by milk and bread and pink ribbon, Janey Mack would have walked over hot coals to oblige Merriment in anything she asked.

'This is Anne,' Janey Mack announced. 'She's looking to buy a present for her friend.'

Merriment nodded. Anne removed one of the worn grey gloves she minded with great care and pointed to the perfume stand on the narrow shelf beneath the lines of soap.

'The expensive one, the bud of Jericho perfume. It's for Stella.'

'Right.' Merriment was about to fetch the bottle when Anne stopped her. She flushed a little, her pale eyes darting quickly to Janey Mack.

'She wants to set up a savings account,' Janey Mack explained. 'Can't pay up front in total.'

'I see.' Merriment slid behind the counter, pulling a red ledger from the cubbyhole under the cash drawer.

'How much would you like to pay off a week?'

'Told ya.' Janey Mack patted Anne's hand. Anne relaxed. When she smiled, two dimples popped in her heart-shaped face. The girl was no more than sixteen and worked full-time for the widow Byrne living on Hanbury Lane.

'I can spare four pennies a week,' she said, chuffed to watch Merriment write her name in the account book. 'It's Anne MacCarrick. I mean, some weeks it might be less, might be more.'

'Whatever you can afford,' Merriment told her.

'See?' Janey Mack nodded, pointed at Merriment and said to Anne, 'They got it wrong about her.'

'What do you mean?' Merriment stopped writing.

'It's the shop,' Anne said turning, showing her long brown curls almost down to her waist. 'It's put-offish.'

'Is it?' Merriment looked at the neat shining stacks of shelves and gleaming cabinets.

'I mean, it's lovely and clean and you've got great soap, but it's very hoity-toity and this end of town's not used to such things.'

Merriment thought of the gold brocade coat being flaunted in the tailor's window round the corner. Crowds gathered to ogle it. The tailor's was always busy. But then she remembered most of his stock was linen and wool with only one or two silk pieces.

'Don't get me wrong.' Anne's hand waved, the grey glove loosely flapping. 'It's intimidating is all.'

'Plus, people don't know what to make of yer breeches,' Janey Mack said earnestly. 'Ye'll have to start wearing a skirt.'

Merriment laughed, a short derisory burst. 'I am not putting on stays to improve business.' Then realising she sounded shrill, she added by way of apology, 'They pinch.'

'She's adamant,' Janey Mack told Anne. 'But you tell yer friends there's a slate and not to be put off by the quietness and the shining glass and sure Merriment will give you a bit off the perfume for bringing in business.'

Merriment caught her breath, taken a little off guard.

'Yes,' she smiled, recovering, then adding to Janey Mack's selling spiel, she told Anne, 'I have all cures, powders for the vapours, lemon drops for a sore throat, silica for abscesses, *Urtica* . . . I mean, stinging nettle for chilblains.'

'Chilblains?' Anne was interested. 'How much for the cure?'

'Three pennies.' Seeing her eyes cloud a little, Merriment altered the deal. 'But I can give you half a jar of salve for one and a half.'

'Can you?' That was it. Anne nodded and stood up straight.

'The widow Byrne is crucified with chilblains, they're always cracking open and bleeding on her. This will sweeten the ol' lady.'

Merriment fetched an empty tin box, took the green waxy cure from its storage jar and began spooning it out.

'And tell anyone ye meet' – Janey Mack was working hard for her new pink ribbon – 'that she never shot no one. The song got it wrong.'

'It's a great song. I can play it on the whistle,' Anne said.

'Can ye?' Janey Mack almost sprang off the stool. Everything seemed to amaze the little girl.

'I can.' Anne put on her glove and tugged her shawl tighter around her, glancing at the soft raindrops sliding down the glass. She passed over one and ha'penny to Merriment and took the tiny box, then three pennies for the perfume deposit.

'You won't let on to Stella,' she said. 'It's a surprise for Christmas for her. Poor love has had a hard year. Lost her mammy three months back and her father's a pig dressed in oilcloth breeches. Gives Stella an awful time.'

'Poor Stella,' Janey Mack sympathised. 'She should drug him.'

Merriment's jaw swung open as two sets of eyes looked hopefully at her.

'Absolutely not,' said Merriment.

Anne glanced away, pinching her mouth, her eyes skipping over the cabinets, but Janey Mack didn't give up.

'Has he a shockin' awful temper?' she asked.

Anne nodded.

'And what colour is his skin?'

Merriment smothered a smile; this was Janey Mack's first diagnostic attempt.

'Mottled,' Anne shrugged.

'And what about his piddle?' Janey Mack's little eyes bulged, as she earnestly tried to interest Merriment in acquiring a new client.

'How would I know?' Anne made a face.

'Colour of his piddle is important,' Janey Mack said. 'Ye have to check the chamber pot, if it's brownish . . .'

'All right,' Merriment interjected. Janey Mack sucked in a breath.

'Have you thought of something to cure him?' Janey Mack whispered.

Merriment didn't speak, and for a moment the room filled with an anticipatory silence. At last she asked, 'Is he prone to ulcers?' and the question pricked the atmosphere, releasing the tension.

'Ulcers? God, I think so,' Anne answered.

Merriment rattled off a list of questions. Is he always cold? Is his urine and other bodily secretions pungent? Does he have a tendency to have warts? Is he selfish, self-centred? Hold long grudges? Does he feel that everyone is against him? Does he fly into rages and take offence easily?

At last she said, 'There is a pacifying herb.'

'There.' Janey Mack tapped behind her head to feel her new pink ribbon. 'She's a cure for everything.'

Anne was intrigued. 'Could she slip it to him, in a sup of ale or something?'

'Or sprinkle it over his dinner. Depends on what I prescribe.'

Anne's forehead crinkled as she concentrated.

'Don't know what colour his piddle or sweat is, but the man flies into rages and barely lets Stella out. The girl is allowed only to go to the shops and back, that's the only time I get to see her. No wonder she has digestive complaints. She can't stomach her life.'

Anne put the chilblain salve into her pocket and told Merriment she would drag Stella in tomorrow.

'Don't care what it costs. If you can pacify that man, it'd be worth all the gold in China.'

When Anne left, Merriment looked across at Janey Mack.

'You hungry?' she asked.

Janey Mack looked confused. She was full from the bread and milk this morning, but if she could get more food she would take it.

'Come on.' Merriment went into the back room and cut more bread. This time she lifted a fancy platter lid and exposed a delicious lump of hard crumbling cheese. She fixed two plates and was about to heap pickled onions onto Janey Mack's plate when the little girl squeaked.

'Sorry, miss, not for me.'

Merriment dragged two chairs over to the fire, helped Janey Mack sit up and placed her onion-less plate on her lap.

'Now,' Merriment began, sitting down, 'tell me more about Hoppy John.'

*

By seven o'clock it was lashing rain, and the light was a curious greeny-grey colour. Merriment shut up the shop and put one of her jackets around Janey Mack's scrawny shoulders. The little girl had her burnt hand washed, covered in pink ointment and freshly bandaged. She pinched the jacket closed with her bandaged hand and slipped her free hand into Merriment's palm. The simple gesture made Merriment turn her face into the rain, trying to push back the horrible worry that Hoppy John would be hard to convince. Who would let such a little girl go at any price?

They walked through the Christchurch market as the hawkers packed up their stalls. Lumps of sodden straw, vegetables turning past their best, stray cabbage leaves and dropped crusts littered the cobbles. The curious smell of manure mixed with the tart odour of curds and whey hung about the air. Janey Mack looked up at the statue of Lucifer, her little feet hurrying to pass him. She squeezed Merriment's hand tight and whispered, 'He's terrible imposing, miss, isn't he?'

Merriment smiled. 'It's only a statue.'

'But the devil is real,' Janey Mack said suddenly, whipping her hand out of Merriment's and making a quick sign of the cross to protect herself.

They took the back entrance into Saint John's Lane, which was practically empty. The city was winding down for the night. Only a few workhorses pulling bags of fuel or empty milk barrels clopped down the narrow twisting streets. Farmers brought their cows back to graze on the common ground over in Oxmanstown and shopkeepers locked their premises, pulling their collars up and their hats down against the rain.

'There's a cess on everything, isn't there, miss?' Janey Mack chattered, her bare feet splashing in the muddy runnels running along the broken pavement. 'You can't fart but they'll tax ya for it. Hoppy John is always going on about it. Said if I get any taller I'd have to pay him a cess, in accordance with the fact that my height is blocking his light. Sometimes he can be funny, but I think the war did things to his head.'

'Do you mind if you have to leave Hoppy John?'

'It's not going to happen,' Janey Mack suddenly blurted.

'Why not?'

Janey Mack stopped dead and looked at the dark glistening ground. She didn't know how to tell Merriment that there was no such thing as a perfect day. So she just shrugged, used to experiencing the inevitable disappointment that life dished out. She looked bleakly ahead, wishing the world would just melt and she could melt with it, walking hand in hand with a lovely lady.

'I can handle Hoppy John,' Merriment reassured her.

Janey Mack nodded miserably.

'I'll explain everything.'

'It won't improve his temper, miss, 'splaining nothin'. "Scavengin' has to be done, 'splaining or no 'splaining," that's what he'll say.'

Janey Mack could feel her fairy-tale day coming to a close. She wanted to slow down, not rush to the quayside and back into a whole lot of trouble.

'We will come to some sort of an agreement.' Merriment clutched at straws.

'He'll agree to yer face, miss, but the minute your back is turned, he'll wallop me and redden my ears.'

'We can't have that.' Merriment squeezed Janey Mack's fingers.

'What ye can't have and what turns out to be are two different things, miss, and Hoppy John has a fearsome temper.'

The little girl was crestfallen. Her eyes became faintly wild, glittering with a fearful anticipation as she considered the angry reception she was going to get from Hoppy John. They turned onto Essex Quay. The Liffey was cluttered with low barges and small boats. Stacked along the quayside wall and sloping in haphazard arrangements were shacks of all sorts and descriptions, each constructed from stray boards and scrap picked from rubbish dumps. There were shacks with porthole windows and cabin doors, shacks with leaning roofs and others roofed with upturned boats to provide shelter from the rain. In the greeny twilight the grey constructions shone gloomily. The rain stopped and when Merriment glanced behind she saw the sun sinking, pale and yellow over Essex Bridge. Janey Mack was silent now. She waved at a sad-looking young boy poking a stick into a lump of silt. He stared back, numb and cold, barely interested. Merriment saw an old sailor stooped in his doorway picking at a herring, his shoulders hunched by years of hard labour and grotesque poverty. She threw him a nod and walked on, oblivious to the runnels of excrement and foul water seeping towards the river. Janey Mack's hand slid from hers. The little girl stopped, her bare feet resting on a cracked brown slab. She took the ribbon from her hair and solemnly handed it to Merriment.

'Ye've been very kind,' she said. 'And I've had the best day I ever had.'

'It's not over yet.'

'I was purchased for to help Hoppy John. He gave two shillings for me and took me from the orphanage. If I break me contract I'll have to go straight back there and you'll be flung into jail on account of tamperin' with the law.'

Merriment tugged on her waistcoat and shook her head.

'We'll see about that,' she said. 'And why can't you keep your ribbon?'

'Wouldn't be right,' Janey Mack said, swinging the jacket from her shoulders. 'Here's yer coat.'

'Why wouldn't it be right?' Merriment was fascinated by the little girl's innate sense of fairness.

'Some things just aren't right.' Janey Mack walked on. Merriment shook her head. The strand of pink ribbon rose and fell like it was a living thing between her fingers. She watched Janey Mack make her way towards an old man bent crooked over a barrow flinging bits of a broken chair into a pile of rubbish. His hips were lopsided, his thick blue coat smeared with grey streaks. His right leg was balanced peculiarly. When he spun round Merriment understood why. There was a carved stump where his shin should have been.

'There she is,' the old man called, his wizened face contorted with disgust. He hobbled towards them, his crooked finger out, his coat flinging open, his walking stick tapping the muddy slabs. He glared down at Janey Mack, his grey eyes popping.

'Where the hell were ye?' he croaked, his grey cheeks suddenly livid. 'Were you bothering this lady here?' He swung the stick up, brandishing it like he intended to crack it across Janey Mack's back.

'She's giving ya money, Hoppy John,' Janey Mack hollered.

The raised stick dropped slowly.

'She fixed my hand.' Janey Mack showed him her new bandage. 'She's a physic. She'll fix yer sore stump.'

Hoppy John's thin face pinched and set hard. His chin was

curiously rounded and swooped up towards his nose. He scrutinised Merriment, noticing her bright breeches beneath her cloak. She didn't impress him. He flicked his eyes back to Janey Mack.

'Where were ye the whole day?' he rasped. 'Ye'll get no supper. Off dodging work, playing with yer notions. There's bees in yer head, Janey. I never met a girl to daydream more. Yer useless so ye are, useless. Chatting to the wind.'

Merriment stepped forward.

'My name is Merriment O'Grady. I was hoping to come to an agreement with you.'

'Oh, aye?' Hoppy John curled his lips, his walking stick held across his body, his gnarled hands ready to use it if necessary. 'What kind of an agreement? I'm not paying for her hand being fixed, if that's what yer after.'

'No. I was thinking . . . I'm very busy over in my shop. I was wondering . . . I was hoping you could spare Janey. I'd like to make her my apprentice.'

This news made Hoppy John laugh. His mouth burst open, dark and empty of teeth.

'What? That bundle of scatterbrained nonsense standing there? Sure, the girl's a hindrance, she'll get in yer way, burn the house down around ya and tell barefaced lies straight to yer face.'

'I would not. I would not,' Janey Mack screeched. 'You're a big fat liar.'

'It's all right, Janey.' Merriment raised her palm. 'You just let me and Hoppy John work something out.' She turned back to Hoppy John; his eyes flashed quickly from her pockets to her face. He was totting things up.

'Naturally, I would like to reimburse you for any inconvenience,' she said. A canny expression cut across Hoppy John's face.

'Reimburse, ah now, ye see there we have a problem.' Hoppy John lowered his walking stick and leaned on it, his whole frame keeling to one side. 'We have a problem, see. See this?'

He stood up straight, tapping his wooden leg with his walking stick. Merriment heard the low dull thud of wood knocking on wood.

'Lost the limb doing me duty. Where once I had a lively wage and the fine company of hardy sailors . . .'

'Let me stop you there. See this?' Merriment stepped forward and unbuttoned her high-necked shirt to reveal a small anchor tattooed into the base of her neck.

Hoppy John's nose twitched, his white eyebrows rising slightly.

'Ah,' he said. 'You've been to sea.'

'So we'll tell no tales,' replied Merriment.

Hoppy John nodded, looking over the river a moment at a brightly painted frigate.

'She fetches my firewood. Cooks me meals. Scavenges for thru'pence a day and prevents me from falling in the river.'

Merriment nodded.

'You could get a boy from the foundling hospital to replace her.'

Hoppy John shrugged.

'Suppose I could.'

'I'll give you two pounds to buy her apprenticeship.'

'Two pounds!' Janey Mack squawked. 'Are ya mad?'

'That'll do.' Hoppy John spat on his large palm and reached out to Merriment to shake on the bargain. Merriment spat on her own hand and shook on the deal. She pulled two folded pound notes from the pocket inside her waistcoat and listened as Hoppy John chuckled and chided.

'I'll tell you this much for nothin',' he said. 'I'm not buying her back. When you show up here looking to get rid of her, I'll only say I warned ye. She's as dizzy as a jinny-joe, always chattering, never thinking in a straight line. She never gets nothin' done beginning to end and she's a mouth on her. She's an answer for everything so she does.'

'That's a pack of lies, you one-legged rusty guts.' Janey Mack wanted to thump Hoppy John in the side; she wanted to send him head over heels into the brown stinking river.

'There ye are,' Hoppy John sniggered. 'What did I tell ya? She's a mouth on her would drive a nun to murder.'

He snatched the money from Merriment's hand and shoved it into his coat pocket. Merriment couldn't help smiling. She had secured Janey Mack and secured her cheaply. She looked down at her new charge.

'I think she's just the kind of girl I am looking for,' she told him. 'Janey here is very capable.'

'Now, melodeon legs, what do you have to say to that?' Janey Mack wanted to know.

Merriment patted her head.

'Have you anything to pick up, Janey?'

'What?'

'Any belongings?'

Janey Mack's huge eyes widened in the fading light.

'Oh, yeah.'

She dived into a tottering shack, leaving Merriment and Hoppy John to look at one another. Neither spoke. When Janey Mack came back out she was carrying a bedraggled shawl and a tiny rusty box.

'Me collection,' she said.

That made Hoppy John splutter with laughter.

'Her collection,' he roared, patting his pocket. 'She's all yours, madam. Good luck to ya.'

And without a single goodbye he turned his back, walking his hobbled walk down along the docks to the nearest tavern to break his pound notes and drink till Christmas.

Merriment took Janey Mack's hand and found herself babbling as they walked back along the quays.

'I'm going to give you a good scrub. Tidy you up. Wash your hair. You'll need a new dress.'

'Really?' Janey Mack clutched her shawl and the tin box with her bandaged hand, holding on for dear life to her fairy godmother with her other hand. It was dark now, and the torches on Essex Bridge sent long rippling flames up into the night sky.

They climbed the steps up to the road and left the poorly lit teetering shacks behind. The houses along the quays were tall and slender and those who could afford to lit candles in lanterns above the doorways. Merriment decided not to walk the back alleys. Instead she turned up Parliament Street, passing the night watch, an old man with a hawthorn stick for a weapon. The owner of a cutlery shop was closing up late, he tapped the rim of his tricorn hat and bid Janey Mack goodnight. They passed row after row of businesses, all filled with an expectant darkness, like the shops and music rooms and vacant tea rooms were all waiting for morning, eager to be busy again.

'Everything looks lonely at night,' Janey Mack whispered.

'Does a bit.' Merriment flung the jacket over Janey Mack's shoulders and held it there with her hand. They turned up a side street full of tall houses. The soft glow of fires and candlelight emanated from the mullioned windows as people settled down to eat their supper. Some houses were brightly lit and Janey Mack stared into the radiant interiors, her heart rising in her chest.

'Look in there,' she said, filled with awe at a chandelier sparkling from a stuccoed ceiling. 'Is that where the King stays?'

'No,' Merriment laughed, 'it's a gentlemen's club.'

They turned up Fishamble Street and Merriment fetched the shop key from her pocket.

It had been a long, eventful day.

'Do you think Solomon knocked on the door when we were out?'

'He's probably in a chophouse working on his broadsheet,' Merriment said. 'He'll be back. I'll leave a candle in the window, let him know we're in.'

'I was supposed to put a chop on for his supper. Do ya have a bit of mutton?'

'I never thought.'

'We'll have to get him sausages tomorrow to make up for having no supper this evening.'

'Do you like sausages?' Merriment enquired.

'Only ever had one. It was tasty-tasty.'

'Then we'll get some sausages to celebrate the start of your apprenticeship. What's in the box, Janey?' Merriment tapped the rusty tin box.

'Teeth, miss.'

'Teeth,' Merriment chuckled. 'I see.'

As she unlocked the shop door and pushed it in, she was fully aware that her life had altered. On a whim, a curious burst of mothering desire, she had adopted a little girl and her life would never be the same again.

5

Blood and Beast

'Are ye in or out, Harry?'

Harry winked at Solomon. 'Ye always know when Badger has a bad hand. He gets very surly.'

'Throw down yer money or move on,' Badger growled.

Harry looked at his cards, calculating his chances slowly to annoy Badger. The man next to him began to snore, pretending to have fallen asleep.

'I'm still in,' Harry announced, ordering another quart of ale. He glanced at the neat pile of coin in the centre of the table where the best of his week's wages was hidden.

'Right,' Badger sneered sourly and, looking at the swarthy man next to Harry, said, 'You in or out, Gus?'

'Yer in an awful hurry there, Badger. Let me tot up.' After a pause, Gus called for one more card.

'I'm in,' Solomon said.

'That's his tell,' Harry told Solomon, his boyish face grinning from ear to ear. 'See the way Badger's gritting his teeth there.'

'Shut up you, you muckwork,' Badger yelled.

'Oh, profanities.' Harry blessed himself. 'He's a bad hand for certain now.'

'Who asked you? Ye whiddler.' Badger's fist landed on the table. 'Go on off home and do what you always do of an evening.'

'What's that then?' Harry beamed, unperturbed by Badger's hot temper.

'Polish the dolphin. Beat the Jesuit. Introduce the hand to the pizzle,' Badger roared. The table burst out laughing.

Harry stayed smiling.

'We have him by the short and curlies,' he told Solomon. 'As sure as his face is turning purple, we have him now.'

'Show your cards, gentlemen,' Gus said.

Solomon laid his cards flat and Badger lurched across the table at Harry, grabbing his head and pulling him out of his seat.

'Ah now, lads.' Gus held onto his ale.

Solomon read the cards. He had lost. He sighed. Harry's diversionary tactics were excellent, the man had won and wrestling free from Badger he pulled the pile of coin towards himself.

'Yer a sore loser,' he yelled, kicking Badger and sending him knocking to the floor.

A row broke out, punches were thrown; a chair was knocked over. Solomon squeezed out of his seat, grabbed his belongings and took refuge at the bar, sipping the last of his ale. At first no one paid a blind bit of attention to the squabble; there was a row every night in the Cock and Hen. While Badger and Harry threw wild, useless punches, huffing and puffing and dancing in comic circles around one another, Solomon looked at the clientele who frequented the tavern. The place was packed to the seams, full of jilts and thief-takers, bullies and fences, receivers and pimps, every mix of ne'er-do-well and vagabond. Every table and snug seemed to house a criminal fraternity. He saw two bawds drinking cherry-brandy tickling a large man with a ruddy face, while at the same time picking his pocket, but they were the small fry; in the darker corners were the more serious lawbreakers, not footpads and sharpers but organised villains, quiet and plotting and unruffled by threats and blades. The Dublin underworld was bulging with a staggering array of lowlifes and scoundrels, and while London could be cut-throat, Dublin's low life seemed more volatile. The city housed an enormous variety of felons and crooks with loud and notorious personalities, who wore their scars like a badge of honour, boldly carrying weapons and wearing their clipped ears and branded faces as a proud display of their chosen profession. Solomon was faintly amused by the brash confidence of the bandits that mingled with ordinary traders and merchants, surprised by the diversity of rogues and vagabonds and chilled a little by the unabashed violence that could erupt at any moment.

Badger and Harry were more pathetic than dangerous. They screeched abuse at one another and did more damage to the air around them than each other. As Solomon watched them wrestling, amused by their ineptitude, he noticed a man with a deep scar down his right cheek glaring at the commotion. There was a particular air of menace about this man. He had piercing blue eyes and a sneering mouth fixed with a malicious half-grin. His jaw line was jagged and his nose had been broken in more than one place. He wore his jet-black hair scraped back in a ponytail that accentuated his large brow. Solomon couldn't help but be fascinated by the man's expression. There was a certain razor-sharp calculation in his piercing stare, an economy of movement about his body and a magnetic quality to how he behaved.

A confidence, no doubt, that comes with power, Solomon thought.

The man commanded attention, without doing anything, so it seemed. Everyone sitting at the table next to him bristled with a kind of fearful respect. Even as they talked to one another, they seemed distracted by the scarred man, stealing glances his way as if keeping an eye on him. Solomon thought of the crime bosses he had known in London, they all had the same unreliable air about them, constantly close to erupting, their hazardous moods unpredictable, their inclination towards excessive violence and savagery the one thing that secured their reputation. The only comfort, Solomon reasoned, was that the bloody and brutal lives they led were in general short.

The scarred man tapped a small pyramid of brown snuff onto the back of his enormous hand and flung his head back, while everyone around him became curiously attentive to the ritual. It was almost humorous to see so many large men suspended in action by the presence of a single individual, watching breathless for a motion of judgement coming from a man they feared and maybe even revered. All the scarred man had to do was move his index finger in the direction of the fight. An inch of air, stroked by a finger was all it took. A profound silence swept through the crowd as two bullies the size of plough horses jumped up, pulled Badger out of the fray, dragged him to the scarred man's table and shoved him into a quiet corner. Harry leaped to his feet blustering, quickly realised what had happened and meekly slipped back to the table to count out his winnings. Once he had sat down, the banter and chatter of the patrons started up again. Solomon finished his drink, took in a deep breath and licked his lower lip. He would be glad to leave such a disorderly place.

Jenny the barmaid refilled his tankard, pulling him a little to one side.

'The man with the scar is Billy Knox, keeps things in line this side of the river. Badger is one of his lads.'

Jenny peeked to one side, her eyes glancing swiftly over the crowd.

'Everyone owes Billy Knox,' she grinned. 'He dishes out favours like hot potatoes at Donnybrook fair. Helping people out of tight spots, and then . . .' Her face darkened. 'Well.' She tapped Solomon's fingers. 'You know a favour is never without a price.'

She sniffed, letting the jibe land. Solomon ignored her meaning.

'Good job ye lost,' she said, her eyebrows lifting as she nodded sagely, 'or you'd have owed Billy something and that is one lad you want to steer clear of.'

Solomon winked good humouredly. 'I'm too inconsequential

for Knox to notice the likes of me. Now' – he stroked Jenny's hand tenderly – 'I'm off to the Black Dog.'

'Here now, Sol,' Jenny whispered. 'When you get there, tell Boxty I sent ya. Ask him where Olocher got the blade. He knows right well so he does. He's up to his neck in it.'

'Boxty, right. You're a gem, Jenny, a little gem.'

'Ye'll be missed, Sol.' Jenny's mouth pinched a little.

'Sure, I'll come back to see ye.'

'That O'Grady one is as odd as two left feet.' Jenny couldn't understand why Solomon would want to go into digs when he could bide his time in one of the rooms upstairs, drinking and playing cards at night and having pub stew for supper.

'She wears breeches,' Solomon smirked.

'I know,' Jenny said. 'And was at sea from the age of nineteen. Probably whored her way round the Bay of Biscay.'

'Do you think so?'

'No, I don't. She's as tight as a bee's arse. Sure, most of the time everyone thought she was a man. She's not like normal women, there's no go in her. Not into that kind of thing, ye know.'

'What kind of thing?' Solomon teased, one eyebrow raised.

'Ah, go way ou' that.'

'What kind of thing?' Solomon repeated, feigning innocence. 'The kind of thing you showed me last night?'

'Shh.' Jenny blew through her lips and looked around. 'Don't go tellin' tales.' Her eyes were bright and giddy. 'That was a once-off, Sol. I've to go to confession tomorrow.'

'Don't go apologising to God for a good healthy appetite,' Solomon beamed. 'Anyway, you've a lovely bottom.'

Outside, the night watch called the hour and two floosies at the door bawled at the top of their lungs, 'Ten o'clock and all is well.'

The men around them clapped and whistled and asked them to show what they got.

'I better go,' Solomon said.

Jenny nodded.

'Nice knowing ye, Sol. Stay in touch.'

'With a beautiful damsel like yourself? Of course I'll be in touch.'

Solomon grabbed Jenny across the counter and kissed her full on the lips before picking up his carpet bag and tripping out the door into the dank rainy night.

The back alleys to the Black Dog were deserted. Rain splashed down on the slippery cobbles and Solomon wished he had brought the last of his stuff over to his new lodgings earlier. Still, he'd won seven shillings in an earlier card game, had a new hawking licence and a fine lead in the Olocher scandal. He stood a moment trying to get his bearings. It was pitch black. He orientated himself towards a distant speck of light palely throbbing at the end of a high wall. The weight of his old law books shoved into his carpet bag along with the last remnants of his hopeful youth dragged his left arm heavily down. He could smell hops brewing. A rat skittered past his wet feet. His buckled shoes were leaking; his silk stockings were spattered with mud. He took a deep breath and marched up the dark, narrow road, his fingers occasionally reaching for the high wall on his right side.

A large blazing bowl burned at the gate, throwing wild red shadows onto the wet road. Solomon looked up the grey steps leading to the imposing doorway. A light glimmered in one of the side glass panels; through it he could see a gathering of people.

The place chilled Solomon's heart. How often had he nearly ended up in debtors' gaol?

Still, you managed to keep out of it, he comforted himself. Always one step ahead of the sheriff.

He sighed. At the age of thirty he was running out of steam. His vagrant life was catching up with him. He'd left Dublin in a blaze of scandal only to run from London ten years later, with Stanley Jordon looking for his head on a plate. Suddenly,

Solomon was tired. Sick and tired of looking over his shoulder. Sick and tired of trying to patch together a living, of scrimping and saving and making no headway. He was worn out and worn down and riddled with guilt, wishing he was anybody else. He shivered, a single drop of rain sliding down the nape of his neck and trickling along his spine, reminding him that he had no backbone.

Don't be a pansy, he told himself. *Buck up and get inside.*

Solomon took a deep breath and pushed open the large oak door only to find mayhem in the reception area. All the tradesmen who normally plied their trade during the day had returned to conduct their business. One cobbler weighed down with a basket and toolbox was jabbering loudly, 'But we were banned earlier, packed off. I've six pairs of mended shoes here to be paid for.' Another man with a shifty eye was pointing back out the door, saying, 'I've a horse and cart full of ale to be brought down to the tap.' Hell-cat women screeched that they had assignations and messages to deliver. There were wig-makers and tailors, tobacco dealers and coal merchants, women with baskets of candles and soap, and all were bawling and complaining to a line of guards standing in the way of the door.

'It's orders,' one of the guards hollered, his large, unshaven chin jutting forward, his gun gripped over his chest. 'Get back,' he growled. 'Back.'

A man with a large boil the size of an egg bulging on his left cheek prodded the air with his finger and grumbled, 'The Cut will not be pleased about this. He'll want his money. I'll send him to you to collect, will I?'

The crowd stiffened and became still, everyone looking at the line of guards to see where the threat would land. It was the gruffest-looking guard who responded.

'The Cut'll get his money, it's a matter of timing. Now out yez go.'

The throng grumbled. One of the women screeched, 'But Betty Handshake is in there and Fred and Jessop.'

The guards were having none of it.

'Until this Olocher malarkey has quietened down, yer not allowed to pass. Them's the orders.'

The crowd was not for turning. When the entrance door knocked open and a coffin maker carrying a fresh coffin barged in, faintly stunned by the constricted reception area, there was a fresh outburst that drowned out the coffin maker's protest, 'But it's a delivery for O'Meara, who's to be executed tomorrow.' The horde harangued that if the coffin maker could get in they could get in.

Two of the guards launched forward, poking people with the barrel of their guns, trying to herd them out.

'Go on,' they cried as they pushed. 'There's to be a shutdown of usual trades until the Olocher matter is done.'

Solomon tugged the sleeve of the least rough-looking guard and leaned in to whisper. 'The Board has requested I carry out a survey,' he lied. 'Matter of geography.'

The guard jolted a little on hearing a reference to the Board. He narrowed his watery eyes and jerked his arm free of Solomon's light grip to go and mutter something to his fellow turnkey.

When Solomon was unceremoniously pushed into the corridor and the door briskly slammed and locked behind him, he heard howls and gripes of 'what the hell' from the disconsolate throng. A scuffle quickly erupted into a belligerent row, forcing one guard to let off a shot to quell the possibility of a riot.

Solomon stood a moment and peered down a green corridor lit by nests of candles cluttered in filthy niches. He heard voices in the distance. People laughing. A woman squealed, her laugh a high, piercing volley that echoed, disturbing the candle flames, making them flicker. Solomon walked towards the noise, passing locked cell doors. Obviously the keeper had tried to give the impression of a tidy shop, at least while members of the Board might be sniffing about. Now that the Board were anxious to discover how Olocher managed to get a weapon to kill himself, and keen to explore the governance of the gaol, the Keeper was doing his best to convince all and sundry that he ran a respectable establishment. Solomon imagined what a regular night in the Black Dog might be like, doors flung open, the corridors and rooms full to the brim with doxies and gamblers, brewers and hustlers, periwig menders and rag traders, the walls ringing with noisy bustling vendors eking out a black living among the hardened and hopeless. But Olocher's suicide had put a stop to the usual trading customs and diversions. Solomon heard someone sobbing softly. The door to the room where the laughing was coming from flew open and a man wearing only a shirt stumbled into the hall and threw up. Someone yelled and clapped, shouting, 'Go on, Charlie, flash the hash, good lad.'

Charlie crumpled to his knees, his stockings wrinkled about his ankles, a bottle hanging loosely in his fingers. Someone slammed the door shut after him and the sound of a melodeon tripped brightly through the air.

'You all right? Charlie, is it?' Solomon asked, reaching down to help him up.

Charlie was dissolute, pumped full of opium and bitter brandy. His eyes spun in his head, trying to focus.

'You got any money?' he asked, staring at Solomon's outstretched hand.

Solomon slipped him three pennies.

'I'm looking for Boxty,' Solomon said.

Charlie nodded, hugging his empty brandy bottle close.

'Do you know where he is?' Solomon looked towards the end of the corridor.

'Down in the nunnery,' Charlie slurred. 'Splashing about in Olocher's blood.'

Charlie pointed to the faraway wall.

'Boxty's in trouble,' Charlie whimpered. 'I'm in trouble.' He started to cry.

Solomon left him bawling on the filthy floor and followed Charlie's directions. He turned down steps, listening to the odd sounds of men calling, shouting for a piss bucket, for a bitch, for a second chance.

The nunnery was down the last flight of dripping steps. It was the place where whores and female cozeners were locked up, in the bowels of the earth. Tonight there were no prisoners. A patch of orange light glowed in the distance. Solomon heard a voice.

'Hello. Is that you, Martin, ye blackguard?'

'Hello,' Solomon called back. He sounded artificially cheery.

Out of the pitch black shadows a scrawny old man – wearing a faded red coat and filthy white waistcoat first issued to him forty years ago when he became a guard at the Black Dog – shuffled forward. He held a torch that dripped occasional blobs of flaming pitch onto the damp floor.

'Who are you?' the man barked, his gaunt face hollowed out by flames and shadows.

'Solomon Fish. Are you Boxty?'

'Could be.' The old guard jutted his chin out, the fingers of his left hand tapping the sling that held his long musket draping from his left shoulder. 'What's it to ye?'

'Jenny, the barmaid down in the Cock and Hen, told me to ask for you. Said you'd be in the know.'

The old man grunted. 'Jenny has a mouth on her. You could drive a horse and four through her wide gob. I've nothing to say to you, now fuck off.'

'So you are Boxty.' Solomon drew out his notebook.

'Get lost,' Boxty hollered.

'You don't know what I'm looking for,' Solomon protested.

'Well, you're not here to ask what I'd like to eat for me supper.'

'It's Olocher,' Solomon said.

'Course it is. Turn around and go back out the door there.'

The index finger of his left hand flicked towards the steps.

Undaunted by Boxty's abrupt behaviour, Solomon adopted another tack, tapped his pencil off the moleskin covering of his little notebook and officiously announced, 'The Board just want a few things cleared up. Part of the official inquiry.'

Boxty's grey eyes bulged and he jutted out his chin as he shook his head, denying everything.

'The Board.' He spat the word out, almost choking on it. 'Fuck me, this is out of hand. Totally out of hand. That bastard Olocher is dead and look at all the shit he's brought down on us. Even dead he's still trouble. I've done nothin'.' He pressed his lips, defiantly snapping out his innocence. 'Do you hear me? Nothin' but me job.'

Solomon stood expressionless. He flicked his notebook open. 'Just go over the events of the evening.'

'For what?' Boxty said gruffly, walking to the iron holder fastened to the wall and slipping the torch into it. 'So you can twist the facts and I can get kicked out on the street, stripped of me wages and pension.'

'You were guarding him as normal,' Solomon directed. 'Doing the usual eve-of-execution stuff, seeing what he wanted for his last meal, asking if he would like to get anything off his chest, to see a priest.'

'A priest!' Boxty snorted, removing his gun and leaning it against the wall. 'Him? I'll tell you what I told Lord Beresford and Judge Coveny' – he pointed at a red door that was slightly ajar – 'and it's not a word of a lie.' He sucked on his teeth and sniffed. 'I looked in.'

Solomon took two steps towards the red door.

'This his cell?' he interrupted.

'Don't go in there.' Boxty stepped to block him. 'It's still covered in blood. Like I said I looked in. Olocher was sitting staring, so I moved away. Next thing I hear a thump and when I go and check, there he is on the floor, blood squirting from his neck. No knife in sight, no weapon, like his throat was sliced open by the devil himself.'

'The Board are unconvinced.' Solomon's mouth was firm. He clamped his jaw and kept his gaze steady and unflinching.

'Fuck them.' Boxty waved the threat away. 'What do they know?'

'Someone gave Olocher a blade.'

'Well, it weren't me,' Boxty squirmed.

'Did you search him?'

'Three times a day we patted him down, emptied out his pockets. This is a joke.'

Boxty dragged a low stool out of the shadows and sat hunched under the flickering torch.

'Me and Martin were chatting,' he said weakly.

'Martin?' Solomon scribbled down the name.

'The other turnkey, Martin Coffey. He should be here. It's after ten bells. He'll vouch for me.'

'Did Martin give him the blade?'

'No he didn't.' Boxty looked away.

'You looked in at Olocher. Olocher was staring. Where was Martin standing?'

'There.' Boxty waved vaguely. 'I don't know. Nearby. Look, you've no idea what we were dealing with.'

Boxty's eyes filled with a timid light. He ran his fingers across his brow, brushing his thin grey fringe to one side.

'He wasn't the usual. Wasn't normal.' His voice trailed a moment and Solomon gave him time to gather his thoughts. 'Down here, on yer own, guarding a man like that. It'd jangle any man's nerves.'

'What do you mean?' Solomon softened his tone.

'He didn't talk once. Didn't try to make friends, didn't bargain or beg.'

'Or bribe?' Solomon interrupted.

'Yeah, if you like.' Boxty shrugged as though extortion was all in a day's work when it came to pacifying prisoners. 'He didn't look for favours. I mean, Olocher, he took to the place like a worm takes to dead flesh. He burrowed in. Sat quietly, like he was drinking in the damp and the dark. Relishing the experience. I'll tell you this much, down here at night on me own, listening to the rain drippin' and not a sound from him, not a murmur . . . Got to the point where I'd be afraid to look in.'

Boxty seemed genuinely disturbed. His eyes darted to the farthest corners of the old cellar. He gripped his hands together, squeezing his fingers like he was trying to wring out his exposed fear. Solomon peered at the red door. A square of deep darkness cut by the bars in the window appeared to move and slither away from the light. A seam of oppressive blackness swelled, engorged along the door jamb. He pulled his eyes back to Boxty.

'So, Olocher didn't talk,' he said flippantly. 'That's hardly frightening.'

Boxty shook his head, his white hands flipping open, revealing his wrinkled palms.

'That's what I'm trying to tell you. I'm forty years working here, forty years, and not once have I met anyone like him. Even with me gun I didn't feel safe. There was something lurkin' in his bones.'

Solomon looked back at the red door, it stood ominously still, bulging with a seething darkness that made the hairs on the back of his neck stand up. He shook the chills away and pasted a fake smile onto his face.

'Sounds a bit florid to me,' he said.

Boxty shook his head, unconvinced. 'You didn't have to deal with him. And what he did to those girls. He was evil. Sure, Judge Coveny said it himself.'

'That Olocher was evil?' Solomon scribbled the judge's name.

'When he saw Olocher's corpse spread out on the floor. He

was poking at it with his cane and saying it was hard to think the man was dead.'

'Why?'

'Because there was something about Olocher that we all thought couldn't be killed.'

Solomon smirked uncomfortably.

'I can't describe it.' Boxty looked earnest now. His eyes narrowed as he tried to explain what he was feeling. 'He was a danger when he was alive and here is his putrid spirit wreaking havoc now he's dead. The man bled like a stuck pig, but look at it.' Boxty extended his arm incredulously. 'His rank energy can still reach out of the grave. Even dead he's left a stink behind him.'

Solomon reached into his jacket pocket and produced a small bottle of whiskey, offering it to Boxty.

'God bless ye, sir.'

'It'll please you to know he's been cut open by eager medical students over in the College of Surgeons.' Solomon's brows rose a little.

Boxty took a deep, greedy glug.

'That so?' He dragged his hand over his moist lips and nodded approvingly. 'That does please me. Don't get me wrong, I'm glad he's gone, but I didn't kill him. Not me, not Martin. If truth be told I'd have been too afraid to do it.'

'Did you get into a row with him?' Solomon probed.

'No, I did not. I told you I didn't talk to the man and the man didn't talk to no one but the devil.'

'And you didn't give him a knife and tell him to do us all a favour?'

'He came up with that idea himself.'

'And the knife?'

'I don't know,' Boxty barked, tired of being grilled. 'This is horseshit. If Martin was here he'd tell ya.' Solomon nodded, unfazed by Boxty's outburst.

'I'll have to interview this Martin Coffey, corroborate the facts.'

'You do that,' Boxty said truculently. 'He'll tell you the same.'

'When does he start duty?'

'Half an hour ago. He's tardy. Wait a minute.' Something in Boxty's addled brain began to join the dots. He took a quick sip and leaned forward, resting his elbow on his left thigh. 'What has Jenny got to do with you?'

'Sorry?' Solomon pretended to misunderstand.

'Jenny over in the Cock and Hen. You said she sent you here.'

'That's right.'

'Well if she sent you here, what have you to do with the Board?'

Solomon didn't miss a beat. He kept his pencil hovering over his notebook.

'I'm a collator of information. A kind of clerk. An accumulator of facts. Would you describe Olocher as squat and round-faced?'

'Huh?'

'Short with piggy eyes and ladies' fingers? Would you say he was a nondescript man? Ordinary?'

'I told you he'd curdle yer stomach to look at him. And what he did to that little one, Jo-Jo, poor little lass. He was unnatural.'

'Yes. A preternatural fiend, you've said.'

'He was oily.'

'Oily?'

'Had a slippery way. A sheen on his skin.'

'Unctuous?'

Boxty didn't give the whiskey back. He fondled the bottle, looking for a moment at the filthy straw gathered in damp clumps at his feet. 'A quick death was too good for him. And I'll tell you something else. I don't like being down here on me own.' He quickly scanned the thick blackness bulging against the red door. 'I never used to care, but since Olocher . . .' He shifted uncomfortably. 'When you've been near to that kind of man, it's like he left a trail in the shadows. Like he's still skulkin' about, slitherin' in the dark somewhere.'

Solomon nodded sympathetically. 'It's gloomy down here,' he agreed. 'And thinking about what Olocher did and listening to the rain drip, it'd be hard not to let your imagination run away with you.'

'Aye. I suppose.'

'Anyway.' Solomon pocketed his notebook, satisfied that he had got all the information he could. 'I'll clear your name with the Board.'

'You tell them what I told you. No dereliction of duty done by me. I'm upstanding.' Boxty pointed a crooked, thin finger at his hollow chest.

'I'll be back to interview the other turnkey,' Solomon warned him.

'He'll say the same.'

Of course he will, Solomon thought. 'I'll head off so. Good night.'

'Right.' Boxty feebly returned the cork stopper to the slender bottle of whiskey and held it out for Solomon to take back.

'Keep it,' Solomon said, keen to leave the oppressive nunnery.

'Bless ye,' Boxty mumbled, watching Solomon climb the steps and disappear. 'Ponce,' he hissed as the door closed.

Solomon paced quickly, moving down the gloomy corridors following a thin trail of candlelight, listening to the inmates mumbling and shouting and crying. He was keen to exit the building, to get away from all the destroyed lives, the oppressive monolithic walls, the pervading sense of agitated gloom, the stench of mould and excrement. He hurried up steps and was on a second-storey floor when he realised he was lost. He stood a moment looking down the grim, dimly lit corridor, his heart beating curiously in his chest, the grey-slabbed floor reflecting the pallid light cast by the wall braziers and for a moment everything was silent. No wailing, no whispering, no clang of metal or raucous laughs, instead a creeping silence seemed to slide thickly from the cold grey stone. He stared along the line of shut doors. The distant darkness at the end of the corridor seemed to coil with black shadows and unfamiliar nuances, the light of the braziers unable to penetrate the morbid gloom. Solomon's skin prickled. His scalp bristled as he gazed at the faraway pitch black and imagined Olocher's ghost stumbling from the inky air. A small man, his gaping throat bubbling blood, his white face twisted in the agony of death throes, his small eyes bulging as he reached out with dripping fingers, staggering towards Solomon crying, 'Devil's here. Devil's here.'

Solomon shivered and recoiled his head, spooked by his own imagination.

'Stupid,' he mumbled, backtracking.

He pinched back a half-smile; if Boxty's stories about Olocher were having this effect on him, think what a craftily written broadsheet could do. He heard the muffled peel of the Christ Church bells. It was eleven o'clock.

'Damn,' he cursed, thinking of Merriment locking up. 'She'll bar the door.'

He looked forlornly up and down the narrow passage. He recognised a brazier; an iron prong hung loose from its base. He ran towards it.

'Come on,' he hissed.

He maddeningly rounded a corner and stared at the black door that led back down to the nunnery.

You fuckin' eejit, he thought, clenching his jaw angrily. Solomon flung the door open, ready to ask Boxty how the hell you got out of this place, when he jolted to a stop. There was something down the steps, crawling on the floor, an enormous creature, its spine undulating, rising and falling, inching forward, masked by shadows. Solomon couldn't move. The walls seemed to oscillate, softening like melted wax. He fixed his eyes on the creature heaving its weight along the ground, a dull red spreading across its broad back as the orange candle flames caused shadows that danced over the earthen floor. Solomon's eyes flared. Rigid with fear, he froze, a single thought burned a funnel through his reason.

It's Olocher, slithering.

There was a limb. A searching antennae, probing the gloom. A spread of skeletal fingers. Solomon's knees buckled. It was a hand, deathly white like a corpse. The vault of the nunnery reverberated with a miserable, chilling groan. Solomon's body drained. He couldn't run.

Olocher was slithering.

A long, thick trunk of torso dragged itself into the pool of flickering light beneath the brazier and, weak with fear, Solomon swallowed back the gorging nausea that shot up his oesophagus. Below him the grey head painfully lifted and a terrified face luminous with horror contorted in a dreadful spasm and let out an appalling shriek.

A cold sweat burst through Solomon's pores.

Boxty was on the floor, crawling towards the steps, the orange torchlight throwing macabre shadows across his back. He dragged his left side like half of him was dead. When he looked up his face was distorted, grotesquely malformed – half his mouth weighed down, his left eye drooping, traces of blood dripping from his lips, a dark bruise forming on his cheek. He looked like he had been beaten.

'Hlp me,' he groaned. 'Hlp me.'

Solomon bolted down the steps.

'Boxty. Are you all right, man? What happened?'

Solomon rolled Boxty over, lifting his head onto his lap. The old man's chest was covered in a brackish-coloured blood.

'Have you been shot?' Solomon searched, patting down Boxty's heaving chest. Boxty clawed at Solomon's jacket, his whole body arching, desperate to say something. Half his mouth opened, his right eye bulged, bloodshot.

85

'De . . . Devil.' He pushed the word out, the dead side of his face ashen.

Solomon looked frantically up the steps, but there was no one to hear him if he shouted for help.

'You've taken a turn,' he told Boxty. 'You'll be all right. We have to get you out of here.' Solomon went to get up.

'No,' Boxty shouted, grabbing him back down.

'I have to get help.' Solomon tried to prise himself away.

Boxty thrashed in distress, trying to stand up, desperate not to be left alone.

Solomon supported him. 'I have you.'

He reached under the old man's back and helped him to his feet, taking his paralysed left arm and hauling it over his shoulder. Boxty stumbled forward, intermittent grunts of fear bursting from his shattered mouth. He was heavy. Solomon dragged him up every step, aware of the pervading acrid smell emanating from the bowels of the dungeon. He fumbled with the door and pulled Boxty out into the passageway, leaning the old man against the grey oozing wall and wiping his brow with the edge of his sleeve. Boxty began to cry. His breeches were stained with urine and filth.

'You're going to be all right,' Solomon tried to reassure him. 'Come on now, I'll look after you. Get you to a hospital.'

'I was . . .' The words came a little clearer. Boxty's left eye blinked. He was improving.

'There, see, you're getting better already,' Solomon grinned painfully.

Boxty shook his head, his good hand clawing at the air, his whole body craning forward trying to tell Solomon something.

'He's back.'

Solomon just wanted to go.

'This is his blood.' Boxty's voice dragged, every word pushed urgently out of his distorted mouth. 'He's back from the grave.'

Solomon looked along the dark corridor, unnerved by Boxty's

illness and disturbed by the strange turn of events. He wondered if he should chance calling out. Where the hell was the other turnkey?

'I'm telling you.' Boxty grabbed Solomon's arm, squeezing it tight. 'He's back.'

A line of foamy spittle slid from the left side of Boxty's mouth.

'Who?' Solomon's heart teetered on the edge of his ribs.

When Boxty spoke, the word came out mispronounced, but there was no mistaking what he was trying to say.

'Dolocher,' he gasped. 'And he has the head of a black pig.'

6

The Dolocher

Merriment opened her eyes. Janey Mack stood at the side of the bed staring down, her pale face ghostly white, her huge eyes blinking expectantly. She smelled of sweet dog rose soap. She had been scrubbed clean in a tin bath the night before and dressed in an old shirt Merriment couldn't throw away. A thin shaft of morning sunlight slipped through a narrow slat in the bedroom shutters. It cast a shaft of ruby light over Janey Mack's puzzled face.

'Morning.' Merriment sat up in the bed. 'Everything all right?'

'Just checking.' Janey Mack grinned, her little face suddenly bursting with an excited light. 'Thought ye were dead.'

'In my bed? You thought I was dead in my bed?'

Janey Mack shrugged.

'I woke up in the middle of the night and thought I was dead,' Janey Mack said, implying there was nothing unusual about mistaking life for death. 'The bed was so soft and I was so warm and cosy I thought God had carried me off.'

Merriment glanced over at the crumpled makeshift bed before the small fireplace. She'd thrown a couple of cushions down on the floor and folded an old blanket in half and Janey Mack thought she'd died and gone to heaven.

'And this isn't a dream,' Janey Mack told her. The little girl unhooked the long latch fastening the shutters and pushed them open. A blazing red sunrise flooded into the spartan bedroom. The grey painted walls blushed, the embroidered throw shone, and crimson sunlight fell in a rectangular pattern across the varnished floorboards. Merriment puffed up the pillows behind her, not for one moment regretting her spur-of-the-moment decision to take on an eight-year-old assistant. Janey Mack climbed onto the window seat and stood looking down at the street below.

Already Fishamble Street was busy. She could see hawkers making their way up to the Christchurch market, some had barrows stacked high with barrels of winkles and cockles, others had hot pies and freshly baked bread. She saw a milkmaid coming in from the country. The maid drove two cows before her and carried a stool, a pail and a quart jug to measure out her milk.

'Two whole pounds, miss,' Janey Mack said, not taking her eyes from the view. 'I can't get my head around it.'

'You know what I can't get my head around. That there was a little girl underneath all that muck.'

'Are ye a bit touched, miss?' Janey Mack swung round. 'I mean, don't get me wrong, I'm delighted you're not the full shillin' since I benefit hugely from your ailing mind, but two pounds, miss, for me . . . it beggars belief.'

Merriment nodded.

'Well, try and believe it.'

'Oh, no doubt I'll get over the shock of it, in time. But Hoppy John, I think he thought all his Christmases had come at once. His head nearly fell off when you suggested the exchange.'

'I see it as a prime investment.'

Merriment bounced out of bed and grabbed her breeches, tugging them under her nightdress and rummaging underneath the bed for her stockings.

'See, there ye'll be sorely disappointed, miss.' Janey Mack jumped down and stepped across the brightening floor. The sky turned pale pink and yellow.

'Why will I be disappointed?' Merriment pulled on her shirt, shivering a little in the sharp morning air.

'There's no way for me to sweeten the salt in me words, miss, but ye've set a high expectation with the price ye paid for me and I can't help but fall short of all the grand things you think that two pounds measures in my person.'

Merriment laughed.

'You're serious in the morning, Janey.' Then she added, 'You don't think you're worth two pounds, is that it?'

Janey Mack frowned, fiddling with the brocade fringe on the bed cover. 'On reflection,' she announced, 'and according to the church scriptures, a person is a priceless thing, worth more than money and possessions.'

'There we are. Exactly.'

'But.'

'There's a but?'

'What the scriptures say and how it turns out to be are two very different things.'

'You're worth two pounds, Janey.'

'It's like Solomon's mother.'

'King Solomon?'

'No. Solomon Fish, with his mother calling him Solomon on account of her expecting him to become rich and move to Babylon to play the harp and pick fruit in the garden.'

Merriment laughed, bewildered. She dragged on her boots and buttoned up her waistcoat.

'I'm going to have to teach you to stick to the point, Janey. Although on the other hand I do like your circumvent ing.'

Janey Mack wanted to ask if her circumventing was near her head. Instead she made her point. 'Solomon's mother thought by giving him a fancy name he'd have a fancy life. And you think by buying me for two whole pounds you'll get the fairness of your price out of me. But I'll never fulfil the task and you'll quickly realise that I don't concentrate and that will set your teeth on edge and then you'll sit and consider. And the long and the short of it is, miss, ye'll regret the overpayment for my purchase and resent the burden of my employment and be forced to conspire to be rid of me.'

'I see.' Merriment stopped making the bed. 'Is it always an opera with you, Janey?'

'I say it as it is, miss.'

'You say it as you perceive it to be. How you see it and how it is may not be one and the same thing, and anyway that's not the point. You think all of this is too good to be true. Well, it's not. I mean, it is true, and you are now an apprentice to an apothecary and you'll have chores to do. It won't be all dilly-dallying and pleasantries.'

'But, Janey Mack, two whole pounds. How will I live up to the price of it?'

'I'll decide that.'

'We're doomed.'

Merriment laughed, her whole face radiant and suddenly youthful.

'We are not doomed. You have the most baroque imagination. Well, you know what they say.' She brushed her long auburn hair, clawing in the wayward silky curls and fastening it with a leather thong. 'If it's not baroque don't fix it!' Merriment laughed warmly at her joke, showing the gap in her neat teeth. 'Get it?' she asked Janey Mack.

'No, miss. And that will be another thing that will gall you and turn you against me. I won't get your jokes.'

Janey Mack looked troubled. She stood twirling the brocade, mulling things over. Once all the silt was washed out, her hair was honey gold not dirty brown. Her features were small and pert. But her eyes were her most haunting attribute; beneath all their innocence they were filled with a shocking depth of wisdom. She stood in a square of yellow sunlight, trying to explain to Merriment that this arrangement was going to fall apart.

Merriment tipped the end of her hair brush, pushing it further onto the narrow table.

'Janey,' she said, choosing her words carefully, 'you've had an uncertain existence. It has made you unsteady. So here's my promise. You're going to live here and train with me, and come under my care. And every day you will work with me and soon it will be so familiar that you will forget you were ever worried about me throwing you out and leaving you to fetch for yourself. The only way I can reassure you is to keep you safe and in a routine. That will quieten your insecurity.'

'But . . .' Janey Mack didn't want to tempt fate but it was her training – no stone could be left unturned. First rule of scavenging – you root and poke and make certain you've missed nothing.

'But?' Merriment said softly.

'Why would you be so kind?'

'No reason. Kindness can exist in and because of itself. We are human beings, Janey, not animals. Kindness is in our nature.'

'All I know, miss, is people are self-pleasing. All good things come with a price.'

'That just isn't true.'

'That's 'cause you're a romantic, miss, ran away to sea because you thought that lad downstairs was worth it. What good did it do ya? Where's he now? Off dallying with his shipmates and here you are parting with good money to buy my company.'

'You think I bought you because I'm lonely?' Merriment smarted under the little girl's keen observation. 'I'm not lonely, Janey. I'm not sad. I'm content and ambitious. I like my studies. I like dry land. I like my life. For God's sake, I like you, Janey.'

'What's to like? Hoppy John says I've a blistering tongue clacking about in my head and I'll never have any friends on account of it.'

'Hoppy John's a bitter man. You're a very bright, lovely girl. Now, have a little faith that sometimes good things just happen.'

'Suppose.' Janey Mack scratched her knee. 'If such a bad thing can happen like what happened to Jo-Jo Jacobs then . . .' Janey

Mack paused and looked about the brightly lit bedroom, taking in all its spare and elegant details. 'Then maybe a good thing can happen too for no rhyme or reason.'

Merriment tried to quash the sudden pang of pity she felt. Life was hard, for everybody, and Janey Mack was not fooled by soft cushions and scented soap. She knew that the fragile balance between relative happiness and desolate, unremitting despair could be disturbed by a light breeze at any moment. Merriment wanted to reassure her, but she understood that words would not do the trick. Only the gentle, repetitious familiarity of being kind and thoughtful would help Janey Mack to believe that sometimes good things just happen.

'After breakfast,' Merriment said, flinging a shawl towards the little girl, 'we are going round to the pawnshop and buying you some clothes and a pair of shoes.'

Janey Mack bounced, jumping from one leg to the other, throwing off her previous mood. She clenched her fists and squeezed them to her cheeks, her whole body shaking. She spun around in circles and squealed with delight.

'Really? Really?'

She was just checking the air with a question; in reality she wasn't listening. Instead her imagination was already full of elegant shifts with neat ribbons and long sleeves. She even allowed herself to dream of a cream-coloured petticoat trimmed with broderie anglaise.

'I can't have you working in the shop in a tattered old shirt. I threw your dress into the fire last night.'

Merriment flung the door open and tripped lightly down the stairs, followed by Janey Mack, who was laughing because she'd never known good fortune and she was drunk on the experience. She patted the wallpaper saying hello to the yellow canaries trapped in brown cages and ran after Merriment through the shop and into the anteroom.

They had bread and butter for breakfast. Merriment stoked

up the fire and Janey Mack sat with her feet extended, roasting her soles in the delicious heat. Merriment washed Janey Mack's hand, reapplied a nettle salve for the burn and wrapped it in a fresh bandage. She brushed Janey Mack's hair and took a look at her prescriptions, beginning to make up the simple recipes.

There was a rap on the shop door.

Janey Mack froze, her bread suspended before her lips. She stopped chewing, a big wodge of bread bulging in her cheeks. She blinked her huge eyes, her heart pounding hard against her thin ribs. Was this it? Was everything going to come tumbling down? Was it the orphanage? A beadle? Had Hoppy John double-crossed her in some way?

Merriment wiped her hands and stood in the doorway, looking across the shuttered shop.

'I'll get that.'

Janey Mack scarpered from her chair and with a wild instinct for self-preservation hid behind a large ceramic jar over near the back door. She heard the bolt on the shop door slide back. Voices. Female voices. They came in. They were coming towards the anteroom.

'Had to drag her in here,' a girl said. 'Would you look at her, her eyes popping out of her head like her face might burst. Come on, Stella, for God's sake.'

It was Anne MacCarrick. Janey Mack dashed from her hiding place and was standing at her chair eating her bread when Merriment led the two girls in.

Anne looked about the dark room and sniffed.

'You work in a bit of a dungeon there, Misses O'Grady. Well, look at this.'

She stepped toward Janey Mack and flung her gloved hands onto her hips.

'By God, that's not little Janey, is it?'

'It's meself.' Janey Mack straightened up.

'Don't you polish up neat as a shiny new penny? And hasn't

she the softest hair? I wouldn't have recognised you.' She spun round to Stella. 'She was mucked up to the eyes yesterday, like something you'd find at the bottom of a cookin' pan, and now look at her, pretty as a dove.'

Janey Mack nodded, feeling she deserved every compliment thrown her way, all because rose-scented soap and Merriment O'Grady possessed some kind of transformative magic. She had been dusted with fairy dust and had come up sparkling.

'I'm gettin' a new dress,' she announced.

'Lucky sausage.'

Anne sat down and laughed at Stella standing petrified in the doorway ready to run if the occasion required.

'Would you look at her, Misses O'Grady, shaking in her boots. She's terrified, so she is.'

'Did you get a fright, love?' Janey Mack asked.

That made Anne laugh louder. She pointed her thumb at Janey Mack and said to the others, 'She's like a little aul' one, isn't she?'

'Can I offer you two girls some blueberry cordial?' Merriment took a huge glass bottle from a shelf and poured the dark purple liquid into four cups.

'That's very nice of you.' Anne removed her soft grey gloves carefully, bobbed her cup in the air and made a swift toast.

'Bottoms up.' She took a long glug and smacked her lips together. 'Now,' she said, getting down to business. 'Stella, come in, for God's sake. You're not going to go to hell.' Anne looked up at Merriment. 'She's convinced that my suggestion, what I was chattin' to yous yesterday about, is a sin and that she'll be damned to roast in Satan's fires if she so much as tries to calm her father down.'

'He's . . .' Stella stuttered. She had long dark curls and a sombre, pale face, a large nose and thin lips and when she frowned a deep line shaped like a Y cut into her forehead.

'He's a blackguard, Stella, plain and simple, and he needs his wings clipped.'

Janey Mack leaned onto the arm of the chair. 'Does his piddle smell funny?' she asked.

Merriment pressed her lips between her teeth but the smile danced in her eyes. Janey Mack was a quick learner. Stella looked east and west.

'Well . . .' She seemed confused. Anne waved her hand.

'You've looked in his pisspot, Stella, you're the only one to clean it. Tell them.'

'It stinks to high heaven.' The words burst from Stella and all her pent-up reservation escaped on a tide of full disclosure. 'He's very bad-tempered, Misses O'Grady. Thinks everyone is again' him. Men. Women he's only bumped into. He's convinced they've insulted and slighted him by a look, never mind a word. And if he takes a skunners against someone, that's it, he'll think bad of them for life. He's suspicious of everyone and everything. He hates me, 'cause I'm "as bad as the rest of them", he says. He's very selfish, wouldn't share the crust of his bread with me, never mind the dog. And then there's his rages. They come sudden and out of nowhere.'

'Her nerves are gone,' Anne chimed in. 'Sure, look at her, she's destroyed with nervous exhaustion. Wouldn't you say so, Misses O'Grady?'

'Does he complain of ulcers in the mouth?' Merriment asked, pulling out her large red ledger.

Stella's eyebrows rose in surprise.

'He does.'

'And does he get sharp stabbing pains?'

'All the time.' Stella was amazed.

'Piles?'

'Never shuts up about them.'

'Acid in the stomach?'

'Worse after he has had milk.'

Merriment put on a large pair of thick leather gloves, tied a scarf over her mouth and took a small vial down off a shelf.

She undid the cork carefully, holding the jar out at arms-length. Stella and Anne stepped back to stand beside Janey Mack.

'One sniff will kill ya,' the little girl whispered.

Merriment nodded and Janey Mack retreated towards the back door.

'I don't want to do him in,' Stella whimpered.

Merriment squeezed out ten drops of shiny liquid into an empty jar. Everyone watched the procedure in a reverential silence. She fetched a thick syrup from the press and mixed it into the drops. She re-corked the dangerous vial, removed her scarf and kept stirring the jug.

'You're not going to kill him, Stella. It's just that raw *nitricum acidum*, or aqua fortis, is extremely corrosive. The fumes are choking and if truth be told one whiff and your heart would stop. This' – she patted the syrupy edge of the jar – 'is an extremely diluted portion. I've mixed it with molasses and I want you to give a spoon of it each morning to your father mixed in warm water. Tell him it is for his gut complaint and to ease the piles. You'll notice a change in his outlook and demeanour in a week, he'll have improved health and disposition in three weeks. We'll reduce the dosage over time.'

She sealed the jar and held it up for Stella to take. Stella stood tall and uncertain, the candlelight falling in a slant across the chequered pattern of her woollen shawl. She couldn't move.

'She's not helpin' ye to murder yer father,' Janey Mack blurted. 'Sure she'd be flung into the Black Dog for that. It's a cure.'

Spurned by Janey Mack's reassurance Stella tentatively took the jar.

'How much do I owe you?'

'Two and nine,' Merriment said, scribbling in the ledger. 'You can pay me one and four now, one and five when you have it.'

Stella sighed, relieved. 'Thank you.'

'There now.' Anne finished up her cordial and changed the subject. 'The widow Byrne woke up in a great mood this morning. She came down to breakfast singing the praises of your chilblain cure.'

Someone knocked firmly on the shop door.

'Busy this morning,' Anne said, watching Merriment leave to answer it.

'Who's that?' she asked Janey Mack.

'Do I look like I can see through walls?' But the minute she heard his voice, she recognised it.

'It's the lodger,' she whispered hurriedly. 'Didn't come back last night, probably off galavantin' with the ladies. He's new to town. Likes cards and writes broadsheets.'

The two girls drank up the information.

'Very handsome,' Janey Mack told them and they both instinctively touched their hair.

'I was all night in the hospital,' Solomon said as he stepped into the room. He halted, his eyebrows rising quizzically. Anne's long hair and casual manner caught his attention. Stella retreated half hidden into the shadows.

'Ladies,' he bowed politely. Merriment stepped in behind him and introduced everyone.

'Mister Fish tells me he has a great story.'

'Please, no formalities. Call me Solomon.' Solomon left his bag on the floor, perched on the edge of the table, crossed his legs and folded his arms, confident and happy to be in female company. He looked pale, his features drawn, but his eyes were smiling. He shook his head and scratched it.

'It's the damnedest thing,' he said. 'The damnedest thing. I went over to the Black Dog to interview one of the guards, a man named Boxty, to enquire after Olocher. Get a bit of information on how he killed himself, what he was like, that kind of thing.'

Solomon's captive audience nodded. Merriment quietly mixed and stirred and wondered how in the space of two days her laboratory had become so cluttered. Solomon started by describing the nunnery.

'Dank and cold as the grave, and Olocher's cell was still knee deep in blood.'

He told them all how unsettled he had felt, how Boxty quaked in the torchlight saying that Olocher used to sit and mumble to the devil, whispering like he was listening to something instructing him. He told them of the way Boxty's gullet swallowed down lumps of fear and how his eyes shifted nervously.

'So I left him. Told him I'd be back to interview Martin Coffey, the other turnkey, and I headed off.'

'Janey Mack, the poor man. I wouldn't like that job.' The little girl looked at the poker resting against the fender, thinking it would be handy to defend herself with if a robber broke in.

'That's not the crux of the story.'

Solomon waved his index finger from side to side. His hands were stained with black ink. The girls were rigid with attention, their faces locked in an expression of intense concentration, intrigued by the fact that there was a crux. He strode to the fire, lifted the tails of his jacket and warmed his cheeks, his hands behind his back.

'I lost my way out and ended up back at the nunnery. I thought to myself, *Boxty will have to show me out.* So I opened the door and what did I see at the bottom of the steps?'

There was a faint pause. Anne shifted to the edge of her seat. Stella emerged from the shadows. Janey Mack stepped forward.

'Boxty was crawling towards me covered in stale blood.'

There were three loud gasps. Only Merriment didn't react. She listened as she worked, methodically weighing out fine powders, fascinated that Solomon could saunter in and within minutes have everyone hanging on his every word.

Wouldn't last a wet week at sea, she thought to herself. *No sailor would put up with his palaver.*

Solomon stood tall and, keeping his right side erect, he collapsed his left arm and leg as he described Boxty's grotesque condition the night before.

'He dragged himself across the floor, crying out, "Don't leave me here, don't leave me here." Then . . .'

Solomon paused for effect.

'What he said next beggars belief.'

Everyone strained to hear.

Solomon whispered, 'Dolocher's back.'

No one took a breath. No one moved. Seconds passed, until unable to bear the burden of the widening silence, Anne hoarsely said, 'Dolocher?' her eyes popping wide mixed with a frisson of terror and excitement.

'That's what Boxty said: he couldn't speak properly. He'd had a fit. Something frightened him so bad that he'd been paralysed down one side of his body.' Solomon craned forward and very slowly and deliberately announced what had happened.

'He'd seen Olocher's ghost.'

There was a communal intake of breath, swift glances exchanged and the word 'never' whispered incredulously.

Solomon nodded. 'Worse than that, Olocher's ghost was half man, half black pig.'

Janey Mack shook her head and swallowed.

'How? Why?' she shivered.

Solomon shrugged, 'That's the mystery. The chilling mystery. Boxty said he heard a noise in Olocher's cell, crept in slowly, with his musket ready when out from behind the door jumped the malignant ghost of Olocher, a grunting black pig with hands and legs and the strength of the devil.'

'Holy God.' Janey Mack's right hand clutched at the back of the chair, her knuckles white. 'Is it true? Is Olocher back? From the grave?'

Solomon licked his lower lip. 'All I can tell you is what Boxty told me and what I saw with my own eyes. I went with him to the hospital and he spent the whole night fretting, staring at his own shadow flickering on the wall, howling that "the Dolocher" had come to fetch him down to hell.'

'Mother of divine . . .' Anne breathed. Stella reached down and held Anne's hand.

'That's not the worst of it.' Solomon moved to one side, out of the direct heat of the fire and leaned on the mantle, looking a moment into the flames.

'The nurse said he was bruised peculiarly. I mean, I saw the bruises myself, ugly big things on his ribs and arms.'

When Solomon looked up, he frowned like he didn't believe he was going to say what he was going to say next. He glanced at Merriment. She caught the look, unsure of how to read it. Was he afraid? Perplexed? Guilty, maybe, of telling tall tales?

'Boxty told me he had proof that Olocher's savage spirit was after him.'

Merriment tapped a little box and crimson powder snowed into a tiny brass pan, yet despite appearances she was just as interested as everyone else to find out how you prove that the dead have come back to life.

'He said he ripped something off Olocher's ghost, something belonging to him.' Solomon stroked his forehead and spoke a little slower, like he was working out some mathematical problem that needed to be articulated with caution in case a stray digit got lost in the mess.

'What did he mean?' Janey Mack stood near Anne, instinctively taking her other hand.

'I didn't know,' Solomon said quietly. 'He kept telling me to go and look behind the red door. So this morning I went down to the Black Dog and the guard that was on last night gave me a candle and let me into Olocher's cell.'

Solomon looked over at Merriment. She had stopped working and was standing with scales in one hand and a tiny weight in the other, waiting with the others to hear what was worse than a demon with a pig's head.

'I found it in a corner under the bench.' Solomon shoved his hands into his pockets, not sure how to formulate his discovery.

'It was a lump of flesh, torn from Olocher's throat.'

The girls gasped. Merriment raised an incredulous eyebrow. Solomon smiled, faintly embarrassed by the implications of his story. But as the girls babbled with intense excitement, overwhelmed with the idea that some preternatural creature had returned to exact a grisly revenge on its captors, Solomon perked up.

'That is shockin', so it is. Janey Mack, shockin'.' Janey Mack looked up at Merriment, swallowing back the terror. 'Up from the dead.' She panicked a little. 'Walked off the surgeon's table with a new head and went to find his jailors.'

Anne patted her face, holding her fingers by her lips, shielding her eyes a little as she peeked at Janey Mack, watching the little girl's outburst.

'His flesh falling off, decomposing.'

'Exactly what I wrote.' Solomon grabbed his bag, pulled out a leaflet and handed it to Anne.

'What's it say?' Janey Mack rushed to her side.

Stella read the words.

'"Olocher's Ghost Returns to Haunt the Black Dog – The Dolocher."'

'I wrote it while I sat with Boxty last night,' Solomon said proudly. 'Took his name for Olocher's phantasm: the Dolocher. I thought it compounded the idea that what attacked him was neither a living nor a dead thing. Had to pay over the odds to get the printer to print me two thousand copies so I could have it out at this morning's market. He'll have the full batch ready in an hour.'

'She sold Ringsend oysters,' Stella announced, the cream leaflet shivering in her hands. Anne and Janey Mack both asked, 'Who?'

'Jo-Jo Jacobs. They think that's how Olocher met her first. He bought oysters off her.'

'Holy God.' Anne shook her head. 'How much is this, Mister Fish?'

'A penny to you, Anne.'

Anne rummaged in her pocket. 'The widow Byrne will want to hear about this. She's done nothing but curse Olocher from one end of the week to the other. She knew Jo-Jo's mammy.'

'And I'll have one.' Stella timidly handed Solomon a penny.

He pocketed the money. 'I've to hurry along and get the stall organised. It's a chastening story, isn't it, ladies?'

'If you could believe the half of it,' Merriment said brightly.

'Sure, he saw the lump of flesh himself.' Janey Mack's eyes blinked, defending Solomon. 'And he sat the night with the lad in the hospital fighting off the huge shadows on the wall.'

'The man was raving,' Merriment said confidently. 'It's one of the preliminary symptoms of apoplexy. The burst of blood to the brain causes the person to experience intense fear. They imagine all sorts, even demons.'

'How do you explain the bruising?' Solomon asked.

'He fell down the stairs.'

'And the lump of flesh?'

Merriment paused. 'I'm sure there's a rational explanation.'

'It slid off Olocher's dead bones,' Janey Mack said. 'That's the rational explanation.' Her face looked gaunt and troubled. 'His flesh melted off him, stinkin'.'

Solomon gave a short, bright laugh and pulled his shoulders back. 'She's a great turn of phrase, hasn't she?' He cocked his head to one side and narrowed his eyes. 'Did someone dip you in a bit of water?'

Janey Mack nodded vigorously, confused by being half frightened and half delighted at the same time.

'You look very civilised, amazing to see the improvement a splash of water can make to an ugly face.'

Janey Mack's jaw dropped. The girls giggled.

'Yer own noggin is nothing to write home about.'

Solomon pinched Janey Mack's cheek as he passed. 'Ah now, don't lie, if there's one gift God gave me it was the gift of beauty.'

'Be careful ye don't fall over and destroy yerself with the weight of yer big head. Sure, y'er as plain as a plank of wood.'

'We all know that's not true,' Solomon grinned, his eyes glittering with boyish glee. He had a cracking story to sell, a once-in-a-lifetime opportunity to turn a decent shilling and a chance to maybe alter his own fortune.

'Bye, girls,' he chirruped. Then, turning to Merriment, he flicked his head to one side, signalling that he wanted to speak to her alone for a moment. They stepped into the shop.

'I wanted to go up to my room. Leave my bag there. Have a quick shave.'

'Go ahead.'

'Thank you.'

His mouth moved like he was about to say something else. Whatever it was, he shook it off, smiled, bowed slightly and went upstairs.

Merriment pulled back the shutters on both windows and flipped the sign on the door. Shop was open. She was heading to the back room when the bell tinkled behind her. A footman entered; his gloves were snow white, his livery especially fine, made of the most expensive red cloth and trimmed with gold braid. He held the door open for a stylish young lady dressed in mother-of-pearl grey silk. She wore a black ribbon around her neck and as she entered, her tall white wig decorated with pink bows listed a little to one side.

'Good morning,' the lady said, unfazed by Merriment's breeches. It was then that Merriment realised that for the first time in years she'd forgotten to put on her holster. Her pistol was still upstairs.

'Hello, m'am.' Merriment bowed politely.

'I believe you sell something I require.' The lady moved towards the counter, her fine eyes gliding over the contents in the glass cases. Anne and Stella emerged from the back room with Janey Mack close behind. Both girls staggered to a halt, drinking in the exquisite gown the powdered lady was wearing.

'Girls, don't gawp,' the young lady smiled. She was very pretty, with high cheekbones both flecked with the barest dab of rouge, her lips were tinged a soft berry red, and her eyebrows were shaped into gentle arches that rose and crinkled expressively.

Anne smoothed her gloves and shook her long locks back, her competitive streak believing that she could hold her own natural beauty up to scrutiny against a rich lady any day. She caught sight of the lady's pink-trimmed shoes and all her confidence crumbled. The lady caught the gleam of envy emanating from Anne's blue eyes.

'Aren't they darling? I picked them up in Paris.'

'You wouldn't want to wear them down Dame Street,' Janey Mack piped up. 'They'd be covered in shite in no time.'

The lady laughed with her whole body and Anne forgave her her riches and her fine garments because anyone who knew how to laugh like that had a sense of humour.

'That's why I have a sedan chair outside,' the lady finally said.

'They'll be glad with your fare,' Janey Mack told her. 'I saw a woman fat as an ox getting into one on George's Street. The poor carriers were buckled under the strain.'

'Yes, I eat very little,' the lady told Janey Mack. 'I'm as light as a feather.'

Anne and Stella said goodbye. Merriment sent Janey Mack into the back room and politely shut the door. The lady dismissed the footman to wait outside with a discreet wave of her hand. Then turning to face Merriment, she quietly leaned forward and said, 'I believe you sell Misses Phillips' Engine.'

'That's right.' Merriment nodded.

'I will require twenty please,' the lady said, drawing out a crisp five-pound note from her studded purse. 'I want my girls to be clean and safe.'

Merriment didn't blink.

'I don't have twenty, but I can get them for you.'

'And you can give my girls the once-over?'

'Of course.'

'I don't want them traipsing through your shop, gives the impression they are contaminated. Can I employ you to make a house call?'

The lady slipped a card across the countertop. In simple black copperplate it read: *Margaret Leeson, 17 Henrietta Street.*

'You can call me Peg,' she said cheerfully. 'Can you come tomorrow evening, sometime around seven?'

Merriment said she could.

Peg smiled and stood a moment scrutinising Merriment's face.

'You know,' she said, tilting her head to one side, her wig teetering a little from the movement, 'Beresford did mention your remarkable eyes, but said nothing of your fine tresses or figure.'

The remark landed a two-pronged sting in Merriment's heart; on the one hand, she was intrigued and hopeful about the fact that Beresford had spoken about her in a flattering way; on the other hand, there was something about Peg's tone and glint of possessiveness in her eye that shot Merriment with a pang of jealousy.

Smiling broadly and slipping on a pair of cherry-coloured gloves, Peg waved her hands coquettishly and piped up, 'Men, eh?'

Then, leaving Merriment with the vaguest sensation of having being ambushed, Peg flitted out the door calling to her footman to take her to the nearest confectionary shop, while Merriment stood a moment washed over by a sudden wave of loneliness. She sniffed wryly, faintly amused that when spoken by a woman Beresford's name could still sting her.

7

The Keeper

Solomon had to pay five and two for the stall, despite Gloria's recommendation. Jody Maguire chewed on a wedge of black tobacco and glared about him, patting his walking stick against his thigh.

'It's the best spot in the whole market.'

A long streak of black spittle darted from his mouth and landed with a splat near Solomon's battered shoes.

'But the average stall . . .' Solomon didn't put up a fight. Long years of card playing had furnished him with the ability to quickly assess a character. And Jody Maguire was not for turning.

'Ye're not asking for an average stall. If ye want the spot, ye'll be charged for it.'

Jody Maguire rattled a glob of mucus at the back of his throat and noisily masticated.

'Right.' Solomon extended his hand to shake on the deal.

'Two weeks up front.'

'But . . .'

Solomon's jaw dropped. He quickly snapped his expression into a fake smile covering up the fact that two weeks' rent would clean him out. He'd spent a fortune at the printers, bought his licence, paid for lodgings and now this. If the market manager got a whiff of penury he'd walk away, give the spot to someone who could pay a steady rent.

'Ten shillings four pence it is so.'

Solomon watched the silver and copper mix in Jody Maguire's

dark greedy palm. The market manager didn't even nod; he just walked away, slipping the money into a satchel strapped across his wide chest. Solomon looked up at the statue of Satan. *You better be worth it*, he thought, folding out his stall and waving across to Gloria.

'Morning, Solomon,' she called brightly. 'See yer keeping bad company.'

'I've a cracking story,' Solomon told her. But she was being asked for three pies, one with meat, so she wasn't listening. Solomon folded out his stall. He lifted up the backboard and pinned several broadsheets to it. He weighed down others with stones and a bleached sheep's skull he'd found kicked behind a gate.

'Penny a sheet,' he hollered. 'Read all about it, Olocher is back from the grave. Haunting the Black Dog. One man has already been struck down by Olocher's terrifying ghost. Come and buy a true account of everything that has happened. The prison guard who saw Olocher slit his own throat is now paralysed down one side of his body.'

A small crowd gathered.

'What happened?' a woman wanted to know.

'Olocher's back from the grave,' Solomon grinned, jumping onto the base of the statue and clinging to Luicifer's trident, using the prop to underpin his words.

'The guard said Olocher is a demon now, half man half pig, made from the rotting flesh of Olocher's autopsied corpse and the malignant substance of his evil spirit. The guard, his name is Boxty, suffered an apoplexy as a result of the encounter and christened the fearful apparition that attacked him "the Dolocher". Look here, I have written word for word every gory detail, the horrible chronology of the gruesome events.'

And waving the broadsheet over the heads of the thickening crowd, Solomon broadcast in a clear, deep voice, 'Here you have a vivid and clear description of all that befell last night in the Black Dog Prison. Ladies and gentlemen, "the Dolocher" is as true, as real as I am standing here. As solid and dark as this statue of the devil himself.'

The crowd surged.

Broadsheets flew off the stand and word spread through the market like wildfire. There was a demon stalking the corridors of the Black Dog Prison. By three o'clock, Solomon had sold the last sheet. He had to turn two women away.

'They're all gone,' he said, cursing himself in his own mind. *I should have printed up three thousand.*

'I came all the way from Oxmanstown,' the woman with the squinting eye complained. Solomon could have kicked himself; the story had already travelled up as far as Smithfield.

'Will ye have more tomorrow?' the woman asked.

'I will indeed.'

The two women walked away promising to return the next day for a sheet. Solomon folded up his stall. He realised he was hungry, when a young boy of about fourteen, who'd been leaning against a wall watching him, came forward.

'Ye want another bit o' news?' the boy said, checking to see if the market manager was anywhere near. The boy had a pronounced cowlick to one side of his fringe. He was skinny and his legs looked malformed, like he'd a touch of rickets but not enough to make him completely bow-legged. Solomon glanced down at him.

'What do you mean?' he asked, upending his stall and leaving it balanced at Lucifer's dark feet.

'To do with yer story,' the boy nodded.

'Did Boxty die?'

The boy shrugged. 'Dunno.' He stuck his hands into his jacket pockets. 'Just think ye'd be interested in events happenin' right now down in the gaol.'

Solomon nodded quickly. 'You banned from here?'

The boy sucked on his upper teeth.

'Let's just say me and the market manger have an arrangement.

I insult him and he comes tearing after me. What can I say? I like to make the fat man run.'

The boy wiped his filthy nose with his grubby sleeve and grinned. He had a mouthful of crooked teeth.

'There's holy war over in the Black Dog, skin and hair flyin'.'

'Come on.' Solomon grabbed his carpet bag. It was weighed down with shillings and pennies. He swept his hand quickly over the young boy's shoulder, leading him in the direction of Gloria's stall.

'Four pies, Gloria, two with meat.'

'What a day ye've had, Solomon.' Without waiting for Solomon's response, Gloria fixed her bright eyes on the young boy and shook her head. 'Corker, love, yer rootin' for a hidin'. If Jody Maguire gets one whiff of ye he'll chastise ye with his stick from one end of Castle Street to th'other.'

'Have to catch me first.' Corker winked.

'Ye're takin' yer life in yer hands.' She wrapped up four pies. 'Here yez are. Two are on me, give us two pence.' Gloria smiled, her apple-dumpling face full of joy. 'I'd a smashin' day on account of you.' She waved a podgy finger at Solomon. 'Terror makes people hungry and the more that went to yer stall the more stopped here, and sure, the smell of my buttery pastry would tempt Jesus Christ himself down off the cross.'

Solomon gave her a couple of pennies.

'Yer a blessin',' Gloria said. 'Keep the devil comin' and the coppers rollin' in.'

'I'll do my best, Gloria. I'll do my best.'

Solomon gave Corker two pies and watched the boy wolf them down in ten seconds flat.

'Dear God, give your mouth a taste of what your belly is enjoying.'

Corker belched, thumping his sternum with the heel of his hand. 'Can't ponder food in my gaff, otherwise someone will snatch it out of yer maw.'

They left the market just as it began to spit rain. A line of horses were stuck waiting while a funeral cortege tramped down Werburgh Street. Solomon thought about heading back to Merriment's and taking a nap. Corker pointed to the side of Christ Church Cathedral.

'Ye'll want to go that way,' he said. 'Trust me.'

Why not, thought Solomon. They cut down Winetavern Street while Corker tried to negotiate a price.

'It's worth four pence.'

'What is?'

'The information.'

'I'll decide once I hear it.'

'Two pence up front, for good faith.'

Solomon laughed.

'A penny,' he gave in.

Corker nodded. 'And three pence once ye hear.' He deftly slipped the penny into his jacket pocket.

'Go on.'

'The second guard is missin'.'

Solomon stopped in his tracks. That thrilled Corker, who smiled broadly, showing all his crooked teeth. He'd just earned the easiest four pennies in his whole life.

'What do you mean?' Solomon held half a pie close to his mouth ready to bite, waiting for the young boy to elaborate.

'The other guard – the one that was with Boxty guarding Olocher the night he slit his own gullet – he's gone missing. What's his name? Martin something or other.'

'Martin Coffey?'

'Yeah.'

'He's done a runner,' Solomon supposed and, shrugging, he took off down the road again. 'Nothing damning in that,' he said finishing off one pie and starting on another – this had cubes of salty bacon mixed in with mashed potatoes and was seasoned with fresh herbs. Gloria could cook.

111

'Do the authorities think Martin murdered Olocher?' he asked.

'Nope.' Corker shook his head, fairly certain. The young boy had brown eyes and was stabbing the inside of his lower lip with his tongue like he was keeping the choicest bit of information for last.

'Not worth four pence,' Solomon said, flinging a bit of crust to a stray dog.

Corker cocked his head to one side. 'They carried out a big search, looking for this Martin fella up and down the building. They found his gun.'

Corker stopped walking, speaking for a moment to the back of Solomon's head.

'In the sentry box. His clothes were hanging off it. They say there's signs of a big fight. Some of them think Martin What-do-yer-call-him is dead. Everyone's saying he's been devoured. The Dolocher has got him and eaten him up, bones an' all.'

Solomon smirked and turned to look Corker straight in the face.

'Where did you hear this?'

'I hear things.' Corker stabbed at the side of his head with his long wiry fingers and held out his hand. 'Worth four pence, I'd say.'

Solomon was fetching four pence from his bag when Corker told him more.

'The bigwigs were over this morning. Lord Beresford nearly laid an egg. He tore strips off the Keeper, said he was running a shoddy house, beating money out of the inmates and letting prisoners murder themselves with remorse. He said he was going to skin the Keeper alive for cocking things up. Livid, so he was. He tore the wig off his head and flung it at the wall, promising to rip the place down stone by stone and swearing he would get to the bottom of things one way or another. He wanted to

112

interview Martin Coffey and anyone else who was on duty the night of Olocher's death.'

'And that's when Martin Coffey's gun and clothes were discovered?'

'Ye hit the nail on the head.'

They were turning down Cooke Street when a horse and rider thundered past, driving Solomon and Corker into the high wall surrounding the Black Dog Prison.

'That's Beresford,' Corker said.

'In a hurry.'

Corker patted down his coat and torn shirt and shifted his shoulders.

'Lost an eye in some naval battle.'

They stood at the gate of the Black Dog and looked up the steps. The rain fell in bright silver slants; the wind whistled in the wrought-iron castings holding the bowls of unlit pitch.

'There's the next part to yer story,' Corker grinned. 'Thanks for the shekels.'

He tugged a forelock and Solomon wondered if his split fringe had been formed by the habit of grinning irreverently and saying goodbye.

'Are you not coming in?' Solomon said.

'Me and the Keeper don't agree. Ye'd want to watch him, his name is Hawkins, he'd rob the eye out of yer head and murder ye for yer teeth and that's on a good day.'

Corker sauntered away, calling back, 'I'll keep ye informed of any developments.'

'You do that.'

Solomon pushed into the wind and up the steps.

There was a sombre battle taking place in the reception room when Solomon stepped in out of the rain. The door clicked behind him but the bullies leaning over the large rosewood desk only glanced at him a moment before resuming their business,

113

while a weather-beaten warden smoked a long clay pipe and blinked back at them incredulously.

'The Cut's not happy,' a bully as large as an oast house announced.

'Sure, I'm not happy,' the warden retorted, tamping down the tobacco in the bulb of his pipe. 'And Martin Coffey is not happy either, what's left of him, that is,' he chuckled malevolently. 'Don't come in here, threatening me with the Cut.' He grinned, exposing three brown teeth and the black edges of his gums. 'I've me own worries to contend with. Me own boss—' He bit off the last of the sentence and looked at Solomon.

The oast-house bully caressed the tip of a long blade shoved into a leather, patterned scabbard and by way of coercion grinned and muttered, 'He'll have to be given Martin's share.'

'Oh aye,' the warden stoically nodded, lighting up his pipe with three thoughtful puffs. 'Then ye'll have to chat to the Keeper. Naught to do with me. Now young man.' The old warden had seen his share of bullies and reprobates, and brushed the group aside with a weary wave of his hand to call Solomon forward. 'What's yer business?'

But before Solomon could answer, the bullies flung open the door into the prison and disappeared down the corridors shouting, 'Keeper. Oh, Keeper. Knock, knock.'

The wizened warden chuckled to himself, 'They'll rue today.'

Solomon scratched his head. 'I'm here on behalf of Beresford.'

Unperturbed, the warden relit his pipe and, not bothering to hear out Solomon's request, waved him away, not caring where he went. It was by pure chance that he met the young guard who had helped him carry Boxty to the hospital.

'Can you take me to the sentry box where Martin Coffey's gun and clothes were found?'

The young guard's name was Michael and his pale complexion gave him an unearthly quality that was eerily amplified by the greenish gloom of the corridors.

'Has Boxty lost his mind?' Michael asked Solomon.

'Just frightened out of his wits,' Solomon replied.

'And now Martin's dead,' Michael whispered. 'Makes me fearful of working here.'

Solomon didn't answer. They proceeded deep into the gaol, silent, until Solomon frowned and asked, 'Who's the Cut?'

Michael's pale blue eyes flicked anxiously up at Solomon's face. 'No one I know of,' he lied, pointing ahead. They passed into a T-shaped corridor and were bisecting it when Solomon looked behind and saw the two bullies who had been in reception pull out weapons and start banging at the wall and shouting, 'Garnish, garnish.'

'Come on.' Michael pulled him quickly away.

Solomon trotted after him. 'What's garnish?' he enquired.

'Money for cleaning out slop, for the candle maker, for the necessaries. Every inmate is obliged to pay garnish.'

'To the Cut?' Solomon probed.

'Here we are.' Michael led the way down a dreary flight of steps into a narrow room lined with peeling plaster where two men in the process of sitting down jumped to their feet and humbly saluted.

'No need for formalities,' Solomon waved them back to their bench, 'I only have a few questions, for the Board,' he said, and was immediately distracted by the splatter of red stains running up the crumbling plaster. 'Is that blood?' He peered closer.

'It is,' a bearded man with a large growth protruding from his forehead confirmed. 'Did ye know Martin?' he asked.

Solomon shook his head.

'Pity.' The bearded man's eyes glinted quickly at his friend. 'Only, if ye knew him well, ye might tell us if those are his.'

He pointed a filthy fingernail at a pail standing against the wall. Solomon looked into the bucket. There, shivering shiny and black and glistening with scarlet blood, were what looked like two kidneys and a corner of heart on a bed of wobbling intestine.

'Jesus.' Solomon retracted his head.

The bearded man and his friend snorted, choking back the laughter.

'Ah, it's not funny,' the bearded man growled, his bulbous eyes straining to keep themselves attached to their sockets.

Solomon cocked an eyebrow and stared up the wall. 'He was sliced open.'

'Put up a fight,' the bearded man nodded. 'See?'

His discoloured fingernail pointed further up the wall where, lodged in the moist plaster work and gleaming dully, was a musket ball. His companion grunted in agreement and that was when Solomon noticed a wad of shredded rags in the second man's hand.

Solomon made a quick note. *Weapon discharged.* 'Are they his clothes?' he asked.

The second man nodded, stray wisps of hair sprouting from his bald pate, his eyes desolately staring at the mess of bloody material between his palms. He held out the shirt; it fell in strips from a seam in the shoulders and was stained with dark patches of purple-black blood.

Michael let out the faintest moan. 'I'm not staying here,' he whispered. He left and the man with the beard scratched the growth on his forehead and looked at his friend.

'What is it, Smithy?'

The other man clacked his tongue and flung the rags into the bucket.

'Bastard owed me money,' he grumbled.

Solomon left the two men scrubbing the cell and retraced his steps to the reception room. He was closing the door at the top of the narrow steps when he heard someone screaming.

'Stop, stop, leave me alone.'

The cries came from the corridor and there was something

116

about the voice that tugged at Solomon's memory. He rushed into the green passageway, a door was flung open with a loud bang and the inmate ran out, familiarly dressed in only a shirt, his skinny legs white and naked. It was Charlie and he was desperate.

'Someone, help me,' he cried, running towards Solomon, his whole face charged with agonised terror.

Solomon skidded to a halt.

'Come here, ye faggot.'

A slight man, with narrow shoulders thundered after Charlie, grabbed him by the hair and slammed his skull into the wall.

'Hey,' Solomon roared, rushing to Charlie's defence. 'What the hell are you doing?'

The man stopped, still holding Charlie by a fistful of hair. He glared at Solomon.

'Fuck off,' he bellowed.

Charlie crumpled to his knees, his forehead bleeding. He sobbed over and over.

'Leave me alone. I'll get it. I'll get the money.'

Despite his size, the man's free hand curled into a fist and came down hard on Charlie's right arm. Solomon heard the snap.

'Jesus, stop,' he shouted, lurching forward, desperate to retrieve Charlie from his awful predicament. He grabbed the man's forearm, hauling on it, trying to prise it away from its trajectory, aiming this time for Charlie's ribs.

The man pushed Solomon back, sending him flying against the wall, his sinewy body strong beyond belief. Solomon felt his ribs crack. He gasped for air, winded. The man laughed, his breath coming in snorts. He was exerted but in no way tired. He paused to look at Solomon doubled over, still hanging onto Charlie by the hair. Charlie fainted in and out of consciousness with the pain.

'Who the fuck are you?' the man said, noticing the contents of Solomon's bag strewn across the flagstones.

Solomon clutched his stomach and tried to stand upright.

'I've been sent on behalf of the Board.'

The little man didn't bat an eyelid. He had an angular face comprised of blades and indents, a protruding forehead, a jutting jaw and a pointy chin. His eyes were empty and hard and a red scar ran across his purple complexion to the edge of his snarling mouth.

'Bullshit.'

The little man hauled Charlie upright and heaved him into the wall again.

'You owe me fifty pounds,' he said, kicking Charlie, who howled frantically.

'You've broken his arm,' Solomon yelled.

'You going to pay for his accommodation?' the little man asked.

Solomon's heart dropped like a lead weight into the pit of his stomach. The man beating Charlie was the Keeper.

'I – I . . .' Solomon stuttered.

'Is that the arrangement?' and like a light the Keeper dropped Charlie's battered body, pushed past Solomon and dived at the open carpet bag, greedy fingers riffling through Solomon's belongings, quickly snatching up his day's earnings.

'That's mine,' Solomon roared, running to get his things. Before he knew what had happened, the Keeper's fist ploughed into Solomon's face and the pain of his nose being shoved into the middle of his skull sent a shock through his whole body. He was launched backwards into an endless black.

8

The Cure

Janey Mack sat on the high stool, her legs stuck out, checking and looking and rechecking again.

'Aren't they the nicest pair of boots ye ever seen in yer whole life?' She was wearing a sage-green shift with a pale undershirt and a brown short jacket trimmed with two faded orange bows. She admired the buttons running up the side of her boots and the neat little heel capped with a half-moon of steel that made her feet tap wherever she walked.

'They are the nicest boots,' Merriment said, filling out the order form for Misses Phillips' Engine. She sealed it with a blob of wax. It was almost time to close up. The light was waning and the markets were long empty. The only traffic on the road were civil servants heading home for supper or down Dame Street to Lizzy's Coffee House for a pastry or next door to Hannifan's Chop House for a slab of meat and a pint of ale. Business had picked up. Today Merriment had had sixteen customers. She was pulling the shutters across and contemplating cooking something to eat when the door opened and a frail old lady with a hunched back furtively stepped in and looked about.

'Ye closing up?'

Her voice was a whisper. She was weighed down by material. Her long dress consisted of layers of old and battered lace that had once been supported by a whalebone hoop. The skirts hung and dragged and disguised the fact that she had a club foot. Her cloak was lined with moth-eaten ermine and her periwig was discoloured and molten in patches. Everything she wore was a relic of a more prosperous time, when she was young and wealthy, long before her dowry had been swindled and she had been reduced to a penny-pinching old dame.

'Come in,' Merriment said warmly. Janey Mack sidled from the stool, a little afraid of the ancient, tattered lady moving through the twilit room like an injured crow.

'Janey, you head on into the back and I'll be in in a minute.' Merriment quietly flipped the shop sign and lit a candle. 'Now, madam, how can I help you?'

'I live on Hanbury Lane,' the lady began. 'I'm a neighbour of Misses Byrne's.' Merriment nodded. The old lady brushed the edge of her wig near her temple. 'I believe you know her housemaid, Anne MacCarrick?'

'Yes.' Merriment waited.

'And you've provided a friend of Anne's with a cure for a bad-tempered father?'

Merriment nodded. The old lady looked particularly grotesque in the candlelight, her sunken face retained the barest hint of defiance but her general demeanour was one of downtrodden surrender. She reached a gloved finger onto the counter and drew arthritic circles as she tried to figure out a way to ask for what she needed.

'I was never pretty,' she said, swallowing back her pride. 'Always had the hump and the foot. But my father was relatively well off. He ran a little business on the corner of Skinner's Row. I met Harold when I was seventeen and could be told nothing.'

She pinched her mouth together, patting the edge of her periwig and touching her temple, mustering up the courage to tell everything.

'I fell.' She clacked her tongue and snorted with derision. 'When my father discovered I was with child he . . . well.' She waved the end of the story off, looking away. 'I never saw my family again. I married Harold and he has diminished me in more ways than I can count. He has beaten me, reduced me.'

She leaned wearily on her walking stick. 'I'm sorry,' she mumbled.

Merriment waited. The old lady spent a long time staring at the countertop, sometimes sighing, sometimes clacking her tongue, always looking like she was on the verge of saying something. At last she shook her head and turned.

'It was all my own doing,' she said firmly. 'I made my own bed and I've to lie in it.' She looked up at Merriment, her eyes filled with a resolute pain: fifty years of hurt that spun on the thin edge of a decision she had made when she was a young and foolish girl of seventeen.

'I must go,' she said flatly. 'Sorry to bother you. You won't breathe a word to Anne?'

'No,' Merriment whispered.

'All right.' The old lady patted her periwig and took a deep breath, turning slowly.

Merriment watched her hobble towards the door, the sudden terror of her own old age flashing before her.

'Does he have spasms?' she blurted out.

The old lady stopped, half-turning. In profile she was bowed into the shape of a question mark.

'I don't know,' she replied.

'Delirium tremens?'

The old lady shook her head, her hump moving back and forth a fraction.

'All I know,' she said sadly, 'is that he hates me. I enrage him.'

Merriment nodded.

'Wait here.'

When she went into the back room to fetch a jar of dried green seeds, Janey Mack was twirling in her new shift and dancing in front of the fire.

'Is the aul' one gone?' the little girl asked, tottering to a halt.

Merriment made the shape 'no' with her mouth, then

frowning, she added, 'Don't set yourself alight. Move back from the flame. Do you want your legs to end up like your hand?'

She went back into the shop, shutting the door behind her, and placed the seeds on the countertop. The old woman was leaning near the candle now, her lower jaw moving from side to side, her eyes staring intently at Merriment's hands, obviously in two minds about what she was doing.

'This is a pacifying cure,' Merriment told the old lady. 'It has anti-spasmodic and narcotic properties.'

She got the mortar and pestle and ground a portion of the seeds into a fine powder. The old lady stared, her grey eyes following the movement of the pestle. Merriment tipped the powder into a cardboard box and pushed the lid down.

'It's called *Passiflora incarnata*. The blooms remind people of the thorns worn by Jesus.'

The old lady's eyes glazed with unexpected tears. She hid her face a moment behind her crooked, swollen fingers, her whole frame shaking with a mixture of guilt and hope.

'It's a strong sedative,' Merriment told her, sliding the box forward. 'Sprinkle it on his food, or into his drink. Do it three times a day or whenever you feel he's getting out of hand.'

The old lady took the box, looking at it a moment, contemplating it in the yellow throbbing candlelight. Merriment tried to read the old lady's troubled face.

'I haven't given you enough to kill him,' she said. 'Just enough to subdue his mania. Even if you poured the whole box into his dinner he wouldn't die.'

The old lady's head bobbed, her wig slipping a little on her narrow skull.

'All right,' she said hoarsely. 'It's just . . .' She paused, staring at the little box like it contained her soul. 'I was reared religious. Devout. If I do this' – she looked deep into Merriment's eyes desperate for guidance – 'I'm lost, aren't I?'

Merriment took in a long slow breath, her heart swelling in

her chest. The whole idea of God made her uncomfortable. She'd been too long at sea, too far away from the rituals and the habits of the city to remember what being devout even meant. She had long ago lost faith. God was a haphazard concept only to be called upon in high winds and rough seas and even then he didn't respond.

'If you killed your husband,' Merriment said gently, 'then you would most certainly be lost. But since you are helping him to be calm and less poisoned by hatred, then . . .'

She left the sentence hang, wishing she could back track from the moral dilemma the old lady was dragging her into. The old woman nodded sadly. She stared at the box for a long time. Still she didn't move. Merriment heard the town crier ring the half hour. It was half past seven.

'I only have a penny ha'penny,' the old lady confessed, embarrassed by all her failings. 'How much more will I owe you?'

Merriment patted the old lady's hand.

'See if it works first. If it works you can pay me the penny ha'penny.'

The old lady kept her eyes on the counter, filled with the shame of having to beg for favours. She was unable to look up.

'Thank you,' she whispered, slowly turning to leave.

'Here.' Merriment couldn't stop herself. She grabbed a box of green tea mixed with *Aurum metallicum* from a glass case and shoved it into the old lady's hand.

'For your arthritis.'

The old lady couldn't speak. Merriment saw her out and fastened up the door, her heart squeezing in her chest. Unless business improved she may well be looking at a harsh old age herself.

If you keep giving away your stock, business won't improve, she thought, squeezing her chin and rubbing her hands over her face.

She pressed her back to the door and closed her eyes, a cold realisation washing over her that she was out of her depth and there was only one thing for it.

'I'll have to see Beresford.' An old longing unexpectedly fluttered up out of her belly bursting across her heart. It had been so long since she had wanted the comfort of Beresford's steady thinking, so long since she had rested in his arms. Why now? She pinched the bridge of her nose, confused by the ache of tender memories. He loved his wife. She tried to quash the recollection of Peg Leeson's pearly white skin, repressing any notion that they might be connected. *He loved me*, she thought forlornly, swallowing back a lump of regret. Then, by way of rational thinking, she tried to convince herself that they were unsuited. But nothing could quell the idea that she would like to see him. *I could thank him for sending business my way.* She half smiled at her own neediness. *And then ask him for money. Charming.* She took in a long, slow breath and tried to stop the scalding thoughts, pushing all hopes of Beresford away.

Janey Mack popped her head out into the shop and grinned.

'You all right?' she asked.

'Starving,' Merriment rallied and smiled.

'She was like a witch,' Janey Mack said marching into the shop, pounding her new boots hard on the floor to hear the dandy sound they made.

Janey Mack's rattle and hum dispelled Merriment's anxiety. The little girl babbled and twirled and pulled subjects out of the air, intoxicated by her new-found prosperity.

'What'll we have for supper?'

'Fried potatoes,' Merriment said, and the little girl's eyes popped out on stalks.

After supper when Merriment was re-bandaging Janey Mack's hand the little girl looked up at the ceiling and asked, 'What's in the third room, off the landing, next door to Solomon?'

'Rubbish and clutter.'

'Is there a fireplace?'

'I don't know.'

'Maybe we could clean the rubbish out.'

'Could turn it into your room, I suppose.' Merriment tried to hide her smile.

'I was thinkin' that.' Janey Mack grinned from ear to ear.

'You're some operator, Janey. Anyone ever tell you that?'

'Hoppy John said I was made for the law. That there were enough turns and alleys to me thinkin' to bombast a judge. He said I could trick a barge from underneath the feet of a skipper if I put me mind to it. But honest to God, miss, I wasn't operatin' for to take advantage of the situation. It just seems a waste of a perfectly well-constructed room to be sleeping in on top of ye here when yer working at night.'

'Very thoughtful of you.'

Merriment finished up the bandage. She hadn't the heart to tell Janey Mack that the room was used for storage because the roof leaked and the fire smoked and, if truth be told, she couldn't afford to keep four fires burning even if three of them were only being lit at night.

'What time is it, miss?'

'Maybe you should start calling me Merriment.'

'If ye like. I thought Solomon would be home hours ago. He's unreliable, isn't he, miss? Gets away with murder 'cause his face is pretty. I'm supposed to put on a chop for his supper. But sure it could be burnt to a crisp before he darkens the door . . . and I've to set a fire in his room.'

'Oh,' Merriment frowned, looking at the clean bandage. 'I forgot. I'll do it.'

'I'll come with ye.'

Janey Mack carried the candle. Merriment brought the scuttle and the kindling. The stairwell appeared narrower and higher in the gloom. Janey Mack gazed at her lengthening shadow creeping up the dark walls. Occasionally the candle flame trembled on the painted yellow breast of a trapped canary. During the day the wallpaper was cheery; at night it became melancholy and morbid.

'Maybe Sol is gone to see Boxty,' Janey Mack whispered, frightened by her own shadow behaving like a detached being. 'Do you want to go in first?'

She opened the door, too terrified to go into Solomon's room in the dark. Merriment brushed past knowing by instinct the direction of the fire. Janey Mack followed.

'On consideration,' she whispered, glancing across the landing to the third door. 'Maybe it would be better if I slept in your room.'

'That's all right,' Merriment said, holding out her hand. 'Give me the candle.'

The kindling hissed and sparked in the fireplace. Janey Mack was just about to sneak a peek into Solomon's bags when there was a knock on the front door.

'Bet that's himself.' Janey Mack took off. 'Come on.' She waved her bandaged hand. Merriment set two logs on the hissing flames before leading Janey Mack down the stairs.

When they opened the door it was the little girl who reacted first.

'Holy mother of God, what happened to your face?'

Solomon was leaning against the door frame with two black-ened eyes, a broken nose and a loose tooth.

'Maybe you'll let me in first,' he said, clutching his ribs.

Merriment sat him down in the chair nearest the fire. She fetched water, fresh lavender, bandages and arnica, while Janey Mack pumped Solomon for all the information.

'I was robbed,' Solomon groaned.

'Ye poor divil. Where?'

'In the Black Dog Prison.'

'In the prison?' Janey Mack squealed. 'Isn't that shockin', miss?'

'By the Keeper.'

126

'Ye know who robbed ye?' Janey Mack looked from Solomon to Merriment and back again. 'Are ye sure?' Janey asked.

Merriment set about cleaning off the last of the blood caked around Solomon's nostrils.

'Ow.'

'Mind him, that's sore.' Janey Mack stood on the stool to get a better look at things.

'Thank you for that,' Merriment said. Then looking at Solomon, she said, 'You know it's broken.'

He nodded.

'I can fix it straight if you let me splint it up.'

His vanity getting the better of him, Solomon nodded again.

'I've to push the cartilage into place. It's going to hurt like hell.'

'Ye can bite down on a stick,' Janey Mack said, looking at the kindling spilling out over the fender. 'Hoppy John had to when he was gettin' his leg cut off proper.'

Merriment gently rubbed arnica around Solomon's bruised eyes.

'I think Solomon is bold enough and brave enough to do this without the stick. I need to get at the nose and not have anything barring my way. Janey, go to that drawer over there and look for a wooden box with a red circle on it and bring it to me.'

Janey Mack did as she was told, chattering all the while.

'Did ye get the beadles to arrest the Keeper?'

'Pointless,' Solomon groaned. 'He beat an inmate to a pulp, that's how I got involved in the first place.'

'Trying to stop him beating a prisoner up?'

'He took everything,' Solomon winced, retracting his head away from the slightest pressure of Merriment's index finger as it slipped near his inner eye and down along his swollen nose.

'Here you are.' Janey Mack watched Merriment open the box

and pull one nose splint after another out, until she found one that was the best size.

'They're like triangles,' Janey Mack told Solomon.

'It's going to be tight, and I'm going to be firm,' Merriment warned him. 'Ready yourself. Sit with both feet on the ground, both hands holding the sides of the chair and rest your head on the back.'

Solomon did as he was told and Janey Mack took up her position on the three-legged stool. Merriment reached her left arm over the back of the chair. Turning a little to one side, she bore down on Solomon, her right knee crossing the tops of his legs, and, leaning hard on him, she crushed the small splint quickly and firmly along his nose. Solomon let out an almighty yell and launched forward, howling and thrashing and clutching his face.

'Jesus, mother of fucking Jesus.'

'Done and dusted. Now, sit back down and I'll bandage you up.'

Solomon couldn't see, his eyes were watering so much, and the pain was cutting through his head, sending shocks down his whole body. He doubled over, his face buried in his hands, whimpering like an injured dog. Janey Mack dragged her lips away from her teeth, hissing with sympathy.

'That nearly killed him, miss. Are ye all right, Sol? Are ye all right?'

'Bloody, mother of divine . . .'

He pulled his hands away and sucked his mouth in, his eyes still smarting.

'What a bloody day.'

The pain was beginning to subside. He shoved his loose tooth further up into his gum and sat down glumly, ready to be bandaged.

Merriment wrapped him under the ears and across the nose and then under the chin and over the crown of the head so that he looked half mummified.

'You'll have to report the incident to the Board,' she said.

'It's my word against his,' Solomon groaned. 'And who knows me? Who can vouch for my character? The man's a tyrant. I wouldn't mind but I had it on good authority to watch out for him.'

Corker's words still rang in his ears.

'What were ye doin' in the Black Dog in the first place. Ye think ye'd avoid it like the plague considering the Dolocher.' Because she couldn't wring her hands Janey Mack had developed a new habit of opening and closing her right fist as a way of releasing her worry. 'Are ye soft in the head?'

'I'd been given a tip.'

Solomon moaned and grabbed his carpet bag, tugging out a sheaf of paper, a battered tin box containing a quill, some loose nibs and the small cubed bottle of Roman shellac that Merriment had sold him.

'I've to write . . .' He suddenly flung his quill down, grabbed the tin box and lobbed it across the room. It clanged noisily against the wall, and knocking against a huge jar, rang it like a bell.

'What the . . .?' Merriment stepped back.

'I'm sorry.' Solomon stood up. 'I'm sorry.' He sank back down, ashamed and frustrated. 'I can't afford to pay the printer. The Keeper robbed all my money. The one story that has a follow-on and I can't write it to sell it. People promised me they would be back tomorrow for more and I have more and I can't . . .'

Solomon stared at the floor.

'How much do ye need?' Janey Mack asked, creeping closer and looking intently into his face.

'Four shillings. I had twenty times that in my bag. It was the best day's selling I ever had.'

His shoulders suddenly lifted. Something struck him and Merriment drew back her head, straightening up, knowing what was coming next.

Don't ask, she recited over and over. *Don't ask.*

'The deposit. One week, if I could take one week back. You'll have it tomorrow afternoon.'

So used to smiling and dazzling people with his eyes and light manner, Solomon pleaded, oblivious to the fact that his greatest asset was now battered and swollen and wrapped in a bandage. Merriment took a deep breath and pushed her feet into the ground. She felt off balance, tipping sideways. The land was more uncertain under foot than the sea.

'I'm sorry,' she said, remembering her pistol lying up on the table in her bedroom. 'On principle, never a borrower nor a lender be.' She knew she sounded priggish but she folded her arms over her chest and, drawing on her logical side, she quickly outlined the impossibility of giving Solomon back his money.

'It's spent. On stock, on firewood, on the chop for your dinner.'

Solomon nodded.

'Of course, I shouldn't have asked. You don't know me. And it looks bad, a stranger . . .' He rubbed his knee over and over. 'I swear to God.' He shoved the chair back and fetched the tin box he had flung away. 'I feel like I've an albatross about my neck. I'm a magnet for bad luck and misfortune.'

He sat back down and looked up at Merriment, his two eyes swallowed in folds of dark red flesh.

'I should never have asked. I am sorry.'

Janey Mack rubbed the fingers of her right hand over her thumb and stared breathlessly at Merriment waiting for her to fix things. Merriment pulled a chair closer to the fire and sat down.

'Will ye have yer chop, seein' as ye paid for it an' all?' Janey Mack asked.

Solomon laughed his short laugh which made him clutch his side and catch his breath.

'I will, Janey love, thank you.' Then waving his quill, he warned her. 'Don't make me laugh now, or my head might literally fall off.'

Janey Mack fetched a pan and slapped the pork chop into the sizzling lard, every now and again glancing up at Merriment expecting her to say something. Solomon opened his bottle of ink and dipping his quill in, he began writing.

'Are ye still writing a broadsheet anyway?'

'I am, Janey.'

'Even though ye've no money?'

'I might persuade the printer . . .'

Janey Mack looked over at Merriment, who was gazing into the fire, her face picked out by the light, her long curls shining. She crossed her legs, resting her chin on her hand and her elbow on the side of the chair.

'What's to write about?' Janey Mack wondered. Solomon told her. The little girl brought his chop to the table and handed him a knife and fork.

'All the saints and angels in blessed heaven,' she exclaimed. 'Ye think the Dolocher devoured the man!'

'Looks like it.' Solomon dived on the plate, starving, a rush of saliva bursting into his mouth. He sawed a sliver of pork, popped it into his mouth and moaned loudly, realising that it was agony to chew.

'Oh, my teeth,' he grumbled, chewing delicately, trying to get the meat to melt.

'And the gun didn't kill him?'

Solomon shook his head. 'Sure, how could a musket ball penetrate a demon?'

Janey Mack nodded seriously.

Merriment roused herself.

'Time for bed, Janey. We'll put a fire down in my room and I'll leave you with a candle.'

'Sure is it even nine o'clock?' Janey Mack didn't want to go to bed.

'No arguing, you need your sleep. Come on, say goodnight to Mister Fish.'

Solomon paused, aware of Merriment's formality. His request for money had driven a firm wedge between him and his new landlady. Janey Mack didn't move.

'Do ye like me new dress and jacket, Sol?'

'You know what, Janey, you look pretty as a picture. I was so wrapped up in myself I never even complimented you on your lovely dress. And what a pair of boots.'

Janey Mack gave a little curtsey and then quick as a flash pulled off her boots, her jacket and her new shift. She stood in her petticoat, her bandaged arm waving in the air.

'There,' she announced, grinning from ear to ear.

'Well, you'll win a prize for speed,' Solomon told her.

Janey Mack picked up her boots and new clothes and plopped them on the table in front of Solomon.

'Ye'll fetch two and six for these in the pawnshop round the corner.'

'Janey.' Merriment's jaw dropped. She launched forward, touching her forehead, confused. 'What are you doing?'

'Sure, I'll have them back by tomorrow afternoon. He'll make a killin' at the market with that story and get them back for me. Won't ye, Sol?'

Solomon felt crushed, his lungs compressed as he swallowed back a whelp of agony.

'I – I can't . . .' he stuttered.

'I'll give Mister Fish the money,' Merriment said, tapping Janey Mack's shoulders.

'Thought ye'd spent it?'

'Janey, you'd hang the apostles.' Merriment couldn't help laughing. 'I have a little put aside for luxuries like food and fuel. Now, take the candle and your boots and your new clothes. Go on. Up you go.'

She patted Janey Mack's arms, missing the quick wink the little girl gave to Solomon.

'I'll be up in a minute,' Merriment said. 'And Janey. That was a very nice thing to do.'

'You're the best girl in all of Ireland,' Solomon said, grinning painfully. He wished he could crawl into a corner and wake up yesterday.

'See you in a bit.' Clutching her bundle of clothes close to her heart, she took the candle in her injured hand and manoeuvred through the door.

'I'm sorry.' Solomon hung his head again.

Merriment felt a perplexing mix of shame and guilt.

'No,' she shook her head. 'I'm sorry.'

She went into the shop and, unlocking the cash box, took out eight shillings. When she came back into the room Solomon was staring gloomily into the fire.

'You've had a bad day. I will need the full amount back tomorrow.' She placed the stack of bright coins on the table.

'That's more than I asked for.' Solomon couldn't move. His hands lay in fists on the table.

'If you do a double print run, sell it for two pence ha'penny, you will make it back ten-fold, I guarantee you. I heard people talking about the Dolocher in the shop today. Word is spreading. And you've the story, you know . . .'

Merriment shrugged her shoulders. She remembered days like this at sea. When the wind blustered and blew and ripped the sails. Those were the days when the ship listed, and masts creaked, when rations spilt and the churning waters sent foam and fever over the bow. Those were the days Beresford would come below and steal a ration of brandy from the sickbay stores and tell her, 'Stand fast now. Nothing like hardship to build the character.' She recollected that all voyages met obstacles and unforeseen catas-trophes. *The only way to ride out the storm is to go with the wind and the wild water and trust that the sea won't drag you down this time.* She looked at Solomon's broken face and gave a half-smile.

133

'Things will get better,' she said, more to herself than to him. Solomon nodded.

'You'll get it back,' he said firmly.

And Merriment left him, hunched over his broadsheet, his quill scratching furiously on the white paper, his eyes bleary and bloodshot, his jaw throbbing, the recollection of Martin Coffey's remains glistening in the bucket sending a shiver down his spine. He wrote for a good hour, until finally he sat back and looked at the stack of bright coins glowing in the candlelight. He tapped them with his index finger and carefully pocketed the lot. Putting away his quill, he moved stealthily, tiptoeing through the shop. He quietly slipped into the bustling street and made his way towards the Cock and Hen on Cooke Street, convinced that with a good hand he could replenish his losses.

9

The Hiding Well

Sunrise was gold and pink. Janey Mack stood on the window seat looking down on Fishamble Street. She recognised the old man with the cart carrying cockles, and the milkmaid with her quart jug and stool, driving two cows before her. She saw Solomon cross the road, his head like a cracked egg. He knocked on the printer's door and was let in.

'Here you are.' Merriment handed the little girl a pair of green woolly socks.

'Do you wonder why he's so sad?' Janey Mack asked, slipping her feet into her new boots.

'Who?'

'Sol. I mean, he smiles a lot and jokes, but he's sad. Isn't he?'

'He's been robbed and beaten,' Merriment replied.

'Before that. He was sad the first day we saw him.'

Merriment frowned. She hadn't noticed anything particularly melancholy about Solomon. She shrugged. 'I've no idea, Janey, perhaps everyone is sad.'

'You're not.'

'You're right. Now come on, chatterbox, let's have breakfast.'

Merriment fastened on her holster, slipped the Answerer inside and buttoned up her waistcoat.

When she opened up the shop, she was stunned to find a line of middle-aged and elderly women queuing to come in.

'Morning.' She held the door open as five women, all cloaked and gloved and dressed in worsted skirts, filed inside.

A stout woman with ginger hair led the way. She waddled to the counter and, surveying the ladies with her, became their spokeswoman. 'Now then, we believe ye've a cure for all ailments, particularly pertaining to the specific problems of spouses.'

Merriment flicked her eyes over the earnest faces. What had she got herself into? Two women wanted to purge their husbands' bad temper. Another was looking to 'wake him up. Sure, there's no jizz in him at all.' One woman's husband kept crying and needed something to lift his spirits. The last woman's husband was too pious.

Merriment shifted uncomfortably, fumbling a little with her ledger. She had only helped Stella and the old woman out of pity. She knew if she kept offering potions to improve the disposition of cantankerous men she could be charged with issuing unlawful prescriptions and lose her licence.

'I'm sorry,' she began. 'You misunderstand. I am here to provide cures.'

'That's what we heard.' The ginger-haired woman nodded seriously.

'No, I apologise,' Merriment interjected, acutely aware that if she admitted that she had provided powders that subdued extremely difficult men for no other reason than to help unfortunate women, she could be reported. She was in a tricky situation.

'You helped Stella.' The ginger-haired woman's blue eyes locked onto Merriment's face. Her friends clustered tight around her. A cold silence descended while the group which had seemed soft and giddy coalesced into a formidable force full of steely resolve. The women knew what they were asking and without speaking, in that silent collective stare, fully communicated what they wanted. They understood clearly what Merriment had done, and they wanted their share of the 'cure' for their difficult men.

'I don't think I can help.' Merriment swallowed.

'Course ye can, love,' the ginger-haired woman said softly. 'Let's just say we'll not tell, you'll have our business and our gratitude and, well, a cure is a cure, is it not? And that's yer job, is it not?'

Merriment felt backed into a corner; there was enough cuteness in the ginger-haired woman's eyes to expose the veiled threat. If Merriment didn't comply, she may very well be reported to the guild, lose her licence and be flung out onto the street. She glanced over at Janey Mack, sitting blinking on her stool.

'I suppose . . .' And with those words the women achieved their victory, the atmosphere instantly softening. They babbled, flapped and flustered and pointed at powders and labelled drawers while each woman gave Merriment a long list of symptoms, curious to see what the female apothecary would prescribe for cruel tempers and spiteful rages. Once she had committed to her fate, Merriment convinced herself that by giving mild doses the guild could not touch her and the women would get some form of satisfaction. So she prepared gentle prescriptions, undercharged her clients and found herself amused by those gathered around her.

Janey Mack entertained the women telling them about the Dolocher and sending them over to Solomon's stall.

'He's next to Lucifer, ye can't miss him. He's bandaged like a boil.'

Merriment mixed powders and tinctures and scribbled notes. She added and subtracted, made bargains and found herself laughing. All that time in sickbay she had moved among men . . . She laughed back then, she was certain of it, but here, there was some kind of unspoken sympathy, a peculiar unity of understanding that made even the simplest of remarks funny. Merriment was confounded to discover that she enjoyed the company of women.

*

'Holy mother of God and the multitude of saints and angels.'

Gloria's expression was trapped between surprise and horror. Her mouth hinged open and her chin puckered, and her thick, fleshy arm reached tentatively for Solomon's jaw.

'Ye look like Lazarus, raised from the dead with the swaddling shroud still on him.'

'I met the Keeper of the Black Dog.'

'Ye poor morsel. What did ye do to him that made him destroy yer face?'

'I said hello.'

Gloria helped Solomon set up his stall.

'I'll be with ye in a minute, darlin',' she called over to a young woman carrying a barrel of curds.

'You go on.' Solomon patted Gloria's broad back. 'Thank you for your help.'

'I've had three people already askin' after ye.' Gloria wiped her hands on her floury apron. 'They walked over from Crooked Staff Pimlico to get a broadsheet. Ye'll sell twice what ye did yesterday.'

Solomon nodded. When his lips moved his whole face ached.

'I've more to tell.'

Gloria's brows sprang up, lifting her bonnet a little further back on her brown curls.

'Go on.' She licked her lips, dragging her shawl tighter, her bosom lifting with bated breath.

*

That day the market was throbbing. Crowds swelled in from across the river. Solomon's stall was the busiest. He stood underneath the statue of the devil, looking like a revived corpse, the title of his broadsheets attracting everyone. By four o'clock he had sold out and still people were coming.

'I'll have more tomorrow,' he promised.

Corker waited until Solomon had folded up his stall and leaned it against Lucifer's feet.

'See ye met the Keeper,' he whistled. 'Gave ye his signature.'

'Yes, thank you for the explicit warning.'

'He was in a bad mood, Beresford had skinned him. He had to take it out on someone.'

'Lucky me.'

'Get us a pie, will ye, Solomon? Me belly is stuck to me back with the hunger.'

Solomon snapped his carpet bag shut. He'd had an excellent day. Even deducting the money he owed to Merriment, he'd still made a resounding profit.

'Come on.'

They walked to Gloria's stall, Corker keeping a keen eye out for the market manager.

'Give us four pies, Gloria darling.'

'Mother of divine, I have none left. What a day, Sol my darling, what a day.'

Corker shrugged. 'Ah well, never mind, love. Will ye get us two tomorrow, Sol?'

Solomon guided Corker to the side gate and looked about for anyone selling pies. The hawkers were packed up, ready to head home and go about their evening chores. Solomon was in such a good mood, even his aching face couldn't bring him down.

'We'll do better,' he told Corker, pointing down Dame Street and saying, 'Ever been in Lizzie's Coffee Shop?'

*

They had cream pastries and such strong coffee that Corker didn't know whether to spit it out or choke it down.

'Curse o' God on it, it's like trying to swill down a cup of tar.'

Solomon got the boy a glass of buttermilk and took his coffee.

'Where do you live?'

139

'In the Liberties.' The cream cake vanished in three mouthfuls. 'Seen you slip into that woman's shop, what's her name with the breeches and the gap teeth?'

'Merriment O'Grady's. I've a room upstairs. Were you spying on me?'

'I take an interest.'

Corker bowed his head, checking to make sure Lizzie wasn't looking before he licked the cream off the edge of his plate.

'Ye need a pig's head on yer broadsheet. A drawing of a man with a pig's head and a gun leaning against the sentry box with clothes hanging out of it,' Corker told Solomon, a glob of cream smeared on the end of his nose.

'That's a good idea. Can you draw?'

Corker nodded, his brown eyes twinkling.

'Like the lad who painted the ceiling in Rome.'

'Let me see.'

Solomon produced his ink and quill and a sheaf of creamy paper.

Corker stuck his tongue out as he dipped the nib into the ink and scratched a dark swooping line onto the blank page. Solomon looked about, glad of the blazing fire close by – he could feel his feet thawing out. Across the way two dandies were chatting loudly, bandying about Latin quotes like they were an addition to their fine silk suits and eccentrically coiffed wigs. Beside them a solitary diner with wolfish eyes and a strangely turned quiff of black hair ate a chop. Sitting on the table before him was a small mother-of-pearl scabbard containing what looked like a curved blade. When the man saw Solomon admiring the gold filigree inlay of the handle, he stopped eating and stared. Solomon looked away, faintly amused that even the well-off in Dublin seemed to spoil for a fight. Across the way Lizzie was taking orders and making sure the new girl was moving fast enough to earn her wage. A group of men were discussing the problem of the Ormond Street Boys.

'When the patterns come, there'll be war. Let the guilds cancel the parades this year.'

'And let the Liberty Boys win?' a bald man hissed. 'No way. No way.'

Solomon wondered when the butcher's guild was due to march around the city waving their colours and banging their drums. Was it November? He'd heard of the riots last year. One poor butcher was hung up on hooks and left to bleed to death. *Dublin,* he thought hopefully, *might just provide me with enough material to have a regular stall, and maybe even more than that.*

'There ye are.' Corker held up his drawing and Solomon's bruised eyes hurt when they widened with surprise.

*

'Are ye in for the evening?' Janey Mack ran across the shop to say hello to Solomon.

'Back early,' he said, glancing over at Merriment, glad to be able to return her loan.

'I haven't lit a fire in yer room yet,' Janey Mack flustered.

'That's fine.'

'Are ye hungry? I can put on a chop for ye.'

'In a bit.'

'Come on in here.' Janey Mack grabbed his hand and brought him into the back room.

It was half past five. Merriment had a problem that she hadn't foreseen, and she was wondering about how to ask Solomon for a favour. *I have some tea,* she thought, then slipped into the anteroom, wondering if bribing him with tea would be enough to sweeten him up.

'He made a fortune,' Janey Mack beamed as she entered with Solomon.

Solomon counted out eight shillings and handed them to Merriment.

'Thank you,' he said quietly. 'You saved my life.'

'And don't forget it.' Janey Mack wagged her finger.

'I have to go out,' Merriment blurted. 'I'll pay you a shilling to watch Janey. I'll be back by half nine. I'm certain. I think. I've no one to look after her.'

'I can mind meself.'

'Ye've been minding yourself for too long already; it's my turn now.' Merriment's eyes pointed to the new bandage wrapped around the little girl's burned fingers.

'Half nine, you say?' Solomon knew he owed her one, and besides he could go to a later game. 'Don't see why not. I'll teach you the ciphers of your name,' he told Janey Mack and the little girl nearly choked at the very idea.

'Janey Mack, will ya? Did ye hear that, miss? Me own name.'

'Let me just take a look at his wounds first, before you start with the alphabet.'

Merriment checked Solomon's eyes. She undid the bandage exposing the black-and-blue bruises and reapplied arnica before tentatively tapping along the sides of the splint.

Solomon stared up at her. Her eggshell skin was burnished soft orange by the firelight. He noticed she had long lashes, that there were flecks of silver in her blue eyes and near the edge of her full lips there was a thread-like tiny scar that disappeared when she smiled. Her hands smelled of ointment, but her touch was gently perceptive. He followed the line of her neck. Her shirt collar was unbuttoned and when she moved he noticed a small blue anchor tattooed into her pale skin.

'You'll get worse before you get better,' Merriment told him.

'Yes,' he replied.

Janey Mack butted in. 'What about me bandaged hand?' She waved it in front of Solomon. 'Won't that stop me holding the quill?'

'Can you pinch your index finger and thumb together?'

Janey Mack could.

'You can hold a quill.'

That sent the little girl into a spin. She rooted in his bag without asking, pulling out the ink and quill and paper. When she saw Corker's drawing her mouth swung open.

'Did you do this?' she gawped.

'That was drawn by my assistant.'

Corker had done a deal. For a ha'penny and two pies he would sketch for Solomon and attract more to his stall. Merriment paused to look at him.

'What?' he asked, picking up on the question in her eyes.

'Nothing.' Merriment shook her head and cut three slices of bread and some crumbly cheese, putting the food on three plates.

Maybe we all manufacture ways to tie ourselves down, she thought.

At half six she fetched her cloak and filled her medicine bag with an array of purgatives, purifiers, three of Misses Phillips' Engines and four bars of sweet-smelling soap. She packed a new ledger and two sharpened pencils. Instinctively she patted the pistol hidden beneath her waistcoat and popped a tricorn hat on her head.

'You heading?' Solomon asked, looking up.

Janey Mack was sitting on his knee, bent over the paper, her bandage full of black splodges that fanned out and spread with every mistake she made. She squeezed her lips between her teeth, frowning with the strain of trying to make the slippery quill form the lines and swoops of a capital J.

'I'll try not to be long,' Merriment said, checking the address written on the card – *17 Henrietta Street*. 'Better go.'

Janey Mack looked up, her huge eyes blinking. Two candlesticks framed her small round face and the glowing light made her look almost healthy.

'Be careful, won't ya, miss. There's blackguards and thieves out there.'

'You won't even know I was gone,' Merriment smiled. She

143

was completely unfamiliar with the feeling of saying goodbye to a small child. Usually when she made a call, she just slammed the door and left. Now there was a little girl who needed her to come back, and for the first time, the songs that spoke of sweet, sad parting struck a chord in Merriment's heart.

'Right,' she said, hiding the pang by turning abruptly and leaving.

She'd have to step it out; it would take her half an hour to walk briskly to the Northside. The rain had stopped but the streets were still wet and slippery. The lamps had been lit and already the theatre traffic was blocking the road in front of the opera house. The coachmen parked wherever they could. Addled footmen opened carriages, helping out ladies in fine cloaks and shimmering gowns and gentlemen in brocaded jackets trimmed with the new winter colours. Merriment pushed her way through the throng, listening to the shrill high squeaks of young ladies as they recognised each other. There were elaborate embraces, earrings glittered, feathers flounced, some women spoke French while groups of young bucks eyed up the females, both sexes flirting and fluttering with guile and anticipation. *The Beggar's Opera* was on and Thomas Sheridan over in Smock Alley was going mad because 'Who wants to see Shakespeare when there are songs to be sung?'

Merriment practically ran up Sackville Street. She should have left earlier. The night watch outside the Lying-In Hospital shouted to her as she passed.

'Take it easy, ye'll burst something, yer in such a hurry.'

It was quarter past seven when she knocked on the door with the number 17 neatly displayed in polished brass on the raised panels. Peg Leeson lived on a beautiful, brightly lit street that even on a damp night looked elegant and refined. Every entrance path was tiled and every doorway was framed by Ionic columns. The fanlights, lit by glowing lanterns, picked out the neat beadwork curling in garlands and swags and delicate tendrils like fine ribs through clear glass.

144

A footman opened the door. He had a long nose and pinched lips and, despite being done up to the nines, gave the impression that nothing pleased him.

'Yes?'

'I'm here to see Miss Leeson.'

He stepped to one side, curtly inviting Merriment into the glittering interior. There was a painted gold armoire with mirrored panels standing to one side of the enormous, blindingly lit hall.

The footman lifted a gloved hand and stiffly pointed for Merriment to go through. She aimed vaguely for the first door to her right, pausing to check with the footman. He nodded and she went through, wondering why he had not announced her.

Peg Leeson was sitting on a green velvet chaise longue in a peach gown, wearing paste diamonds that looked real, an ostrich feather dyed silver and flapping a silver fan. At the sight of Merriment, the man caressing her fingers jumped to his feet and opened his arms, his face beaming wildly.

'Merriment O'Grady, as I live and breathe.'

Merriment gave a short laugh, masking her surprise as she quickly assessed the scene. Ashenhurst Beresford was coming towards her genially smiling, seemingly thrilled by her presence, but her heart plummeted, her ribs closed in as she quickly realised that she had interrupted an intimate moment. She remembered the time he had come back sad, after a long furlough, and had told her that he intended to be true to his wife. She had nodded meekly, but she had cried later, on her own, in her cabin. It took them some months to steady their relationship, to return to the roles of captain and surgeon. It had taken time for her to put away her hopes, to learn to see Beresford as a friend. Now, here he was in all his glory, lavishing attention on none other than the renowned madam Margaret Leeson: his commitment to his wife it seemed, did not exclude a casual encounter with an expensive courtesan, and this rankled with Merriment. Her feelings chaffed, she was careful to keep her emotions well hidden. She glanced at Peg, who

145

smiled knowingly, sitting back in her chair. Peg, it seemed, had staked her claim. Lord Beresford was hers. Merriment concealed her disappointment and irritation beneath a cool politeness and, unable to stop herself, let Peg know she had enough history with Beresford to intimately use his first name.

'Ashenhurst.' Merriment's brows rose good-humouredly. 'Are you well?'

He swooped his arms around Merriment and held her tight.

'By Christ, you're a sight for a sore eye.'

His eyepatch cut across his distinguished face, and Merriment couldn't help but respond to his warmth. He seemed genuinely pleased to see her and comforted by that small fact at least, Merriment found her feet.

*

While Merriment checked the girls working for Peg Leeson, Solomon Fish taught Janey Mack how to write the letters J and M.

'Now you have your initials.'

'Will this hand forget tomorrow what it learned today?'

'No.'

'Ye sure?'

'It's like falling off a chair. Once you've done it once, you know how to do it again.'

The wind rattled the back door and Solomon asked what was outside.

'A yard. There's a way into the back, halfway down the street, a little alley; ye have to cut through a pigsty, though, and, sure, the swill and the swine would destroy yer buckled shoes.'

Janey Mack slipped from Solomon's lap and taking the poker she rattled the cinders and flung another log on the fire.

'Did ye ever marry, Sol?'

Janey Mack sat on the fender checking out Solomon's injured face. The bandages hid his expression.

'No.'

She pointed to the little oval portrait standing on the shelf across the room.

'That's the lad Merriment murdered.'

'Is it? I thought she didn't kill him.'

Janey Mack shrugged. 'She could be on the run. She's not here long. Three months at most.'

'How long are you here?'

'Two days.'

'Oh.' Solomon had taken it for granted that Janey Mack had been assisting Merriment for a lot longer.

'I never seen a ghost.' Janey Mack stared into the fire. Then turning her huge eyes on Solomon, she said, 'What if the Dolocher came up this street here?'

Solomon shook his head, his face hurt. 'He haunts the Black Dog: that's where his demon spirit is trapped, inside the grey dark walls of the notorious prison. That place is his tomb, his sarcophagus, a mausoleum encasing ... Actually,' Solomon jotted a quick note, 'I like that.' Then looking at Janey Mack's troubled face, he called her over.

'He's not real, Janey.' Solomon winked, his upper eyelid crashing down on his lower, sending a shooting pain through his jaw. 'It's just a good story.'

'But how do ye explain all the things?' Janey Mack wanted to know.

'Prison fever.' Solomon tried to smile, his whole head ached. 'You can't let truth get in the way of a cracking good tale. It's a story. Now you don't be worrying yourself about it. This week it's the Dolocher, next week it'll be a phantasm over in the hospital or a spectral ship out at sea or a headless horseman.'

'But yer man's guts were at the bottom of a bucket, ye saw that yerself with yer own eyes.'

'Yes well,' Solomon sighed. 'It's an intriguing story, but a story nonetheless. Now, will I show you how to write Merriment's initials?'

Janey Mack struggled with the letter G, while Solomon gazed into the fire remembering the anchor on Merriment's neck and the feel of her fingers stroking the edges of his eyes. Suddenly a knock came on the back door.

'Jesus.' Janey Mack pounced to her feet, running to grab the poker. 'Who's that?' she whispered frantically, staring at Solomon.

'Hello,' Solomon called, his heart pounding despite himself.

'It's Corker, Sol, let us in.'

Solomon dragged back the latch and pulled open the door. Corker stepped into the warmth, a gush of wind bursting in with him. His quick eyes swept across the interior, resting a second on Janey Mack's face. They each recognised a faint feral streak in the other which made them instantly suspicious and competitive.

'How do you do.' Janey Mack took the lead.

'Miss.' Corker tugged his forelock.

Solomon shut out the wind and looked down at Corker's filthy feet.

'Stand in by the fire. This is Janey. This is Corker.' Solomon swept his hand back and forth, bouncing the introduction along. 'Is everything all right?'

Corker shook his head.

'Got a bit of information for ye. Ye're going to want to hear this, Sol.'

'Go ahead.'

Corker paused, shoved his hands into his breeches pockets and licked his bottom lip.

'One shillin'.'

'Not a chance,' Solomon laughed.

'It's worth twice the price. It's to do with the Dolocher and I've a place to send ye and someone to interview.'

'Did the Dolocher cough up the bones of the missin' turnkey?' Janey Mack asked.

'Worse,' Corker said, crinkling the bridge of his nose. 'He's out of the Black Dog and prowlin' the streets of Dublin.'

'What?' Janey Mack swallowed, her face suddenly pale. She turned to Solomon. 'But you said about his sarcophagus. You said he wasn't real!' She squeezed her right hand into a fist, opening and closing it, her heart thumping loudly in her chest.

Solomon threw Corker a shilling and sat down, listening intently.

'Florence Wells is a weaver. Lives down the Liberties. She was over visiting her sister-in-law in Copper Alley. On her way back she took a short cut down Saint John's Lane. She said she was halfway down the lane when she got this peculiar feelin' that there was somethin' behind her. She looked back.'

Corker looked over his own shoulder, and Janey Mack gave a little whimper, hiding her mouth behind her bandaged hand.

'She saw nothing.' Corker held his hands out and froze. 'She took no more than three steps forward when out of the shadows, running at her, with this massive head and black cloak came this beast.'

'Oh Janey.' Janey Mack squashed herself close to Solomon and clutched his hand, barely able to breathe. Corker looked a little shaken. He brushed his tongue swiftly over his lower lip and glanced into the corner of the room.

'She said it all happened in a flash. She dropped her lantern, but not before she saw the light bounce off a black pig's head. It lunged at her laughing and she ran, but he grabbed her cloak and swiped at her face. She slithered and screamed and kicked and managed to wriggle free and off she took, like the hounds of hell, belting away with the sound of the Dolocher pounding after her.'

Janey Mack gave a little squeal. Solomon swept his arm about her, drawing her protectively into his chest.

'Where is Florence now?' he asked.

Corker nodded seriously. 'She came screaming into the Liberties like a banshee. Her neighbours took her in. She's in

O'Dwyer's cottage. They're pouring whiskey down her throat she's that hysterical with the fright.'

'Right.' Solomon stood up.

'Where are ye going?' Janey Mack clung to his arm.

He'd forgotten he was babysitting. He sank back down and sat the little girl on his knee. Janey Mack was trembling like a leaf.

'Damned interesting story,' he said.

'Thought it would intrigue ye.' Corker eyed the crusts of bread left on one of the plates. Solomon pulled out his notebook and took a few quick notes.

'When did it happen?'

'Only about half an hour ago. They've sent for a doctor.'

Janey Mack heard the key turn in the shop door. She hopped from Solomon's knee and ran to the end of the table, waiting for the door to the anteroom to open. When Merriment came in she was stunned to find Janey Mack in a panic and a young boy standing, warming his feet by the fire.

'He's out of the Black Dog, miss,' Janey Mack babbled, tears popping in her frightened eyes. 'Haunting Hell.' She pointed towards Christ Church Cathedral. 'He's got the guards and now he's back to catch women.'

'Who has? What's going on?' Merriment swung off her cloak and put her bag on the table. Solomon grabbed a lantern off a shelf and lit it.

'I've to head. There's been a development. Janey will fill you in.'

Before she could say wait, Solomon and Corker were out the door and picking their way through the backyards, past a rubbish pile and a pigsty, making for O'Dwyer's cottage, where Florence Wells was shaking and rocking and telling her story.

Janey Mack was in such a panic that Merriment gave her a few drops of distilled Star of Bethlehem oil and heated a cup of hot milk for her. Still, the little girl chattered.

'When she looked up, there was the Dolocher, with his pig's

head and his evil laugh and he took a swipe at her, meaning to drag her back to the grave with him. But yer woman, Florence, fought him off and took to her heels.'

'There now, you see. He can't be fleet of foot.' Merriment poured herself a little milk and sat sipping it, watching Janey Mack hunched over on the little three-legged stool, staring into the fire.

'The Dolocher?' The bridge of Janey Mack's nose pinched into a frown.

'He didn't catch her.' Merriment smiled reassuringly. 'Besides, we don't know anything about Florence Whatever-her-name-is, she may be sick.'

'Sick to the stomach after what happened. The thing about spirits is they can creep in, miss, they can drift under the door-jamb and slip through keyholes and Olocher was a bad one. Solomon said the Dolocher wasn't real, but he changed his mind after what Corker told him. What if he comes here, down the chimney, looking for me?'

'Why would he be looking for you?' Merriment's head retracted, confused.

'Dunno. Bad spirits are slithery things, miss. Hoppy John said when he was lying on deck the day his leg was swiped off him, he saw men dying and when they died their spirits came out of their bones. Hoppy John said they looked agitated, very displeased. They could walk through walls, miss. And he said they were bad when they were alive, but they were cursed awful once they were dead.'

'Hoppy John was telling sea tales.'

'But we're not safe, miss.' Janey Mack scanned all the places the Dolocher could gain entry.

'Look.' Merriment stretched and reached up the side of the chimney breast, her fingers tugged at a loose brick. She pulled it out, and Janey Mack came to her feet, wondering why Merriment was tearing the chimney breast apart. Was she showing another way for the Dolocher to get in?

'What is it?' Janey Mack's bandaged hand touched her lips, petrified.

Merriment removed two bricks and reached into the dark gap. She hauled out something that crinkled and whispered like rain hissing. It was tissue paper and Janey Mack in all her terror thought it was a dead, white ghost. She stepped back, watching Merriment pull out a bundle and gently lay it on the table.

'Now,' Merriment said, 'ghosts and spirits wander because they are disorientated.' She did her best to sound authoritative; she needed to convince the little girl that what she was saying was true or Janey Mack would be up the whole night, too terrified to sleep and making herself sick with worry.

'Their spirit eyes don't see the way we do,' she went on. 'They feel things, get attracted to things.'

Janey Mack nodded, her huge eyes unblinking, staring at Merriment's hands as she unwrapped the tissue and pulled out a baby's hat, a little pair of knitted booties and a dress.

Janey Mack reached for the soft pale material and whispered, 'What does it mean, miss?'

Merriment looked back at the hole in the chimney breast.

'It's a magnet. It's called a "hiding well". It's a trap. Any spirit that comes looking for souls to steal will be drawn to this hidden stash and leave us alone. It's an old folk mechanism for keeping rambling spirits occupied.'

Janey Mack nodded, but years of scavenging had trained her to make certain she was missing nothing.

'It will hardly satisfy Olocher, who killed all those girls,' she said breathlessly.

'His spirit, if it is abroad, will be confused.'

'He's out there.' Janey Mack pointed. 'Ask Florence Wells.'

'We don't know anything about that woman: her mind may never have been sound and she could be looking for attention or have such a wild imagination that she may have convinced herself that she saw what she saw. The point is' – Merriment folded away the baby clothes and returned them to the hiding well – 'this is a perfectly tried-and-tested way of protecting a household.'

Janey Mack nodded, satisfied. This was the first time she'd lived in a house, and while the security measure was new to her, she could see that the stones in the chimney breast were loose for some reason and she trusted the folk methods, since they had been tested by people who lived in the past and somehow that gave the hiding well veracity.

'Ye sure?' she asked.

Merriment patted the little girl's head and let her crawl up onto her knees. They sat by the fire. Janey Mack curled in Merriment's lap, her head resting on Merriment's breast. When the night watch called out that it was eleven bells, Merriment took Janey Mack upstairs and laid her on the cushions before the fire. She stoked the ashes and put another log on the dying embers, left the candle on her dressing table and tip-toed downstairs to sit and read.

She was dozing in her chair when two sharp raps came to the back door.

'Yes?' she whispered hoarsely, her heart jumping.

'Merri, it's me. Solomon.'

Merriment let him in. He was drowned, the rain was coming down strong and the lantern had fizzled out. He pushed into the anteroom shaking, his bandages half undone.

'My God, get your coat off, you're soaked through.' Merriment found him a towel to dry himself with. Solomon shivered, his teeth chattering. He grabbed the dangling bandage and unwrapped his head, flinging the wet linen strip onto the table.

'Thank you for letting me in. Sorry I missed curfew, extraordinary circumstances.'

'Yes, I know. How's the lady?'

Merriment fetched a decanter of brandy and poured Solomon a stiff drink and a small one for herself.

'I don't think she's the full shilling.' Solomon took the brandy, gratefully. 'I just can't decide if she's unhinged because she got an awful fright or if she was unhinged and frightened herself.'

With the wooden splint like a false nose and his eyes black and his upper lip cut, Solomon looked like a masked man, like something from a medieval painting. He slipped out of his shoes, his socks soaking, steam evaporating from the back of his mud-spattered breeches.

'It's a cracking story,' he grinned. 'I mean, a demon. The details are just fantastic. Lumps of rotting flesh. Florence said her hand slid along the Dolocher's chest and his flesh was cold and clammy and slippery to touch and that he stank like a corpse.'

His eyes flicked to Merriment's face. She was sitting cross-legged, the brandy glistening in her glass, one hand draped across her lap. He thought about the tattoo. She appeared to wince for a moment.

'You think I'm grotesque?' he said quietly.

'I didn't say a thing.' Merriment gave a slight smile.

'You don't need to. You've very piercing eyes.'

Solomon sipped his drink, the warm liquid making a hot channel to his belly.

'And you'd be right,' he sighed. 'My principles are grubbily concerned with profit.'

'We all need to eat, Solomon.'

Merriment raised her brows and waited.

'Thank you.' Solomon rolled back onto his heels, straightening up. 'You could have lectured me.'

'Hardly. When I profit on the poor health of others.'

'You heal and mend and provide comfort.'

Merriment laughed, her whole face suddenly youthful and alive.

'You mightn't say that if you had to take mercury drops for an ailment. Besides, you provide entertainment.'

'And moral corruption.'

The unexpected remark sent Merriment back into her chair.

'Good lord,' she exclaimed. 'There's a high-minded, self-righteousness living deep in your bosom. Who'd have thought?'

Solomon grinned sheepishly, staring down into his glass.

'Only comes out when I'm tired. I did consider the church as a profession once.'

'Really?' That made Merriment smile.

'And law,' he reminded her. 'I've fallen far from my aspirations.'

'Haven't we all. Life has a neat way of trimming us back. But you know what they say – our character is formed in adversity and spoiled by indulgence.'

'That's a very puritanical idea.' Solomon frowned. 'I don't like to suffer.'

'None of us do, but it's probably not as bad for us as we think.' Merriment stretched out her legs and let her head rest on the back of her chair.

'No.' Solomon shook his head and finished his drink. 'There I think you are wrong. Suffering makes people savage, drives them to despair and cruelty, makes them irresponsible.'

Merriment looked at Solomon's profile: his jaw had hardened. 'Like Olocher?' she asked.

'Olocher? You think despair made him murder? That he suffered? No. He was something else altogether. Everything about that man, all that I have been told, what he did: he was born with something dark living inside him. That kind of appetite is not manufactured by neglect and hardship. No, Olocher was an animal.'

'Funny, I heard he was an inconspicuous little man with a pudgy face and beady eyes.'

'Born with an urge to abduct and murder. I mean, six girls.'

Solomon thought of Olocher's corpse lying on the surgeon's table, remembering the waxy white fingers draped by the dead man's side. He thought of what those hands had done.

'It's the old argument.' Merriment pulled the book she'd been reading out from her side where it had slipped and placed it on her lap. Solomon read the words *Boyle* and *Chemyst*.

'What argument?' Solomon asked.

'Nature or nurture? You think Olocher was born that way. I think . . .'

'You think suffering distorted him until everything that was human about him was driven out?'

'No.'

Merriment's answer confounded Solomon.

'Neither nature or nurture drove him to kill those girls. Something more tricky was operating.' She gazed into the fire. 'Anyway, the man is dead and that's a good thing.'

'Is he?' Solomon's voice was light, mischievous. 'What about his rank spirit out there hiding in the shadows?'

'Very funny.' Merriment smiled.

'I thought you believed in spirits?'

'What makes you say that?' Merriment frowned.

'Isn't that what you meant by something tricky operating in Olocher?'

'No.' Merriment shifted uncomfortably. Her fingers tapped the book on her lap, reminding herself of the grand world of logic and the intricate multitude of causes, all rationally interconnecting, driving the universe like an elegant machine. Solomon detected the uncertainty in her voice.

'You don't think Olocher has come back from the dead to exact revenge on his tormenting guards?'

'Any decent doctor will tell you that a burst of blood to the brain prior to an apopleptic fit leads to hallucinations and fever. Poor Boxty thought he saw a demon with a pig's face and some kind of guilt or fear made him think of Olocher.'

Solomon interrupted, 'And Martin Coffey has just absconded because he knows the authorities want to talk to him, leaving behind his viscera to convince us he's dead, and Florence, well who knows? My broadsheet is probably responsible for

156

her encounter with the Dolocher apparition.'

'Exactly.' Merriment released her breath in a low, soft sigh.

'So you don't believe in spirits?'

Solomon searched her face, noticing the faintest twinge, a flutter of her eyelids, an unspoken thought. He saw her chest rise as she took in a deep breath, collecting herself.

'I'm a scientific woman, Solomon. I believe anything is possible. But . . .' She paused, her lips partially open. 'When it comes to matters of the supernatural kind, I think we have to be circumspect. Evidence of the spiritual world is less easy to capture.'

For a moment neither of them spoke. The wood crackled in the fire and spit out little red splinters that burned brightly before fading to ash on the flagstone floor.

'There's something damned peculiar going on,' Solomon said at last.

'Do you believe in ghosts?' Merriment asked.

'I wish . . . I'd like to think . . . The idea of surviving death, of returning, of seeing loved ones who have passed on.'

His gaze was directed at the floor but he didn't see the flag-stones. He was peering into the past and Merriment wondered what he was pondering. She was intrigued by Solomon's answer.

'You'd like to be haunted?' she asked.

'Perhaps I am.'

Solomon shifted awkwardly, feeling suddenly exposed.

'You sound full of remorse, Solomon.'

Solomon pulled back his shoulders and smiled.

'Yes, I do. And there's nothing more boring than a man filled with regret, particularly when I should be happy. This story is a gem. I was thinking of titling the broadsheet "The Dolocher Haunts Hell".'

'Very appropriate.'

'I thought so.'

Solomon pulled a chair to the table, drew his equipment out

of his bag and began writing. Merriment left him stooped over the table. She took a candle with her and slipped quietly up to her room. Janey Mack was not sleeping before the fire. The little girl had climbed into Merriment's bed and was lying sideways beneath the covers.

10

The Girl in the Gutter

For three days throngs of people packed into Christchurch market, barging their way to Solomon's stall. Corker had decorated the backboard with sketches of Florence Wells rushing along Saint John's Lane, her cloak billowing, her face twisted with terror, being pursued by a tall demon furnished with the monstrous head of a swine. He drew Boxty creeping along the floor of the subterranean dungeon in the Black Dog and Martin Coffey in a grotesque pietà, nakedly draped over the Dolocher's knees while the beast ate him. The broadsheet print run had expanded to four thousand, with men and women buying three and four copies in one go. The frenzy of excited terror set the crowd talking. The possibility of a supernatural manifestation sent a buzzing thrill through the populace. People laughed and joked that the 'divil' himself had popped up on the banks of the Liffey to sample a bit of Dublin. They teased one another about having to watch out because 'ye've more sins notched up on yer black soul, the Dolocher will want a taste of you'.

But shivering beneath their mirth was the unmistakable nervousness of the possibility that the boundary between life and death had been blurred. The very idea of the Dolocher turned people's thoughts to the phantasmagorical. Now, not only was there the worry of corrupt governance, crime, cesses and poverty, but on top of the everyday anxieties there was the preternatural to consider. And the idea of a demon sent such a frisson of horror through the city that lords and ladies became intrigued by what was happening on the Southside. 'He's taken to his prayers,' Solomon told the crowd buzzing before him. 'Poor Boxty is only half right after the shock of it. Corker, give that lady five sheets.'

Solomon was paying Corker eight pennies a day to help him out on the stall. The market manager, Jody Maguire, was disgusted he hadn't charged more for the prime spot. But Solomon knew the story would fizzle out and he would soon be peddling common-or-garden gossip. So he took full advantage of this opportunity to turn a shilling and threw all his energy into the enterprise. He brought Corker back with him to Merriment's and spent a good portion of his evenings in the anteroom, devising new angles to twist the Dolocher story, giving it a spin to last longer. He got Corker to come up with suitably gothic sketches to illustrate the macabre details. And every morning he bounced into MacCambridge's Printers to place his hurried order. Now, as he stood on the feet of the statue of Lucifer, shouting out his broadsheet cry, 'Read all about it: Florence Wells gives a full account of the Dolocher's rank breath,' he was so engrossed in pitching and selling that he was oblivious to the tall man in a dark frock coat and purple cravat leaning against one of the buttresses of the cathedral, watching him.

*

For three mornings Merriment opened her shop and watched as the queues lengthened.

'He's getting worse,' the woman with the pinched face complained. 'What ye gave me isn't working at all.'

'There's no cure for her aul' fella,' the stout woman with ginger hair told Merriment. 'My cure is working big time. I've never known me aul' man to be so happy. Sure, yesterday, ye know . . .' She winked and chortled loudly and the other customers laughed.

'Can ye give me something else?' the woman with the pinched face persisted.

'Sure, that lad quoted the scriptures ever before ye got wed. Ye knew he had a poker up his fundament long before ye agreed to the bans,' the ginger-haired woman ribbed her skinny friend. 'That's what ye get for marrying a holy Joe, no joy in the bedroom and an earful of Bible quotes to bring ye down on a sunny day.'

'Ye're crude as black tar, Molly Jenkins,' the pinched-faced woman exploded. The morning drifted into the afternoon and the steady stream of customers thinned out after two o'clock.

It was when Anne dropped by to put down an instalment on Stella's perfume that a frail man of fifty stepped up to the counter and, quietly throwing his eyes to one side, curled his fingers to beckon Merriment to a corner.

'Everything all right?' Merriment touched his shoulder. He gave the slightest shake of his head.

'I was wondering . . .' He paused, making sure that no one was looking or listening. Anne was chatting to Janey Mack. Two women were over by the glass cabinet deliberating over what to buy as a present for a coachman.

'Yes?' Merriment could see a touch of jaundice in his eyes; the man definitely had liver complaints. He patted his tattered periwig and tugged on his starched shirt. Swallowing down his pride, he raised his eyebrows, looking up at Merriment hopefully.

'Would you have a potion?'

'Yes?'

'Or a talisman or an amulet to protect a soul from evil?'

Merriment laughed softly with surprise and cut the laugh off as soon as she realised that the old man was absolutely serious.

'No,' she whispered.

The old man nodded forlornly and gripped his hands squeezing his fingers.

'You have your faith,' Merriment tried to console him.

The old man didn't answer. He looked blankly at the floor; a vein in his neck throbbed, beating out the irregular pattern of his pulse.

161

'If I had that,' he whispered hoarsely, 'I'd be on my knees in the cathedral and not here looking for help from you. God and me . . .' He shook his head, implying that that relationship was damaged.

'The devil has other plans for me.' The man stood wringing his hands, his breath coming in shallow drafts, his jaw clenched tight.

'You don't need an amulet,' Merriment said.

'I saw him,' the old man whispered.

And even though he'd spoken the words under his breath, Anne, Janey Mack and the two women by the glass cabinet all responded by becoming completely silent, their ears straining to hear every last word.

Merriment frowned sympathetically and the old man clutched at his sternum like his heart might burst out and abandon him.

'The Dolocher,' he hissed.

Janey Mack didn't blink. She sat frozen to the spot, her eyes fixed on the bristly edges of the old man's face.

'And he's like they say, tall and cloaked, with a man's body and a pig's head and breast and a man's hands. And he had tusks and he looked at me. He stepped out of the shadows and he looked at me.'

The old man suddenly gripped Merriment's hands, startling her. His touch was cold and clammy and he dug his fingers into her flesh, obviously afraid for his life.

'I will be next.'

'What do you mean? Why would you be?'

'He saw me. He pointed at me.'

'Jesus, you poor love.' Anne moved from the counter and called the other women over. 'He's seen the Dolocher.'

The women glided closer to hear the story. Janey Mack clenched and released her right fist.

'I—' the old man shook his head, flustering under the strain of all the attention. 'I have to go.'

'Wait.' Anne tried to hold him by the elbow, but the man shook free, rushed out the door and fled.

'Well, now.' Anne patted her palm over her heart. 'If that doesn't beat all.'

*

While the women chatted and buzzed about this latest sighting of the Dolocher, Solomon sold his last sheet and was folding up his stall when the tall man in the dark frock coat approached him and handed him his card.

'The name is Chesterfield Grierson.' He had a freshly powdered wig and a silver-headed cane. He pulled a snuffbox from his pocket, took a quick pinch and snapped the lid, waiting for Solomon to be suitably impressed.

'Solomon Fish.'

Solomon quickly scanned Chesterfield Grierson's finely tailored clothes and immaculately pressed cravat. Admiring the understated garments, he felt a pang of envy.

'Corker, run over to Gloria there and grab us four pies before she sells up completely,' he said.

Corker did as he was told and Chesterfield stepped to one side to let the boy pass.

'I've sold out,' Solomon told him. 'Finished up early. What time is it? Two o'clock?'

Chesterfield confirmed the time by nodding his long face and shifting his raised eyebrows higher. His face seemed permanently fixed with an incredulous expression. His grey eyebrows were constantly arched like they were posing a never-ending rhetorical question. His lips were suspended in a half-smile and his eyes were lit with a sardonic intelligence that exposed his shrewdness and encouraged some to call him a 'conniving bastard'. Truth was he understood economics. He had a strong puritan streak counterbalanced by a rash capacity to fall in love with the wrong women.

163

'Do you play cards, Mister Fish?'

The question took Solomon by surprise. This was the first time in years, the first time ever that he had a decent sum of money to throw into the pot and Chesterfield's attire promised the possibility of a game with high stakes.

'I do,' Solomon said, interested.

'I have a proposition. Call it a gamble if you like.'

He was using the card game as an analogy. Solomon felt let down.

'Perhaps you know of me?' he continued.

Solomon shook his head. He still wore the splint – Merriment had fixed it with a ribbon that tied at the back of his skull. Gloria had laughed and joked about how it looked like a snout, 'And sure ye look half-pig yerself, standing there bawlin' about the Dolocher. One pig callin' out about another!' Then by way of comfort, she had added, 'It'd make ye weep to see yer good looks ruined.'

Solomon's bruises were turning yellow now and the swelling of his upper eyelids was reducing. He checked Chesterfield Grierson's card, looking for a clue.

'Should I have heard of you?' he asked.

'Perhaps you've heard of *Pue's Occurrences*?'

Solomon shook his head.

'We've a wide circulation.'

Before Chesterfield could continue with his proposition, Corker barged in and shoved two pies into Solomon's hand.

'We've to go,' Corker said, his mouth full of food.

Chesterfield turned his astonished look upon the boy, his jaw swinging open to protest.

'There's a development.' Corker wolfed down his pie, crumbs cascading down his filthy waistcoat. 'Over in the Tholsel.'

'There appears to be an emergency, sufficient to prevent this young man from chewing his food correctly,' Chesterfield told Solomon, before turning his attention to Corker. 'Does it have anything to do with the Dolocher?'

164

Corker stopped mid-chew and narrowed his eyes suspiciously.

'I don't report to you, sir,' Corker replied. 'This is business between me and Mister Fish here.'

'Very good.' Chesterfield lengthened, his tall form unwittingly mirroring the statue of Lucifer glowering down over them. He nodded and smiled; his eyes bright, his face so full of the one expression that he was completely unreadable. Corker couldn't tell if he was offended or delighted.

'Mister Fish, do me the honour of calling to my office on Skinner's Row at your earliest convenience.'

Chesterfield Grierson bowed deeply and set off out of the market towards Werburgh Street.

'What was that about?' Corker frowned.

'I think I'm about to be offered a job,' Solomon said brightly.

The news struck Corker hard. His chest caved and his heart plummeted into his stomach. It had been less than a week since he had met Solomon but somehow in that short time he had become entangled in what, to him, was a grand enterprise and a storybook adventure. He was drawing and getting hot pies to eat. He had tasted cream pastry and disgusting coffee. He'd sat in a warm room in the evenings drinking milk and kidding with Janey Mack as he and Solomon worked out which parts of the broadsheets needed to be illustrated. Now, in one short sentence – nine little words, 'I think I'm about to be offered a job' – all his prospects had evaporated. Somehow, in the space of a few days, he had tethered his future to Solomon Fish and now Solomon was moving on.

'What's in the Tholsel?' Solomon asked.

Corker told him, and they both raced over.

*

Solomon stared up at the mechanical clock housed in a medieval tower, surrounded by saints carrying bolts of material and shears, indicating that the Tholsel had originally been built as a linen merchant's hall. The clock told him it was half past two. Today the building was being used as a courtroom and a woman named Ester Murphy from Rhys Lane was waiting to be called to the stand. Surrounded by a gaggle of men and women, there to support her in her ordeal, Ester took a quick sup of gin while smoking a clay pipe.

Solomon and Corker squeezed into the public gallery.

'Do your best,' Solomon said, handing Corker three sheaves of paper on a piece of board and two pencils. He looked across at the judge's bench and immediately recognised an old student friend of his from his days studying law. It was George Sweeny, and George Sweeny looked well. His wig was expensive. He wore the traditional black gown and sober suit. But there was something different about George: he had an accomplished air, he had outgrown his baby face and his nervous tick of tugging at his shirt collar. Qualified, George sat up tall and straight at the bench, looking through files and taking brisk notes. Solomon sank back into his seat, suddenly aware of his own battered face and threadbare jacket. The mace pounded on the floor, three loud raps. Solomon stood with the crowd, all rising for the Right Honourable, an octogenarian with a bad case of gout and a swollen lower lip the size of a fat slug and the colour of port wine. There was the usual palaver of legal ritual, a reciting of the cases, a calling to the stand and a lot of 'me lords this' and 'me lords that'. Corker sketched the Judge, over emphasising his lower lip and deepening his scowl. And everyone waited, as case after case rolled by.

When the mechanical clock chimed four times. Solomon pulled out his notebook and watched Ester Murphy take the stand. She was sworn in, her credentials read and the Judge informed that she was here to give an account of an attack, which happened yesterday evening as she was making her way to Cutpurse Lane to visit her ailing mother.

'It was almost nine bells, yer honour. I heard the night watch callin' out the time as I was coming along Copper Alley at the back of Christ Church Cathedral to me mother's house. I was trottin', yer honour. And I had me lantern and a short stick with a nail in it, to protect meself. I was afraid, yer honour, not on account of Olocher, ye understand; I was afraid because the city is dangerous at night, full of brigands and thieves. But I had no choice: me poor mother is very ill and I'd a bit of bread and cheese in me basket for to give to her. I was coming along Saint John's Lane, just by the back wall to Hell. It's a lonely, quiet road along there, yer honour, all I could hear were me own heels poundin' on the cobbles, echoing into the pitch-black sky and not a sinner nor livin' thing close by. I was getting a stitch in me side from marchin' so quick, but I was too afraid to slow down or stop, for fear of what might jump out at me from the shadows.'

Ester turned her plump face to the stuccoed ceiling. The rims of her eyes were red and her complexion was a greyish yellow from lack of sleep.

'I was about to turn out of Saint John's Lane on to Christchurch Lane . . . I saw a chink of light. I knew it to be the streetlight that burns on the corner there and I ran toward it, but me side split, yer honour. I got such a cramp. I doubled up to catch me breath and in that one moment, out from the wall stepped the Dolocher.'

A thick silence descended on the courtroom: no one breathed, no one blinked, no one moved. Everyone sat on the edge of their seats, waiting.

'I heard him first. He come from me right side and I saw his boots. It happened so quick, yer honour. I saw his great big head and his tusks and I couldn't scream. He flung out his hand and he grabbed me shoulder and I made a swipe at him with me stick with the nail in it. And he let out a roar and I dropped me basket and me lantern and I swung at him again and this time I struck him so hard that when I pulled the stick away the nail dragged a lump of muscle with it. But that didn't stop him, yer honour, he kept coming at me and I fought and kicked trying to get away until I managed to get me chance and I took it, leaving all I had behind, including me cloak. Me cloak got caught on his tusk, yer honour.'

Solomon stared down at Ester Murphy, searching her face, looking for some trace of dementia or latent hysteria. But there was something about her manner, a gravitas in her tone which made it obvious she was struggling with having to recount the experience: the very centre of her being, loaded with common sense and practicality, couldn't quite believe what her mouth was reporting. When he interviewed her friends later, Solomon discovered that Ester Murphy was a sensible woman with no interest in religion, known to be down to earth and the giver of sound advice. She particularly frowned upon gossip and told people off when they exaggerated facts or embellished the truth for the sake of a good story.

The Judge rattled out a statement – a summary of Ester's account was to be recorded – and rounded off the acknowledgement with a quote from the Bible and a warning for everyone present to guard their souls by pious devotion and a rigorous adherence to the Ten Commandments.

On the way home, neither Solomon nor Corker spoke for a long time. Corker was preoccupied by his bleak future, Solomon was confounded by the Dolocher. He looked along the winding streets, dodging the passing men and women all busy about their everyday tasks. On the horizon he saw the distant spires and domes of four churches pressed against the baleful yellow sky and an uncertainty crept into his bones. He'd seen the surgeons carve up Olocher's body; the corpse had split with a sucking noise as the ribs were pulled asunder and the heart was produced. There was nothing left of the man but limbs and cold flesh. No inkling of Olocher's appetite had been retained in his organs, no sign of his lust for murder or taste for young girls was to be detected in his dead, expressionless face. And yet, had something imperceptible to the naked eye, his malformed will, managed to keep a hold on this earth? Had Olocher's black soul the power that Boxty insisted it had? Could he really have come back from the dead?

Solomon remembered the other corpses he knew. His mother's worn face, waxy smooth and unlined as she was laid out on the kitchen table and waked for three days before being buried in a wicker casket. She'd have fought heaven and all the angels to come back and console Solomon in his grief.

He thought of Eliza, dragged from the river. Unable to bear the recollection, he shivered and shook himself, pushing the memory back, a wave of guilt crushing his heart.

'Have ye me eight pennies?' Corker said sharply, drawing Solomon out of his dark thoughts.

'Sorry?' Solomon seemed confused.

'Me eight pennies.' Corker had decided to withdraw all his charm and affection and to keep a businesslike tone with Solomon.

'Of course, yes.' Solomon rooted the money out of his pocket and Corker squeezed his mouth tight as his fingers closed over the coins.

'This story has legs, hasn't it, Corker?'

'If you say so.'

Corker sulkily turned his face away and shrugged.

Solomon frowned. 'Are you all right?'

'What would be wrong with me?'

'I don't know. You seem . . . off.'

Corker kept looking away.

'Is it something to do with the Dolocher?' Solomon asked softly.

'Don't be a thick—'

Solomon took hold of Corker's shoulder, drawing the boy to a halt.

'You're annoyed with me about something. Come on now, spit it out, you're having a fit of pique like a woman, cross on some account and expecting me to read your mind.'

Corker shook his head.

'Nothin' wrong with me,' he sniffed. 'Ye've a bag full of money there, more to write about and the prospect of a new job in the offing, so everything's fine and dandy.'

'I see.'

Solomon scratched his ear. The splint over his nose was coming loose. He walked on.

'Now why would I take a job offered by Chesterfield Grierson when I can rake in three times what I would earn sitting at a desk in his office?'

Corker's eyes lit up and he trotted after Solomon.

'That's right,' he nodded. 'That's right.'

'Chesterfield sees I have a talent and, well, let me put it this way, the only person I will let exploit me is myself.' Solomon pointed to his own chest. 'And you and me make a great little team, don't we?' he added.

'Yes, we do.' Corker beamed, showing all his haphazard teeth. His solemn mood vanished and, galvanised by the good news that Solomon and him were still in partnership, he pointed to the paper under his arm and rattled out a proposition. 'I've to do up these sketches proper, Sol, they'll be brilliant and we'll get seven thousand copies printed.'

'Ah now,' Solomon interjected.

'Five hundred each of the first, second, third and fourth broadsheets and the remainin' five thousand of Ester Murphy's testimony.'

Solomon hadn't thought of reissuing his previous copies.

'That's not a bad idea. People can collect all the instalments. By God, that's genius, Corker. And we can charge five pence for the package or a penny ha'penny for a single sheet.'

As they turned onto Cooke Street, Solomon's chest

instinctively constricted. His fingers tightened around the handle of his carpet bag. The sun was low, casting a jaundiced yellow light and to his right was the high imposing wall of the Black Dog Prison. He thought of Charlie, lying in his bed, and felt a surge of guilt.

I should go in and visit him, thought Solomon. Then his sensible side interjected. *And have the Keeper refresh his signature and steal my best day's earnings yet? I don't think so.*

As he was staring up at the monolithic gateway, two men burst out onto the streets laughing. One of them, a wizened little man with leathery skin, crashed into him, knocking his bag onto the cobbles.

'Hey,' Solomon blustered.

'Hey,' the little man yelled back, 'you watch where y'er going.' His high-pitched voice was electrified by a touch of insanity; he danced from one foot to the other and wagged an accusatory finger. Behind him, his companion, a colossus with hard suspicious eyes and a jowly face, looked bleakly back at the steps and poked his little friend's back.

'Come on, Fred, go on before Hawkins gives us another job.'

Fred did a little jig and sucked on his false teeth, then, picking up the bag, he shoved it into Solomon's stomach and said, 'Here, you, don't be dropping yer things.' He flicked Corker's nose and turned back to his large friend.

'Fuck Hawkins,' he chuckled gleefully, 'we've a new thing going. Come on, big man.'

As they made their way to the quays, Fred skipped up onto the pavement and down onto the road while his enormous companion grumbled and huddled close to the prison wall.

'One for the lunatic house,' Corker snapped.

Solomon glanced into the forecourt of the Black Dog: a small group of villainous-looking rogues were offloading crates and barrels from a battered cart and bringing the goods down into the cellars, while over at a storehouse next to the prison

171

graveyard a fresh delivery of lime was being carried out back.

'What a sink of vice,' he grumbled, turning away, 'a nursery for thieves and robbers.' Then, ruffling Corker's hair, he grinned. 'You don't want to end up there.'

They weren't ten paces from the Black Dog's gates when an incredulous voice called out his name and made him spin on his heels.

'Solomon Fish, as I live and breathe.'

Coming across the road, carrying an empty basket and wearing a ruby-coloured shawl, was a stout woman of about fifty.

'Maggie.' Solomon's eyes widened with delighted surprise. 'Maggie Fines.'

He scooped the old lady up in his arms and swung her about while she protested.

'Put me down. This is no way to treat an old friend.' The woman patted down her skirt and tugged her shawl tight. 'I wouldn't have known ye from yer face,' she said, tapping his jaw lightly, 'but I'd recognise yer gait anywhere. I said to myself it is Solomon and I took the chance of calling out yer name, and here ye are.'

She grinned down at Corker and asked, 'Is this yer young fella?'

Corker jigged his shoulders, feeling curiously proud.

'This scallywag is my employee,' Solomon said, patting the boy's back.

'Employee, no less. So ye got the bar, Solomon. I am glad to hear. Yer mother would have been very proud.'

'Not quite.' Solomon smiled, a little pained, instinctively looking down and shuffling his feet like he used to do when he was a boy of five and trusted to Maggie Fines' charge.

'He does this.' Corker grabbed an old broadsheet from his pocket and gave it to Maggie.

'I see.' Maggie was still impressed. Then taking a quick scan of the headline, she gasped. 'Olocher is back from the dead?' Her jaw dropped.

172

'It's a peculiar story.' Solomon dismissed his hack work with a quick wave of his fingers. 'How have you been, Maggie, how long is it since we last met?'

'It has to be ten years, Solomon, has to be. Poor Jack passed away, God rest his soul.'

'I'm sorry.'

'We all wondered what happened to you, ever since, ye know, Eliza.' Maggie looked softly into Solomon's face and Corker wondered what the old lady was alluding to.

'That was ten years ago, Maggie. Though you won't believe, I was just thinking of her, not twenty minutes ago.'

'Course ye were, Sol, God rest her. Who'd forget that blessed girl's face. Ten years.' She shook her head. 'Seems shorter. It weren't yer fault, ye do know that.'

Maggie patted Solomon's arm and reassuringly left her hand softly pressed in the crook of his elbow.

'Eliza always had a bit of tragedy about her.'

Solomon winced and looked away.

'And what became of ya, when ya left?'

'Ah, this and that.' Solomon tried to shrug off his chequered past, but the images of his old lodgings, his card games, the miserable journeys over land and sea, the constant running and dodging and diving kept intruding as he chatted to his mother's old friend.

'We all thought ye'd run off with Sally Loftus when she went missing.'

Solomon shook his head and smiled sadly.

'Ye didn't think much of me so.'

'Ah, Solomon, ye were a young lad, sure the heart recovers quickly when it's young, and ye were as handsome as the moon itself. It pleased us to think ye might be happy after yer mam going so sudden, and after Eliza did what she did, and Sally had always given ye the glad eye.'

Solomon nodded bleakly and Maggie saw his pain. She changed the subject.

173

'So y'er livin' in the city now?' She tugged her bonnet down further and shifted her basket to her other arm.

'For the moment,' Solomon said, squirming under the inquisition. 'Don't know if I'll be here too long.'

Corker's heart sank again.

'It's very noisy,' Maggie complained. 'Wouldn't be for me. Do ye ever think of comin' back to Saggart?'

'No,' Solomon said flatly. 'No, Maggie. Those days are gone. Anyway . . .' He buoyantly tossed off the dark mood and asked Maggie what she was doing in the city.

'We come in once a season. I'm here with Gertie Baker, Misses Baker's youngest, sure she'd have been only a wee little thing when ye left, Solomon. Gorgeous little young one now. We're after sellin' all our lacework.'

Maggie patted her right hip and her joint rattled with the sound of silver.

'We've made a tidy sum for the comin' winter.'

She paused and smiled up into Solomon's bruised face.

'Did ye get yerself into a spot of trouble, Solomon?'

'Oh, this.' He tapped his nose, the splint fell, and Corker and Maggie laughed. 'I don't think I need this anymore.' Solomon put the curved triangular piece of wood in his pocket and smiled his boyish grin. His face was still discoloured but at least the swelling had gone down.

'I had a bit of an altercation,' he told Maggie, glancing up at the wall beside them. Then sweeping his arm around Maggie's shoulder, he told Corker, 'This fine lady used to babysit me when I was a toddler.'

'When his mammy worked in the big house.' Maggie squeezed his waist.

'Will we go for a dram?' Solomon asked her.

'Sure why not. I don't have to meet Gertie till seven.'

Corker said he'd go on to Merriment's. 'I'll get on with the sketches and give ye two a chance to catch up on old times.'

174

As he was leaving, Maggie Fines gave him a penny.

'Don't spend it in one go.'

'Sure, what else would ye do with a penny,' Corker quipped, running off and waving back at Sol.

'He's a good lad,' Maggie laughed. 'Has a bit of yer quickness about him. Now where will we have the dram, young man?'

Solomon took Maggie to a coffee house and treated her to supper. He flirted with the waitress and Maggie teased him about his love of the women and prophesied that he'd never settle down.

'These are my carefree days,' Solomon said with a wink, feeling more cursed than blessed.

They chatted and laughed and reminisced while they ate pigeon stew, followed by sponge cake filled with cream and fresh tea all the way from India. Afterwards Solomon walked Maggie to the side gate of the Christchurch market.

'This is me,' Maggie said, 'You go on, Solomon, Gertie will be along any minute now. There she is.'

Maggie pointed down the road, past a phaeton being pulled by two glistening black horses. A young girl in a pale cloak waved and started running towards them.

'You go on, Solomon.'

'All right so.'

He gave her a tight hug and kissed her cheek, the sudden memory of his mother making his eyes sting. He said a fond goodbye and pushed through the traffic, sidestepping a huge hole in the pavement and rushing down to Fishamble Street, keen to be in before it started to rain.

*

There was something about the warmth of the anteroom that made Solomon fidgety: the amber light thrown by the fire, the chatter of Corker telling yarns to Janey Mack, Merriment preparing prescriptions. He ate his dinner quickly, frantic to get away. He glanced over at Merriment, watching her move. As she stooped over her powders and scales, her face illuminated, her eggshell skin radiant, reading and rechecking her lists, he watched her fingers tap and measure and move with authority. Her whole form was intelligent and unflappable and that made him curiously restless. He washed his dinner down with milk and asked Janey Mack if there was a fire lit in his room.

'There is.'

'Good.'

And without giving a reason why, he told everyone he was writing upstairs.

'Leave your sketches there on the table for me for tomorrow and then head off home; your mother will be looking for you,' he told Corker.

Corker didn't nod.

'I'll be heading out later,' Solomon told Merriment and, grabbing his bag and a candle, he stormed out of the room and up the stairs.

'What's got into him?' Janey Mack asked.

'He's not staying long,' Corker said. 'He did something to someone called Eliza and then everyone thought he ran off with a girl called Sally Loftus.'

Merriment paused, silently taking in the information and reflecting on it.

Solomon flung his bag on the floor, got on his knees and pulled up the loose floorboard where he had stashed his most prized possessions. He put five pounds into a tin box among his belongings and kept out two pounds for himself, intending to go to the Cock and Hen later and try his luck in a game. He'd had enough. He wanted to get lost, be with a woman who could laugh and distract him. He felt reckless, like taking all his money and heading to a club and flinging it in the centre of a card table and shouting out, 'Cut me in.' He wanted out of his own skin. He pulled open his bag, agitated, full of shame and anger and the unbearable weight of knowing that the past was something that could not be undone. He grabbed a sheaf of paper and some ink, hardly able to sit still. He drew his chair to the dresser and caught his breath when he spotted his own reflection in the oval mirror Merriment had left him to use for shaving.

His eyes were surrounded by dark bluish circles tinged with yellow, the side of his nose was discoloured and his lip was scarred a little, but it was the sharp, bitter glint in his expression that shocked him. Was this it? Was this who he was? Solomon Fish, a vagrant writer, fleeing from town to town, flirting with barmaids and shop hands, scribbling salacious broadsheets that either inflated terror or inflamed scandal? He tried to look away but couldn't. When he was young and fond of philosophy he used to believe in right action, in the law of responsibility, in the idea that there was a noble, aspirational quality in man and that all good deeds were rewarded. His oratory dazzled then and he was so oblivious to his own hypocritical behaviour that he seduced whoever he wanted and bore little of the consequences, until one day someone showed him who he really was and that day the whole course of his life changed.

He stood up abruptly and took to pacing the room. He would do anything to get out of his own mind and away from the memory of that awful day when he hauled Eliza May out of the river.

'Damn this.' He grabbed his jacket and, looking at the blank paper on his desk, told himself, *I'll write about Ester Murphy later.*

He emptied out his box, leaving two pound notes behind. He hurried down the stairs and slammed the shop door behind him, leaving Corker, Janey Mack and Merriment staring at each other.

'He's hightailed it,' Corker said. 'I better go too.'

He left the sketch of the Judge on the table and shrugged.

'Safe home, Corker,' Janey Mack whispered, as she stood at

the shop door waving him off. 'Hurry in out of the dark. Don't let the Dolocher catch ye.'

She watched him run up towards the cathedral, his pale, crooked legs vanishing behind a passing curricle as he sped home, keen to be off Dublin's haunted city streets.

*

The Cock and Hen was full to capacity, the atmosphere thick with blue smoke and rank with the putrid stink from the tanners, who despite scrubbing couldn't get rid of the stench of their profession from their pores. In one corner there were fiddlers and melodeon players; before them a knot of drunken women did gigs and reels, egged on by a rowdy group of plasterers who'd come over from Italy to carry out the stucco work on the ceilings and walls of the city's mansions. Jenny winked at Solomon from behind the counter and waved him over.

'The usual, Sol?'

He nodded and was sifting through the crowd looking for Harry and Badger when a tall man with granite features and a mean expression approached him. His gruff demeanour incongruously counterbalanced his refined attire. The man was wearing a crisp white shirt, a blue nipped jacket trimmed with gold braid, a sage-coloured waistcoat with brass buttons and pristine silk stockings tied with lime-coloured ribbon.

'Y'er doing well at the market,' he began as he blocked Solomon's way, his head tilting malevolently to one side, his eyes sparking with a flinty hardness, his voice so low it sounded like it was emerging from a deep cistern. Solomon tried to grin his way past, but the bully stopped his progress, spanning his large palm across Solomon's sternum.

'Ye've an invitation.' The bully grinned, exposing surprisingly good teeth and a single dimple that depressed his rugged cheek. Solomon had begun to shake his head, declining whatever the man in front of him was offering, when the bully cast his eyes over to a table deep in the corner away from the music and the dancing women.

'Ye've earned enough to get you into a real game,' the bully sniffed. 'The invitation is from Knox and, sure' – he ran his index finger under his nose – 'ye might win.'

Solomon's heart sank. Across the room he could feel the glint of Billy Knox's glacial eyes staring at him. He knew he wasn't getting away and, determined to pretend he had less money with him, he followed the bully to the card table and promised himself he was never ever coming back to the Cock and Hen again.

*

Some time after Corker had left, Janey Mack turned to Merriment and said, 'Solomon's in a bit of a mood. I bet he's gone out to drink. Do you like him? Would you shoot him if he annoyed ya?'

Merriment smirked. 'I wouldn't shoot anyone.'

'Wouldn't ya?' Janey Mack looked at her injured hand. Merriment had taken the bandage off to let the air at it; it was definitely improving.

'I'd shoot loads of people just to shut them up,' Janey Mack said, gazing into the fire. 'Imagine, he's from the back of beyond,' she started up again. 'He's a country lad, you'd never think it to look at him, with his city coat and buckled shoes. He's kind of bookish, isn't he? But you'd like that. I think there's a rake in him. Hard to fasten that lad down. He likes to laugh, I think; even though he's sad, he laughs a lot.'

'He was sombre the other night,' Merriment said, wiping her hands and coming to sit by the fire.

'Was he?'

'Said he regretted something.'

'Playing cards and losing money no doubt.' Janey Mack clicked her tongue.

'No. It was more than gambler's remorse.' Merriment shook her head a little.

179

'How d'you know?'

''Cause I know,' Merriment grinned.

'Did ye see it in his eyes?' Janey Mack tilted her head slightly, her tone fluttering nervously.

Merriment smiled craftily and pitched her brows, reiterating that somehow, after years of training, she had a magical ability to uncover the secrets of the mind that lay hidden in the body and emerged as ailments with specific symptoms.

Janey Mack's face darkened. She stared for a moment into the fire, the fingers of her right hand rubbing her right thumb, mulling something over. She looked up at Merriment and sat upright on the three-legged stool.

'Can you see if someone has done something bad, miss?'

'Well,' Merriment nodded, 'signs do pop up in the body.'

'Do they?'

'Oh, yes. For example if a person lies, a black line develops down the middle of the tongue. Let me see your tongue.'

Dutifully, Janey Mack poked her tongue out and Merriment craned over to inspect it.

'Very good, no lie has tripped off that tongue.'

'What else, miss, shows up in the body?'

'Let's see, a person who does a crime with their hands, little scarlet spots burst up on the palms.'

'Jesus,' Janey Mack hissed. She quickly inspected her hands and Merriment's eyebrows rose quizzically.

'Is there something you need to tell me, Janey?'

'God no.' Janey Mack blinked. 'Are they big spots, miss?'

'On the hands? No. Very small. You need a professional's eye to see them, but they're there.'

'Janey Mack.'

'Don't worry, I'll train you up. By the time you're qualified, you'll be able to read a person like a book.'

Janey Mack nodded. She threw another log onto the fire and watched as sparks flew up the chimney.

'What do you see in Solomon, miss?'

Merriment folded her hands across her lap and thought for a moment.

'I think Solomon has a secret.'

'Do ya? Do you think he murdered anyone?'

'No,' Merriment laughed. 'No.' She shook her head doubtfully. 'Janey, all this business with Olocher has inflamed your imagination. Solomon is, well . . .' She paused, contemplating just what she thought of Solomon Fish. 'Something depreciated his worth, reduced his character, put him to the life of a vagabond writer.'

'We've all had knocks.' Janey Mack shrugged. 'I think it was his looks that spoiled him.'

Merriment stared at the little girl poking the log in the fire and nodded approvingly. Janey Mack was bright as a button and somehow that made Merriment proud.

'Go on,' she said encouragingly.

'That's it. He was a pretty baby and got what he wanted, a pretty boy and got what he wanted, and then one day he was all grown up and didn't get what he wanted. And in a fit of disappointment he had a tantrum and took to the road and has been slidin' downhill ever since.'

*

Solomon looked bleakly at the pile of notes and coins that had only hours earlier been carefully stashed in a battered tin box in the floor in his bedroom and were now being counted out by Billy Knox's bookkeeper. Billy himself looked barely amused, his penetrating eyes glimmering with a cruel, detached light. He ordered brandy and muttered something to the man next to him while Solomon glared dismally at his losses.

'And of course there's the tariff,' the bully in the fine clothes informed Solomon. His nickname was 'Pearly' on account of his teeth and fondness for fashion. 'Seven pounds, I reckon.'

Solomon bristled. 'I wrote no promissory notes.'

Pearly showed his gleaming smile. 'Ah now, when ye play with the big boys, ye follie their rules. It was seven pounds to sit in the game.'

'You never said.' Solomon's eyes danced frantically over the table. 'You never mentioned a game fee.'

'Didn't I?' Pearly feigned a concerned frown, tutting at himself sardonically. 'Shame on me.'

'But—' Solomon panicked.

'Don't be blusterin' now.' Pearly wagged an enormous finger and, pulling out a notebook and pencil, astounded Solomon by writing. 'Yer address?' Pearly enquired.

'I owe nothing,' Solomon protested.

Pearly nodded sympathetically and very pointedly said, 'I'll put down the apothecary shop, will I?'

Sickened that Knox's gang already had tabs on him, Solomon stood up from the table, desperate to get away, but Pearly grabbed his arm.

'See, how it works' – Pearly's voice rumbled as he hauled Solomon down beside him – 'is ye pay what ye owe or ye find a friend who might loan ye the money and assist ye.'

Solomon's stomach lurched, his whole body flooding with regret. Why had he come out? Why hadn't he stayed safe inside Merriment's lodgings? Why hadn't he just written about Ester Murphy's witness statement?

Pearly licked his lower lip, his purple tongue glistening as it emerged from his mouth. 'A lady businessman might give ye an advance,' he proposed, his thick dark brows rising towards his hairline, his eyes staring meaningfully into Solomon's face.

The full force of Pearly's suggestion hit Solomon like a cannonball to the chest. They knew about Merriment . . . They intended to extort . . . In a casual moment he was now embroiled . . . up to his neck . . . and now Merriment was dragged in. She had been targeted. He began to panic.

'Absolutely not,' Solomon snapped. 'Absolutely not.' Then, desperate to get away, scrambling to mask his dread, to hide his terror, he launched to his feet and growled down at Pearly, his words slowly punching the air, 'You will get your money and then you will fuck off.'

Solomon stormed away to howls of laughter.

What was he going to do? He felt sick, claustrophobic, hemmed in. The room seemed to spin about him, the crush of bodies, the shoving and shouting, the noise and grubbiness. His thoughts burned and boiled, torturing him. He owed money. It was London all over again, only now Merriment . . . He felt sick. What the hell had he done? He swayed on his feet, stumbling, pushing past a knot of thieves pulling candlesticks from a sack and asking Judy the Fence to take a look. Solomon couldn't squeeze by them. He was going to throw up. He needed air. Space. Seeing the trapdoor to the cellar open, he took his chances and dived down the steps, gulping in mouthfuls of the cold, rank atmosphere. Jenny was there. He grabbed her and kissed her, forcing his tongue between her teeth, his arms dragging her close, pulling her behind the casks into the shadows, hungrily disrobing her, opening her blouse.

He was damned.

Jenny succumbed, letting Solomon lift her skirts and take her. The cellar was damp, a candle threw a pallid light over the blackening barrels, and as Jenny heaved and squirmed beneath him, Solomon thrust deep, only stopping when she pushed him back and asked him what was wrong.

'What ye crying for?'

Solomon sank against the wall, grimly holding his breeches, looking bleakly into the shadows. He winced at the grubby surroundings, at Jenny's confused face, at the stink of mould and stale beer. And he couldn't bear it, couldn't bear that he was a dissolute, lascivious gambler, a whoremonger, tipping a barmaid in a vault, dragging Merriment into his nefarious dealings, contaminating her good world with his polluted compulsions. He blinked, confounded by his own tears.

'I'm not drunk enough,' he muttered, quickly fastening his buttons.

'Is that so?' Jenny hissed sharply. 'Well, fuck you and yer attitude. Ye ponce. Ye weeping Mary, get yerself up the stairs and out the door, ye lobcock, and don't dare step in here again.'

Jenny smoothed her skirts and grabbed the pitcher of ale she'd come down to the cellar for, leaving Solomon resting against the wall, shaking his head miserably.

When he appeared in the bar, Jenny was standing over a card game, laughing raucously.

'Weeping like a toddler he was,' she bawled loudly.

There were loud guffaws; someone banged the table with their fist and elbowed Jenny.

'Sure, I'd bet ye'd bring tears to anyone's eyes with your tricks and japes and expectations.'

Solomon slinked out into the night, closing the door to the Cock and Hen quietly behind him.

It was a cold night. He welcomed the chill wind; it naturally cooled his overheated mind as he walked along the quays watching the boats bob on the tide. The lights in the galleys reflected on the dark water and on the quayside people sat in clusters inside their lean-to shacks, the dull flame of their home fires casting a crimson glow in the tiny windows. He walked and wondered what he should do. He knew how Knox's gang worked. It was the same with the London gangs, the fee he owed would never be paid. Billy Knox would squeeze every last drop from him, keep ratcheting up the expense of the game, adding percentages. He had two pounds under the floorboard and for a moment he wondered about asking Merriment for the balance.

'Christ.' He bit his teeth together, pushing away the vision of her face. What the hell had he done? He ran through the list of people he could ask. Gloria? The printer? He sucked on the inside of his cheek cursing and damning himself, cursing and damning the situation. He was in hell, locked in a cycle of constantly owing money, of escaping debt, evading criminals, disappointing women, disappointing himself. How had his life come to this? Again! He groaned, miserable and tormented.

Maybe Maggie, he wondered. Then, revolted that he could even consider calling out to Saggart to fleece poor Maggie of her earnings so he could extricate himself from the tangle created by his own bad character, his own lack of inner resolve, he balled his fist and dragged his knuckles off a low wall until they bled. He was furious and frustrated. Hadn't he promised himself on the voyage over that he was done with cards? Done with women? Wasn't Dublin a whole new start? Seething with self-loathing he walked blindly through the narrow streets, full of shame and regret and torn by a longing to be with Merriment, to say something to her, to hear her voice.

She would despise you, he thought, rolling his eyes towards the cloudy sky, the last remnants of his pride shredded by the unassailable truth that he was a creature of destructive habits, destined to ruin any prospect of hope for himself and those near him. He had undone in one evening all that he had successfully achieved in a month.

He was at the top of Winetavern Street when a pale hump by a step near the back door to one of the guilds groaned and reached out a bloody hand.

'Help me,' the voice whimpered, 'help me.'

'Jesus.' Solomon jolted, recognising something in the tone, something familiar about the corner of the shawl, a ruby-coloured shawl. He ran towards the woman.

'Maggie! My God, Maggie, what happened?'

The left side of Maggie's head was dripping, blood streaked along her face and curled into her mouth, staining her teeth. Her

185

clothes were torn, her bodice half ripped open, her skirts loose and one of her shoes was missing. She pawed at the air, trying to haul herself upright. She rolled over and vomited, splattering Solomon's shoes.

'Help me,' she sobbed, not recognising Solomon.

'It's me, Maggie, Solomon Fish, remember? I'll help you. I'll help you.'

Solomon swept an arm under her shoulder. He saw his breath coming in a white puff. He could hear his own voice echo off the walls and in the distance was aware of the sound of approaching hooves.

'Try and sit up, good woman.'

He looked frantically about. Behind him the blazing streetlight hissed and sizzled, the flames dancing from the pitch.

'Hey,' he bellowed at the top of his lungs. 'Someone help me, there's a woman here.' He balanced Maggie Fines on the step and ran to the top of Skinner's Row, shouting at the top of his lungs for help.

*

It took three men to carry Maggie Fines to Merriment's shop.

'Open up,' Solomon hollered, hammering on the door.

Janey Mack sprang from Merriment's lap, disorientated and teetering.

'What is it? It's murder, miss, don't open the door. Who could it be?'

'It's me, Merriment,' Solomon hollered. 'It's urgent, let us in.'

Merriment had her pistol in her hand as she unbolted the door, aware of the voices of a crowd gathering outside. Solomon burst in, his face gaunt, his white flesh eerily contrasting against the dark circles surrounding his eyes. Two men followed him, bringing in a faint and blood-smeared Maggie.

'She's been attacked.' Solomon barged past. Janey Mack stood shivering, holding a candle.

'Did the Dolocher get her?' she gulped.

'Will you look at her?' Solomon swept his hand over his brow as Merriment passed.

'Put her in the chair,' she said, grabbing a basin, spirits, clean cloths and fresh bandages.

The anteroom filled up. Maggie was lowered into a chair and given brandy to help revive her. Merriment set about wiping her face and inspecting her body for other wounds, while all around her an anxious crowd pressed close, waiting to hear what the injured woman had to say.

'She's been hit badly on the head. Something sharp.' Merriment lifted a piece of scalp the size of a fried egg and gently mopped away the blood. Maggie hissed and flinched; her hands shook.

'Sshh. Maggie, it's me. Remember?' Solomon knelt down beside her. 'Remember me?'

A confused expression shifted across Maggie's battered face. Merriment patted down the torn scalp and gently rubbed a soothing ointment along the frayed edges, pausing for Solomon to feed the woman more brandy.

'She was in town selling lace,' he told the men standing near him. 'She was with a girl called Gertrude.'

'Gertie,' Maggie repeated, recollecting the name.

'That's right, Maggie. What happened?'

'He was waiting in the shadows. We were going to catch the coach out to Saggart.'

Maggie reached for Solomon, clutching at his arm, her face suddenly frantic.

'Tell Jack to come and fetch me, Sol. Run along and tell him, I'm ready to go home. Go on now.'

'I will, Maggie. I will.'

Solomon looked helplessly at Merriment.

'I think there's a couple of ribs bruised,' she told him. 'I can make up a plaster.'

'She can stay in my bed,' Solomon said.

One of the men stepped forward and coughed a rasping, chesty cough. He turned out to be the night watch and in all the hue and cry he had managed to lose his cudgel. He clutched his lantern close to his thigh. His round face was full of folds of flesh, like a pug dog, his ancient eyes drooping, the lower lids hanging, the exposed rims scarlet and weeping.

'Ask her where her money is?' the old man suggested.

'Where's your money, Maggie?'

'I don't have it,' Maggie said, hissing and jerking away from the touch of Merriment's fingers. 'I lost it and me basket. He took Gertie, whisked her away and he tried to fetch me with him, but I say me prayers.' Then her eyes darted quickly. She dropped the glass and, as it rolled noisily along the floor, she clasped Solomon's hand and uttered in a low terrified whisper, 'Where's Gertie, Solomon? Where's she gone?'

'The Dolocher took her,' Janey Mack whispered, her huge eyes blinking with horror. The night watch and the three men with him stood motionless. Two women, who had been watching Merriment assiduously, looked meaningfully at each other but said nothing.

Solomon came to his feet.

'We have to set up a search party. We're looking for a young girl. She's wearing a pale cloak. Long hair. Fair, I think.'

Solomon wracked his brain, trying to conjure up the image of Gertie, but all he could remember was a speck, a young blur waving at Maggie as she approached.

'Right-oh,' the night watch said, 'we'll work in threes, considering there's a villain out there.'

'Time is of the essence. Get as many neighbours together as you can. See if we can get more beadles over here.'

Solomon grabbed a lantern, shepherding the crowd out. They splintered off into groups, dividing the area into quadrants and setting up a meeting point to report back to.

Maggie Fines sat in the chair, her head lolling as she rocked back and forth. She looked at Janey Mack accusingly and, pointing at the little girl's heart, she asked, 'How can it be that the dead are up and walking?'

*

'Over here,' someone hollered.

The rain came down in sheets, driven sideways by the rising wind. Two men were hunched over a long, pale streak and Solomon knew as he ran towards them that Gertie was dead. A lantern was placed at her head, throwing enough light to illuminate her pale face and staring eyes. She lay half naked in the gutter. Her belly had been cut and her intestine bulged from the gash. Her bare breasts looked blue and were streaked with rills of muddy water. Her skirts were twisted and soaking wet, her thighs were bloodstained and her feet were bare. A simple chain with a carved wooden cross hung about her neck and her hair spread into a fan of amber gold. She was sixteen years of age at the most and the last look in her eyes was one of abject horror. Solomon threw his jacket over her, shaking his head with disbelief.

'Has to be her,' he whispered.

'She was strangled,' the night watch informed him. 'The marks around her neck.'

Blue patches like darkly eclipsed moons clustered around her throat.

'She was raped, poor thing,' a woman said as she lowered Gertie's skirts, made the sign of the cross on the young girl's forehead and began reciting the Confiteor. Solomon swallowed down the surge of bile rising in his gullet and wondered how he was going to tell Maggie Fines. He was about to stand when something caught his eyes. It shimmered a moment when he moved the lantern, and swinging back to inspect it, he pointed behind the praying woman, asking her, 'What's that?'

Underneath the sloping branches of a shrub, something

sparkled wet with rain. The woman reached her hand in and screamed, jolting back.

Solomon had to kick it out. They all looked down at the pale mound quivering in the hissing lantern light next to Gertie's head. There were striations of red muscle marbled with white fat in the mound, and when they turned it over, black dark bristles beaded with small globes of rain fanned out, hideously grotesque.

'It's a lump of rotten flesh!'

And Solomon shivered, afraid of everything that the pound of flesh implied.

11

Pyrrho of Elis

Solomon tapped softly on the back door. Merriment opened it, her blue eyes wide with expectation.

'Well?' she whispered.

'Dead. Raped.'

'Oh.' Merriment's hand swept to her mouth. She watched Solomon as he sank into a chair, shaken utterly and completely to the core. He was battered in body and mind. He was soaked through, his feet were spattered with mud, his breeches, shirt and jacket dripped, rivulets of water slid off the ends of his hair. But more than anything it was his pinched, haunted expression that alarmed Merriment. She fetched a blanket from a cupboard and handed it to him.

'How awful,' she said quietly. 'I really am sorry. Where?'

'One of the side streets near Smock Alley.' Solomon could barely stop his hands from trembling. He looked blankly at the walls as he told Merriment about Gertie's bruised neck.

'She was brought to the Lying-In Hospital, to be cleaned, put in a shroud.'

Solomon looked at the blanket.

'The poor thing.' Merriment patted her heart. 'It's dreadful.' She pulled the cork out of a cut-glass decanter. 'To have met with such a cruel, violent end. Her parents will be devastated. Such horrible news.' She poured two glasses of fortified wine, gazing a moment into the shadowy shelves where jars of ointments stood in neat rows.

'What a night.'

She offered Solomon the wine. 'You've had a dreadful shock.'

He took the glass, faintly dazed, and slumped back into the chair.

'You should get out of your wet clothes,' Merriment suggested. 'Wrap up in the blanket, get warm.'

But Solomon didn't move. He stared miserably into the fire, his eyes glazed with tears. He hid his face, barely able to contain his misery; he felt cursed and destroyed and overwhelmed by everything.

'You all right?' Merriment asked.

Solomon nodded bleakly.

'What a thing to see,' he muttered. 'What a thing for someone to do. She'd been cut open.'

Merriment grimaced, stopping in her tracks.

'Slashed her belly.' Solomon held the side of his head. 'Like what Olocher did to that girl.'

He looked mournfully up at Merriment.

'She was so young. Last time I saw Gertie she was running and waving.' Then he remembered Maggie. Solomon's head rolled back.

'Is Maggie . . .?' He couldn't finish the question.

Merriment paused. 'She's,' she began, then, sighing, said, 'I don't know. Her right pupil is blown out. She's got a fever and I'm not sure I have the skill to siphon off a haemorrhage.'

She tried to soften the prognosis but knew enough not to get Solomon's hopes up.

'The body can rally, you know. Maggie could easily make a full recovery. It's just . . . fever is tricky. She's sleeping now . . .' Merriment trailed off.

Solomon sat for a while peering into the flames, a thin trail of vapour rising from his damp feet. All was grim and grey and miserable. Merriment sat quietly opposite him, concerned, encouraging him to drink what she had given him.

'You look . . .' she started, gazing at Solomon's distressed profile. He looked grief-stricken and shattered.

'Drink a little more,' she said softly.

And he sipped, silently locked in an agony of emotions, the wine slowly softening and blurring the edges of his self-loathing and shock. The silence spanned out between them. The warmth of the fire, of Merriment's patient gaze, of the fortified wine, worked on his agitation until, after a long spell of listening to nothing but the flames fluttering in the hearth, Solomon began to feel his mind release a little, his breath relax. He let go. Let go of Billy Knox and Pearly, of Jenny sneering, of Maggie balled in a bloody heap in a doorway, of Gertie sprawled on the cobbled street. He sank into the subtle comfort of the anteroom, imbibing all the warmth, the tender looks from the woman across the way from him, the fire, the wine. Merriment poured him another glass.

'This is a grisly business,' she finally said.

Solomon nodded, frowning as he recollected the lump of flesh ghoulishly glittering in the rain, the black spiked bristles menacingly echoing with Boxty's account of the Dolocher.

'It's the devil's work,' Solomon said flatly, 'an evil act born in a putrid soul.'

Merriment watched him sink into his dark thoughts, his eyes half closing, the corners of his mouth pulled down by sadness.

'It is evil to have cut a young life so short, so horribly,' she softly agreed. But Solomon shifted in his chair.

'What if . . .' He looked into the flames dancing in the dark hearth. 'There was a lump of flesh, with coarse black hair, the same as the piece I found in the Black Dog.'

Solomon looked over at her, for a long time studying her face, the eggshell delicacy of her skin, the plump broadness of her lips, the defined edges of her cheekbones, the intelligence of her brow. And as he stared, Merriment understood clearly what he was implying, yet sat quietly, giving him room to explore the idea that perhaps, somehow, a fiend had emerged from the debtors' prison on Cooke Street and was now prowling the dark alleyways of Dublin.

'I cannot shake the idea,' Solomon said bleakly, 'that Olocher has somehow returned from the dead. The witnesses, the evidence . . .' He turned away to stare into the fire, contemplating the tortures of hell. He was in his own hell, locked in misfortune and put upon by thieves and bullies. He was shadowed by forces that brought him ill luck and misery. He was wretchedly hounded and plagued by hardships and adversities and so uniquely obstructed from life's opportunities that it took nothing more than a little nudge to convince him that a demon sat on his back. If he in some small way could sense an evil shadow cast over his own existence, it did not take too much more reasoning to suppose that a devil could erupt into the physical world and carry out its own dark desires.

Merriment let him sit for a while mulling over the preternatural possibilities of the Dolocher until at last she said, 'There cannot be a demon.'

'Why not?' Solomon glanced sideways at her. 'Because it goes against reason? Because if there is a devil, there's a God, and this new science will collapse? Because you don't want to believe it?'

'All of those things,' Merriment answered, 'and none of those things.'

Solomon shifted uncomfortably but didn't speak. Instead he listened while Merriment told him a story from her seafaring days.

'We'd been sailing off Port Royal.' As she spoke, Solomon's shoulders seemed to slump and soften, lulled by the tone of her voice. 'We'd had such a run of bad luck. Stupid things like unfettered barrels that broke loose and shattered one sailor's leg. There was a breach in the hull. A plague of weevils in the biscuit. Really, the usual stuff. But the men took it badly, believed the trials we had been experiencing were omens. They read portents in the clouds and began to fix all their frustration on one man. A single sailor with a deformed arm. They blamed him, said he was attracting the misfortune. And when we were attacked by pirates, which by the way the region was notorious for, they lynched the poor man, hung him from the yard arm, all of them standing mute while he screamed his innocence.'

Merriment stopped, pausing as she remembered trying to rush to cut the poor man down. Beresford had hauled her back and hissed at her under his breath. 'Stay, or you'll swing beside him. This is the law of the sea, and unpalatable as it is, it will purge our bad luck.' And because she still wanted to save the poor sailor, Beresford glared at her and reminded her of her own precarious position. 'Bad luck to have a woman onboard. Don't give them ideas. This should quell their ardour. Stand fast.' And so she stood and watched.

She pushed away the recollection of the poor sailor crying for mercy and topped up her wine glass, sighing as she tried to convince Solomon that Dublin was in the grip of some kind of demon fever.

'You didn't see the things that I've seen,' Solomon muttered in response, and Merriment sat deep into her chair and rested her head back, listening to the wind beginning to rise outside. The wood hissed in the fire, the candle flame stuttered a moment, sending fluttering shadows skipping over the wall while they both sat contemplating the darker aspects of human nature.

'Did you ever hear of Pyrrho of Elis?' Merriment asked, lengthening up, her face suddenly animated.

Solomon shook his head, his blond curls shivering a little.

'He had four questions that he recommended we should always ask to really know and understand a thing.'

Solomon turned his torso so that he could look at Merriment, engaged by her solidity, wishing he had her firm belief in scientific methodology, her measured stoicism, her conviction that the walls dividing the natural from the supernatural were strong and firm and impenetrable. His eyes slipped a moment to her lips, sliding down to the notch in her throat. He had to fight to pull his gaze away, to stop himself from muttering 'you're beautiful'.

'The first question we must ask,' Merriment told him, 'is what is it? Define it. Then we must consider what the thing is made of? How are we related to it? And after that we must enquire what is our attitude towards it?'

She leaned forward, the wine in her glass a ruddy glow between her pale fingers, the top button of her shirt was open and the collar had slipped back to expose the long, soft line of her neck. For some time they both sat silently applying Pyrrho of Elis' logic to the current case. Solomon was the first to give his account.

'What is the Dolocher?'

His eyes searched the flagstone floor, the answer coming in broad waves, punctured by long pauses.

'A demon. A creature from the paranormal depths. An amalgam of dead things, human and swine, somehow animated by a wilful desire to seek revenge, to murder and destroy. A corpse revitalised by an insatiable hunger. A cadaver sliced open by surgeons. But before that, did Olocher make a demon or attract a demon? Did his wicked heart construct the demon from the pit of his reeking lusts? As Olocher sat muttering in his prison cell did he summon up enough bile to infuse his own flesh with an occult essence that was so powerful that by the time he was lying on the surgeon's table, he had transformed his body, transfigured it with such great evil that like an automaton his cadaver was galvanised to continue fulfilling Olocher's compulsions, raping and murdering and haunting Hell? Or did something latch onto him, use him like a parasite, and manipulate his corpse, turning it into an instrument for a swine-headed fiend intent on murder and revenge?'

Solomon let Merriment pour him more drink. He felt strangely better, as the crimson light in the room cosily enveloped him.

'What was Pyrrho of Elis' other questions?' he asked.

'How are we related to the thing and what is our attitude to it?'

Solomon nodded, licking the taste of wine from his lips.

'So the Dolocher is a demon' – he held up an index finger – 'made of dead flesh and dreadful deeds.' He raked his fingers along his cheek. 'How are we related? Well, that's easy, we are its quarry. The Dolocher hunts us out and our attitude is one of fear.'

Satisfied, Solomon smiled sardonically at Merriment and said, 'Here we are in the eighteenth century confounded by demonic forces. What a time.'

Merriment nodded but disagreed. 'And if it is not a demon all your supposition collapses and crumbles away.'

'Trouble is,' Solomon countered, 'if it walks like a duck and quacks like a duck, then it's a duck.'

Merriment pinched back a disbelieving smile. 'I can't argue with your logic. If it looks like a demon and acts like a demon, then it's a demon. But' – she swept her hand over her glass – 'I have had patients in the past with strange ailments: the symptoms pointed at an illness in a certain organ when in fact the disease lay in another part of the body. Nature has a tricky, slippery quality.' She let her eyes rest on Solomon's hands. 'We need to keep a cool mind, to sift the facts from the clutter of information that diverts our attention.'

'By clutter, you mean the murder of Gertie, the attack on Maggie, on Florence, on Ester, the striking down of Boxty and the dismemberment of Martin Coffey? Isn't that rather a lot of evidence to brush aside because you cannot countenance the idea of a demon?'

Merriment sighed, her head falling thoughtfully to one side. 'Put like that,' she said, taking a sip.

'Now you have to wonder . . .' Solomon wanted to reach for

her, wrap an arm over her shoulder, have her sink into his chest; instead he sat forward in his chair and asked, 'Are we resisting the evidence, the eye-witness accounts, the murder victims, because our faith rejects the very existence of a devil? You the "sceptical chemist", the scientist, want to quash the very idea of demonic forces because how can you bring religion into scientific experiment; and I want to deny the Dolocher because, God damn it, if there is a devil then there is a God and that won't do. That won't do.'

'You want to deny?' Merriment seemed genuinely amused; her eyes sparkled as she smothered an incredulous chuckle. 'But you have argued vehemently that the Dolocher is a demon, that the creature exists.'

Solomon shrugged. 'I think perhaps it does exist, but the best part of me wants to believe we are safe from angels and demons and sprites of every kind. We have enough trouble in the world without spectres and ghosts creeping in.'

Buoyed by the drink, by the garnet-coloured light and the compelling attraction of Merriment's company, Solomon felt emboldened. Strength emerged from an unknown quarter. A stray thought suddenly filled his mind: perhaps he could outwit Knox, perhaps he could change, perhaps he could stay.

He watched Merriment drink, her eyelids an opalescent white beneath her dark brows, her lips sensually parting over the glass, closing sweetly as she sipped.

How many men has she lain with? he wondered. *How could they have left her? Maybe they didn't leave her, maybe she left them.* He remembered Jenny the barmaid's remark, 'Probably whored her way around the Bay of Biscay.'

Sitting here beside the fire talking to the woman who wore breeches and carried a pistol, Solomon understood implicitly that Merriment possessed the most intriguing attribute of all. She was mysterious. And intoxicated by fortified wine and the heady combination of a bright, sensual woman and gentle light,

Solomon found his eyes drifting from Merriment's mouth to the base of her neck and down to her breasts, his whole being filled with longing.

He could stay.

'Can I ask you something?' Solomon enquired. 'Did your luck change after they hanged the deformed sailor off Port Royal?'

Merriment blushed suddenly; a rosy flare crept up her neck and fanned out into a blaze on her cheeks. She smiled, showing the gap in her front teeth, her whole being illuminated. Her fine spirit glittered in her blue eyes.

'Well then, you have found me out.' She laughed a peppery laugh full of spice and bite. 'Strangely enough, our luck completely changed.'

Solomon found himself laughing too. How had that happened? How had a gentle mirth emerged from the obliterating events of the day?

They both sat back in their chairs, their amusement ebbing away, softening into contentment, a long silence opening up between them, filled with the sound of the fire crackling, the wind blustering and the rain pounding a rapport on the side of the house. And cocooned in warmth and comfort Solomon began to contemplate how he might outwit Billy Knox. He still had two pounds and another instalment of the Dolocher tale. It pierced his heart to think he could use poor Gertie's murder to pay off his gambling debts, but his back was to the wall. He could not forsake his chances in Dublin and, horrific as the truth was, he would rather stay and try and make good than run and leave all this behind. *This?* his conscience enquired as his mind sloped away from the one thing that truly made him want to stay.

Merriment.

He ran his fingers through his hair and thought of Pearly's suggestion: *Ask a friend for a loan.* And looking at the glowing cinders collapsing in the hearth, he took in a deep breath, deciding to take his chances.

'I should work,' he said to Merriment.

He would invest his two pounds in broadsheets and start again.

'There's Gertie's murder to report, Maggie's condition, Ester Murphy's testimony.' He put his glass down on the floor. 'Bloody distasteful,' he growled, more to himself than to Merriment, 'but I have to do it.' He wanted to add, 'Don't judge me.' Instead he turned his face away, afraid to see disapproval in her eyes.

'Of course.' Merriment felt curiously self-conscious. For a moment she wondered about staying in the room and reading her book, but the atmosphere had been disturbed between them, the balance of intimacy tipped a little off-kilter. She intuited that Solomon wanted to be alone and, taking the cue, rose from her chair and put the glasses on the sideboard. She pointed at the large ceramic jar near the door. 'There's bread and cheese there, and some butter under that dish.'

'Thank you.' Solomon smiled sadly. Then he stood up and, digging into his jacket pocket, opened his wallet and said, 'Here.' He took out three shillings.

Merriment frowned, confused.

'For Maggie,' he said, and counting out two more shillings, all he had left, asked her to do him a favour.

'His name is Charlie. I think his arm was broken the night the Keeper did this to my face. He's in the Black Dog. Will you look in on him and let me know how he is?'

'Good lord,' Merriment couldn't help but tease. 'Is the Dolocher chastising you to do good deeds?'

'No,' Solomon said flatly. 'You are.'

Merriment crumpled, completely disarmed. She wanted to swat away her feelings with a quip, wanted to say something clever to diffuse the intensity of the emotions suddenly boiling in her heart. But she could think of nothing. She looked into his face, surprised, her fingertips touching his as he gave her the money.

'I will,' she promised.

Solomon wanted to kiss her. Instead he gazed at her steadily, watching her eyelids lower. Her thick auburn hair, richly burnished by the firelight, shivered a little as she turned, her long curls flowing beyond her waist.

'Night,' she said softly.

And he watched her leave, the scent of her perfume delicately mingled with the longing in his heart. If only he could make good.

12

Two Houses

When Corker called early the next morning, the sun hadn't come up yet. By instinct he came to the back door and tapped. Solomon was slumped over his work, the fire had died down, and when the raps roused him, he thought for a brief moment he was a young boy again and had dozed off while reading by candlelight after a hard day's work. The darkness was familiar, warm, full of the past and who he used to be.

'Yes,' he whispered hoarsely, expecting his mother's voice to say, 'Sol, you stayed up the night long, come on like a good lad, have a bit of soda bread and butter, ye'll be late.'

'Sol, is that you?' Corker responded; he had been expecting Janey Mack or Merriment.

The latch to the back door drew back with a clank and Solomon, wrapped in a blanket, leaned against it sleepily, letting Corker in. The candle guttered in the wind and settled once the door was shut.

'Met the night watch.' Corker rubbed his hands together and made for the dead fire. He rattled the ashes, uncovering the barest glow. 'Bloody cold out there.' He hunkered down, desperate to soak up the last dregs of the heat.

Solomon lit another candle and looked for kindling. 'Is it the middle of the night?' He gazed bemused at his surroundings.

'It's six thirty. I was up. Me mam—' Corker cut off, not bothering to explain what he was doing up so early. 'I thought we'd get started soon as possible seein' as we have to be over at the civic offices for one or so. Heard about the young one being strangled and cut. Heard about the chunk of flesh found with her. I found the night watch hiding. He's the one who told me. I fell upon him. He's terrified out of his wits, the poor old man. Says he's going to the Aldermen's to give in his resignation. He must be seventy if he's a day.'

Corker shovelled the ash into a bucket and grabbed a handful of kindling, taking Solomon's candle to light a fresh fire.

'Cut us a slice of bread, Sol, would ya?'

Then, glancing at the pile of damp clothes on the floor, he grinned, his crooked teeth on full display.

'What'd you and Merriment get up to last night?'

'Nothing.' Solomon scowled. 'I got half drowned looking for that poor Gertie girl. Here.' He handed Corker a thick slice of bread. 'I've to go up and get changed and look in on Maggie.' He was about to open the door into the shop when he paused and turned, tilting his head. 'Why do we have to go to the civic offices?'

'After what happened last night.' Corker wolfed down the bread, barely chewing on the crust. 'The two houses are meeting, the Aldermen and the Sheriff's, one will want to blame the other for the Dolocher business. They'll have to explain themselves to the head buck cats, the city elders, beadles and night watches. All the bigwigs will want to know what's going on. There'll be a crackdown on criminal gangs, watches doubled. Something will come out in the mix, ye'll see.'

'Right.' Solomon scratched the side of his face. His eyes were itchy. The idea of a crackdown on criminal gangs set off a chain of thoughts. Maybe Pearly and Billy Knox would go to ground, keep a low profile, get off his back. He pointed to the table. 'You grab a sheet of paper and do a quick sketch of a girl dead in a gutter. I'll go up and get dressed. Give me my wet clothes, will you?'

Corker did as he was bid, admiring Solomon's worn shoes.

'If ye ever want to chuck these, I know a set of feet would welcome their comfort.'

'They leak,' Solomon said, before blindly making his way upstairs.

Maggie was sleeping deeply, her breath catching in her throat with a slight rattle. He tip-toed past her, unaware that slumped at her feet, sitting on the chest she had purchased in India, was Merriment. He quietly opened his bag, drew out a shirt and was slipping into dry breeches when a voice softly whispered.

'Is it morning?'

'Jesus,' Solomon hissed, spinning, his chest gleaming in the dim light of the shuttered room. His arms waved palely as he instinctively clutched his shirt and staggered upright. It took him a moment to realise it was Merriment.

'Sorry,' she whispered.

'No, I just . . .' Solomon wiped his brow; he was shattered. 'I need to get dressed.'

Merriment unhinged the shutters and drew them back, letting a damp grey light into the room. Maggie Fines was sitting propped up, her face haggard. The patch of injured scalp had risen and blotches of dried blood were caught in her wispy grey hair. She was surrounded by pillows and covered by a pale quilt. Wrapped in her fingers were a set of rosary beads, and visible beneath the white shift Merriment had loaned her were the tight pink bandages of a comfrey plaster that squeezed and nourished her fractured ribs.

'She looks awful.' Solomon crept close.

Maggie stirred, her face wincing, her whole being aching as she slowly opened her eyes.

'Solomon Fish,' she smiled painfully. 'What happened to yer face, Sol?'

'Hey, Maggie, how are you this morning?'

Maggie turned to Merriment and nodded politely, despite the pain shooting up from her side.

'This yer wife, Sol?'

Solomon looked at Merriment.

'I . . .' he began to say.

'Poor Eliza, she'll be disappointed.' Maggie rested her head back onto the pillow. 'I feel sore all over. True as God, I feel like I've been put through the mill.'

Merriment sat on the bed beside her, checking her face and inspecting the side of her head.

'Don't touch that, dear.' Maggie retracted, her head slowly turning to watch the door creak open. Janey Mack stepped in, her night shift dragging along the floor. She was wrapped in the tattered shawl she'd taken from Hoppy John's, her large eyes blinking with fearful expectation as she stepped towards Maggie.

'There ye are, Misses. I thought we'd find ye dead in the bed.'

'Janey,' Merriment tried to signal to the little girl to say no more, 'will you fetch Maggie a sup of warm milk?'

Merriment patted Maggie's hand. 'Would you like that, Maggie, some warm milk for breakfast?'

'Thank you, dear.'

Maggie rubbed the rosary beads with her left thumb and wagged a finger at Solomon.

'What did ye do with Sally Loftus, Solomon?'

Solomon looked away in a panic.

'I'm late,' he grumbled, tugging on his shirt and grabbing a pair of stockings.

Merriment watched him scurry from the room, taking Janey Mack with him.

'Breaks everyone's heart,' Maggie whispered. 'He'll break yours too no doubt.'

Maggie let her head sink into the pillows. She gave a little moan as she shifted, clutching at her painful ribs.

'You need to rest,' Merriment told her. 'Janey Mack and I will look after you today.'

The door slammed downstairs. Merriment got up to look out

the window. Across the way a skinny man hopped up and down off the kerb, his hands in his pockets, his wizened face peering left and right, amusing himself with idle skipping. He appeared to be waiting for someone. A dairymaid dawdled up the road, tugging a reluctant cow towards the market. A huge man wearing a blue nipped jacket, a neatly pressed shirt, cream breeches and polished boots idly leaned on a windowsill and hailed the dairymaid over to buy a quart of milk. Merriment watched him gulp it down, interested in his particular manner as he carefully sipped from the quart jug. He glanced up at her and their eyes momentarily met. Merriment thought he might have smiled at her. Unnerved, she stepped a little back, watching him as he sauntered away into the crowd while the shambles began to thicken with fishwives arriving with the morning's catch.

'Is Sol gone to get my Jack?' Maggie tried to lift herself up.

'Yes,' Merriment lied as she gazed down into the street below. The man in the blue jacket had vanished. She saw Solomon run towards the printers with Corker hot on his heels and wondered why the name Sally Loftus had scalded him so much.

*

All that day, the shop was phenomenally busy. The news of Gertie Baker's murder had shot through the community. The city buzzed with the startling report that a supernatural force was strangling and attacking women, cutting them open. Strangers commented with strangers, stopping in their tracks to throw their tuppence-worth into overheard conversations, trading titbits of information.

'Olocher used to stalk them when he was alive. I know one girl so maltreated by him that she's been confined to the lunatic asylum ever since.'

'Olocher's predilection was to slice off slivers of flesh and eat them before his victims' eyes.'

The populace worked itself into a tumult. That a man so

heinous as Olocher could extend his wrath beyond the grave sent several quarters running for the safety and succour of the Church. People flung themselves onto their knees, renouncing their sins, gathering up bottles of holy water and buying scapulars as a meagre protection from the hideous grasp of Satan himself. The attacks were considered awful, the fact that they were carried out by a 'fiend from hell' was believed to be some form of dreadful retribution that may very well be a precursor to Gabriel's trumpet announcing the cracking open of the earth and the arrival of the Four Horsemen of the Apocalypse. No one could understand why Dublin had been chosen to be the starting ground for the end of times, but several wagged their heads and told anyone who would listen that the city was awash with every imaginable vice and only by banishing whores and lowlifes could the Dolocher be driven away.

All day Merriment had to make up potions, the majority for anxiety and fear, others for ailing, unloving or bad-tempered spouses; a small few were for sadness and despair. She was so busy in the shop that she barely had time to eat. Janey Mack crept downstairs and fetched some bread and cheese for herself and another cup of milk for Maggie late in the afternoon.

'You all right?' Merriment asked her, noticing the little girl was very quiet.

'Yes,' Janey Mack blurted, startled by the question. 'Just getting bread.'

'How's Maggie?'

Merriment was crushing the dried corpses of two imported spiders, *Latrodectus mactans*, black widow, to extract the benefits from their bulbous bodies for the whimpering woman trembling with trepidation over by the doorway.

'Maggie's talking,' Janey Mack said, her face clouded and preoccupied. Merriment knew something wasn't quite right; she simply hadn't the time to address the matter.

'Don't give her anything to eat,' she warned.

207

Janey Mack nodded, slipping into the anteroom and coming out five minutes later with a plate of bread and cheese which she intended to eat herself, and a large mug of milk. The bell over the door to the shop kept ringing as customer after customer entered, all of them eagerly discussing the dreadful events that were unfolding in the area called Hell.

*

Solomon gave Corker an extra shilling to mind the stall and keep selling.

'What about the meeting?' Corker asked him.

'I've something to do first.'

Solomon made his way through the throng, barging past Jody Maguire, who snatched his elbow and dragged him back.

'Funny how the Dolocher turns up the minute you show yer face to this plot.'

Solomon tugged his arm free.

'Let me go,' he scowled. Jody Maguire grinned grotesquely, his skin rough and purple, his mean eyes glinting viciously.

'What happened to yer face?' He tapped his walking stick against his thigh.

'Fuck off,' Solomon countered. That made Jody Maguire laugh.

'Nasty little tongue in yer head, haven't ye? For such a pretty boy.'

Solomon marched away making for the undertaker's on Purcell's Court. In the fresh light of day, he was full of conflict, last night's surety slipping into doubt. He knew the mechanics of criminal gangs all too well. The idea that he could just pay off his debt and walk away was overly optimistic; however, he also knew that a weekly stipend paid to Knox might keep the bully off his back. Despite last night's resolve, the idea of moving on appealed to him once again: pay the two pounds' balance and scarper. But the snagging tug of Merriment's power kept bringing him back to the same centre: perhaps he could change his stars. And there was Corker. His emotions swung unevenly from dejection to hope, back and forth, between all possibilities. Preoccupied and uncertain, he weaved his way through the busy streets, not seeing the world around him. When he got to the undertaker's, he made arrangements to have Gertie Baker's body taken from the Lying-In Hospital and carried to Saggart by a single dray. He paid a messenger to bring the carefully worded note he had composed to the Baker family, warning them of their coming sorrow. On his way down Skinner's Row he tripped and, looking at his shoes, noticed one sole was loose and flapping and in bad need of repair.

He felt the nine guineas earned that morning rattling in his jacket pocket and on a whim bought himself a pair of calf-leather boots buffed and polished the colour of oxblood. Billy Knox could have some money, but not all that was owed him.

'Can you mend these?' he asked, removing his battered buckled shoes.

The shopkeeper nodded, giving his assistant the shoes to patch up and stitch. 'They'll be good as new,' the shopkeeper promised.

'I'll be back in two hours,' Solomon said, leaving the cobbler's and heading towards the quays.

He was mounting the steps to the civic offices, following a line of flustered officials, all cloaked and trimmed and rushing to the emergency meeting called for two o'clock. The meeting was late to accommodate the travel arrangements of one Lord Beresford and the court sessions of one Judge Coveny. A crowd had gathered at the offices to shout abuse at anyone going inside and insisting on justice as they passed by.

'Do yer jobs. What do we pay cesses for? The city is not safe. More street lights. Fix the pavements. More night watches.'

There were jibes and jokes about the Dolocher.

'He'd choke on yous, yer face would sour milk, curdle his stomach, he'd take one look at ye and scream.'

Line after line of officials poured into the building, shoving past the irate crowd and pouring into the high chamber at the top of the stairs. They took their seats around a polished deal table, waiting for the more prestigious city elders and the chairmen of the relevant houses to take their places. The bicameral houses responsible for the security of the city created a natural divide. The House of Aldermen, who were dressed in lime green and yellow, sat directly opposite the House of the Sheriff and Commons, who wore powder-blue waistcoats and pink garters. Each side muttered about the ineptitude of the other, both houses shirking full responsibility for the payment of night watches and lighting as they snapped snide remarks, defending their positions across the table.

Solomon squeezed into the room, hiding behind three cloaked gentlemen and adopting his most officious air when a valet questioned him for identification.

'I'm here on behalf of the Board of the Black Dog,' he lied, noticing to his horror that Chesterfield Grierson was sitting cross-legged at the table, leaning into his chair with one arm looped over the back, delicately waving a scented hanky and staring intently into Solomon's face.

'You can't sit at the table,' the valet told him.

Solomon nodded brusquely and, finding a spot by the wall, he drew out his notebook, pretending to be preoccupied to avoid Chesterfield's gaze. The room filled with every notable representative from all districts, all vying for a spot at the table, or as close to the head of the table as could possibly benefit their career advancement. The room hummed with categorical propositions, everyone emphatic in their own way about what had to be done to staunch the flow of this current crime wave.

When Lord Beresford was announced with the city chairman and his secretary, Lord Rochford and Judge Coveny, everyone stood up and bowed. Solomon looked at Lord Beresford, remembering him galloping away from the Black Dog the day after Olocher had killed himself. Beresford had a very presupposing manner. He was a tall man in his fifties, handsome with a wiry frame, a sharp angled face and a long mouth. His hair was silver, his wig was white, but his brows were dark. A black leather patch covered his left eye; his right eye was the palest blue and filled with a hawkish expression. The man was sharp and flinty and everything about his movements clearly expressed that he was not one to suffer fools gladly. Even with one eye missing, nothing escaped his notice. Solomon immediately jotted down the word 'astute' by Lord Beresford's name, oddly feeling that he might like the man. Lord Rochford grimaced, his mouth turned down, his eyes flicking disapprovingly from one face to another, disgusted with the very notion of having to sit with such an unaccomplished throng. He waited to have his seat drawn out for him before begrudgingly sitting down, laying his fur-lined hat on the table and resting his hands on his walking stick, while Judge Coveny flustered and guffawed and smacked someone's back. The chairman lifted a gavel and roundly pounded it three times to officially start the meeting.

All hell broke loose.

*

While Corker roped in two of his sisters to help him sell Solomon's broadsheets and while Maggie Fines terrified Janey Mack, Merriment cut and measured and crushed one herb after another, dishing out medicine and raking in money to the point where she thought she really would have to bring in a more accomplished assistant.

Anne called in, dragging Stella after her.

'Look,' she announced, beaming, while Merriment tried to count out change and package another salve.

'What do you think?' Anne beamed.

Merriment was confused.

'Isn't she greatly altered?' Anne prompted. Stella looked the

211

same, her long gaunt face staring seriously about her. 'Your treatment has done the trick.' Anne carefully removed her gloves and nodded to the waiting customer. 'She's dandy with the cures,' she said. 'Aren't ye, Merriment?' Then waving her gloves at Stella, she said, 'Tell yer woman how good Merriment is.'

Merriment smiled, exhausted. 'There you are.' She handed the salve to the woman and gave her her change. When the customer left, Merriment sighed and sank onto the high stool.

'My God, it's been unbelievably busy today.'

'Her dad let her out.' Anne didn't care that business was improving.

Stella wandered over to the perfume stall. 'He's been on much better form,' she told Merriment, turning to sniff the samples. When her back was to them, Anne slipped a further three pennies to Merriment, with a quick wink and a winning smile.

'Where's Janey Mack?' she asked.

'Upstairs.' Merriment didn't want to mention Maggie Fines, she didn't want to bring up the Dolocher; she'd had enough of the subject for the day. Anne nodded, tapping her fingers a moment on the counter.

'And Solomon?'

'Over in Hell.'

'No, he's not,' Anne contradicted. 'That young fella with the funny teeth is there, surrounded by other children with funny teeth. I swear to God there must be ten of them. I bet his mother is Catholic.'

'Anne,' Stella exclaimed.

'I'm only saying. They breed like rabbits, it's a known fact. Anyway,' Anne confided as she patted the lace ruffle at her chest, 'there's a brood of ugly children manning Solomon's stall and Solomon is nowhere to be seen.'

Merriment shrugged, pretending to be unconcerned, but she did wonder where Solomon was.

'Bought his two broadsheets, though.' Anne produced the

sheets from her pocket and flattened them on the counter. 'The widow Byrne is fixated on the Dolocher. We frighten the livin' daylights out of ourselves at night, reading these things over and over. Misses Lennon does pop in. You remember her.' Anne stared into Merriment's blank face. 'Ye gave her a sedative thingy for her husband, made from the bloom of the flowers that look like the thorns around Christ's head. The old lady, doubled up with arthritis?'

'Yes.' Merriment was exhausted.

'We do sip milk with a drop of brandy in it and the widow even asked me to sleep beside her, she's that afraid. Grand for me, though,' Anne giggled. 'Her bed's warm and comfy, and I do have the best night's sleep, honest to God.'

The shop door opened and Merriment instantly recognised Dolly Shelbourne, the skinny woman with the holy husband. Dolly looked frantic. She peeked back out the front door and rushed to the counter, her behaviour instantly piquing Anne and Stella's interest.

'Misses O'Grady,' Dolly hissed, her pinched face animated with greater than normal anxiety and, ignoring Merriment's customers, she craned over the counter to announce.

'It's Thaddeus, he's it in for ye. He found the drops ye gave me. I've come to warn ye.'

Merriment could feel her heart skipping, instinctively knowing what was coming next.

'On account of his religious convictions.' Dolly rocked back and forth on her toes, she wrung her hands, her neck craned, her eyes constantly skipped to the window to inspect any passers-by. 'He has it in his mind y'er a witch.'

Anne gasped. Stella blanched. Merriment raised her hand: the gesture was a calming one, done to convince Stella that nothing untoward was taking place.

'Of course I'm not a witch,' Merriment faltered.

Dolly's head bobbed anxiously. 'I know,' she repeated over

213

and over. 'I know. But there's no talking to him, he thought I was trying to poison him. I had to run to my sister's house. He flung me into the street. Look, he tore my dress. Beat me with birch. Floggin' me on account of what it says in the Bible.'

Merriment tried to swallow, but her mouth was dry.

'Has he gone to the guild?' she enquired, her heart racing in her chest.

'The guild?' Dolly's eyes rolled. 'He's gone to the parson, talks about getting a petition. He means to have you tried.'

Anne hissed out, 'Jesus.'

Merriment sucked in a deep breath, struggling to keep her mind from rushing to the worst conclusions.

'He's like a terrier cornering a rat when he gets an idea into his head,' Dolly explained. 'Nothing will deter him.' Tears popped in her eyes. She was scared. 'I'm sorry,' she blubbered. 'Only I have to go. I thought it only fair ye should know. He's determined to chastise ye, have ye chained in the stocks.'

Dolly tiptoed quickly to the door, where she peered left and right, searching the crowds for her disgruntled husband. She shot a quick glance back at Merriment.

'I blame that Molly Jenkins one for draggin' me here.' She pulled open the door, hunkered down beside a passing sedan chair and scurried away, using the chair as a shield to hide her.

Merriment pressed her fingers to her lips, concerned that she would be called before the apothecary guild to explain what was going on. Anne looked at Stella and shook her head.

'Now, Stella,' she began. But Stella paced out of the shop, muttering a low goodbye.

'She's easily affrighted.' Anne smiled apprehensively. 'I better follow her.' Then, realising that Merriment looked very worried, she added, 'I'm sure it's nothing, Merriment. Yer man's probably a craw-thumper, full of mea culpas and is about as Christian as Attila the Hun. I wouldn't worry about what that lady said. There's bigger things to be concerned with.'

Then she frowned nervously as it dawned on her that the city was in the grip of Dolocher fever and, by implication, if a demon could exist why not a witch, and tried to skip over the holes in her reasoning. Anne sniffed and pinched her lips together. 'I better go after Stella. All I can say is ye did her father the world of good. The world of good.'

Merriment leaned on the counter wondering what to do.

As the doorbell tinkled its last chime, Janey Mack came thundering down the stairs and launched into the room, frantically shouting.

'Maggie's frothing at the mouth. Come quick, she's thrashin' about like the devil has her.'

*

Over at the meeting of the two houses, men were on their feet, blustering and shouting and slamming the table with their fists.

'Double the night watch.'

'Reform the prisons.'

'Send in the militia.'

Lord Beresford leaned back into his chair with a faintly amused expression on his face and Lord Rochford scowled and tutted. It took the general secretary pounding on the table with a borrowed cane to bring the room to order.

'A bloody demon,' one man spluttered in a gap of silence and the room erupted with a mixture of laughter, scorn and genuine concern.

It took a few hours of negotiations to come up with a plan. There would be a general tidy-up of the city, a sweep to arrest and imprison any ne'er-do-well, but first the prisons would have to be flushed through and that was where the problem lay. All the city's gaols were bulging at the seams, and siphoning off the least offensive prisoners by either early release or prompt execution was a matter for the courts. Once this was discovered there was another hue and cry about the inefficiency of the legal

215

system. Someone suggested that some of the military barracks could serve as a gaol, but that was immediately abandoned and by the end of the meeting all that had been resolved was to put on a double watch, since the introduction of a curfew was shot down by all of the merchants and businessmen present.

Solomon tried to bolt quickly from the meeting, but the refined tone of Chesterfield Grierson called his name loud and clear.

'Mister Fish.'

Solomon had no choice but to turn and bow politely.

'Mister Grierson.'

'Skinner's Row is not so far from your stall.' Chesterfield pulled out his little silver snuffbox.

'Events have been unfolding thick and fast,' Solomon reminded him.

'Indeed.' Chesterfield tapped a streak of brown powder onto the back of his hand, brought it to his nostril where he took a quick, sharp sniff. 'My proposition is simple.'

They stood in the elegant upper landing, surrounded by pale blue walls finely decorated with Italian stucco work. Clerks hovered near their masters, while most of the officials hung about in conspiratorial groups, satisfied or annoyed by the decisions signed off by both houses. The House of Aldermen had insisted that the House of the Sheriff and Commons were trying to muscle in on their area of responsibility, while a major power struggle between both houses seemed to solidify as a result of the decisions passed. Chesterfield Grierson waved regally at one or two people, and bowed solemnly to others, all the time outlining to Solomon why he should come and work for him at *Pue's Occurrences*.

'Your style is ornate, baroque. I enjoy your flights of fancy.' Chesterfield tapped his yellow cravat. 'You err a little on the side of verbosity. However, you have flair and an understanding of what it is the populace wish to digest.'

Seeing that Solomon wasn't interested in his critique, Chesterfield got to the heart of the matter.

'You will be paid twelve shillings a week with a quarterly review of your salary, which will be increased incrementally depending on the distribution figures. *Pue's Occurrences* needs updating. I have a certain world view that is currently out of vogue; you, on the other hand, seem to hold no boundaries. Perhaps between us we could aspire to become the definitive news herald?'

Solomon shook his head. 'I write what I want, because I know what will sell. You start tampering with me and we will row.'

Chesterfield Grierson didn't smile; his deeply arched eyebrows rose towards his hairline in an almost clownish fashion. He glared into Solomon's face and seemed to read something in the line and contour of his jaw.

'We would discuss, I am sure.' He tapped his wig and a fine hail of powder puffed into the air. 'I have no fear of robust discussion, Mister Fish. After all, we are in pursuit of grander principles, aren't we?'

Solomon pushed his hands into his breeches pockets.

'Principles are the luxury of the rich; the rest of us mere mortals eke a living in the shadow of the greats and report life as it is, not as we would wish it to be.'

'Quite right, quite right.'

Chesterfield tilted his head. His immaculately pressed jacket was beautifully tailored and tastefully restrained, with only the barest brocade visible around the buttonholes.

'Twelve shillings is no mean sum.'

'I earned eight pounds in the last two weeks.' This remark cut, reminding Solomon of his losses to Knox at the card table.

'The Dolocher story will pass; all scandals pass.'

Solomon smirked. 'All scandals refresh themselves.'

'Not this one. The Dolocher is a once-in-a-lifetime story. It has captivated people's imaginations, quite right that you should

217

profit on the grisly details. However, the story will expire and scandals such as love affairs and the antics of the Ormond Street Boys won't be as lucrative. Then' – Chesterfield tugged on the cuff of his sleeve – 'a steady wage in a nice office, warming your toes by the fire and mixing with gentlemen in coffee houses, that surely must be attractive.'

Solomon nodded. 'Thank you for your offer, Mister Grierson; however, I don't think I will be staying in Dublin for much longer.'

Though he had swung between possibilities all day, at that moment Solomon had settled on leaving.

Chesterfield didn't miss a beat. He looked around the room, faintly repelled by the insincere smiles and overt politeness.

'Despite the fact that the young boy that draws your sketches has fastened his hopes on you?'

Solomon felt the sting and resented the charge.

'Corker is a street lad, he's resourceful. He knows better than to . . .' Solomon cut his explanation in half and revised his intention. 'Once I've milked the Dolocher story for all I can get, I will be leaving.'

'Back to London?' Chesterfield enquired, stunning Solomon into a nervous silence.

Chesterfield suddenly bowed deeply to Lord Beresford as he approached and shook his hand.

'Ashenhurst,' he smiled.

'Don't grin at me, you blackguard,' Beresford hissed, leaning in. 'How much are you looking for from me this week?'

'Maybe a naval vessel? What about a clipper?' asked Chesterfield, the ever-present look of surprise still on his face.

Lord Beresford laughed and smacked Chesterfield's back.

'Good to see you, Chesterfield. Still in love with Peggy Leeson?'

Chesterfield Grierson looked instantly wounded, his face falling in one long movement.

'There now.' Lord Beresford elbowed him. 'She's asking after you.' Then, turning to Solomon, he said, 'How do you do.'

Solomon gave the slightest bow. 'Do you know,' he asked, still smarting with the knowledge that Chesterfield had researched him, 'that the Keeper in the Black Dog Prison, Mister Hawkins, is beating prisoners and robbing them?'

Beresford turned his sharp pale eye to inspect Solomon's face. Chesterfield coughed. 'May I present Mister Solomon Fish, future news editor with *Pue's Occurrences*.'

'I'm not working for your paper,' Solomon snapped. Then, turning to Lord Beresford, he sharply enquired, 'Have you any comment you'd like to make on the matter? A direct quote that I can use in my pamphlet.'

'A pamphleteer.' Beresford laughed heartily, Solomon's sudden threat vanishing with the revelation that he was nothing more than a street hawker. 'Dear God, Chesterfield, things so bad that you're canvassing pamphleteers to come run your business?'

Solomon bowed curtly. 'I'm off,' he announced. 'Mister Grierson, Lord Beresford.'

As he left, Chesterfield turned to Beresford and whispered, 'I'd sack the Keeper in the Black Dog, if I were you. That man has a way with words.'

*

The bells of Christ Church Cathedral rang out four times. Rain clouds were gathering over the rooftops, piling up over the slender chimneys. The streets were bustling, horses and carriages rattled by, while livestock were driven back out of the city, bothered by stray dogs and children throwing stones. Solomon was exhausted, his heart churned up by the seething confusion of the last few weeks. Skinner's Row was busy. A cart had upturned and an old man was cursing and beating the broken wheel that had let him down; the turnips he was carrying rolled over the road and were hastily grabbed by ragged children who seemed to appear from nowhere. Solomon collected his buckled shoes. As he watched the cobbler wrap them in brown paper and tie them with string he heard a male customer grumbling.

'That new apothecary on Fishamble Street is concocting potions for the women to poison their husbands with. She should be charged for malpractice, reported and shut down.'

Solomon paid for the repair and turned to the customer, a tiny man with a lopsided face, and defended Merriment.

'That apothecary has a wonderful reputation,' he said firmly.

The shrunken man pointed a gnarled finger.

'She's drugging the men so that they are sitting drooling in the corner, fit for nothing. She wears breeches. She's contrary to nature, so she is; contrary to nature.'

Solomon laughed and walked away.

It began to rain as he passed under the gateway to Christchurch market. Most of the market was empty, the detritus of the day's trading littered the flagstones, one or two horses were tethered to the railings, but the crowds had cleared. All the stalls were folded up except for Solomon's. Instantly he knew there was something wrong. Corker and a bevy of filthy-looking children were massed behind his stall, while Gloria and one or two other traders were standing alongside them, all shouting and protesting at one man.

'What's going on?' Solomon ran to them.

Jody Maguire rounded on him and grinned broadly.

'Speak of a queer and he will appear.'

Corker was livid. He rushed to Solomon's side, blurting out the gross injustice of the market manager's thinking.

'This fat lump of useless lard wants me to pay him one whole pound on account of I am not the official licence holder of this stall.'

'He's my assistant,' Solomon asserted.

'That's right,' Gloria and the other traders agreed.

Jody Maguire chewed a wodge of tobacco and spit a long,

dirty streak onto the ground before declaring, 'His name is not on the trading licence. It's a point of law and ye can fume and bluster all yez want, but the law's the law and unless ye pay me the fees due, ye can give up yer prime spot and buy a licence for Spittlefield.'

Jody Maguire smacked his walking stick down hard on the wooden stall, sending the last few copies of Gertie Baker's story floating onto the wind. Solomon gritted his teeth; this always happened, events always conspired to fleece him and reduce him and diminish his chances. There was always some bastard ready to rob him and bring him down. He took the carpet bag that Corker was guarding with his life and counted out one pound.

'Don't,' Gloria whispered. 'Solomon, ye can't.'

Solomon looked at Corker. The boy's huge brown eyes blinked; he was aghast, stung by the unfairness of the situation and confounded that Solomon would part with such an astronomical amount of money.

'You're right.'

Solomon turned to face the market manager, who was tugging on the strap of his satchel, scratching his enormous belly. Solomon leaned towards him, whispering loud enough for everyone to hear.

'You can take your stall and shove it where only the Dolocher would look.'

Gloria laughed.

'That's right,' she howled, 'you tell him, Solomon.'

Solomon pocketed his money and stormed away, followed by Corker and a multitude of ragged children, including two infants barely able to walk.

'You'll regret it,' Jody Maguire barked, utterly confused. 'Ye hear me, ya ponce, ye had a prime spot here.'

Corker swooped a little girl with the filthiest face up into his arms and trotted beside Solomon. The rain spattered onto his tattered jacket, leaving huge blotches the colour of dark pennies.

221

'What'll we do now, Sol?'

'Corker, you have to go home.' He handed Corker two shillings and the parcel he was carrying.

'What's this?' Corker asked.

'A gift.'

One of the children, a girl with huge sorrowful eyes and a threadbare shift, shivered miserably. She looked hungry. They all looked hungry.

'Will I see ya tomorrow?' Corker asked.

'Where's your mother?' Solomon wanted to get away. He didn't want to see hungry children, he didn't want to see a young boy looking anxiously up into his face, he couldn't bear the awful desperation in Corker's eyes.

'Don't come tomorrow,' Solomon snapped.

'But, Sol . . .'

'Go home, Corker. Go home.'

Solomon turned and left, his whole being squirming. How could he have travelled to Dublin and in the space of one month used the city up? He thought of Jenny laughing at him, of Eliza May pleading with him, of Sally Loftus crying in his arms, of Gertie dead under his jacket, of Maggie Fines lying sick in his bed. He thought of Billy Knox and Pearly and he started to run, through the rain, down Wood Quay. He ran until he could run no more. And on a side street somewhere near the river, he slipped into a tavern called the Brazen Head.

13

The Confession

Merriment and Janey washed and prepared Maggie Fines' body. They hid Maggie's swollen scalp under a crisp white bonnet and dressed her in a clean nightdress, fastened the ribbon at her throat and entwined her rosary beads around her interlocked fingers. Merriment placed two old pennies on either eyelid, forcing Maggie's corpse to keep its eyes closed. She clasped the shutters and lit a candle, leaving it on the little table by Maggie's bed. She was about to usher Janey Mack out of the room when the little girl whispered, 'We shouldn't leave her alone.'

'She'll be all right,' Merriment insisted.

'No, miss. The dead get lonely. I stayed three days with Mammy.'

Merriment caught her breath.

'Did you?'

'Told her stories to keep her company and kissed her face.'

Merriment turned away, concealing the pain she felt for the poor little girl. She'd never thought to ask Janey Mack about her family. She had assumed she was a foundling baby, abandoned at the orphanage by a destitute woman.

Janey Mack looked into the clean hearth.

'We should light a fire, make the room cosy. We could have a sup of milk up here, Maggie would like that. She said she was afraid of the worms squeezing their way in.'

'Janey, I think we should wait downstairs.'

The little girl shook her head and wrung her right hand, blinking miserably at Maggie Fines' waxing corpse.

'I'd want somebody to sit with me, miss.'

Torn between pity and care, Merriment gave in to Janey Mack's request and went to her room to fetch two more candles, to brighten the atmosphere. She wished to God that Solomon would hurry home. He was late. She lit a fire and sent Janey Mack to bring up some bread and cheese and two cups of milk.

'Will you manage them on a tray?'

'Yes, miss.'

The rain pattered against the window, the flames from the fire danced on the opposite wall, and Maggie Fines' still corpse glowed like white marble in the gloom. Janey Mack stuck her tongue out as she tapped the door open, concentrating on keeping the milk from sloshing and spilling.

They sat before the fire, Janey Mack on the trunk and Merriment in the chair.

'Night's a lonely time, miss,' Janey Mack said, glancing over at Maggie. 'And it's raining out.'

'Solomon will be home soon.' Merriment felt it was a bad idea holding a vigil at Maggie's bedside, but she couldn't think of a way of convince Janey Mack to go downstairs.

'He didn't come back with Corker.' Janey Mack sipped on her milk. Then, taking a big bite of bread, she said, 'He has a hidey-hole, miss.'

Merriment frowned.

'Who has?'

'Solomon, look.'

Janey Mack put her bread and milk carefully down and deftly prised up the loose floorboard where Solomon had stashed his money.

'Janey.' Merriment stood up, appalled that the little girl had pried into Solomon's private life. 'Put that back.'

224

'There's twenty-four pounds here, miss. That's a fortune. Maybe he's saving to get married.'

She shook the box but there was no sound. She looked confused, then opened it.

'It's gone, just two pounds left,' she exclaimed, shooting a meaningful glance Merriment's way. 'What do you suppose he's done with it? Bought a horse? We'd have no place to keep a horse.'

'Just leave it back.' Merriment pointed to the gap in the boards.

'There's books here too.' Janey Mack produced a large volume from the cobwebbed darkness. 'Is this the Bible, miss?'

Merriment saw the word *Tort* embossed in gold on a red leather spine.

'It's a law book.'

'Then this one's the Bible.' Janey Mack drew up a small dark book and Merriment nodded.

'Janey, put everything back this minute. You have no right to go through Solomon's things.'

'He's a rope here, miss.'

Merriment drew back, surprised. Janey Mack held up the wheat-coloured coil.

'What's he a rope for?' Janey Mack whispered. 'Do you think he ties people up, miss?'

Merriment shifted uncomfortably, her left hand pressed down on the knuckles of her right hand.

'Janey, put everything back,' she said sternly.

'But maybe this is his secret, miss.'

Merriment took the rope and flung it on top of the tin box.

'You've got to respect people's privacy, Janey. Now arrange everything as it was and put the floorboard back.'

Janey Mack did as she was told. She brushed down her dress, took her cup and stood at the end of the bed drinking her milk and checking on Maggie, who lay motionless with two huge penny pieces flattening her dead eyes closed.

'Did you have a baby, miss?'

'What?'

Janey Mack pointed to the chimney breast, reminding Merriment of the hiding well downstairs. 'The little bonnet and the booties in the fireplace, miss. Did you have a baby?'

Merriment's mouth hung open, ready to lie. She looked at the corpse in the bed, at the candle on the table, at the flames quivering in the fire.

'It was long ago,' she said quietly, astounded to be speaking about something buried so far in the past.

Janey Mack didn't mind. She licked the butter off her bread before eating the crust.

'Did it die, miss?'

Merriment took a long, deep breath.

'She died of croup.'

Janey Mack sat back down. She'd finished her supper. For a while she looked at her hands, inspecting them front and back. Her burns were healing nicely.

'I found a baby once.'

Merriment's eyebrows rose; she hadn't expected to hear that. She looked at the little girl sitting with her legs tucked under her on the trunk. Janey Mack nodded as she spoke, turning the hem of her dress over and back, fidgeting nervously.

'On a rubbish pile,' she said. 'A scrawny little thing. Bald as an egg. Whimpering, so it was. I wrapped it in a scarf and carried it all day. Fed it pease pudding. It got sick all over me. It was a little boy, with a wrinkly face.'

Merriment held her breath, listening, wondering what kind of world would leave a child on a rubbish heap. The land was more merciless than the sea.

'What happened to him?'

Janey Mack shrugged and averted her eyes.

'Lost him, miss, down by the river.'

She hopped down off the trunk and checked on Maggie,

patting the woman's dead hands to let her know she was not alone. She adjusted the ribbon on Maggie's nightdress and told Merriment, 'She's freezing.'

Janey Mack was checking under the pennies to see if Maggie's eyes would stay closed, when she asked, 'Did your fella know you had a baby, miss?'

'No.' Merriment shook her head, faintly confused that for the first time in twenty years she was speaking about her daughter, and to an eight-year-old child.

'Did you never tell him, miss?' Janey Mack replaced the penny.

'No.'

'Pity.' She left Maggie and coming back to the end of the bed, she leaned against the post and tilted her head to one side.

'Did ye ever find yer man in the frame downstairs, like the song says, miss?'

Merriment gave a little smile, and nodded.

'I did.'

Janey Mack launched forward, her eyes wide, her right thumb excitedly rubbing along the fingers of her right hand.

'Did ya?'

'We met when he was eighteen years old and his name was Johnny Barden and I loved him with all my heart.'

'I knew it, miss. I knew ye were romantic.'

Merriment recollected who she used to be when she was eighteen years old. She was light-hearted and free. She gazed at her hands. *All those years ago*, she thought, recollecting the disintegration of her heart. It took a full eight years at sea, searching every port they stopped in, asking endless questions, looking and putting out word. Eight years of hanging on to hope by a thread and during that time Merriment had altered. Her bright philosophical spirit that loved to dance withered and hardened into a scientific shell. Facts and figures nourished her waning soul, treatises on medicine and logic and mathematics held her together and made her strong, until one day she was

227

strong enough to stand on deck and look out to sea and give up on the girl she used to be. She let go of her longing to find Johnny Barden. Let go of the idea of their love and put away her old romantic thinking.

Merriment glanced at Janey Mack, who was waiting with bated breath and sparkling eyes, waiting to hear the story of how Merriment O'Grady found Johnny Barden and killed him for betraying her. The eagerness of the little girl's expression sent a wave of love through Merriment's heart. How could such a little girl have become so important to her in such a short space of time? Her chest stung with an unfamiliar, remote feeling, stirring the memory of the love she used to feel for her father. *My God, if anything should happen to you.*

Janey Mack crept closer. 'Go on,' she said encouragingly. 'Tell us what happened when ye found him.' Her face was bright with expectation, delighted to be hearing the true story, direct from the horse's mouth. Merriment crossed her legs and looking into the cup of milk she held on her lap, she recalled those days when she was eighteen years old and believed the world was a golden place filled with possibilities and endless pleasure.

'Johnny was press-ganged and taken to sea and I was inconsolable.' She sipped at the milk, amazed that the pain she had thought she could never recover from no longer undid her.

'Course you were inconsolable.' Janey Mack arched forward, her hands reaching out theatrically. 'That'd be you, miss, on the shore with yer long hair and yer cloak, and you weeping and wailing and crying out to the ocean – *Come back, Johnny, come back.* But he couldn't hear you on account of the wind on the waves and the far distance between yez.'

Merriment smiled at Janey Mack reliving what had happened so long ago.

'I cut my hair,' Merriment said.

'And dressed yerself up like a sailor and tarred yer face and took to wearin' breeches and swearin' and spittin' like the men.'

'And I enlisted aboard the *Unflappable*, a frigate heading for China.'

'Janey Mack, were you scared, miss?' The little girl held her breath.

'Initially, but no one found me out.'

Merriment put the cup down on the fender and leaned a moment looking into the fire.

'I learned to scale the rigging and hide my face and blend in with the crew.'

'Until one day your blouse flew open and out popped yer breast.'

'No.' Merriment laughed suddenly.

'But that's what the song says. After a skirmish, the silver button flew off yer jacket and there appeared yer snow-white breast.'

'Nothing like that happened.' Merriment looked over at Maggie. The corpse's huge penny eyes gazed back.

'I discovered I was pregnant and once we docked in Spain, I sneaked away and took up lodgings in a tavern. There I had my baby. Joanne.'

Janey Mack nodded and waited. When Merriment didn't speak, the little girl reminded her.

'Who died.'

Merriment lifted her head and licked her lips, surprised to think that Joanne would be twenty years old now, if she had lived.

'I kept her boots and bonnet and cried for a whole year.'

'Did ye, miss? That's shockin' lonely.' Janey Mack sat on the edge of the trunk. 'And then did ye come back home?'

'I signed back up, this time on a bigger ship.'

'Really, miss?' Janey Mack was on her feet, waving her arms again. 'Rovin' the rollin' waves looking for Johnny Barden and you found him strollin' along with his lady gay, and ye took out a brace of pistols that ye had at yer command and ye shot him with his lady at his right hand.'

'I found him in Liverpool.' Merriment couldn't suppress the strange joy of watching Janey Mack utterly enraptured. The little girl's huge blue eyes popped, she stood with her fingertips touching, waiting for every morsel of exotic information that dropped from Merriment's lips. 'I found him in Liverpool, thirteen long years after we had first parted.'

'Thirteen years, miss.'

'I saw him walking down a street, as casual, as inconsequential. If you were looking on, you'd never have guessed, you'd have seen a woman in breeches carrying a medicine bag glancing over at a man in a frock coat, leading a fine mare.'

'Janey Mack, he wore a frock coat and owned a handsome horse.'

'He had long given up the sea. He'd escaped and settled in Liverpool.'

Janey Mack gasped, genuinely shocked.

'He never came back to Ireland to look for ye and tell ye he was all right?'

Merriment lowered her eyes and shifted in her chair.

'He had become an ostler and he looked well. I'd have known him in a crowd. I did know him in a crowd. He was broader than I remembered. He had filled out and he had a beard now. But I recognised him immediately.'

'And did he see you, miss?' Janey Mack swallowed.

'He did.'

'And did he drop the mare and come rushing to sweep you up in his arms?'

Merriment shook her head.

'He didn't know me.'

Janey Mack bounced back. 'Didn't he, miss?' Then looking at Merriment's boots, she said, 'Must have been the breeches, miss.'

'I followed him.'

Janey Mack slid down to the trunk, her little face pale and washed out.

'Did ya, miss?' she whispered. 'And did ya kill him on account of him not recollecting ye?'

'I didn't kill him.' Merriment half frowned and half smiled. 'I followed him home. He was married with three children.'

'Ah, Janey Mack.' The little girl flung her arms in the air, and then, remembering Maggie dead in the bed behind her, she hoarsely whispered, 'That's awful so it is, miss, and you nursing a broken heart this thirteen years and for what? A man that dropped ye like a hot potato. That's very disappointing, so it is.'

'That's the thing.' Merriment removed the thong that tied her hair back and shook her tresses free, letting them tumble over her shoulder in a long auburn sweep. 'I wasn't disappointed.'

This revelation astounded Janey Mack.

'Weren't ya?' She frowned, her forehead creasing, drawing her thin brows into little zigzags above her eyes. 'Had he got fat, miss?'

'No.' Merriment stroked the ends of her hair, loosening out the knots. 'What I'm trying to say is, somehow, in the middle of all my travels, through all my friendships and training and all that I had learned, I had changed.'

She paused, giving a little sigh.

'If things had been different. If life hadn't intruded, if . . .'

'If ifs and ands were pots and pans there be no need for tinkers,' Janey Mack rhymed off stoically.

'That's the thing exactly, Janey, exactly.'

Merriment looked strangely beautiful in the firelight, her fragile skin had a delicate glow, her freckles appeared more pronounced, and her hair sweeping in a long tide over her shoulders reminded Janey Mack of the picture of a lady in the clouds embroidered on a chair she'd once seen in a shop window.

231

'We all like to think we make our own destinies, but the Romans had it right.' Merriment smiled gently.

'Did they, miss?'

'Fortuna – fate – the gods decide our lot in life.'

'Oh.' Janey Mack wasn't satisfied with that notion.

To cheer her up Merriment finished her romantic story.

'I was made a ship's commander, though.'

'Were ye, miss?'

'For a short period, when the commander got very sick and I had to take over for a night. After that I was promoted to ship's surgeon, earned my living that way. Made enough money to set up my practice here and take on an assistant.'

'And a lodger.'

Merriment nodded. 'And a lodger.'

Janey Mack stood up and wandered over to Maggie again.

'Where do you think Sol is?'

Merriment shrugged, doing her best to look indifferent. Truth was she wished he would come home. The beadle had yet to be informed about Maggie and arrangements had to be made to bring her to Saggart.

'Do you think the Dolocher has him, miss?'

Janey Mack could barely breathe, her huge eyes were wide, staring anxiously, no longer distracted by Merriment's sea tales.

'Don't be ridiculous,' Merriment smirked. 'He's in a chophouse, having supper. He had a bit of business to do with some man,' she lied.

'Did he, miss?' Janey Mack nodded uncertainly. 'Maggie told me he was to marry.'

'Solomon?' Merriment's heart jumped. Janey Mack's head bounced back and forth.

'A girl called Eliza May had her sights fixed on him. She flung herself in the river.'

Merriment's lower lip dropped, a small gasp escaped. She looked away, trying to conceal her shock.

'Do ye think Eliza May found out Solomon's secret and drowned herself on account of it?'

Merriment stood up, not knowing where she was going, and moved for the door. She stopped herself, feeling trapped by the needs of a corpse and an eight-year-old girl.

'Who knows why Eliza May did what she did.'

'And then he ran off with Sally Loftus and where is she now? Not with him. What do you suppose he did with her, miss?'

'Nothing. Honestly, Janey. I think we should go downstairs.'

'No, miss, Maggie won't like it.'

Janey Mack moved to the foot of the bed and looked at Maggie lying in repose, propped up on pillows, her dead face white as chalk and grotesquely marred by two huge pennies staring darkly from her sockets.

'Will ye have another baby, miss?' Janey Mack whispered.

'I'm too old, I think.' Merriment felt a curious pain, a dull, dragging sensation in her heart. 'I don't think so.'

'I wanted to keep the baby.' Janey Mack looked at her fingers, pushing them along the twisted moulding that decorated the end of the bedstead.

'The one you lost?' Merriment stepped beside her, gently stroking the back of the little girl's head.

'He was very sick.' Janey Mack's voice faltered. 'He went quiet as a mouse, but I got some milk for him.'

The little girl stared at her scarred hand, looking for the telltale signs of guilt, for crimson pinprick spots. She stared a moment at Maggie, before gazing beseechingly up at Merriment and asking, 'Do you think God let the devil out, miss?'

Merriment snorted a quick, derisory laugh.

'No. What do you mean?'

'The Dolocher, miss, to catch sinners and drag them to hell.'

Merriment reassuringly touched Janey Mack's hand.

'No. Sure, what did poor Maggie do, or Gertie? They were good people. Good people who were unprotected . . .'

'But what if they did something bad and we didn't know it, but the Dolocher did and he was told to fetch them to hell?'

Merriment scratched her head, sighing impatiently. 'Listen to me.' She brought Janey Mack back to the chair and sat the little girl on her lap. 'There is no devil out there, there are only bad men, bad men who want money and . . .'

'The devil's real.' Janey Mack started to cry.

'Come on, we're going downstairs.' Merriment had had enough.

'No.' Janey Mack's whole body trembled.

'What is this about?' Merriment tried to hold the little girl's face.

Janey Mack wailed, obviously distressed.

'What if he comes to get me?'

Merriment's mouth swung open. She was shocked and confused.

'Why would the Dolocher want you?'

Janey Mack refused to speak; instead she trembled and wrung her hands and sobbed, her whole body convulsing with terror.

'Janey, come on now. It's all right, you're all right. Tell me what all this is about.' Merriment stroked the little girl's back, anxious to calm the child down. 'Is it about the baby?'

Janey Mack nodded, slipping from Merriment's knees.

'What is it about the baby?' Merriment asked softly, her heart stuttering in her chest, her breath shallow.

Janey Mack pinched her lips together, her face streaked with tears. It took her a long time to answer. She stared at the fireplace, too afraid to speak. Merriment stayed rubbing her back, trying to ease the words up from the pit of the little girl's stomach.

'What about the baby?' Merriment repeated.

Janey Mack started sobbing again. She cried so much her face turned bright red and snot dribbled from her nose.

'Ye won't like me,' she bawled, afraid that this one confession was going to tear the house down. 'Ye'll give me back. I shouldn't have taken him to Hoppy John. I should've hid him like I intended.'

'What happened to the baby?' Merriment struggled to keep her voice neutral.

'I killed him.'

Merriment's hand stopped moving, she couldn't breathe, couldn't believe what she'd just heard, she felt faint, her fingers floated away from the little girl's spine. And the break in contact snapped Janey Mack in half. Grief-stricken, the child crumpled to the floor and cried and cried until Merriment dragged her up onto her lap and hugged her tight.

'There now,' she hushed the little girl. 'There now. Tell me everything.'

Merriment felt sick; she rocked Janey Mack back and forth, wishing desperately with all her heart that this wasn't happening. The world was turning on its head and dragging her with it and all she wanted was to go below deck, batten down the hatches, fling herself into her bunk and listen to the raging sea. A stormy night with a leaky hull was preferable to the stomach-churning situation she was now in. A corpse in the bed and a child murderer on her lap.

Janey Mack pulled herself away from the comfort of Merriment's arms and sat rocking on the sea chest. Merriment swallowed back the taste of bile in her mouth. She waited, watching Janey Mack muster up the courage to tell all.

'I should have hid him,' the little girl whimpered. 'I argued with meself and thought maybe Hoppy John would let me keep the little mite. So I took him to Hoppy John and said look what I found in the scrap, and he pulled the baby away and flung it in the river and I watched it sink and I waited and waited for the little mite to come back up but it never did. And I kicked and punched Hoppy John and he shoved my hand in the fire and told me he'd slit my throat if I told anyone and now the Dolocher is out to grab me to hell because I knew Hoppy John would murder the baby and still I took it over.'

Janey Mack started a fresh wave of tears. Merriment couldn't suppress her relief. She exhaled loudly, pressing a hand to her heart as she slid onto the chest beside the little weeping girl.

'You didn't murder the baby, Janey. Hoppy John was the one who did the deed. Shh, now, shh, it's not your fault. That baby didn't stand a chance.'

'That's not how it works, miss,' Janey Mack sniffed. 'God knows what yer thinking, and if ye know something will end badly and don't try to avoid it, he punishes ye for not being vigilant.'

'You didn't kill the baby, Janey, and God is a bit more tolerant than you think he is.'

'I brought the baby to its executioner. If I'd just hid him.'

'That's enough, you're not to blame. The murderer is Hoppy John.'

Janey Mack took in a long deep breath.

'You don't think my part in it . . .'

Merriment shook her head. 'You found a baby and cared for it as best you could. Night was coming and you knew you couldn't leave it out in the dark and cold.'

'I know, miss, but I could have found a little hidey-hole for it.'

Glancing at the corpse in the bed, Merriment worked hard trying to convince Janey Mack that she was innocent.

'You knew the baby would be lonely on its own the night long.'

'I did, miss. No one likes to be on their own.'

'You wanted to tuck him into bed, beside you.' Merriment cuddled Janey Mack, giving the top of her head a little kiss. 'So you asked Hoppy John for permission.'

Janey Mack thought for a while.

'Do ye think . . .' She wiped her face on the sleeve of her dress. 'Do ye think the Dolocher will catch him?'

Merriment shook her head.

'Janey, I don't think anyone is going to hell.'

'That's 'cause yer a romantic, miss. I think Hoppy John should go to hell.' Janey Mack looked sadly into the crackling fire. 'Thing is, miss, I don't get off scot-free. I knew in me gut, miss. I knew he'd do something to the baby and now God is callin' on me to explain meself.'

'You don't have to explain yourself to God.'

'To the Romans then.'

Merriment laughed; a sudden ping of mirth bounced around the room.

'Why do you have to explain yourself to the Romans?'

''Cause of what they said about fate making our destiny. I've to explain meself to someone.'

Merriment snuggled into Janey Mack, squeezing her tight.

'You are the most confounding little girl I ever met in my whole life.'

'Ye're not going to turn me into the magistrate then, miss?'

'You tried to save a sick child from the rubbish heap, an abandoned little boy. That makes you an angel. Now, no demon is going to come and get you. You're not going to hell. You are safe as houses here and you are going to grow up and marry and have children of your own. So, no more blaming yourself. You are a good girl, do you hear me? A good girl with a good heart.'

Here, Merriment took a candle and went into her room. She rummaged for the little tin box shoved into the back of the drawer of her dressing table.

'This is just for your peace of mind.'

'What is it, miss?' Janey Mack peeked in the door at her.

'This is for you. You can wear this about your neck.'

Janey Mack tiptoed in, glancing a moment over her shoulder, afraid that Maggie's voice might call out after her to come back.

She took the painted box and prised it open. There on a bed of folded lace was a simple crucifix.

'On a gold chain.' Janey Mack's eyes popped incredulously. 'Oh, miss, are ye sure? It's the nicest necklace I ever seen.'

'And it was blessed by a bishop,' Merriment fibbed. 'So no demon, even if he accidentally ran into you, could touch you on account of the power of this cross about your neck.'

'Janey Mack, it's the dandiest thing. That's lovely, so it is. Are ye sure, miss? What about yerself?'

'I'm safe as houses.' Merriment smiled. She helped the little girl to put the crucifix on and tilted the table mirror for Janey Mack to admire herself.

Her eyes flicked anxiously back out the open door.

'He wouldn't come to fetch the dead, would he, miss?'

Merriment rolled her eyes and patted Janey's head.

'Come on, you need warm milk and sleep.'

But Janey was having none of it, insisting on keeping Maggie company. They returned to their vigil. Janey Mack finally fell asleep curled up on Merriment's knee while Merriment stared at the loose floorboard wondering where Solomon was and why he carried a rope.

14

The Apparition

Solomon was uproariously drunk. He swept his arms around the blonde girl's shoulder and said, 'What are the four questions we must always ask if we want to know what something really is?'

The blonde girl looked at her friend and giggled. She took another swig of gin and held up her empty glass. 'Can I have another?'

Solomon grinned. 'Is that question number one?'

When she nodded he called for the barmaid to bring them more gin. The blonde's friend, a dark-haired girl with a pronounced mole on her chin, shoved her glass into the middle of the table.

'Me too,' she said. 'You're great craic, Solomon.' Then, turning to the barmaid, she whispered, 'Leave us the bottle, Molly, we've a live one here.'

Solomon kissed the blonde's pert bosom, one kiss on each breast.

'No.' He hauled himself upright. 'There are four questions the philosopher Pyrrho always asked.'

'Is that right?' The dark-haired girl poured herself a generous glass of gin and, knocking it back in one gulp, leaned forward and whispered, 'D'ye want to do it with us two?'

Solomon froze, his head swaying, his brain washing the question back and forth. He smiled broadly and laughed. 'You sirens, you bacchanalian beauties, you temptresses of flesh. Let me paddle my fingers.' Solomon slid his hand under the blonde girl's skirt and she gave a loud shriek, swatting it away.

'Not here,' she chided, looking coyly over at the two men sitting by the window muttering seriously to each other. 'See if Molly has a room.'

Solomon nodded. 'Question number one.' He waved a finger before the two girls. 'We have to ask what things are and what are they made of?'

The blonde girl giggled. 'I'm a girl and I'm made of sugar and spice and all things nice.'

When the dark-haired girl laughed her painted red mouth split wide open. She was having a good time.

'Molly,' Solomon bellowed. 'Molly.'

The barmaid strolled over, flinging the grey towel she was carrying over her shoulder.

'What is it?' she growled, folding her arms.

Solomon leered at her enormous hips.

'I need a room.'

'That'll be one and six up front.' Molly held out her grubby hand. 'And two and four for the drink.'

Solomon bobbed his head. 'A fair charge for such a fine establishment. A fair charge.'

He gave Molly the money. When she left, Solomon swayed to his feet. 'Come on, girls, I can take on the two of you, let's go.'

The blonde hauled him back down.

'It'll be three shillings each.' She kept her blue eyes steady. The powder on her face looked white and ghastly in the yellow candlelight. Her rouged cheeks hid craterous pox marks, yet despite the make-up and the scars she was still pretty. Her face had a natural symmetry; her features had genuinely pleasing proportions.

'If you hadn't been riddled, you'd be prettier than Helen of Troy.'

The dark-haired girl slid her stocking foot up along his thigh.

'You pay us half up front and half when ye've finished. Go and get the key off Molly, get the room number and we'll follow ye up.'

Solomon was drunk, but not that drunk. He got the key, sent the blonde ahead and sneaked the dark-haired girl and the last of the gin into his room, triumphantly throwing his arms open and flinging himself on the bed.

'Let us lose ourselves in the arms of Venus.'

While Merriment kept a vigil over Maggie Fines' corpse, Solomon bounced and laughed with two prostitutes on a hard and un-giving bed. He pleasured one and lost interest in them both the minute he had come. The satisfying of his carnal desires had been swift and short and curiously sobering. He rolled off the dark-haired girl and looked away when the blonde presented herself. The room was filthy, covered in dust. The bed sheets were soiled and the stench of boiled cabbage seemed to issue from the walls.

'Three shillings,' he said flatly, rummaging in his bag for his wallet. He handed the dark-haired girl the money and pulled on his trousers. 'You both better go.' He dragged his hand through his hair and went to sit by the window seat.

'God, don't the shine wear off him sudden?' the blonde girl smirked at her friend, then laughed and shrugged. 'Ye finished him off too quick, Marie. Saves me the work.'

They left with coin rattling in their pockets and went downstairs to spend it on gin. Solomon looked at the rain streaming down the glass, gazing at the watery runnels bursting and sliding to the mullions, unable to stop his mind drawing comparisons.

Turns out, he thought wryly, *that a conversation about Pyrrho can produce more heat than taking two women to bed.*

He hated that he was thinking of Merriment. Hated that he wondered what her mouth on his would be like, hated that he imagined kissing her, dragging her to him, making her yield. He knew she would push him away, disgusted by his whoring, disgusted by his spinelessness, by his weak character, by the fact that he was always running, leaving a trail of misfortune in his wake. He envied and loathed her steadiness: attracted to the

241

quality of fortitude she possessed, repelled by the fact that she represented such a stark contrast to his own changeable soul. He was weak, she was strong, and being near her only magnified his appalling flaws. Depressed, he dragged on his boots, buttoned up his shirt, washed his face and toyed with the idea of hurrying back to his lodgings to see her.

When he got downstairs the Brazen Head was filling up, the snugs thickening with labourers and sailors. A troupe of players were toasting some actor wearing a red ermine cloak and a fake crown. The two bawds he'd taken to his room were over at the bar supping on gin and guffawing loudly while down in a well-lit corner a group of dandies were shuffling a deck of cards. Solomon's eyes snapped to the table, reading quickly the quality of the players. They were wealthy enough to pander to the latest fashions, flighty enough to carry rapiers but not crass enough to know all the dirty tricks a good card player could use to improve his takings. Solomon was thinking of joining them in the hope of winning money to fob Knox off for now at least when he spotted a small man with an angular face. He instantly recognised the pronounced forehead, the red scar running to the edge of his mouth, the empty eyes. Hawkins, the Keeper of the Black Dog, was slipping onto a bench and opposite him was a man with an immaculate row of teeth, finely dressed and sporting a blue nipped jacket. What was Pearly doing with Hawkins? There was a peculiar exchange that Solomon couldn't completely read. Pearly handed Hawkins a well-wrapped parcel which he quickly disposed of, slipping it inside his jacket pocket. The two men conferred quietly, hunched over the table with Pearly looking curiously subject to Hawkins, whose manner was slightly more dominant. It was odd to see Pearly's brow creased, his eyes downcast like he was at one and the same time brooding and smarting. Hawkins was shaking his head and snarling while Pearly occasionally muttered a cowed response. It was Hawkins who left the table first, leering down over Pearly, growling some kind of parting shot, perhaps an instruction. Either way Solomon didn't wait to see. Keen to get away before he was spotted, he scurried out the door and hurried into the darkness.

He pushed into the rain, flicking up his jacket collar, his blond curls blowing loose in the wind and sticking to his skull the more wet they became. He passed a couple heading down to the tavern and wished he had a lantern to help him make his way. The night was pitch black. There was one streetlight burning at the top of New Row, and even though he couldn't see one foot in front of the other, he made for the distant flickering blotch at the corner of Corn Market House.

He strode as quickly as he could, aware of his own breath, of the wind whistling through the railings surrounding a disused house. The city seemed empty. Somewhere behind him he heard the distant clop of hooves and a horse whickering, but mostly all he could hear was his own footfall echoing off the high walls of the empty buildings on either side of him. He gripped his bag tight, suddenly wishing he carried a stick, something like the weapon Jody Maguire carried, or a pistol. Merriment carried a pistol. He was thinking of Merriment again.

He hurried, taking a left turn down Cutpurse Row to High Street. Two of the cottages at the end of the narrow alley had candles burning in the window. An insipid, dim glow reflected off the distant cobbles and blindly Solomon pushed forward, half running, keen to get out of the darkness and away from the sensation that something lurked in the shadows. He was rounding the back of Newgate, cursing himself for choosing to walk in the most deserted spot in the city, when he paused a moment, examining the slab of darkness stretching out before him. He saw the barest suggestion of grey. Outlines that slithered, vanished and reappeared as his eyes tried to organise them into recognisable shapes. Was that a doorway, a gate, a person? The darkness seemed to move with an oily viscous quality, the air was thick and shifting, black sliding over black.

He felt interred.

The clear awful image of Gertie lying dead in the gutter suddenly flashed in his mind. He recalled Boxty grotesquely crawling along the filthy floor of the Black Dog, his spine undulating, his face warped, his mouth a dark uneven gap. A primal, paralysing fear gripped Solomon, unable to repress the sudden conviction that at any moment the Dolocher could burst through the membrane of night, its swinish head glowing eerily, its hands thrashing wildly, lunging and ripping and biting and tearing.

Solomon started to run, one hand held up before him, the other gripping his bag and clutching it to his heart. His chest tightened, squeezing his lungs, crushing his breath. He staggered to a halt, gasping down air, blinking, trying to refocus.

There was something there. He peered deeply, scrutinising the shadows, his skin prickling. The hairs on his arms standing on end. Halfway up a high wall the blackness moved, folding over and back. There was a dragging sound, a low thump. Something landing. Descending? Solomon gulped and swayed, teetering back on his heels. To his horror a buttery yellow streak emerged from the brickwork. There on a ledge, crouched and malformed and staring down at him, was the enormous bristling skull of a black pig set on hunched shoulders. The Dolocher's fierce head moved. A swell of dark prickly flesh poured in folds from his neck. His dull tusks and snout suddenly vanished. The source of light disappeared, sucking the Dolocher away with it.

Solomon bolted forward, his ears pulsing with the horrible rush of blood to his head. He ran pushing his chest forward, his lungs rasping, his breath squeezing tight, hurting his ribs, his legs pounding, taking long blind strides. Could he outrun the devil? A low sound emanated from his throat, a desperate cry. Was the Dolocher flying through the air after him? He kept running, instinctively turning corners, heading straight, looking for light, frantic to get to a thoroughfare, to people, to be inside, to be safe.

The Dolocher was real: he'd seen it with his own eyes, emerging from walls. Would it burst up from the ground, defying time and space? Solomon wanted to retch. He would be pulled asunder by a hellish fiend, ripped limb from limb for all the ways he had transgressed. He glared wildly behind him, searching the impenetrable night. Stumbling forward, patting a wall, he fell through a doorless aperture and landed with a noisy thud on the floor. He pulled down a stack of planks, sending the wood crashing. The ear-splitting clatter echoed loudly through the empty building. Solomon doubled up and sucked in air, desperate to fill his lungs and stop the pain in his side, while all he could think as he fell was, *It's too late. This is how I'm going to die.*

Solomon lay gasping, staring at the point he had fallen through, waiting to see the snorting visage of the Dolocher's barbed skull plunging through the doorway with wide dripping jaws snarling open, ready to tear him apart. He couldn't move. He was frozen in a distorted curl, his spine arched upwards, his fingers rounded like talons, his lips pulled back, his eyes wide. He didn't flinch, just stared.

A noise erupted above him – his whole body riveted, thrashing as a jolting shock pulsed through him, bouncing him from the floor to his feet. A sharp pain cut through his ribs; he tried to sprint away, but his body was rigid. Thuds pounded from the ceiling.

The Dolocher was upstairs.

All Solomon needed was air, but his heart was spinning in his chest, slicing at his flesh, shredding his lungs. A pinprick of light appeared from somewhere high up, sending a slender pale shaft through the ornate staves of a banister. And Solomon cried out, his voice a hoarse, broken shriek.

'Who's there?' a man gruffly bellowed.

A lump of nausea gorged up Solomon's throat.

'I have a weapon, ye blackguard. Now, who's there?' the gruff voice threatened.

A woman pleaded, 'Come back, Lar, come back,' and Solomon clambered towards the bottom of the stairs almost sick with relief.

'Help me.' He stumbled up a few steps, weak and shaken.

On an upper landing a huge shadow crept along the wall and a tall man dressed in filthy garments, his eyes wide, rounded the corner and stood glaring down at Solomon.

'You don't live here,' he barked, taking in Solomon's jacket and new boots.

'I saw the Dolocher . . .' Solomon faltered and the man froze, checking Solomon's pale face for veracity.

'Did ye?' he snarled, 'or are ye addled with drink?'

The tall man sheltered the candle from the wind, throwing a spectral light up onto his own lopsided face in the process. The eerie light made him look ghostly, a grisly phantasm cruelly drawn by the anaemic candle flame, but Solomon was never more pleased to see another human being in his whole life.

'I swear to you, as I live and breathe.' Solomon clung to the banisters, his chest heaving. 'It was up a wall, looking down.' Solomon's knees buckled; he locked them to prevent himself from collapsing. 'Jesus Christ.' His face was bloodless. His body began convulsing as the adrenaline washed out of his tissues, throwing his muscles into spasm.

'He's real. The Dolocher is real.'

The tall man took three steps down and quickly assessed him. 'Ye look shook enough to have seen something,' he said. 'Come on.'

He waved a large hand and, seeing that Solomon couldn't move, assisted him up two flights of stairs. The stairwell was dark and crumbling; the smell of damp and urine hung in the air. As they climbed, the lone flame flickered casting distorted shadows onto the peeling walls. A gust of icy wind channelled down from the upper landing almost snuffing out the candle.

'Blast,' the man grumbled, saving the flame and flicking back a tattered sheet that served as a door into his living quarters. 'Come in.'

He held the sheet upright and Solomon stepped into a forlorn room furnished with four sickly children and a pregnant woman.

'Ye all right, Lar?' The woman looked petrified. The children were settled in a straw crate, all of them in a row, peeping like frightened mice from under a burlap sack that served as a quilt.

'This lad's had . . .' Lar said, suddenly cutting off. 'Go back to sleep.' He pulled a battered screen out, somehow convinced that the thin partition would serve to block out the adult conversation.

'He seen the Dolocher,' Lar whispered to his wife and the woman sank back into the wall, gripping her chest with horror.

Lar drew over the stub end of a barrel and sat down, signalling to Solomon to come and settle by the fire. Solomon sat on an upturned box, relieved to be in company, glad of the heat. He paused for a moment, his hands fanned before the flames, his body slowly undoing the severe shock he had experienced. He glanced at the pregnant woman. She looked sick, her skin had a polished hue, her eyes were deep-set and dark rings circled the sockets, her hair was stringy, she looked old, even though she was no more than twenty-five.

'It's awful.' Lar's wife patted his shoulder. 'Get him a bit of ale, Lar.'

'There's none left.'

Lar pulled a wooden bowl from the mantelpiece and spooned a greenish liquid from the cauldron simmering on the fire.

'Bit of cabbage broth.' He handed the bowl to Solomon. 'Warm ye.'

Lar lit a clay pipe and folded his arms over his expansive chest, looking intently at his ill wife, waiting for Solomon to give his testimony. Solomon sipped the warm, soothing broth, feeling his innards melting, his bones reviving.

'Thank you,' he said at last, slowly coming to his senses. The room was practically bare; there was a heap of straw in one corner, strewn with a grey blanket, a rickety table, two chamber pots, a bucket for ash and that was it. The broken windows were shuttered but the wind whistled through the cracks, sending cold streams into the room and rattling the shutters nosily.

'Landlord took the doors.' Lar grinned miserably, noticing Solomon looking about. 'Told us it would cost three and six to get them back.'

Solomon nodded like he understood, but he didn't. Lar's wife shifted uncomfortably and, drawing a strand of lank hair away from her face, asked gently, 'Ye ready to tell us?'

Solomon flapped his mouth open and closed; he didn't know where to start. He wiped his brow. His forehead was wet and clammy.

'I felt him. Before I saw him. I felt he was there. He was on a ledge, halfway up a wall.'

The fire crackled, spitting out a hail of crimson sparks.

'His skull.' Solomon struggled to recall the details, the apparition had disappeared so quickly. He closed his eyes desperate to fully recollect all that he had seen. The black eye sockets, the bristling line of dark spines covering the depressed, hollow cheeks, the dull glow of the curling tusks, the suggestive outline of a snout, the silvery glint of fine black hairs sprouting from the pointing ears.

'He has a black pig's face with tusks and a row of teeth. There was a light, faint, far away. I don't know. He was only there a split second. He emerged from the brickwork, came out of the wall, peered down at me and vanished. I thought he was coming to get me. I was sure I dead.'

Solomon licked his lower lip and turned away, his eyes stung with a film of tears. He didn't want to cry. He blinked, shaking his head.

'Can I stay here till morning?'

Lar nodded. 'Course ye can.'

Then looking at his wife, he gave a little smile.

'Now, Ruth, ye've nothin' to worry about. Ye've been good as gold all yer life.'

'What about that little girl found in the gutter?' Ruth squeezed her skirts. 'She did nothin', Lar. It's dreadful when the good lord himself is lettin' the devil out. I don't want to bring another child into this world.'

Lar tried to smile. His whole face seemed to flow away from his eyebrows, his features dripping like melted wax. He was a large, ugly man with kind eyes.

'There's no devil will get past me, love.' He held up his two arms proudly. 'I'll mind ye.'

'I'll not sleep, Lar. Not a wink.' Then, turning to Solomon, she asked, 'What's your name, stranger?'

'Solomon. Solomon Fish.'

'I have to ask' – Ruth kept her troubled eyes fixed on Solomon's face – 'do ye think he followed ye?'

Solomon shook his head, but he didn't know.

'No,' he said firmly. 'No. I got away.'

*

Lar and Ruth did sleep: they lay wrapped in each other's arms while Solomon sat by the fire, staring over at the doorway, watching the pale sheet billow like a living thing nourished by swells of passing air. The night crawled by, the only light coming from the wood snapping in the fire, the minutes creeping painfully forward, giving Solomon enough time to relive all his failures.

Why had he ever told Eliza May he loved her? Why had he taken his mother for granted? Why had he left Sally Loftus? Why was he cruel and feckless and incapable of taking on responsibility? Why was the devil after him?

He remembered that first night at the age of eighteen when he sat down at the card table in the Law Club and lost his week's rent. The night he drank himself into a stupor and missed his third law exam. The morning he decided to walk out of Garbelly's lecture to never return. The day he buried his mother. The lazy afternoon he ran into Betty Everton and charmed her blouse off her. He winced, reliving Eliza May's accusations. 'Betty said ye kissed her.' 'I never,' Solomon remembered lying. And the lies blackened and expanded and drove him further into unreachable depths and now the devil was after him.

Every few moments he recalled the Dolocher staring down at him, and the shock of the memory drove his hands together. Was he praying? He couldn't pray. There was no God. He wanted to tell Merriment everything, wanted to talk to her, tell her what he had seen. He wanted to see her, look at her face, wanted her to listen.

He blinked at the dying ash in the hearth, what would she say when he told her it was true? That the devil walked the earth and Olocher's rank soul had crawled up out of dead flesh and had taken the form of a black pig. What were they to do, now that he knew the Dolocher was real?

15

New Beginnings

When Ruth clipped back the shutters, Solomon jolted awake. He had dozed off and slid along the wall, his head resting on a panel that jutted from the fireplace. Lar was still snoring in bed and four hungry children were seated in a line in front of the fender, all gawping at the stranger snoozing in the corner.

'Morning.' Solomon sat up and ran his fingers through his hair. He smiled weakly at the children. They stared blankly back. Ruth offered Solomon a measly chunk of stale bread and patted his shoulder.

'Always better when the sun's up,' she whispered. 'Bless us and save us, it's a calamity having the devil himself abroad. Can't bear the night. Sup of milk, Solomon?'

Solomon dipped his bread in the watery milk and shared it with the littlest child. The room looked even bleaker in daylight. There were rat holes in the skirting and gaps in the floorboards. Chunks of the ceiling plaster had come loose and the slats were visible. The children wore threadbare shifts and a boy, no more than five years old, had a runny nose and sores around his mouth. The sound of feet moving crossed the ceiling above and outside on the landing he could hear someone running up and down the stairs.

'Others live here?' he asked.

'Course.' Ruth tapped Lar and handed him his breakfast, a bigger slice of stale bread and a mug of cabbage broth. 'Twelve families.' As she spoke the whole building seemed to come alive.

Solomon could hear a baby crying, someone shouting to 'watch out below', another woman was calling the name 'Frank' over and over.

'I thought the place was empty. Last night . . .' Solomon stopped. A skinny man with no teeth lifted the grey linen sheet that served as a door and poked his head in.

'Someone scattered the wood,' he complained and Ruth waved at him to come forward. She pointed at Solomon and said, 'He saw the Dolocher hanging from a wall.'

Within minutes the room was crowded. Word was out that a stranger had taken refuge in the tenement and the stranger had just missed being skinned alive and carted off to hell. Solomon told the crowded room everything he had been through and the terrified congregation nodded and conferred, throwing out wild theories as to why the devil himself had come to Dublin to cleanse the putrefied inhabitants.

'What'd ye do wrong?' one woman wanted to know.

'Didn't pray enough,' Solomon said sarcastically, then added, 'I don't know. All I know is Gertie didn't do anything.'

'That's what I said,' Ruth told her neighbours. 'Makes ye dread bringing a child into such a place.'

Solomon stayed an hour talking to the fascinated residents, all of them advising him that his civic duty was to report the apparition to the beadles, with the men of the group insisting on setting up a vigil to guard the street. He left as the men discussed making weapons, fetching scythes and hooks and blades that would later be hammered onto sticks. He picked his way along the musty passageway, past the clutter of scattered planks he had knocked over the night before, and stepped out into the cool dull morning.

He had never been more grateful to see the daylight. The street was narrow and twisting, lined by tenement after tenement. A throng of ragged children swarmed entrances, running in and out, emptying chamber pots into the gutter, kicking vermin out of the way and scolding each other or hollering at their parents that they were coming or going depending on which they were doing. The stench of excrement was overpowering, the gutter was awash with thick clumps of undiluted waste and screaming from a room somewhere overhead was a woman complaining about 'me only decent skirt'. Solomon heard a loud smash as glass shattered and a young bow-legged boy bolted from a dark alley way.

'I hope ye rot in hell, ye bitch,' the boy screamed. 'Sellin' me shoes, ye bitch, ye wicked drunken hussy bitch of a whore.'

'Corker!' Solomon called and Corker rounded on his feet, tears streaking his filthy face.

'Sol.' His jaw dropped, his brown eyes flitting back the way he had come. There was a rustle from the alley; something sailed past Corker's head and landed with a wallop on the cobbles.

'Missed, ye bitch,' Corker hollered. Then running his hand under his nose, he wiped a long string of snot onto his sleeve.

'She's a drunk.' He shrugged and sauntered towards Solomon. 'Were ye looking for me?' he said hopefully and Solomon patted his shoulder and nodded.

'Did she sell your shoes?' he asked.

'Bought a bottle of gin.' Corker sniffed. 'I wish she'd just topple into the Liffey and drown.' He shooed away the toddler coming out after him. 'Go home, Joey, get Effie to mind ye, I'm working.'

The toddler sucked on the corner of a cabbage leaf and shook his head.

'Effie,' Corker bawled at the top of his lungs. 'I'm off to work. Joey's goin' to fling himself under a horse.'

The little girl that Solomon had seen shivering the day before skidded out onto the street. She nodded at Solomon and grabbed Joey up in her arms.

'Get us a bit of poison, Corker,' Effie grinned. 'We'll do her in tonight.'

'Right ye are, Effie love,' Corker nodded. He gave a casual wave and sticking his hands in his pocket asked Solomon, 'What's the plan?'

*

Chesterfield Grierson was smoking a carved bone pipe trimmed with silver. He sat behind a large oak desk that was covered in files and open volumes and wore his usual surprised expression when his clerk announced that a Mister Solomon Fish and associate were asking to see him.

'Show them through,' Chesterfield said, his exaggerated brows lifting a fraction.

Solomon gave his conditions. He and Corker were a package. Grierson did not disagree, but he made it clear that Corker's wage came from Solomon's pocket, only to be renegotiated when distribution figures had been reviewed. Solomon looked about the well-furnished office. There were two upholstered chairs for guests, lines of shelves crammed with volumes and files, two desks holding more files all piled at least three feet high, and a small table laden with decanters and glasses and a globe. Hanging from a cabinet was a map of Dublin, decorated with red dots. Solomon examined it.

'You need to add a new dot,' he told Chesterfield.

'That right?'

'The Dolocher was spotted last night near New Row, in an alleyway not far from Corn Market House.'

'Is that right?'

Chesterfield Grierson's long, meticulous fingers tapped the gold lid of a delicate inkwell filled with crimson ink and without speaking invited Solomon to draw a red dot marking the latest sighting.

Is this where we will be working from? Solomon wondered, rearranging the room in his mind, imagining his desk facing the door, his back to the window, the fire across the way to his right.

Chesterfield slowly rose from his comfortable chair. Today he was dressed in a dark, sleek suit, trimmed with pale grey threads at the cuff that matched his grey silk cravat. He looked very sober, almost funereal, Solomon thought.

'My secretary will show you to your office, Mister Fish. Once we've signed a contract. I like to copper fasten things. If I'm to invest, I expect a reciprocal commitment from my investments. Philmont will allot you your hours, the days we go to print, my expectations of you as editor, your entitlements, your obligations, all the tedious nitty-gritty that this litigious age requires.'

As he spoke, Chesterfield was slowly ushering Solomon out of the room.

'Suffice it to say, I am delighted that you have chosen to come and work for *Pue's Occurrences*. I expect to read your editorial this evening. Meanwhile you can leave the leading headline article on my desk in one hour. We go to print this evening.'

He opened the door and waved to Philmont.

'Seems you've just stepped into the breach.'

Chesterfield bowed deeply and retreated backwards through the door, closing it slowly.

Corker rolled his eyes at Solomon. 'That lad moves like he's dancin' with ye.'

Philmont led them to a tiny room with a single window and a narrow fireplace. There was a desk, a chair with a broken back and a wastepaper basket. A long grey cobweb fluttered across the chimney breast.

'The contract will be on your desk in an hour,' Philmont said, looking forlornly about like he'd lost something. He bowed and slipped quietly away.

Corker got a fire going and Solomon wrote a hurried note.

'Take this to Merriment' – he folded up the paper – 'and don't be long, I want you to hurry back and draw the Dolocher looking down from a ledge, high up.'

Corker nodded and, grinning broadly, tugged at his cowlick.

'Right ye are. But, isn't this dandy, Sol? An office, be the hokey and me workin' as yer assistant.' Corker shoved his hands into his pockets and licking his lower lip, risked asking the question he most wanted to know the answer to.

'Yer stayin', so?' Corker couldn't hide his delight.

'I'm staying,' Solomon said, his stomach surging. He clenched his jaw, forcing a smile, and nodded at the door, sending Corker on his way.

When the boy left, Solomon looked about the tiny office, fighting the rising panic that his decision to stay had created. He felt like he was sinking, plunging into a depth of suffocating responsibilities. In the cold light of morning last night's plan began to fracture. Change, as it turned out, was deeply unpleasant. Biting down, he resisted the urge to get up and head for the docks and take a ship to Scotland. Instead, he forced himself to lift the quill on his desk and smooth out a flat sheet of paper, then began writing his editorial.

'A Personal Encounter with the Dolocher.'

He was indulging in grand adjectives and baroque hyperbole, quoting scripture and musing on Dante when Corker belted into the office in a flap.

'Yer one's dead, Sol. Maggie, yer friend.'

Solomon froze.

'What?' he whispered.

'Sorry, Sol, Maggie has passed away.'

Solomon flung his work to one side and grabbed his jacket.

'When?'

'Last night. And I think Merriment is mad at ye.'

'What did she say?'

'Nothin'. She read yer note and said nothin'. That's when ye know a woman is furious with ye. It was Janey told me about yer one, dead up in yer bed.'

'Right.'

Chesterfield Grierson was standing at his door proofreading some document and telling Philmont where to make alterations when Solomon and Corker ran by and vanished down the stairs.

'He's one of those new breeds,' Chesterfield remarked dryly, 'prone to excessive reaction.'

*

Merriment was serving four customers at once and at the same time giving a statement to two beadles from the sheriff's office when Solomon and Corker barged into the shop.

'Sorry.' Solomon rushed to the counter.

Merriment pressed her lips together and folded mawseeds into a sheet of brown paper.

'This is the man,' she said to one of the beadles. 'He knows where the lady lives. The corpse has to be removed, there's a little girl upstairs won't leave her side.'

Merriment passed the envelope to a skinny woman with wild eyes and took the money, while Solomon ran his hand through his hair, anxious to do the right thing.

'I had an appointment this morning.' He pointed at his note by way of explanation.

'Well, you're here now,' Merriment said quietly, annoyed that she was inexplicably furious with him. She served the other customers while the beadles went upstairs with Solomon and Corker to inspect Maggie Fines lying in the bed, ready to be removed.

Solomon sank onto the trunk, appalled that this was how Maggie had died. All those evenings as a little boy he had crept onto Maggie's knee, all the days she'd spoiled him with apples and honey and milk and sugar. The times she had wiped his cuts and grazes, the stories she had spun, all to entertain and care for him. Little did he know then how she would die or that he would be the one to oversee her funeral arrangements.

'She wasn't alone.' Janey Mack slipped her arm around

Solomon's neck. 'Me and Merri stayed the whole night long with her, told her grand tales and kept her company.'

'Thank you.' Solomon stared down at his hands, his fingers entwined. He wasn't praying.

The beadles looked at the wound underneath Maggie's bonnet, undid the ribbon of her nightdress and looked at the bandages wrapped around Maggie's ribs.

'The Dolocher,' one of the men whispered.

Solomon turned away. As he stood up, he brushed down his breeches and fixed his jacket.

'I'll arrange for her to be brought back to Saggart,' he said. 'She'd no family. No one left.'

The beadles were satisfied, took Solomon's details and told him they would be reporting the matter to the House of the Sheriff and Commons and he may be called before a magistrate to have his statement entered into court records.

Solomon agreed to everything as he guided the beadles downstairs, leaving Janey Mack sitting on the edge of the bed brushing the ends of Maggie's hair and talking to the dead woman very gently.

The beadles left and for a brief few moments the shop was empty. Merriment was in the anteroom and Corker was poised at the front door, ready to go wherever Solomon wanted.

'Give me a minute,' Solomon said, slipping into the anteroom and looking at Merriment standing by the fire gazing at the picture in the oval frame.

'I'm sorry I didn't come home last night,' he said sincerely.

'I'm your landlady, Solomon. Not your mother.'

Merriment forced a smile. Why was she so angry with him? She rested one hand on the mantle and hid her face by looking into the fire. She knew why she was angry with him. He hadn't given her a second thought. He had sauntered out the door and left her with a sick woman to nurse, he hadn't thought twice about her or the fact that she might need help. He was only concerned with himself and that disappointed her.

'I know, but you might have been worried.' Solomon sounded tired.

'I assumed you fell into company.'

Merriment trailed off but she fixed Solomon with her blue eyes, accusing him silently. Solomon smarted, recalling his debauched rollicking with two prostitutes, ashamed of his indulgence.

'But . . .' Merriment smiled a little, her eggshell skin glowing in the dim light of the anteroom, her wild hair tied back, her arms folded, her stance wide and confident. Even in breeches she was elegant. She brushed off her anger, realising that expecting more from Solomon was only part of the problem. The truth was she had wanted his company, wanted to discuss Janey Mack's confession, Maggie's last moment. For some reason she couldn't fathom, she wanted to tell him about Peggy Leeson and Ashenhurst Beresford. Amused by her need for his company, she swept away her annoyance. Solomon didn't think of her, why would he? She was his landlady; besides, she was older than him and dressed in breeches. She was androgynous, a brain to discuss things with. Wasn't this how all men saw her? Hadn't Beresford distanced himself from her and Johnny Barden before him? Why should Solomon be any different?

Merriment suddenly thought of what her life had become. Everything had passed her by. She had had no real relationship to speak of. No bright future. She had used up her best years by locking herself in sickbay and avoiding the world. She was getting older and her confidence had taken more than its fair share of beatings. Why was she fixing her hope on a young man who would grow tired of her? Why was she stumbling? She thought bleakly of her future, her old age. Was there nothing to look forward to? *Will I be old and frail and poor?* Merriment took a deep breath and scrambled towards her logical side.

You're tired and emotional, she told herself. *Facts of reality cannot be changed.* And, realising that there was no point in focusing on such things, Merriment let her disappointment evaporate. She was not going to relive the passion she had once harboured for Ashenhurst and Johnny. Solomon was a young handsome rake and she was a curiosity, an odd woman with whom he enjoyed talking.

'I will be honest,' she said. 'I would have appreciated your company waking Maggie. Janey was—'

'Thank you,' Solomon interrupted, 'for Maggie. For preparing her.' Solomon caught his breath. 'She was a lovely woman. Very kind.'

'I'm sorry.' Merriment felt a wave of guilt cut through her: all this anger and desire had blurred her thinking. Solomon was bereft and all she could think about was suiting herself, of wanting his company.

She moved a little nearer. 'Please, I'm sorry for your loss.'

Solomon looked away and shook his head. 'I should have been here. I shouldn't have left you . . . I shouldn't have left her alone.'

'I thought she was getting better,' Merriment said. 'I thought . . .' She looked into Solomon's eyes searching for some way to comfort him.

'Last night . . .' Solomon frowned. 'I saw something.'

He wanted to move closer, wanted to stand beside her, wanted to slip back the collar of her shirt and rub his thumb along the little blue anchor tattooed on her clavicle.

'I saw the Dolocher,' he said, staring directly into Merriment's eyes, waiting for her to look away and shut him out. Waiting for her to reject the unpalatable reality of what he had seen because it did not match her scientific principles. Instead Merriment's arms dropped open. She stepped forward, her face intensely curious.

'Where?' she asked breathlessly.

'On New Row, somewhere near there.' Solomon swallowed. 'He came out of a wall. I don't know. It was so sudden. One minute there was darkness, then a faint light and a black pig's head . . .'

260

'Are you all right?' she asked.

'Do you mean am I sane?' Solomon whispered.

'Are you sure you saw it?' Her eyes glittered as her expression clouded.

'Certain.'

Merriment didn't contradict him. She didn't smile or rebuff or belittle. Instead she gazed at him, watching every muscle, every infinitesimal twitch his face made, looking for signs of mania or deception.

He was not lying.

The bell over the shop door chimed, puncturing the thick silence.

Solomon glanced behind him and sighed, feeling rushed.

'I have to go, bring Maggie . . .' He faltered. 'I could be away two days. I have to pack. See her interred. I'm working on Skinner's Row, well, you have the note.'

'Hello,' someone called from the shop, even though Corker had told the woman that Merriment would be out shortly.

'Just a moment,' Merriment shouted. 'All right.' She looked at Solomon. 'Two days.' She was surprised that her heart felt sore at the prospect.

'Merriment . . .' Solomon paused, unable to take his eyes off her. 'Don't go out after dark.'

Merriment shook her head.

'I have a pistol.'

'Listen to me.' Solomon strode forward and grabbed her wrist. Up close she smelled of rose and her skin was silky soft. 'A pistol won't protect you. I mean it.'

Merriment swallowed.

'You look exhausted, Solomon. Did you sleep last night?'

'No, not really.'

Solomon wanted to step closer still, wanted to tell her – a woman he hardly knew – that she had spun a web. She had enchanted him, that she was the reason he wanted to stay in

261

Dublin, that something about her stopped him spinning. He could feel his fingers loosening, his fingertips gliding a fraction, wanting to stroke the length of her arms. Merriment noticed the alteration in his touch and blushed. Convinced she was imagining things, she turned quickly and retreated to the fireplace, unsure of why Solomon's insistence that she stay safe and secure should thrill her so much.

'If I do have to go out,' she told him, remembering that Peggy Leeson was waiting on a delivery, 'I will stick to the main thoroughfares, stay under light, make sure I am not alone.'

'Don't go anywhere,' Solomon blurted. 'Just stay inside after dark. I'll be back in two days.' He squeezed his forehead. 'I know you think it is improbable but I swear to you I saw it. The Dolocher is real and dangerous and I don't want you taking chances.'

He looked so pale and worried that Merriment nodded.

'I won't,' she said reassuringly.

'Good.'

Solomon hurried out of the room and upstairs to pack. Merriment slipped the fingers of her left hand around her right wrist. Her skin was warm and tingling with the faintest sensation where Solomon's grip had left a light impression. She frowned at the news he had just given her, convinced by his words and how he looked that what he said was true. The walls of her reason crumbled under the weight of eyewitness testimony and mounting corpses. She clamped her teeth together, frowning at the fact that what she had understood as reality had to be broadened and deepened. For now she had to accommodate the idea that demons really did exist. Chilled to the bone, unnerved and unsettled, she worried about Solomon's absence.

Two days, she thought, tapping the oval frame before heading out into the shop to serve the customer waiting patiently by the tea stand.

16

We Are Legion

Wednesday's edition of *Pue's Occurrences* had the headline 'Staff Editor Encounters the Dolocher'. Solomon had penned a hurried account of his experience near New Row, outlining all the instances and places where the Dolocher had been seen and the two murders committed by the fiend. He made broad recommendations to the public, advising people to travel in groups by night and imploring the city authorities to redouble their efforts to intensify the watch. He left Corker with strict instructions to go to the pawnshop and buy a pair of breeches, a jacket and a pair of shoes and to leave his new clothes at work, changing every morning and evening.

'What for?' Corker was delighted and confused at the same time, looking in the palm of his hand at the money Solomon had given him.

'So your mother won't sell them.'

'The bitch. She'd sell me teeth if she could prise them from me head.'

'When the paper comes out I want you to give yourself a good wash.'

'Where?' Corker squeaked. He wondered where he was going to find clean water, never mind soap.

'I'll give you a note to bring to Merriment's. You wash, scrub up clean and go to all the coffee houses and clubs and sell as many copies of *Pue's* as you can.'

'Right-oh,' Corker sniffed. 'Ye make *Pue's* sound like something that should be used to wipe yer arse.'

'Very funny. Don't let anyone boss you. You work for me. Ignore Philmont and Chesterfield. Use this satchel to put the takings in and bring it back here every day.'

'Right-oh.'

Corker began cross-hatching his sketch of the Dolocher. He had drawn the beast crouched over and peering down from a towering height, its swinish face in chiaroscuro.

The office fire blazed in the hearth. Outside the wind was rising, the sniping rain hammered against the window.

'Beats standing in the market havin' Jody Maguire spitting black juice down at ye, doesn't it, Sol?'

Solomon nodded, writing hurriedly.

'When are ye leaving?' Corker asked.

'Soon as I can dash off this article. Now stop interrupting.'

Corker grinned, all his crooked teeth shining a faint yellow.

*

Solomon bought a second-hand cloak, heavy and dark and warm. He also purchased a tricorn hat and toyed with the idea of a periwig, deciding he hadn't the time to fuss. At four o'clock he jumped onto the back of the cart carrying Maggie Fines' corpse in a wicker coffin, and despite the rain fell asleep as the driver crossed the foothills of the Dublin Mountains to the small village of Saggart.

The rain fell in slants over the cluster of cottages gathered at the crossroads. A young girl he didn't know bowed over the village well, her hair stuck to her face as she peered across at him. The sudden recollection of Eliza May's drowned face flashed before his eyes. He looked down the street past the donkey huddled beneath a bush and remembered running to visit Eliza May that first summer. He had been seventeen and full of passion. His heart ached with the recollection of who he used to be. Young and vital and full of belief, and Eliza May was his queen. That halcyon summer she laughed and kissed him and the endless days were filled with sunshine and buttercups and rolling in the fragrant meadow. That was before Eliza May's moods came, before he discovered that she cried as much as she laughed, before he realised that the girl he loved could not be reached when she was in the doldrums. One evening at twilight he found her sitting on the church stile sobbing like she was grief-stricken.

'You will leave me,' she wept. And though he held her close, rocked her and whispered, 'Never,' Eliza May shuddered, unconvinced.

Now as he stood in the pouring rain looking along the muddy street Solomon squeezed his eyes closed. The rain clung to his lashes as he desperately tried to shake off the weight of Eliza May's memory. But her beautiful young ghost hung about his bones.

'Need a hand?' a familiar voice asked, and Solomon nodded reaching down to lift one corner of the wicker coffin.

Old Jed Ryan and Tom the carpenter came out to give Solomon and the driver a hand bringing Maggie's coffin into the house. Maggie's house consisted of a single living room and a small bedroom. A neighbour had cooped her chickens for the night and left the garden gate open on the superstition that she would come home alive and close it herself.

That night Maggie was waked on her kitchen table. The neighbours came in quietly, filing past her luminous corpse, touching her fingers and kissing her forehead and saying goodbye, praying and muttering at the godawful shock of such a nice woman meeting such a dreadful end. Old Mitchel brought a fiddle and Solomon paid Johnny Patrick one pound to roll five barrels of ale and bring ten bottles of whiskey to the wake. Friends and neighbours for twenty miles walked or rode into Saggart that night and by four o'clock in the morning the festivities were developing a

265

second wind with women dancing and laughing in one corner, men playing cards and telling yarns in another corner while three keeners kept up a gentle wail, careful not to intrude on the high jinks and shenanigans. Solomon was quizzed on London and the Dolocher, about Eliza May and Sally Loftus. Others asked him if it was true that he owed a criminal money and Solomon bristled, remembering clearly why it was he had wanted to leave Saggart in the first place. He dodged the awkward questions with bland rebuffs, keeping everything general and impersonal. It was only when Michael Loftus took a swipe at him that Solomon decided he might go and sleep somewhere.

'Ye took her,' Michael Loftus cried, his plump face red and miserable. 'Ye destroyed me little girl and we haven't seen sight nor sound of her.'

His wife dragged him out the door begging him to 'whist'.

'But he took her. Couldn't keep his pizzle in his breeches, the whoring blackguard.'

'Ah now, Mick.' A neighbour with broad shoulders waved his clay pipe. 'Not over the corpse, Mick. No profanities at lovely Maggie's wake. Go on now. Off ye go.'

Solomon sat in a corner, wishing he could undo all the harm he had precipitated. Johnny Patrick brought him a drink.

'She were keen on ye, little Sally,' he said, sitting down. 'Heard ye got her pregnant.'

Solomon shook his head. For her sake, he didn't want the truth to be known.

Sally had set about comforting him after Eliza May's death. And he had taken the comfort of her arms, losing himself in her peachy soft skin and long blonde hair. Sally was very different to Eliza May. She was a practical girl with sharp edges and she quickly grew tired of his grief. He remembered the day she'd snapped. They'd been fooling around in Paddy Jordon's hay loft and Solomon was lying on his back staring up into the beams where the swallows had built a nest. Sally clacked her tongue impatiently, sick of his faraway staring. She crouched forward and tugged on her stockings.

'She were touched,' Sally said, a hard light glinting in her eyes. 'Everyone could see but you, Sol.'

Solomon hoisted himself onto his elbows and frowned.

'What do you mean?' he asked.

'Eliza May, she was for the birds.'

'She was fragile.' His voice cracked.

'She was unhinged and difficult, but ye'd got yer head stuck in that many poetry books and stories ye couldn't see the wood from the trees. Everyone knew it would end bad and why wouldn't it? This bloody place would get anybody down.'

Sally stared bleakly at the barn floor below, her expression alternating between smouldering rage and wily calculation. Solomon could see she was prickling, desperate to change her stars.

'Take me with ye to London.'

'Who says I'm goin' to London?'

'Maggie told me mam y'er thinkin' of it.'

Her face filled with bright glee at the thought of moving to such a large metropolis.

'No one would know yer business.' She grinned. 'Ye could do yer own thing without tongues wagging or a father to bar yer way.'

'Sally . . .'

'Oh, look at ye,' Sally chirruped, 'y'er white as a sheet.' She bounced to her feet and brushed the straw off her skirts. 'I don't want to marry ye, Sol. Y'er all right for a roll in the hay, but ye know. Me and you don't have that much in common. And I'd love to see London.'

The weeks following that revelation Sally alternated her tactics, trying to convince Solomon to take her with him. Some days she was nonchalant and offhand, showing him that she'd be no trouble and that she had no vested interest in him. Other days she pleaded, desperate to leave Saggart and her humdrum life behind.

Solomon turned to Johnny Patrick.

'She wanted to come to England with me,' he said. 'I told her to stay. She kept crying that she'd be no trouble.' Solomon bowed his head, staring at the honey-coloured whiskey in one of Maggie's good china cups.

'She followed ye so,' Johnny Patrick said.

Solomon didn't answer.

'I heard it from the brother-in-law, he saw her over in London underneath one of the bridges.'

'Did he?' Solomon winced, knowing the inevitable outcome for a young girl making such a rash decision.

'She were begging. One of her teeth missing. The brother-in-law said he did his best to convince her to come home. Said he'd stand the fare for her passage an' all. Sure little Sally wept bitterly, said she couldn't look her mother in the face and that she'd made her bed and must lie in it. The brother-in-law said she was drunk as a newt, sobbin' for gin and sobbin' for to come home and sobbin' 'cause she couldn't come home and sobbin' for money.'

Solomon shook his head, biting on the inside of his cheek, wishing he had just said yes and let Sally come with him. His rejection drove her to desperate measures when a kind word from him would have protected her.

Johnny Patrick nudged him. 'She were always headstrong, Solomon. As headstrong as her father there.' He waved his drink at the open door. 'Sure if the poor lass rounded the door her father'd beat her from here to Kerry for the shame she brought on his house. Sally is not welcome home and the poor divil knows it. Nothing ye can do there, my friend. Nothin' ye can do there.'

The wake carried on until morning, with all the mourners heading home at dawn to freshen up and prepare for the Mass. Late that afternoon, in a tumbledown churchyard, Maggie was laid to rest by her husband's side and Solomon Fish stood quietly by her graveside thinking of her past kindnesses and of his mother. He wanted to go home directly after the funeral but he knew that he had a responsibility to carry out the details of Maggie's will, distributing the little that she had owned among her neighbours. He had to sign off on her tenancy agreement and pay any outstanding bills. He would have to spend a second night there and finish off the last of his duties the following morning. He looked through the bleak rain at the dank trees surrounding the churchyard, wishing with all his heart that when he died he would have someone to be buried beside.

*

As the rain patted against the shop window and Solomon hoped to be interred next to a loved one, Merriment showed Janey Mack how to prepare *Paris quadrifolia*.

'It grows on a single stem. The flowers smell rank but it has a purple fruit which splits open and produces lots of seeds. It's also called True Love.'

That got Janey Mack's interest. 'Is it, miss?'

'Too much of it makes you sick and gives you diarrhoea, makes you giddy.'

'Bit like true love, miss.'

Janey Mack grinned cheekily and Merriment laughed.

'Did ye never love anyone after Johnny Barden, miss?'

'I did.' Merriment crushed the seeds with the mortar. 'It was a long and tragic love affair.'

She remembered the first time she realised she had feelings for Ashenhurst Beresford. He had come below decks to visit the sick, something he did almost every night. They had both got into the habit of drinking a glass of port in the back office. That particular night he looked pale and Merriment remarked on it.

'Are you worried about your wife?' she asked, knowing that his wife was unwell.

Beresford's head jolted back; he fixed her steadily with his bright eye, his eyepatch glinting darkly when he moved.

'No,' he said firmly, but his jaw locked and a nerve danced a moment at the edge of his mouth, like he was biting back a confession. For a while he said nothing, just stared, and Merriment felt pinned to the spot by his oppressive scrutiny.

'You're beautiful, you know,' he said sharply before pushing his glass across the table and walking away, leaving Merriment staring at the door frame listening to his footsteps as they paced across sickbay and up the stairs to the galley above. The remark left her heart sundered. That was the moment that changed everything.

For a full year after that night, they continued to meet and discuss business, both of them pretending that nothing had altered. But they gazed more deeply at each other while they spoke. The conversations lingered long into the small hours and their goodbyes became awkward. A kind of pressure built up between them until one night Beresford came into the back room and, without speaking, slipped his arms around her and pressed his lips to hers. She gave in, forgetting everything, forgetting he was a captain, forgetting he was married, forgetting she was lonely. She remembered Beresford whispering, 'I can make no promises.' Sequestered in a tiny cabin on stormy waters with the wind howling and the lantern flickering, his whispers and embrace were enough for her then.

The passion was brief and laden with guilt. There was a shift in Beresford's manner once his appetite had been satiated. In fact, there were times when he could be offhand. Six months after the affair began, Beresford returned from one furlough a new man. His wife had been well and something in their marriage had been reinvigorated. He cooled his ardour and Merriment retreated, hurt, nursing a fresh, disappointed pain. For a time things were strained. But the days at sea stretched into months and the months into years and their affection for one another slipped back into its own rhythm. They did occasionally lie with each other by way of comfort, but Merriment knew not to indulge in the fantasy of a committed relationship. Beresford's passion waned into a respectful friendship that had intermittent sensual benefits for the times when he felt most in need.

Years passed, full of unresolved intimacy, so that by the time Merriment suggested giving up the sea, Beresford was faintly relieved by the idea. Merriment laughed at his keenness and was amazed to find that she was not cut by his manner but encouraged, particularly when he revealed that he was settling on land too, reinforcing her notion that he wanted to be near her. Confused by his actions, she had remained watchful. Their attachment proved to be more elastic than she had imagined. Somehow, the nights she had cried alone in her bunk faded into the distance. What was exposed was that they both had an affection for each other, a bond of friendship fastened by rough seas and skirmishes abroad. Their connection ran deeper than convention and his insistence on helping her to set up her shop curiously opened a deeper vein in her thinking: perhaps they were bound to always be linked in some way. What should have driven a wedge between them inexplicably consolidated their relationship. Beresford wanted to lend her money; she had taken a little and the small percentage he invested in her enterprise kept them attached in a way that quickened her feelings for him and confused her understanding of what they were to each other. Was that why she felt knocked back when she met him with Peg Leeson? There was a little something in each of them that could not resist the other.

Annoyed that she was pining for Ashenhurst on the one hand, and intrigued by Solomon on the other, Merriment thought of how she had been sculpted by rejection: what Johnny Barden had carved from her all those years ago, Beresford had finished off. Perhaps they had done her a favour. Giving up on love had drawn her away from romantic attachment and channelled her passion, directing it to the secure, flawless realm of logic and scientific rationalism. She thought of Solomon, arched over the table writing, and she frowned. *Stop*, she told herself. *Don't do this.* She looked at Janey Mack and her heart was tugged in another direction. Merriment shrugged off her interest in Solomon and smiled at Janey Mack's expectant face.

'Were ye thinkin' of him there, miss? The lad from the tragic love affair.'

'I was.'

'Don't be wasting yer time, miss. He'll not be thinkin' of you, will he?'

And Merriment smiled, to mask the pang in her heart.

'I don't suppose so,' she said.

*

When Anne called in later that afternoon she was carrying a copy of *Pue's Occurrences*.

'It's seven pence a copy,' she complained. 'I thought that lad with the crooked teeth was having me on. The widow Byrne will not be impressed. Where's Sol?'

'Off burying Maggie,' Janey Mack said.

'Did she die?' Anne gasped. 'God rest her poor soul, the Dolocher has claimed another victim.' She opened out the broadsheet and pointed to the headline. 'And Solomon saw him.' Anne read from the article. '"He emerged, a solid block of thick bristling flesh, his fearsome head glowing ominously in the pitch black. The barbed hairs growing along his extended snout appearing eerily russet along the depressed cheeks that accentuated his pronounced jaw. His polished eyes glimmered with a terrible light and, hunching above me, the demon made to lurch. Immobile and paralysed with fear, I was fixed to the spot, unable to breathe. Then just as suddenly as he had appeared, his terrible form vanished into the impenetrable darkness and I took off, afraid of where the Dolocher might materialise next."'

272

Anne clutched at her throat. Janey Mack's mouth hung open, her face drained white. They both looked at Merriment, waiting for her to speak.

'I . . .' Merriment started, but she was confounded. 'He saw something,' she said quietly and Janey Mack groaned, tears springing to her eyes.

'The Dolocher's after Solomon now. He could follow him home. Solomon must have done something.' Janey Mack stared out into the streets. 'We're not safe, none of us are.'

Anne scowled, pressing her pale fingers to her bloodless cheek.

'My God, the widow Byrne will not believe this. I don't think I can breathe.' Her eyes widened as she sipped in threads of air, clutching her breastbone and shaking her head. 'Poor Sol.' She blinked back two huge glittering tears.

'Anne.' Merriment licked her lips trying to think of a way to comfort both girls. 'We are safe inside . . .' she began.

'You've to say yer prayers, Janey.' Anne tried to pull herself together, her voice high-pitched and false. 'Y'er a grand little girl. Sure, the devil wouldn't be after us. We all stay in. He only comes out at night, roaming around the streets.'

Janey Mack ignored Anne and gazed intently up at Merriment. 'Ye shouldn't let Solomon back in,' she suggested.

Merriment patted the little girl's head. 'We can't bar the door to him.'

'Ye have te, miss: if ye don't, he'll draw the Dolocher here and the two of us will be found dead in our beds or taken like that turnkey from the Black Dog.'

'Oh.' Merriment suddenly remembered Charlie and her promise to Sol. 'Anne, can you bring Janey with you on your errands?'

'Why?' Janey Mack panicked.

'I've something to do. I'll only be an hour at the most.'

'What about the shop?'

'I'll shut it up, leave a sign.'

'Where are ye going?' Janey Mack tugged at Merriment's sleeve.

'To the Black Dog.'

*

Anne took Janey Mack's hand and said, 'Now you don't let go of me. We'll swing by Saint Werburgh's church. I've to meet the widow Byrne there. There's some preacher lad coming and we thought we'd give him a listen to. Anyway, we said we'd get some holy water and say our prayers, it's the only way to repel the devil.'

Janey Mack nodded sombrely. It was a grey, misty afternoon. The bells of Christ Church Cathedral rang out cheerlessly, the steeple vanishing in a bluish shroud of fog. No one liked the poor visibility. Horses and riders emerged out of the gloom like phantoms. People scurried, cloaks and shawls and skirts flapping, heels clicking, dissolving into the mist like they were insubstantial wraiths blending into an anonymous cloud.

'It's bitter,' Anne complained, clutching her shawl and hurrying across Castle Street with Janey Mack in tow. 'Don't this mist creep into yer bones? Gets under the skin, so it does. Come on.'

A huge crowd filed into the church. Some of the throng paused on the steps and clustered into frightened groups, clutching at their Bibles or wringing their hands anxiously, trading Dolocher stories. Janey Mack scanned the crowd. There were young and old, fine ladies with pale, wretched faces, old men with sour, angry expressions, charwomen and weavers, even tradesmen who'd normally take a sup of ale at lunchtime were giving up their luxury to hear the famous Reverend Malachy Jones extol his learned advice on how to approach the current crisis.

The widow Byrne was a plump woman of about fifty with bright blue eyes and a high wig intended for a much younger woman. She wore a dark purple dress and a wool cape embroidered with blue roses. She took one look at Janey Mack and tapped the little girl on the edge of her shoulder.

'The trumpet has sounded,' she said cheerfully. 'Gabriel has blown the last call and the devil himself is rounding us up one by one.'

Janey Mack nodded bleakly.

'You better have no sins, little girl, or you are done for.'

'Misses Byrne, she's half out of her wits with fright as it is.'

'I'm only saying. Unless you've led an exemplary life, there's no hope.'

Janey Mack peered through the mist, watching as people emerged from the shrouded air, ghostly quiet. They moved silently up the steps and past the broad grey columns at the church entrance.

'We'll go in.'

The widow Byrne led the way, stepping into the dark wainscoted reception and moving with a curious kind of lightness that belied her weight. She glided to the top of the pews arranged to look out from a side aisle, insisting that everyone squash up and make room for her and her servant. Janey Mack sat on Anne's knee, absorbing the cold, grey atmosphere. The church was huge and cavernous and bare: there were no paintings on the ceiling, no icons adorning the wall, no tabernacle or side niches holding dying saints or beatific angels. The church was a sparse, restrained Grecian monolith, with a high balcony supported by fluted Ionic columns. To the right of the altar, carved from dark polished wood, there was an imposing pulpit. Janey Mack snuggled into Anne, feeling the creeping anxiety as it moved in waves through the congregation. A low murmur rumbled through the church as people whispered, uncertain of how to deal with the tricks of the devil, how to avoid the terrible wrath of the Dolocher. When the church was crammed to capacity, with people spilling out onto the steps, the sexton hammered his mace three times on the slab floor, sending three resounding booms through the edifice, which echoed up into the rafters. A profound, thick silence descended, while a small man dressed in black, wearing a neat white periwig and thick spectacles, slowly made his way up the pulpit, carrying a sheaf of notes and a small Bible.

For a long time he stared at the congregation, and the longer he waited the more people held their breaths. When he finally spoke, he shrieked, a loud high-pitched elongation of the name Mark. The congregation pitched back. There was a universal groan of communal shock.

'Mark five.' The preacher waved his left hand. 'And so they arrived in the region of Gerasenes.'

Janey Mack squeezed Anne tight.

'When Jesus stepped out of the boat a man possessed by an evil spirit came running out of the cemetery, for this man lived among the tombs and the burial caves and he was insane. He could not be restrained; even chains and shackles could not hold him back. No one was strong enough to subdue him. Day and night he wandered among the burial caves and the hills, howling and cutting himself with sharp stones. And when the man saw Jesus he rushed forward, shrieking and screaming, and Jesus demanded, "What is your name?" and the man replied, "Legion. For we are many."'

The preacher paused, his breath coming sharp and strong, his magnified eyes searching the crowd. The congregation sat pale and quiet and trembling.

'Dublin,' Malachy Jones assured them in a loud sonorous tone, 'is this graveyard, is this very cemetery mentioned in Mark's gospel. Dublin is the haunting ground of Legion.'

Women muffled their mouths with hankies. Men coughed uncomfortably. Malachy Jones held up the Bible.

'And the man cut himself with stones.' He thumped the pulpit. 'Did not Olocher slice his own throat? Was he not possessed by a vile spirit? One of the legion? Did not one of the legion animate

276

Olocher's dead bones? And what happened to the possessed man in Mark's gospel?' The preacher raised both arms. 'Jesus healed him by banishing the evil spirits into a herd of swine. Swine,' he shrieked, the word piercing the air high and shrill. 'Is not Olocher's body a hybrid? A distortion of all that is natural and good? Has his wickedness not fused the head of a black pig to the decaying bones of an autopsied corpse? This is Mark's gospel. This is Dublin. Today we are in the graveyard of one who calls himself Legion.'

The congregation shifted, terrified by the biblical comparison. Some women whimpered and sniffed.

'We have, out in those very streets there' – the reverend pointed to the doorway – 'Olocher's wicked spirit, his malformed, grotesque soul prowling the alleyways and the backstreets. And he is recognised by his visage, for he has been banished from salvation and left to roam this earth in the shape of a pig. This deviant human has risen from his dank grave and we have been warned: we will be snatched away, we will be destroyed by the savage appetite of this fiend from hell, this fiend that roams hell. The devil,' the preacher roared, 'is among us. You will be measured by your deeds and you will be found wanting. Repent your sins. Repent and be devout, repent and be vigilant.'

Janey Mack nuzzled into Anne's neck.

'Me skin is crawlin' up and down me arms,' she whispered, fighting back tears. The Reverend Malachy Jones whipped the crowd into a frenzy of renunciation and suspicion. His sermon warned them that Olocher had appeared ordinary before his heinous crimes were discovered.

'Who are you sitting beside? Is your neighbour evil?' he asked. 'Is the one sitting beside you rotten through and through with wicked sin? Be vigilant and abhor those who blaspheme, those who indulge base pleasures, those who pray with one hand and smite with the other. Be vigilant and mark those who have taken the lower road, those who have turned away from God and court the devil, for if you keep the company of sinners you are tarnished with the stench of corruptible doom. You will be smelled out, your wrongdoing will exude an odoriferous stench, for the Dolocher will recognise you, he will sniff you out and you will be devoured and eradicated from the book of eternal life and left floundering in an agony of pit fire and sulphur.'

The Reverend Malachy Jones battered his wretched audience with a terrifying litany of possibilities, until finally, an hour later, the church emptied and the petrified congregation hurried into the misty streets rushing to get home, lock their doors and fall on their knees in a feverish act of contrition.

The widow Byrne was luminous with morbid excitement. She chatted to her friends while Anne squeezed Janey Mack's hand. Janey Mack heard a group of workmen grumbling on the steps. One man with thick black hair and small narrow eyes sucked furiously on his pipe, only pulling it from his teeth to repeat over and over, 'Shifting his shape, hiding in a herd of swine.'

'That's right,' his workmates nodded, 'hiding in the herd.'

The men huddled tight, their rough faces blotchy with red patches, their eyes shifting, their heads turning, suspiciously scanning the last of the congregation before they continued whispering out the sides of their mouths. When they shuffled off in the direction of Lord Edward's Tavern, Janey Mack watched them while the widow Byrne chuckled and wrung her hands, her face lit with a gleeful kind of horror that made her blue eyes sparkle.

'Well, in my whole life, of all that I've seen and done, I never heard the like of such a sermon. My spine is that affrighted I don't know how it doesn't jump from my back and run off without me. What an appalling predicament we are all in, girls, appalling.'

*

When Merriment returned from the Black Dog she found Janey

278

Mack and Anne at the door of the shop, both of them white-faced and shaking. She was about to ask what they were doing standing about outside when she saw what they were trembling at.

'Oh.' Merriment staggered to a halt.

Daubed in bright red paint over the door and facade of her business was the word *WITCH*.

The crimson letters glistened, the power of the word punching through the thin veneer of rational thinking, reverberating with a menacing authority. The word glimmered in the grey air, in the twilight region between understanding and fear. A witch, a strong woman distorted by a maligned will, in contact with devils and familiars, using evil mystical rituals to conjure up demons and hex neighbours and do harm. Merriment tried to stop her hands shaking, recalling the deformed sailor lynched by the crew swinging from the yardarm off Port Royal. She'd escaped then because someone else had been targeted as the source of the misfortune. But if the crew had applied the superstition that it was bad luck to have a woman onboard ship, she could have been strung up. She swept her fringe to one side wondering, had her luck run out? Was this the law of the land? Would she be purged to counteract the hideous appearance of the Dolocher? Would the belief that she mixed potions and poisons be whispered throughout the city? Would she be expelled from the guild? Taken to trial? Formally accused?

Her breath came short and fast. She swallowed, staring at the word, her eyes widening as she ruminated over the macabre world she now lived in, feeling suddenly cast back in time to an era cluttered with religious zealotry and punctuated by profound spiritual fear. And knowing what fear could do to a crowd, she gazed at the letters scrawled over her doorway, afraid that if not stopped the word could command such primordial power that it could very easily become her epitaph. The thought of a baying crowd gathering outside the shop, armed with stones and torches and legal writs, chilled her to the bone.

She swallowed down her terror. If she had to, she could pack quickly and take Janey Mack with her to sea. For now, she would contact Beresford.

'I know who did this,' she whispered hoarsely.

'Fling them in jail.' Janey Mack squeezed Merriment's hand, her whole body trembling. 'Shoot them.'

Merriment swept her fringe out of her eyes and, smiling to mask her concern, she pressed Janey Mack's fingers. 'Come on. Let's scrub this off.'

Anne said her goodbyes and scurried into the mist, her heart racing as she pattered through the cobbled streets, squinting at every grey shade in the hope that she would catch up with her employer.

'Misses Byrne,' she called meekly whenever she saw someone stout, 'is that you?'

Close to Hanbury Lane, the widow Byrne heard Anne's plaintive whisper and called back through the drear air.

'Mother?'

'No, Misses Byrne, it's me.' Anne ran, her face glistening, her complexion flushed, her eyes bright and shining.

'Oh my God, you look like you've consumption,' the widow Byrne gasped. 'Like a beautiful spectre, bursting back from the dead.'

'Don't be saying that,' Anne quivered, linking her employer's elbow.

The widow Byrne tugged her shawl tighter. 'I'll tell you this much, if you don't die young, you'll be a beautiful bride.'

'Stop frightening me.' Anne poked the old lady in the ribs. Then, squeezing in close to her, Anne whispered, 'The apothecary on Fishamble Street is in trouble.'

17

Pigs

By five o'clock the city was deserted.

Merriment had to mix fresh paint to put on the door to obliterate the accusation scrawled there. All the while she had to outline in great detail for Janey Mack how common sense would prevail and how her dear friend Lord Beresford would quash this outrageous accusation.

'But what if he can't?' Janey Mack wanted to know.

'He will.'

'But now that the devil is true, isn't everything else true?' The little girl watched Merriment blot out the *CH* with a daub of thick paint.

'I'm not a witch.'

'But there might be witches.' Janey Mack shivered. ''Cause there's demons. And the parson said that the quantity of heretics and heathens in this city would keep Satan busy for a good many years since we are living in a place worse than Sodom and Gomorrah.' Janey Mack squeezed her right hand and squinted into the mist.

'What if they burn us out?' she whimpered. 'Maybe all of Dublin will collapse down into hell. Maybe the Dolocher is the start of it, and then the ground will open up and swallow us all down into the pit of sulphurous lakes and we'll be roasting in the scalding, blistering fires, only we won't die but we will feel like we are forever burning.'

Merriment sighed and shook her head. 'That's not going to happen.'

281

'But how do you know?' Little droplets of mist gathered in small sparkling globes on Janey Mack's hair. Her huge eyes blinked with terror. 'You didn't know there were such things as demons until the Dolocher came along and now we're all going to perish.'

Merriment flung the brush into the small bucket and put her hand onto the crown of Janey Mack's head.

'Stop, Janey,' she said firmly. 'You have to govern your feelings.'

'Why?' Janey Mack suddenly bawled, tears wobbling on the rims of her eyes. 'Why have I to govern my feelings? What if they hang ye for being a witch? What if they don't listen to me when I tell them yer the best woman that ever walked the earth? What if they hang me for being yer assistant?'

'No one is getting hanged.' Merriment pushed in the door and brought Janey Mack into the back room.

'But if they burn ye, like what they did with Joan of Arc?'

'Janey . . .' Merriment swept her hands through her hair and for a moment stood clutching the sides of her head. 'We've all had a long day. Now, sit in by the fire and dry yourself. I'll put on a bit of supper.'

Merriment fried potatoes and sorrel, and tried to quell the rising sense of doom that seemed to unfurl into the atmosphere as the sun sank low, leaving a grey bank of mist shrouding the city streets.

'What if he comes to take you away?' Janey Mack poked her food around the plate.

'The Dolocher?' Merriment could feel her patience fraying, her nerves jangling.

'The man who left the word on the door.'

'He won't take me away.'

Merriment had to sit at the end of the table, forced by Janey Mack to dictate out loud what she was writing to Beresford.

'"There is a matter pertaining to the defacement of my

property and a slander on my character that I wish to discuss with you.'"'

'Tell him about the lie yer man wrote.' Janey Mack stood next to her, her fingertips pressing the edge of the table so hard her fingernails were white.

'I'm doing that.' Merriment nodded, adding, 'Janey, we are living in the eighteenth century. The law, believe it or not, is on my side.'

Merriment waved off every counterargument Janey Mack put up, until the little girl switched tack and refocused on the other horror terrorising the city, the Dolocher.

'He could slip in under there,' she whispered hoarsely.

'I told you.' Merriment pointed to the hiding well.

She was pouring two cups of milk when they heard a commotion out front. Janey Mack darted forward, then spun round shaking, her huge eyes fixed wide and unblinking. 'It's yer man.' She darted for the back door and pulled it open. A wall of mist blotted out the yard as the chill air flooded into the room. 'He's come to fetch ye away, have ye tied to a stake. We have to escape,' she whispered frantically. Merriment's hands were trembling as she slipped the Answerer from its holster and put her index finger to her lips.

'*Shh,*' she mimed.

Holding her breath, she listened, her heart thumping, fine beads of sweat popping on her brow.

She could hear men calling, feet thumping on the pavement.

Had Dolly Shelbourne's husband returned, only this time with a mob? Was she about to be carted off? Burned out? Perhaps she should run, bolt out into the night with Janey Mack and head to sea. She paused at the open door to the anteroom and strained to hear.

She could hear voices. Someone called out the name 'Joe'. She thought she heard something metal clang on the cobbles. She peeped across the shop floor. At the edges of the doorjamb she thought she saw a flicker. A passing torch. Footsteps ran by. She heard another shout, this time from further down the street. 'Fred,' the voice called and someone, presumably Fred, called back, 'Jessop, ye mongrel, get up here.'

Janey Mack tip-toed towards Merriment, her little body pitching forward, stiffly making progress, as her panicked face glared up at Merriment, her jaw tight with anxiety.

'You stay here.' Merriment stepped forward.

'Don't,' Janey Mack squealed, instinctively reaching out.

But it was too late. Merriment crept into the shop, her pistol cocked and raised as she quietly made for the front door. Janey Mack followed, her face gleaming in the brown shadows. Through the long hinges of the window shutters Merriment could see flecks of flickering orange. She drew back the bolt and slowly opened the door, her pistol firmly gripped, the nozzle emerging first into the grey evening, Janey Mack clinging to her back. Merriment's head peeped out into the street her face glowing pearlescent with apprehension.

Across the way, in the thickening mist, a group of ten or so men had gathered with blazing torches and sundry weapons. They were clustered together communing among themselves.

'Yes?' she called firmly. Her voice rang out loud and sharp in the mist though she felt her body might collapse, suddenly limp with terror. What if she were set upon and hauled away? She rallied, quickly stiffening, making sure to keep the door only partially ajar, ready, so that if she had to shut it quickly she could.

'There now, m'am.' A slender man with a patchy beard broke away from the others and marched across the road, his hands in his pockets. 'Ye best go in.'

They weren't here to drag her away. Merriment exhaled, her shoulders instantly relaxed as she swallowed back her relief and pulled the door wide, stepping out into the grey chill night.

'What's going on?' she asked, still concerned that the men were so heavily armed.

'There's going to be a cullin',' the man with the patchy beard told her.

'What do you mean?'

Merriment slipped the Answerer back into its holster and looked down the deserted street. The fog obliterated the buildings. Carriages rattled close by but could not be seen. It was twilight and darkening quickly. The men spoke in low, serious tones, comparing weapons and looking eagerly into the mist.

'What do you mean a culling?' Merriment asked again, shivering a little.

'Only one way to make sure we catch the Dolocher,' the slight man sneered, his nostrils flaring wide. 'We kill the pigs.'

Merriment was appalled. 'All the pigs?'

'Every last one of them.'

Janey Mack peeked out, her pale face shimmering with reflected torchlight.

'That's what Jesus did,' she whispered. 'He cast the devil into the herd of swine and drove them off a cliff.'

A large man with a tattered periwig and a great grey cloak spit to one side and, looking at the weapon in his hand, a huge butcher's knife, he nodded in agreement.

'See?' His bulging eyes looked about. 'Out of the mouths of babes.'

'Ye need to fasten the doors and shut up the windows,' the little man with the patchy beard told Merriment. 'We'll not be long now. Bring yer little lass inside and don't come out no matter what ye hear.'

'But all the pigs in the city?' Merriment's face drained.

'Miss, don't leave me,' Janey Mack wailed.

'Shh, I'm not going anywhere.' Merriment stared down Fishamble Street. Coming through the darkening shroud of thick fog she saw a line of torches, a row of dim golden glows and soft red smudges carried by spectral outlines. The phantasms drew near, their forms coalescing and emerging out of the gloom. A row of determined men came forward, all armed with spikes and hooks and knifes and blades. Janey Mack instantly recognised two of the men she had seen outside Saint Werburgh's church that afternoon: one was a colossus with a big slab of a face who peered at the world from beneath his thick brows, the other was his little friend, a skipping man with brilliant eyes and false teeth.

'There they are,' the huge man with the tattered periwig nodded. Then, taking Merriment by the elbow, he hissed, 'Get in, miss, none of this will be pretty.'

Merriment slipped back inside and locked the shop up. Janey Mack nervously squeezed her right hand open and closed.

'Mother in heaven,' she swallowed, 'they're goin' to hunt him down. He'll have nowhere to hide.'

'Pointless,' Merriment muttered, ushering Janey Mack into the back room. 'Such waste,' she grumbled, 'to slaughter every pig.'

'But how else will they get the Dolocher?' Janey Mack tapped the necklace at her throat. 'He hides among the pigs, looks like one of them. This will see an end to him.'

'Janey,' Merriment snapped, but then, seeing how desperate the little girl looked, she took a breath and stopped. Janey Mack stood at the end of the table, her frame quivering, her hands nervously tapping, her forlorn eyes beseechingly looking for comfort.

'I suppose,' Merriment smiled. 'This will put an end to him. Come on, have a bit of supper.'

No matter how she tried to distract the little girl, there was no getting her to sit still and talk. Every sound, every creek and footfall, every horse and carriage that rattled past sent Janey Mack over to the door that led into the shop. She'd slowly draw it open and peeping into the dark interior she'd listen, holding her breath.

'Do ye think they've started?'

She strained to hear, standing on her tippy-toes and angling her head, ready to pick up the slightest indication, the most remote wail. Merriment cajoled the little girl to come and sit on her knee.

'Haven't we a lovely fire?' she said, trying to divert Janey Mack's attention. 'When I was a little girl, sitting on my father's knee, we used to play a game called looking into the flames, and we'd look deep into the fire and see whole kingdoms among the burning logs. I can see a face, can you see a face?'

'Maybe Solomon won't come back,' Janey Mack said.

'Why would you say that?' Merriment wondered.

'He took most of his money and the rope is gone. He left the Bible and the law book.'

Merriment frowned.

What had he intended? A remote niggling doubt seeped into her heart; then, looking up at the mantelpiece and recalling his goodbye, she shook her head.

'He'll be back,' she answered firmly.

'Might not be a good thing.' Janey Mack stared at the gap above the threshold of the back door. 'Maggie said he leaves nothing but tears in his wake.' She pleadingly turned to face Merriment. 'I don't want him bringing the Dolocher here,' she whispered.

'He's not going to bring the Dolocher here,' Merriment said sternly.

'Ye can't convince me I didn't kill the baby.' Janey Mack looked into the fire. 'I know ye said it was Hoppy John, but the devil doesn't care, he's here to take whoever had a hand in any kind of badness, big or small, and I'll never be forgiven for my part in that baby's death.'

Outside, sets of women's heels hurriedly clicked by.

'Well then,' Merriment sighed, resigned that there was only one thing that could calm Janey Mack down. 'We'll have to take you to a priest. Get him to absolve your sin and then your soul will be white as snow and you'll be safe as houses.' She squeezed the little girl tight. 'Mind you, you'll have to say a paternoster or two as part of your confession. But that should do the trick.'

'Will it, miss?' Janey Mack clung hopefully to the notion of a priest.

'Definitely,' Merriment smiled. 'I promise.' She wrapped her arms around Janey Mack and they sat in silence, listening to the wood sizzle and spit, both of them conscious of every sound that emanated from the surrounding streets. Merriment could feel her heart pattering. Her mind wandered to the conundrum of the Dolocher. How had a demon evolved out of the mixture of bad deeds and the decomposing corpse of Olocher? What energies were employed to construct such a demon? How could the most incorporeal of substances, the most elusive of supposed realities come into existence? What initiated the transformation?

She looked about at her potions and tinctures. She understood the relationship between chemicals, the single addition of a dominant ingredient that permeates and alters a mixture, to render it completely transformed by simple infusion. Had a demonic force infiltrated Olocher's dying body, invading every nerve ending, every muscle, taking his cadaver over, or had the mingling occurred earlier, encouraging Olocher to murder, to be an agent of evil on behalf of the demon? She thought of raw nitric acid, *aqua fortis*; it was by its nature corrosive. Had Olocher always, by his own impulses, been demonic?

Merriment gazed up at the mantelpiece. *How does a mortal being wrestle with the devil?* she wondered, appalled that she now had to contemplate such a thing. But her predisposition was towards order and method, and as she considered how a demon could be destroyed, her heart sank. In all the cases she could think of, demonic possession required some kind of spiritual dominance to eradicate it, and this she knew was not where her strength lay.

Sitting with her arms around Janey Mack, she recalled Solomon's broadsheets, disturbed that a preternatural force was operating in the district around her. She stroked Janey Mack's head, thinking of all the subtle energies that wrought great change in the world, all the hidden, secret dynamism of love and greed and envy. To have to include pure, undiluted evil made her skin ripple with gooseflesh. Could Olocher really have been in communication with the devil? The notion appalled her, but in the dark brooding anteroom, listening to the muffled sounds coming from the street outside, she could not quell the rising certainty that something was abroad. Something inexplicable that executed a swift and ruthless judgement.

'There.' Janey Mack bolted from her arms. A rush of feet thundered past the front door. The distant sounds of voices calling cut through the air.

'They're here.' Janey Mack squeezed her hands to her mouth, her eyes frantically searching the walls.

A pitiful shriek sounded in the far distance; a long, awful whine filled with unearthly suffering splintered the night air. It was followed by another baleful cry and the howling grunt of a herd of pigs. Merriment sat upright, squeezing the arms of the chair, her knuckles white. She arched forward, craning to hear. The noise grew closer, the air suddenly alive with the commotion of men running, calling and baiting. Pigs squealed and scattered, the noise a confusion of animal panic mingled with the sound of metal clanging and men screaming. A flurry of thumping feet and rampaging hooves burst up the backyard. There was a tremendous bang at the back door that drove Janey Mack crying for shelter behind Merriment's chair. The back door shuddered and rattled. Merriment jolted to her feet.

'Get him,' two men shouted at once from the other side of the door. Janey Mack grabbed for Merriment's hand. There was a muffled scuffle on the other side of the door. The door juddered and buckled in its frame as a distressed, wriggling pig was pinned against it. 'We have, we have him. Stick him, for fuck sake, stick him.'

And the most horrific, human-sounding scream filled the room. The pig struggled, thumping the door, flailing and shrieking, desperate to live. Janey Mack began wailing, her hysterical sobs indistinguishable from the high-pitched terrified shriek emitting from the pig's severed gullet. A crimson pool slipped under the door, sliding over the threshold, oozing into the anteroom. The grunts from the men holding the beast down was punctuated by the sound of them kicking and punching the wounded animal until finally the creature thrashed one last time. The door shook gently as the body slumped in relief against it.

'That's it,' a man said. 'Put it with the others.'

They heaved the creature, huffing and moaning as they hauled its dead weight over the cobbled yard, bashing and knocking any stray clutter in their path, until finally their voices faded and Merriment let go of her breath, shocked to her core.

'It's over,' she told Janey Mack, but the little girl was wracked with fear. She stood chattering, her pale face streaked with tears, her right hand clenched tight.

'It sounded like a man,' she blubbered. 'D'ye think it was him?'

Merriment threw a sheet over the pooling blood.

'I do,' she said quietly.

'I don't think I'll sleep.' Janey Mack watched the blood soak into the white linen, the crimson spreading and fanning in all directions. 'It sounded shockin' savage, like a banshee wailing. I thought me ears would explode in me head. Do ye think he'll come back, now his throat has been cut a second time?'

'No.' Merriment mopped the blood, her hands turning scarlet, the blood caking beneath her fingernails.

'He screamed shockin' loud. I thought me bones would burst from me skin with the fright and he was hammering at the back door to get in and I thought he was going to flay us. I thought he'd bash the door in and hop on us with his tusks full of gore and rip us limb from limb.' Janey Mack crept close to Merriment, watching her dump the soaking sheet into a tin bath. Merriment went to fetch water, a scrubbing brush and fresh cloth.

'Ye should check,' Janey Mack finally said. 'Ye should draw out yer pistol and check.'

'Check what?' Merriment scrubbed, so disturbed by the amount of blood that her eyes welled with tears. She hid her face by leaning both hands on the scrubbing brush and bowing her head, working furiously.

'Out back, ye should check if there's a lump of flesh, like what he was prone to leave behind. If there's a bit of flesh we know they got him.'

Merriment flecked the floor with soda, scrubbing the flags until a scarlet froth bubbled from the bristles of the brush.

'They got him,' she said firmly.

'But check.'

'Fine.' Merriment flung the brush into the bucket and soaked her hands. She took a candle from the table, drew back the bolt and slowly pulled the door open.

'The Answerer,' Janey Mack whelped, and to appease the little girl Merriment unholstered the pistol.

The candle flame flickered then straightened up, the pale finger of light dully illuminating the bloody threshold and shiny cobbles. Above the rooftops Merriment could hear the distant roar of men bellowing and calling and the eerie shriek of dying pigs wailing through the muffled fog. She held the candle high, looking about her, her heart beating loudly in her chest. The mist was thinning, not enough to let her survey the full courtyard but from what she could see the yard was empty, the network of back walls and slender pathways nothing more than grey suggestions in the poor light. The overlooking buildings were shrouded, the chimneys and rooftops blotted by the mist. Lone windows glowed softly where candles were placed on the sills.

'Well?' Janey Mack whispered, keeping well back.

Merriment searched the cobbles by her feet.

'I see nothing.'

Janey Mack listened, her little mouth open, her eyelids anxiously pinned back.

'They're over on Copper Alley. Do ye hear them?'

Merriment nodded, checking the ground. Blood congealed like slick oil in the runnels between the cobblestones, pooling in cracks and crevices, shining scarlet when the candle flame moved above it.

'Might not have been him,' Janey Mack said, tiptoeing a little closer, shivering as she peeped beyond Merriment out into the dark, thick mist. Merriment saw something silver glint in the grit not far from the ash pit and was squinting trying to distinguish if it was a shard of glass or a coin when the shadows to her right moved. She glanced over, the night air suddenly electrified by the gush of terror flushing through her veins as the candle flame picked out the black glistening spines of jagged bristles floating not six feet away from her. The candle flame dully illuminated a round twist of bony tusk, flatly highlighting the barest smear of dark, dripping snout. In the thick, deep, cloying air the obscure roundels of hollowed eye sockets pierced by ghoulish eyes glimmered a moment. Merriment stared deeply into the bright eyes, recognising a quality, a dark malevolence that shimmered with intent. A sinister knowingness emanated from the gaze. Instinctively, Merriment thrust the candle forward. The visage turned and receded into the folding shadows, vanishing at the same instant that Merriment let out a soft yelp, her heart surging forwards and back, her hands trembling and her knees giving way. She gripped the doorjamb and quickly sprang back inside, bolting the lock hurriedly.

'What is it?'

'I . . .' Merriment rested her forehead on the door, hiding her face, collecting her wits, her pistol limp in her hand.

'It's starting to rain,' she lied, clenching her jaw and wrestling with the waves of white terror softening her bones. She had seen it. Just like Solomon. She recalled its eyes and shivered, certain that she would never forget its malicious gaze. The Dolocher was out there, waiting in the shadows.

'Let's lock up.'

She lit more candles.

'We should,' Janey Mack agreed.

'Every room, every window.' Merriment tried to flatten her voice, but she moved urgently, pulling open drawers and fetching nails and a hammer.

'There's a few planks outside,' Janey Mack told her.

'We'll work with what we have.' Merriment pointed to two lanterns. 'Light those, Janey, and come with me.'

The back door was secure. They nailed the shop shutters closed, and put an extra few nails sideways against the door frame to prevent the front door from opening so that if someone managed to pick the lock they would still have a hard time getting in. As they crept upstairs, the candlelight glinting off the yellow breasts of the little canaries trapped in ivy-bedecked cages, Janey Mack pointed to the door under the stairs.

'What's in there, miss?'

'Rubbish.' Merriment stared at the upper landing cautiously, her mind reeling. Could the Dolocher melt through brickwork? Was it waiting up there for her? She paused, her pupils wide, her face drained, her heart kicking at her chest. Was there something near her bedroom door? Janey Mack clutched at the back of Merriment's waistcoat so petrified she couldn't speak. Merriment took the stairs slowly, pausing with each step, letting the candlelight slowly fan into the darkness, inch by inch.

Janey Mack was right: the Dolocher had followed Solomon home and now it was waiting. It was out there in the shadows, or in here . . . Her brain reeled. She could not deny what her own eyes had seen. A horrible tightness squeezed her chest – how do you fight a demon? Merriment handed the little girl the bag of nails and the second lantern and slowly drew out her pistol, clutching the hammer tight, ready to bludgeon with one hand and shoot with the other. If it lurched at them, Merriment would fight the only way she could. She had no faith to protect her, no prayers to defend herself with, only a pistol and a hammer.

She crept another step closer, turning on the elbow of the stairs, her shadow elongating up onto the ceiling, the window to her left sparkling with reflected candlelight. The stairs creaked as she held her breath and glared into the shadows. Somehow every dull line, every dark form – the base of the chair in the landing, the top of the cupboard door, the door handle into Solomon's room – all seemed threatening and unfamiliar. She took another step. Janey Mack lifted the lantern and looked behind her, squinting into the black pit of darkness at the bottom of the stairs, worried that something was crouching in the press underneath, waiting for them to pass before crawling out and slinking up after them to trap them in one room and corner them there.

On the upper landing Merriment tucked the hammer into her waistband, twisted the handle into her bedroom and pushed the door open. The hinges creaked loudly, sending a long, slow moan into the darkness, groaning through the absolute silence like an alarm announcing their position. Merriment grabbed a lantern off Janey Mack and plunged her hand forward moving quickly into the room, hurriedly inspecting it. A dim grey light washed the windows, the mullions glowed a dull pink. There were people outside with torches, rushing quietly through the mist. The knowledge that there were people close by reassured Merriment.

'It's all right,' she whispered, waving Janey Mack in.

As they drew the shutters they saw two men across the way in the street below, standing tight together, their heads bowed, occasionally glancing around. They were laughing: their humour seemed oddly out of place. One man turned and stared over at the shop front, scanning the shuttered window and filling Merriment with a curious doubt. She'd seen him before. The little man who had skipped from the kerb to the road the morning the milkmaid had stopped to pour milk into the quart jug for the well-dressed man in the fancy blue jacket. The skipping man had a calculated stare and when another man joined the group and looked over at the shop too, glancing up at her window, Merriment instinctively stepped back.

What did Dolly Shelbourne's husband look like?

'What is it?' Janey Mack groaned. The men brazenly seemed to be surveying the shop. Were they going to set it on fire, like Janey Mack had warned? Were they going to attempt to break in? Someone whistled, a beckoning shrill note. All three men progressed down Fishamble Street, no longer interested in the flaming candle burning in the upstairs window of M. O'Grady's apothecary shop. Merriment watched them saunter away, relieved but disturbed, her eyes drinking in as much detail as she could. The little man's skittering walk, the colossus with the sunken eyes and sheepish expression, the man with the hard stare and angular face. She knew him. She'd met him. The man with the angular face had tried to feel her up that very afternoon. It was the Keeper of the Black Dog Prison. She leaned against the glass watching the Keeper and his companions meet another two men. One pushed a barrow load of pig corpses. The Keeper pointed towards the quays and Merriment observed them as they all headed down towards the river and vanished around a corner, leaving her with a deep sense of unease.

'Who is it?' Janey Mack squeezed her nose to the window pane, squinting over the rooftops.

'No one. Come on,' Merriment pulled three nails from her pockets and began nailing the shutters closed. Tucking the hammer into her waistband again, she made for Solomon's room.

What if it's in here, waiting? It took everything she had to push the door open and stride in.

'You keep your eye on the stairs.'

Janey Mack did as she was told, her huge eyes wide and barely blinking. She kept her back to the doorjamb and rested her lantern on the floor by her feet. As Merriment closed the shutters she saw two men coming out of the mist, one of them carrying a torch, the other dragging the pink corpse of a dead pig. The pig's head lolled from side to side, its large tongue dangling from its jaws. Its side was slashed open and its entrails bubbled from the gaping wound. The man dragged the dead animal by its front legs, leaving a streak of bright red on the shining cobbles. He stopped a moment to mop his brow, obviously exhausted from the exercise, and swiped his handkerchief over his unshaven face. His eyes darted a moment up to the window where Merriment looked down. They shared a glance before Merriment closed the last shuttered panel, slipped the bar across the hinges and began nailing the window shut.

'What about that room?' Janey Mack whispered, pointing at the third door. Merriment thought of the hole in the roof. An image of a winged demon plunging feet first through the exposed rafters made her shudder. She ran back into her room, pulled out a drawer and without hesitating smashed out the bottom and broke the sides. Using the planks, she hammered them across the third doorway and when she had finished, she stood back and stared at the uneven barrier. She felt helpless. It wouldn't be strong enough. How could a demon be stopped by a hammer and nails? She looked at the flimsy deterrent and then down at Janey Mack's snow-white face; the little girl was petrified.

'There we are,' Merriment said firmly, disguising her fear. 'Now let's go downstairs and make some hot milk and cinnamon.'

As they sipped their milk, Janey Mack chattered.

'The widow Byrne is stout and has eyes like winkles,' Janey Mack said. 'And she moves like she's gliding. Her wig was too big and her friend Misses Johnston says that the woman on Aungier Street who keeps a tea shop was robbed and a full ten pounds was stolen from her.'

Merriment nodded.

'She said the city is gone to wrack and ruin and that after midnight the night watch should be multiplied by twenty. The night watch on her street gets drunk and abusive and hides in his hut muttering profanities, that's what the widow Byrne says.'

Janey Mack put her cup on the table and took the poker to rattle the ashes and throw two more logs on the fire. She lay down by the hearth and, lulled by the sweet milk and warmed by the fire, she fell asleep. Merriment looked at the chimney breast and listened. The world was deathly quiet. She slipped her fingers around the butt end of her pistol and kept a vigil over Janey Mack, suddenly and irrationally wishing with all her heart that Solomon Fish would stay away and never come back.

18

The Vanishing

Solomon Fish was dropped off at Harold's Cross and walked from there into town. He followed a line of dairymaids escorting their cows into the metropolis. There were women carrying baskets of eggs, others heaving bushels of birch, and men with carts transporting everything from cabbages to turf. The sun was pink in the morning sky and the air was biting cold. Solomon was glad of his new cloak; he tugged the collar tight and sighed, his breath forming a white cloud when he exhaled. The traffic heading up Patrick's Street was thick and slow moving. He weaved through the crowd, hurrying up the steep incline towards Christ Church Cathedral, surprised to have finished up Maggie's business so early. She had left no bills unpaid – her china had been divided along with her other meagre possessions after the funeral – so all he had to do first thing was sign off on her tenancy agreement and that had taken all of two minutes. He hitched a ride into Dublin with the blacksmith and was just turning onto Castle Street when the cathedral bells rang seven times.

Over near the gates of Christchurch market a throng had encircled a horse and cart with two rough-looking men perched in the driver's seat. One of the men hopped down, his large face burnt raw by the cold morning air. He scratched beneath his periwig and tugged on the belt pinching his belly, gesticulating wildly at his companion and calling him down to look into the gutter. Solomon Fish paused. Emblazoned on the side of their cart was the House of Aldermen coat of arms and their light-blue coats trimmed with pewter buttons identified the men as bailiffs.

'Sol, over here.'

Waving from behind the black railings surrounding the cathedral was Gloria. She stood on the butt of stone supporting the iron fence, tugged off her cap and fluttered it in the air to signal to Solomon to come on over. He dodged the horses trotting past and weaved through the line of carriages that had pulled up outside the market.

'What's going on?' Solomon asked.

'The devil's been here and gone.' Gloria flattened her cap back onto her head and shrugged her shawl tight. Her usually jovial face was pasty pale and her eyes were troubled. She glanced furtively to her left and right.

'Ye heard what happened last night?'

Solomon shook his head. 'I was away.'

'They killed all the pigs in the city. Jesus, Sol, the screaming. Must have been how the massacre of the innocents sounded when Herod issued the order to slaughter. It was savage, so it was. Where were you?'

'Burying the last woman the Dolocher murdered.'

Gloria blessed herself, shook her head and tutted.

'And Corker says ye saw him.'

Solomon nodded gravely.

'Mother of God, Sol, what's going to happen to us all?'

Solomon took a long deep breath, quashing the memory of the Dolocher peering down at him from the gloom. Even in broad daylight he could not stop his heart racing at the recollection. His eyes naturally drifted up to the gargoyles poking from the cornice of the cathedral roof.

'Did he say anything to ya?' Gloria licked her lips, clenching her shawl tight over her chest.

Solomon shook his head.

'What did he look like?'

299

'A black pig. Long snout. Bristles. The shoulders of a man. Maybe. Hands. I think . . . No eyes.'

'Jesus,' Gloria gasped as Solomon realised he had not recalled that detail before. The Dolocher was sightless. Blind. Yet somehow could see.

'They thought they got him last night.' Gloria nodded frantically. 'Now there's trouble this morning.'

Solomon saw one woman crying, sobbing into her husband's shoulder as the man guided her away.

'But what will we eat? How will we pay for the loss?' the weeping woman complained bitterly.

Gloria leaned in and clutched the wrought-iron railing with one hand.

'It's a godawful thing, this business,' she hissed, her plump face hardening as her eyes darted to the two men inspecting the ground close by.

'There was a stack of pigs left on the corner there last night. Blood running into the gutter, the whole street was red and stinking with blood. And then the bailiffs' – Gloria pointed – 'came this morning to pick up the carcasses, only they were gone.'

Solomon looked at the empty bailiffs' wagon and at the empty gutter.

'Gone?' he asked, confused.

Gloria's dry lips parted, her left hand flicked open. 'They've vanished,' she whispered. Her face was grey now, drained of colour, her eyes frantically flicking in all directions. 'There's not one dead pig to be found out of the six hundred butchered last night. Not a single beast to be seen. It's horrific, isn't it, Sol? What are we goin' to do now? That's what I'd like to know.'

Solomon stared at the bemused bailiffs. They walked about following one long trail of blood after another, listening as individuals from the crowd told them that the Dolocher had dragged the corpses with it to hell. Corker emerged from the throng, his big brown eyes popping in his pale face when he saw Solomon.

'Y'er back,' he yelled, running over.

'Jesus, Corker, it's awful, isn't it?' Gloria clutched at her shawl, fastening it tight about her throat. 'The whole place is cursed.'

'There ye are, Gloria.' Corker tugged at his forelock. 'Did ye steal the pigs to make yer pies?'

'I did not.' Gloria pursed her lips She was in no humour for jibes.

'That'd be right,' Corker grinned. 'Sure, there's no meat in yer wares. Ye heard of blind stew, that's what she cooks, pies with a suggestion of meat juice.'

'Y'er looking for a clip around the ear,' Gloria grumbled. 'You go ask the bailiff there what happened to the pigs? Did the Dolocher die among them and whip them off to hell with him, or did he outwit the lot that were after him and come back and spirit the corpses away with him just to show how powerful he is?'

'Jody Maguire took them to roast on a spit,' Corker said. He shoved his hands into his pockets and whispered up at Solomon. 'There's a meeting in the civic offices at ten. There's murder over this. Someone stole the lot; the aldermen and sheriffs will be skinned alive. I'm telling ye the city manager will be boiled in oil for mismanaging the whole thing.'

Solomon nodded bleakly. 'Right,' he muttered. He nodded goodbye to Gloria, and with Corker accompanying him he headed in the direction of Fishamble Street.

'Y'er back early,' Corker grinned.

'Miss me?'

'A bit.' Corker shrugged. 'I wasn't sure ye'd be back.'

'I see.'

Solomon stepped to one side allowing two ladies to pass and noticed the hems of their skirts were stained with crimson. In the gutter, thin red spatter marks of blood coalesced into a steady stream flowing from a thick broad spread of purple-black, the

301

obvious site of a killing. The footpath was stained with dark red patches and drag marks. Globs of shimmering scarlet glistened like veins on the grey pavement. Solomon trod carefully, stepping over the gory remains of the previous night's culling.

'After what ye wrote in yer article,' Corker said, 'I thought ye might have hightailed it.'

Solomon didn't answer. Around him, women hurried, some with the ends of their shawls pressed over their faces, shielding their noses from the stench. Men strode purposefully, their eyes fixed dead ahead, their expressions closed off, obviously anxious, wary of the latest development and completely at a loss as to what the vanishing herds of dead swine could mean.

'Did he really change ye?' Corker asked.

'Sorry?' Solomon took out his key and held it suspended before the door to the apothecary shop, bemused to find the door painted a different colour.

'What ye said about facing the devil and burning like Dante in the circles of hell. Did the Dolocher really whisper to ye that ye had to change?'

Solomon winced, painfully self-conscious.

'Figuratively speaking,' he said, turning the key in the lock and, pushing the door, he snapped his hand away, confused by the sticky layer of paint coating his fingertips. It opened a fraction, stopping when it hit the nails Merriment had hammered into the frame the night before.

'Hello.' Solomon pushed again, this time with a single index finger. The door resisted.

Corker leaned against the wall and whistled. 'Looks like y'er barred.'

'Merri,' Solomon called. He heard a door open and Janey Mack's feet patter on the parquet floor. Her face appeared in the slender space between the door and the nails.

'Go away,' she hissed.

'Janey,' Solomon said softly.

302

'Go away and don't come back.'

Janey Mack pushed the door shut and locked it from the inside. Solomon stared at the dark green sheen. His fingerprints had spoiled the glossy surface.

'She's not the full shillin',' Corker said, tugging on Solomon's sleeve and directing him towards the slender alley that cut through the line of shops into a series of backyards and sundry rubbish piles. 'This way.'

The entrance to the narrow alley was low slung and slender as a doorway. The ceiling was barrel vaulted and decorated with calcified stalactites, the walls on either side so oppressively close that a wide man would have to turn sideways to navigate along it. A single gutter split down the middle, carrying effluvia and rubbish out onto the street. The tunnel stank of excrement and the high overnotes of fermenting waste, and Solomon was grateful to step out of it into the fresh daylight and the network of backyards running either side of the exit. They passed a pigsty owned by two sisters who ran a bakery. The sty was empty, the gates left open, the dung stained with pools of red. Solomon picked his way along the cobbles, glancing at Corker's bare feet smeared with filth. There was a sore above his left ankle caked in dirt.

The yard behind the apothecary shop was broad and open. The rubbish pile where Janey Mack had been scavenging on the first day she met Merriment leaned against a wall opposite the back door. Solomon looked up; the tall brown buildings surrounding him jutted into the sky, the roofs hidden by parapets. Circling the chimneys, reaching into the cold morning air, was a flock of wailing seagulls. Pink and golden clouds streaked across the bright blue sky and sharp sunlight glittered on the lead guttering that descended along the red brickwork. He took a deep breath and knocked on the back door, longing to see Merriment. He called out her name, listening, searching the flaking red paint as he waited for her to appear.

Corker spit on the ground, shoved his hands into his jacket pockets and shivered.

'Did ye make it up?' he asked. 'What ye saw.'

Solomon shook his head.

'It's just . . .' Corker ran his tongue over his crooked teeth. 'I thought, for the money, ye know, ye'd embellished.'

Solomon could hear Janey Mack pleading as Merriment slid back the lock. When she opened the door Merriment looked shockingly pale, her long hair thick and wild about her face. Dark circles framed her sockets and her eyes glistened with a feral light.

'What is it?' Solomon reached for her arm. 'What's happened?'

Janey Mack called from the interior darkness, her small round face almost floating in the gloom, 'Maggie said ye were cursed, that a trail of disaster follows ye, that ye have only ever brought sorrow into a house, that all who knew ye died or disappeared.'

'Janey.' Merriment swung the door open. The daylight seeped slowly into the airless anteroom as Janey Mack rushed forward.

'He's not to be trusted.' She clenched her right hand. 'Maggie loved him, miss, and look what happened to her, and his mother loved him and she died young, and his betrothed loved him and she flung herself in a river, and Sally Loftus loved him and she has disappeared, and if he stays in this house we will be found dead in our beds.'

'That's enough.' Merriment swept a hand over her face. In the cold light of day, her skin prickling in response to the chill morning, surrounded by sharp clear sunlight, her lungs filling with clean fresh air, she became uncertain of what she had seen the night before.

'We didn't sleep well,' she said wearily to Solomon. 'The business with the culling has upset us. Come in.'

She stepped to one side and Janey Mack smacked her hand on the table, shook her head vigorously and shouted, 'No.'

'Here we go,' Corker muttered, leaning on the door frame, watching Solomon pause and search Merriment's face.

'This is ridiculous.' Merriment spun on her heels and went to fetch a glass, chiding Janey Mack as she spooned powdered asafoetida into water. 'You can't speak to Solomon like that, Janey. Besides, everyone says the Dolocher is dead now.' Unable to suppress the recollection of its evil eyes staring at her from the gloom, Merriment stirred the water briskly and frowned, hiding her agitation.

'No, he's not,' Corker piped up. Solomon pinched his arm. 'Ow, what did ye do that for?'

'This will help calm you down.' Merriment tapped at the glass.

'Ye can't stop me saying what I have to say,' Janey Mack protested, defiantly jutting out her chin. Her pale face looked furious and upset. 'I know ye like his face and his manner,' she whimpered. 'I know y'er going to send me back to Hoppy John 'cause I'm cheeky and didn't I tell ye I say it like it is. I warned ye I had a blisterin' tongue.'

Then, pointing at Solomon, she started to cry. 'It's yer fault. That's what ye do, ye ruin things 'cause people get attached to yer face and wit and don't see yer badness. I'm only saying,' she sobbed, and folding her arms onto the table she buried her head and cried and cried. 'He has a rope.'

Merriment closed her eyes and sucked her lips between her teeth. She felt exhausted, trapped in a bind, with Janey Mack weeping on one side and Solomon looking wounded on the other.

'Did Maggie say all those things?' Solomon whispered.

Janey Mack nodded and went back to crying.

'And if I told you that I was that bad, that selfish, but that I wanted to be better, would it matter to you?'

Janey Mack shook her head.

'No,' she sniffed. 'Ye brought the Dolocher with ye,' she blubbered. 'Ye came to Dublin and he appeared. And I like ye

305

an' all, Sol, but I can't let me heart rule me head. Facts is facts.'

Corker laughed scornfully. 'Yer brains are loose, rattlin' about in yer skull like a dried pea in a jar.'

Janey Mack stuck her tongue out and then went back to crying. Solomon stepped across the threshold.

'Eliza May killed herself because I abandoned her. I was seventeen. I had just got a place in King's Inn.'

Solomon avoided Merriment's eyes. He could feel her watching him as she slid into her chair, feel her reading his face, searching his body language for truth. The air in the room was thick and stale as he tried to explain why he carried a rope. He moved closer, stepping into the gloom, feeling the weight of all the accusations hurled at him. He wanted to crawl away from his bones, climb out of his skin and take to his heels. He gripped the back of the empty chair, anchoring himself to the spot. The Dolocher's deep black sockets flashed in his mind. Swallowing back his resistance, determined for once not to wriggle free, he glanced at the polished flagstones. He wanted Merriment to know. He wanted to tell her everything. He took a deep breath.

'I got Sally Loftus pregnant,' he blurted.

Merriment looked away. He felt the withdrawal of her gaze like a physical blow. He stayed gripping the back of the chair, satisfied that he was to be rejected. The punishment was apt. He thought of all the reasons why she would be better off without him. He was feckless, a magnet for bad luck, a whoremonger, a gambler. He recalled Pearly suggesting that he should borrow money from her and he knew it was only a matter of time before Billy Knox's gang squeezed him for more money and pressured him to drag Merriment into the mix. For her own sake, it would be better if he moved on. Trouble was, before he left, he wanted Merriment to know the truth. Somehow, losing her, sacrificing the possibility of ever being with her, felt in a strange kind of way like atonement. Perhaps he had changed.

'Sally followed me to London,' he continued. 'She lost the child and is currently drinking herself into an early grave.'

Janey Mack stopped crying. She didn't lift her head from her arms; instead she rested in the crook of her elbows, her eyes closed, listening as Solomon Fish confessed all his bad doings.

'My mother died young because she was sick.'

Solomon stared at the candle butt in the centre of the table.

'Eliza May,' he whispered, 'destroyed me.'

For a long time nobody spoke. Merriment stared at Solomon's face. He looked gaunt and haunted. His cloak draped across his slumped shoulders, all the mirth and light-hearted blitheness she had seen in him that first day was gone.

'The evening we pulled her from the river . . .' He hung his head as he squeezed his eyes closed. 'Her lips were blue and her eyes were open and all I remember is the birdsong. She was laid out on the bank, her hair tangled with weeds and . . .'

He shook his head trying to empty the image from his mind.

'The birds sang all around her. She had been so beautiful. So young.'

He paused a moment, looking for a way to explain.

'The thing with Eliza May, she was either laughing or crying. There was no in-between for her . . .'

Solomon trailed off. He could feel the gap in his heart widening, Merriment's silence crushing him. Outside, the thrum of carriages rattling along Fishamble Street grew louder. A hawker selling rags and bones shouted out his sing-song rhyme to draw people's attention and somewhere in the distance a dog barked.

'I got a rope the day she was buried and' – Solomon smirked shamefully – 'I intended to hang myself. Some grand gesture.' He bit the inside of his cheek, smiling scornfully. 'Of course, I couldn't do it. I like my pretty neck too much.'

Janey Mack lifted her face and wiped her cheek with the back of her hand.

'I didn't want my mother to find me swinging from the rafters,' Solomon tried to explain. 'It would have killed her. She worked hard to save for my tuition fees.'

He shrugged off the memory of his mother's desperate face.

'I didn't hang myself. I couldn't.'

He wanted to say, *I hadn't the nerve.* Instead he said, 'I like life too much,' and was faintly surprised. 'So,' he continued, 'I carry the rope from that day to this. A grisly memento, really, of a pretty girl who drowned herself.'

'That's awful.' Janey Mack blew her nose in her skirt and then showed Merriment. 'Sorry, miss, it's habit. Ye'd never have known with me old skirt.'

Then, turning back to Solomon, she stood staring at him, waiting, like she expected more.

Merriment shifted forward in her chair. 'Janey, we all need a second chance, don't we?' she said.

Solomon glanced at Merriment's face. She sat poised regally, her long fingers smoothly falling along the arms of the chair, her legs crossed, her shirt collar open, the line of her lips soft and plump, her eyelids glistening pearly pink above her sheer blue eyes. In the half-light, with her hair falling in long auburn tresses she looked like a Renaissance oil painting of a heroine dispensing fine judgement, saving his head from a noose.

Janey Mack examined her healing hand.

'Suppose,' she acquiesced.

Solomon lengthened his spine and flung his shoulders back. Standing up straight and tall, he drew in a deep breath. Despite his stance he felt curiously vulnerable. Now that Merriment had the full measure of his character she would retreat, observe a cautious distance. Righting past wrongs had to come with a price, he thought solemnly, and the notion that such an intricate woman as Merriment would consider him as a worthy partner combusted with the incendiary accusations Janey Mack had levelled at him. His broken attempt to show his remorse didn't come across as noble, of that he was certain. He knew he sounded flush with self-pity, but he was tired of running, tired of evading and slipping into the shadows, tired of living on the edge. For the first time he was willing to take his punishment. He fumbled with the rim of his tricorn hat, awkwardly wondering how to salvage the last shreds of his tattered confidence. He was about to excuse himself when Merriment looked at Corker and asked, 'You looking for water?'

'If it's not too much trouble,' Corker sniffed.

'Bring him upstairs into Solomon's room,' Merriment said to Janey Mack.

'But—' the little girl protested.

'And maybe you should lie down in my bed, get a bit of sleep,' Merriment continued. 'Solomon and myself have something to discuss.'

Reluctantly, Janey Mack led the way as Corker told her how all the pigs were missing, that the Dolocher was 'after stealing them. To show how powerful he is.'

Merriment closed the door behind them and signalled to Solomon to sit down. She left the back door open to refresh the air and draw more light into the room.

'Have the pigs vanished?' she asked, pouring them both a glass of milk.

Solomon nodded. 'Everyone's baffled. The bailiffs are scratching their heads at the top of the street.'

'All of them?' She frowned, calculating the logistics of the operation necessary to remove so much livestock. When Solomon nodded, Merriment perched on the edge of her chair and pressed her fingers to her lips.

'I saw something,' she whispered. 'Last night, when they were killing the pigs. Out there, to the right of the door. I saw . . .' She dragged her lower lip between her teeth like she was uncertain of letting the words issue.

'I think I saw the Dolocher.'

Solomon sat back, letting out a long, slow exhalation.

'Spiny black bristles, large head, tusks, deep black sockets?'

Merriment nodded. 'And a cloak.'

'Half man, half beast.'

Merriment's heart raced. 'Now what?' She searched his face.

Solomon stood up. 'You did right to bar the door.'

'I know this is foolish.' Merriment frowned, her hands shaking. 'But I am thinking of getting the place blessed.' She stood up and left her glass on the table, twisting it restlessly, unable to keep easy, uncomfortable with the shift in her thinking. 'Funny how fragile logic is in the face of primal fear, isn't it?' She tapped her left temple.

'It'd be folly not to respond instinctively,' Solomon reassured her. 'This is no time for grand theorising. We've both seen something profoundly strange, inexplicable.'

'And we rush to church, to rituals I have no more faith in . . .'

'The best of us are confounded,' Solomon said. 'Nobody knows what is going on. How do you explain it?' He stepped closer, his voice soft and caring. 'I knew when you opened the door that something was wrong. You've had a shock. You look exhausted. Perhaps you should leave the shop closed for the day.'

Merriment shook her head. She thought of Dolly Shelbourne's husband and worried that she hadn't heard the last of him. Over on the mantle the hurried note to Beresford lay propped against a candlestick. What was she going to do? What if Dolly's husband returned? What if the Dolocher returned?

Solomon slipped his hand gently across Merriment's back, letting it rest in the natural curve of her spine.

'You need sleep.'

'I . . .' Merriment moved, turning slightly, stepping back, confused by Solomon's touch. He removed his hand, his fingertips still tingling, his heart falling away, realising he'd been too intimate.

'Janey Mack is convinced . . .' Merriment bowed her head, her thoughts spinning. *What if?* she wondered before briskly asking, 'Is it following you?'

Solomon's jaw dropped. He stared out the back door. The sunlight spilled over the threshold and he noticed a red hue like a fine film gleaming on the cobbles. Outside a gull cried shrilly; its plaintive caw rang through the bright sky, mournfully acknowledging Solomon's loss.

'You want me to go,' he said quietly, shaking his head, understanding that there was some kind of universal moral law that made this the right thing to do. He could set up in a tavern and Billy Knox and Pearly could lament the possibility of extorting money from Merriment. Without him, Billy Knox would have no conduit to her. At least she would be safe. Still Solomon could not move. Could not take his eyes off her. Merriment didn't answer, instead she gazed out the door, preoccupied.

Her fingers were fanned out, gleaming as they pressed against the table, her long, lean form muted by the cool shadows of the room. The longer she remained silent the more Solomon convinced himself that it would never have worked with Merriment. He had been vain enough to think that there was something in her gaze, a quality in her eyes that hinted at her favouring him. He had been so fixated on the way that she moved, seeing every movement of her fingers as they wandered over objects as a sure measurement of her sensuality. He had wanted to unravel her.

But she was too clever for him, too astute and too well travelled to be fooled by his pretty face and light-hearted manner. Merriment had a wisdom and certainty and what had he? A misspent life pitted with failings. He had left a trail of disaster after him, and now he had fixed his longing on the finest woman he had ever met. Should anything happen between them it would fail, as sure as every other relationship had failed. It was bound to. He was contaminated by misfortune.

Solomon clenched his jaw, biting back his despondency, and summoned up the strength to do the right thing.

'I see,' he nodded, patting his hat against his thigh. 'You're right, I should go.'

And before she could reconsider Solomon strode away and up the stairs to pack his bags.

*

It's for the best, Merriment thought. *He was going to leave one way or the other. Eventually.*

She sank into a chair and rested her head back, staring up at the ceiling. She knew this feeling. She had said goodbye before. She knew the process of shutting down, of retreating inwards, of cauterising all hope and lopping off future dreams. She was familiar with the cool, shrinking feeling of self-reliance. She understood that Solomon was an indulgence, a peculiar whimsy, some kind of fascination that sprang from her loneliness. She entwined her hands, folding one thumb above the other. She had let herself become interested, watching him move and talk, enjoying his company. It was her own fault. She shut her eyes, remembering Johnny Barden, remembering the moment she gazed out on the Aegean Sea and realised he was never going to return to her. That was the moment she learned to turn her back, to let go, to stand alone and face the world unaided. That was the day she learned to be strong. This was a feeling she was familiar with, the sensation of making a decision that moved like a blade, slicing off all ties. She could turn away again. Who was Solomon to her anyway? A fleeting encounter in her busy life.

She listened; she could hear him moving about upstairs. Outside, the bells of Christ Church Cathedral chimed in the crisp, clear air.

It's the right thing to do, she told herself as she slowly got up and fetched the hammer. She moved into the shop and began to prise the nails from the door and the window frames.

It's the right thing to do.

19

Malleus Maleficarium

Skinner's Row was chock-a-block. Shopkeepers were out scrubbing away the blood from last night's slaughter and cautioning passers-by to watch out as they flung buckets of soapy water over the pavement. The whole city buzzed with the latest news. The Dolocher had caused the swine to disappear; somehow its diabolical power was increasing. Solomon barged through the crowd, his brain boiling, his carpet bag bulging with belongings. Corker quietly trotted by his side, searching his face, certain that something had gone bad.

'Is it the office first, boss?' Corker ventured, desperate to break the ice.

Solomon didn't answer. He'd stay in the Turk's Head, he thought. He ploughed swiftly up Skinner's Row. At the fringes of his consciousness he wondered if the Dolocher was following him, disconcerted by the fact that the demon had crept into Merriment's backyard. He clicked his tongue, trying to shake off the possibility, pushed open the door into *Pue's Occurrences* and took the stairs two steps at a time. He halted halfway up when the door to Chesterfield Grierson's office opened and Lord Beresford came out.

Beresford turned his good eye quizzically on Solomon.

'You poached him,' he laughed, genuinely amused. 'I'll tell you this much, Chesterfield, he does turn a gothic phrase. We howled with laughter at the club.'

Solomon arched his brows, piqued by the comment.

'Glad to amuse,' he grinned, disguising his annoyance. 'You should look at the gothic horror that is currently unfolding in the Black Dog,' Solomon suggested archly. 'Aren't you on the Board there?'

Corker sped into the office, wincing as he looked back and slicing his index finger along his throat, encouraging Solomon to stop talking. Solomon was eager to fight: he'd had a bad morning.

'And since you've the ear of parliament members you should inspect the tenements on New Row over near Corn Market House, they're a fine symbol of a thriving city. I mean that sarcastically, of course. Those slums are a resounding statement of disinterest from the ascendency. How the nobler classes distain to grubby themselves with charitable duties. I suppose you are of the ilk that propose that the poor enjoy living in squalor, that they relish slopping about in foul conditions, with no doors to shut out the wind, while their landlords employ cruel agents to extract exorbitant rents.'

'Dear God, you've employed a zealot,' Beresford guffawed. 'I couldn't be more pleased for you, Chesterfield, the two of you can bore the breeches off each other day in, day out. I'm sure to walk in here of an afternoon and find you both on your knees praying like Catholics and wearing sackcloth.'

Solomon pressed his teeth together, furious that Beresford was right – he did sound self-righteous and pious. There was something about Beresford's height and hawkish handsomeness that made Solomon suddenly want to take him down a peg, something about his knowing manner that made Solomon feel his own ineptitude keenly. The truth was that Beresford had all the self-confidence and unshakable self-belief that was required in a sea captain who would have well over five hundred souls under his command at any one time. Had it been a better day and had Solomon been in a better place, he might have enjoyed Beresford's company. But today was a bad day, so Solomon glared, his face flush with frustration, his heart crushed by rejection, his manhood diminished by his own feeble character.

Beresford pulled on a glove.

'Well, while you two puritans are whipping the city into a religious frenzy, you leave the inquiring work to me.' He smiled.

'What do you mean?' Solomon asked, looking for a chink in Beresford's implacable armour.

'Who ordered the cull?' Beresford's eye glinted with a scalpel-like sharpness. The man possessed the kind of keen precision that could deftly extract the potency of a brooding problem, long before it developed into a situation. Solomon sensed that Beresford was extremely shrewd and so, with enough wit to outpace his own black mood, he stopped looking to contradict and paid attention.

'There was no official order given by the town elders.' Beresford raised a brow. 'No aldermen or beadles, no one from the Sheriff's office involved. The populace cannot take the law into their own hands: someone needs to be prosecuted. The city is practically lawless as it is. The amount of robberies the courts have had to handle. And now the slaughtering of livestock. It's abominable, utterly unacceptable. I'm instigating a curfew and sending men out to investigate who organised the killing.'

Then, patting his perfectly coiffed wig, he rolled his eye. 'I blame that ridiculous preacher. He went from church to church yesterday, calling on people to repent.' He smacked Chesterfield's back and teased, 'You'd have liked him.' Then winking at his friend, he needled him softly. 'Peggy says she looks forward to seeing you.'

The barest spots of red appeared on Chesterfield Grierson's cheeks. He coughed softly in an effort to conceal his discomfort.

'Sol.' Corker reappeared on the landing dressed in his fine

breeches and jacket and wearing battered shoes on his bare feet. He had thirty copies of *Pue's Occurrences* under his arms.

'Yes?' Solomon asked.

'Why don't I leave a few copies in Merriment's? She can put them on the counter, sell them to her customers.'

Solomon smarted. He shook his head quickly, averting his eyes.

Beresford's brows raised, his eyepatch moving slightly upwards.

'Merriment O'Grady?' he asked.

'A past dalliance of yours?' Chesterfield's mouth barely grinned, but his eyes danced, glad to be able to sting Beresford a little for his previous remark.

Solomon's heart tumbled, his chest contracted. He watched Beresford smile, his jaw sharp and pronounced.

'Ye know her?' Corker innocently asked. 'She wears breeches, carries a pistol.'

'I taught her how to shoot it, lad,' Beresford announced proudly. 'She's a damn fine creature. If I wasn't married . . .' He tugged his pristine collar higher up his throat, patting the emerald-studded pin fastened to the bulge of gleaming white silk about his neck. 'Those lips,' he smiled. 'Nothing more fascinating than a headstrong woman, eh, Chesterfield?'

Chesterfield grumbled, pulled his ornate pipe out of his top pocket and lit it, making little sucking sounds. Solomon looked away and clamped his jaw tight. Of course, Merriment had chosen a fine lover, a capable sea captain. He was everything Solomon was not. A warrior, a gentleman, a married man. The last fact spun like a blade in the pit of Solomon's stomach. Was she still seeing him?

'Come over to the club later,' Beresford said to Chesterfield. 'We'll talk about things then.'

Tapping the tip of his walking cane to his forehead, he bowed quickly and headed down the stairs, whistling lightly.

Impervious to the general mood in the city, he flung the door open and marched down Skinner's Row, breathing in the crisp air and soaking up the flattering glances he received from passing ladies.

Solomon's mind reeled as he imagined the handsome sea captain teaching Merriment to shoot. Had Beresford taught her anything else? Solomon winced at the idea. Stung by the discovery and wounded by his departure from her lodgings, Solomon tried to pull himself together. He pointed at the papers under Corker's arm and asked Chesterfield how much money there was for a second edition.

'In one week?' Chesterfield's incredulous face lit up.

'We need further instalments. Let's go for a second print run, include the taking of the pigs,' Solomon told him.

Chesterfield nodded then shrewdly enquired, 'Will you be carrying the loss of the first-edition papers that haven't sold?'

Solomon grinned. 'All right then, let's sell a supplement to accompany the first edition. An insert.'

'A broadsheet you mean?' Chesterfield entwined his long fingers and left his pipe dangling from the side of his mouth as he waited.

'Exactly. Only it will be called *Pue's News* and can be purchased for an extra penny with the first edition, or for three pennies unaccompanied.'

'Excellent.' Chesterfield Grierson clapped his hands together, took out his pipe and entered his office, shutting the door with a click, leaving Solomon and Corker standing on the top of the stairs looking at one another.

Solomon waved his hand. 'Right, let's get started.'

He tried to muster up enthusiasm for the day as he followed Corker into his office. Truth was, Solomon Fish felt full of holes.

*

318

Merriment had no time to sit and regret the departure of Solomon. The shop was so busy that when Anne popped in to buy hand cream for the widow Byrne, she ended up helping out.

'Where's Janey?'

'The little mite fell asleep and I hadn't the heart to wake her,' Merriment told her.

Anne followed Merriment's instructions carefully, writing names and addresses and ailments in the ledger and organising appointments. Merriment gave quick examinations, aware that most of those who had come to the shop were suffering from intense bouts of fear, presenting all the symptoms usually associated with acute anxiety. The customers came thick and fast, and the queues were three lines deep behind the counter when the door was flung open. The bell rang so arduously that the entire shop turned to look, and there, standing panting and surrounded by a dour-looking set of companions, was a righteous man waving a Bible.

'You heathens,' he shouted, his large face purple with passion and contorted with frenzy. His companions stood mute, their sour faces blinking disapprovingly while their enthusiastic leader swept into the centre of the floor and began shouting accusations and pointing wildly at the sheepish throng before him.

'She is a witch.'

His voice was shrill and loud.

'A succubus that calls the devil to us and you are supplying her with a ways and means to stay among us.'

Merriment tapped the holster by her side. Dolly Shelbourne's husband was taller than she had imagined.

'She is issuing potions and bitter drops to incapacitate the men of this city, to make us weak in body, to take our power so she can fulfil her devil's work.'

A woman sneaked away, nervously creeping out the front door and scurrying off.

'And all of you are courting her business. It is her foul spirit that has conjured up the Dolocher. Her foul practices that have attracted him to this God-fearing city.' His eyes bulged, popping wide in his head. A mist of spittle sprayed from his mouth with every word he hollered.

'Did you hear me? She is poisoning fine healthy men, reducing them to babbling idiots!'

'Sir—' Merriment began.

'Do not speak to me. "For out of their falsehoods . . ."' He rattled out a series of Bible quotes and those who could escape slinked off and disappeared.

Merriment produced the Answerer, much to the shock of everyone present. The pistol had a very sobering effect on her accuser.

'Excuse me for interrupting,' she said firmly, 'but I am not a witch. I administer healing tinctures and salves. Now' – she cocked the hammer – 'I do have a treatment for hysteria.' Everyone wondered if her cure for hysterical religiosity was a musket ball to the head and they stepped back, keeping out of the firing line.

Merriment's voice was cool, her hands were hot, she could feel the blood rushing to her face, the pound of her pulse throbbing in her ears, but she was practiced enough to disguise her nervousness, had enough experience of conflict and aggression to project a very poised and self-assured exterior. To everyone there she looked level-headed and unflappable.

Her brows arched mildly. 'May I suggest that you leave quietly, sir, and I will do no more about it; otherwise I will have to defend my property and my reputation with a writ from the assizes forbidding you to ever step foot in here again, or . . .' She tipped the pistol in her hand up slightly, indicating that she just might shoot him as an alternative if he didn't leave.

Her imperturbable demeanour and confident handling of her weapon unnerved the man before her. His cohorts grumbled that he should leave her be, that there were other tacks to take. Desperate not to lose face, Mister Shelbourne stared at Merriment and smirked.

'Look at you. You are an aberration of femininity, a deviation from all that is encased in the very term "woman", with your breeches and your pistol. You are a repulsive rejection of all that is ladylike, demure, soft and compassionate. You are a viper, a blight on the face of God's will, an abhorrent distortion of true nature. A hermaphrodite suckling on the teat of a devil.'

Merriment waved her pistol, indicating that he either get out or she would shoot.

'You have won for now, you succubus bitch, but all is not over.' And turning on his heel, he marched out the door, his four companions quickly stepping after him.

'Jesus,' somebody sighed, relieved that he had gone.

Merriment carefully uncocked the hammer and returned the Answerer to its holster, the blood draining to her feet, thoroughly shaken by the confrontation. Her knees buckled and she sank down onto the high stool, her head spinning. Anne fetched her water, while one by one the customers made their excuses and filed out of the shop, taking their business elsewhere. Anne stood behind the counter blinking uncomfortably.

'He's put the wind up them,' she tutted and then, seeing that Merriment was worried, she added, 'He'll not take it further. The likes of him is all bluster and blast.'

But in her heart Merriment knew to never underestimate the conviction of a fundamentalist.

Anne took the widow Byrne's ointment and smiled pitifully at Merriment, trying to sound flippant and untroubled by what had occurred as she said her goodbyes.

'I'll pop in tomorrow.' She grinned, her eyes pained as she tried to disguise her discomfort. Merriment nodded and patted Anne's back with a 'thank you'. She wanted to pay Anne for her help; instead they came to an agreement that she'd knock down the price of Stella's perfume. She latched the door when Anne left, flipped the sign and pulled over the shutters. She retired to the anteroom, stoked up a bright fire and lit as many candles as she could, to drive away the shadows and dispel the sense of impending doom. Perhaps she should pack up and go, take Janey Mack, seek refuge somewhere. Then she thought of her hurried note to Beresford and, wondering if he had received it, apprehensively mused over how he could help. Not for the first time, she wished she was back at sea.

As she sat wondering what to do, her eyes drifted to a pile of books cast on a low shelf in one corner. Among her books on surgery and herbs she saw a thin volume she had picked up in a marketplace in the Baltic. She had bought the book because it was written in Latin and contained curious woodcuts. She plucked the narrow volume from the pile and flicked it open, the image on the flyleaf enough to make her blood run cold. Emblazoned on the page were the words *Malleus Maleficarium*. Merriment remembered smiling at the title years ago, amused by the folksy terror that had driven two Alpine monks to write a book that translated as *The Hammer of Witches*. The opening quote was from Exodus: 'Thou shalt not suffer a witch to live.' Merriment shivered recollecting Mister Shelbourne's livid fervour. The tone of what she was reading curiously mirrored his convictions and she knew how awful the consequences of such conviction could be. The image of the old sailor with a deformed arm swinging from the rigging was a brutal reminder of a dark desire living in all communities to purge. She turned the thin pages over; her mouth went dry as she swallowed back her fear, looking at the woodcuts of women accompanied by familiars and riding brooms. She could feel her heart constricting, the strange images working provocatively on her mind. She stopped at one page, her curiosity piqued by an etching of a demon drawn by Durer. This demon was squat, its body covered with lizard scales, thick talons sprouting from its feet, black bat wings swooping from its back. It had a long protruding, hairy face with a single horn bursting from its goatish skull. It was emerging from a hole in the ground, ready to attack an innocent passer-by.

Merriment had dismissed the book years ago as a relic of a dark age locked in by superstition and stunted by religious myopia. Now she attentively searched the etching for details, questioning whether the phenomenon of devils had been long catalogued and captured by previous generations to warn anyone living in the future not to be lax, not to suppose that the world is a flat reality consisting only of things that are normal and mundane. Had the monks writing the *Malleus Maleficarium* written in earnest? Had they seen demons and devils? Had they known the supernatural world was close by? Had they understood that certain events can produce a malignant spirit? Had they a Dolocher of their own? Had they known how to ward off evil? Had they known how to destroy the devil?

Merriment quickly read the section on the manifestation of a demon, her breath fluttering in her lungs.

How does a demon appear? the monks asked. First, it uses a speck of dust. With wicked intention, it harvests moisture from the atmosphere, and using more dust it coalesces into form. The curiously scientific tone made her shudder. She thought of the dark shadow of Pyrrho of Elis's questions, appalled at how rational inquiry could be applied to irrational subjects. By the meticulous application of a particular perspective, the authors of the *Malleus Maleficarium* had developed an intriguing argument that lent such a tone of authority to the text that the existence of demons and witches seemed totally plausible. Her mind reeled at the idea of an invisible creature, nothing more than a cluster of disembodied consciousness using dead material to carry out its will.

She thought of Olocher's proclivities still festering in his autopsied corpse. She thought of the slippery, fetid flesh dripping from his chest, his spiny coat dark and coarse. She thought of the horrific melding of beast and man. An incubus slithering through the streets of Dublin. She couldn't stop the thoughts and with every page she turned a fresh image triggered a new gothic digression. The monks who composed the *Malleus Maleficarium* had meticulously contemplated all mechanisms of manifestation, had analysed and considered the most bizarre possibilities. Beneath the picture of a hideous succubus mounted on a mortal man was the explanation, *Devils do indeed collect human semen, by means of which they are able to produce bodily effects; but this cannot be done without some local movement, therefore demons can transfer the semen which they have collected and inject it into the bodies of others.*

She thought of how Gertie had been raped, wondering if the Dolocher had intended to impregnate her, so that her womb would produce his malformed offspring. The book worked hard on her imagination, filling her with such anxiety that she sat a moment with her eyes closed terrified of what was going to happen. Scenes of an excited crowd keen to rid Dublin of all things demonic rose up behind her eyes. She imagined an agitated mob coming to fetch her, to drag her to a pyre, to tie her to a stake. She opened her eyes, scattering the images, faintly amused at the notion that she and Joan of Arc bore the curious similarities of wearing men's clothing, carrying a weapon and being hounded by witch finders. She did her best to dispel the notions of perishing in flames, her thoughts instead dancing at the possibility of Mister Shelbourne going to the guild of apothecaries to instigate a malpractice suit. Perhaps Solomon's knowledge of legal matters . . . She thrust aside the half-formed idea. He wasn't coming back. Her heart squeezed tight, emitting a strong sore pressure, an ache of longing and remorse that manifested as raw pain in her body. Why hadn't she told him to stay? Tears popped into her eyes. She gazed at a woodcut of the devil, depicted in this engraving as an ebony-skinned creature with a long, spiky tail and recalled the elusive blur of bristling strokes that had emerged from the shadows last night. She desperately tried to bring focus to the unclear edges of her recollection, to draw a distinct face, but like an insubstantial wraith the phantasmagorical form evaded clear scrutiny. *I saw his eyes*, she told herself, glancing at the peculiar volume in her hands. But her certainty vacillated. Had she seen a curl of bluish tusk? The russet grey folds of pig flesh? The hint of blue irises? Or had she constructed the Dolocher from all of Solomon's broadsheets, from a hot and feverish imagination destabilised by the screams of the slaughtered pig? She couldn't stop her mind reeling or her mood plummeting as the walls closed in on her, a tumult of emotions rising from the depths of her being undercutting her stoical rationalism. The Dolocher disassembled all that she had held to be dear and true. The demon heralded a new world. A world rippling with supernatural creatures, full of dark crevices from which all kinds of noxious fumes could infect the unsuspecting mind. And looking down at the *Malleus Maleficarium*, she realised that simply owning the book could be considered suspect, a totem of her interest in the occult, not a bizarre relic from a medieval mindset but rather a book hinting at her guilt. She became terrified that an accusation of witchcraft could very easily be levied against her and couldn't dispel the rising trepidation as she pondered what to do.

She prepared a tincture to calm her nerves and tried to find a chink of light to console herself, but all that came to mind was the fact that Solomon was gone, Beresford was seeking the company of Peggy Leeson, her customers had vanished, her business was affected and there was a religious zealot whipping up the fear of others that could very easily convince some official that Merriment O'Grady should be investigated. She was squeezing the *Malleus Maleficarium* between her hands, trying to construct some kind of solution to her problems, when Janey

Mack appeared at the door, rubbing her eyes, her hair poking up in parts and her face criss-crossed on one side where it had been pressed into the pillow.

Merriment surreptitiously sneaked the small volume into her pocket and plastered a smile onto her face.

'Hello sleepyhead,' she said stretching out her arms to invite Janey Mack in for a cuddle. 'Did you sleep well?'

'What time is it?' Janey Mack seemed confused. 'The shop is closed.'

Merriment began to fetch food from the larder. 'It's half past three in the day. The shop was very quiet,' she lied. She hid her anxieties from Janey Mack, feeling the slow release of her calming cure beginning to at least take the sharp edges off her fear.

'Now.' She placed an array of produce on the table. 'How about something to eat?'

'And then we'll go to the priest,' Janey Mack reminded her.

'Oh.' Merriment pinched back her frustration; the last thing on earth she wanted to do was seek out some churchman. What if Dolly's husband saw her? He could very easily cause a scene. 'Perhaps tomorrow . . .' she demurred.

All the little girl had to say to make Merriment crumble was, 'You promised.'

'All right.' She gave in, chopping up some potatoes to throw into a stew. 'We'll go later.'

They were eating dumplings, which Janey Mack declared was her most favourite food of all time, when a sharp series of knocks came to the shop door. This time it was Merriment who jumped to her feet, telling Janey Mack to wait as she slipped out of the anteroom, her heart racing, her hand on her hip ready to produce the Answerer.

Lord Rochford was not amused. He pushed past, grumbling, 'What is this nonsense? Locking up early? Let me in.'

Merriment flicked the sign to *Open*, asking Janey Mack to keep an eye on things. She needed the little girl out of the anteroom so she could examine his lordship.

'You take the high stool.' She patted the seat, calling Janey Mack over. 'Watch the place,' she said quietly, waving Lord Rochford into the back room. He walked imperiously in, glowering as he passed, his lips curling into a natural and consistent sneer of revulsion.

'We won't be long,' Merriment whispered to Janey Mack before clicking the anteroom door shut. She took a breath, collecting herself before she fetched her red ledger and quickly scanned her last entry.

'How are things?' she asked, masking the disturbed emotions stirred up by the day's events.

'Better,' Lord Rochford grumbled, making the statement sound like a complaint. 'I need more of that ointment.'

He unbuttoned his breeches to show Merriment how he'd improved and put his member away once she'd finished examining him.

'Another dose should do it, something a little milder,' she said, pulling a sachet of powder down from a shelf. Her fingers worked deftly as she weighed and measured, adding a few drops of tincture with a tablespoon of oil to three ounces of the noxious-smelling powder. She moved quickly, aware that Lord Rochford was glaring at her, his left hand rubbing the hilt of the sword strapped to his hip.

'As a matter of interest,' he enquired, looking around the room scornfully, 'do you terminate, you know, things?'

Merriment stopped mixing the salve she was preparing. She held the slender wooden paddle suspended over the bowl, understanding full well what Rochford was getting at. This was all she needed, another reason for the citizens of Dublin to have her arrested and flung in gaol. She shuddered.

'It's against the law,' she said firmly.

'But in certain circumstances,' Rochford pressed. 'For issues of health.'

'It's against the law,' she repeated, spooning the mixture into a tiny glass jar.

'So you'd let a mother die rather than . . .' Rochford stopped toying. 'You're telling me as a handy woman, that you have never terminated a pregnancy?'

Merriment didn't answer. Her heart pounded in her chest. Her ears began to ring. She tried to keep her hands steady. A godawful convergence of events was conspiring to undo her existence and now a powerful man was pressing her with such zeal that she could feel herself panicking. She wanted Beresford's calm resolve to make this all go away. She wanted Solomon . . . If only he would come back.

Lord Rochford's nostrils flared, his eyes flicked across the dark shelves, his lips snarled with disgust.

'I want you to carry out an abortion. I will pay you handsomely.'

Merriment knew from his tone that he was not requesting but rather ordering the termination.

'There's a girl, lives on Henrietta Street, one of Margaret Leeson's bitches. She's trying to blackmail me, says my son is the father.' His jaw clenched. 'I want you to see to it that the pregnancy is terminated.'

'No,' Merriment repeated, her hands beginning to shake. She grabbed a tea towel to hide the tremor.

Lord Rochford's expression didn't change; he didn't flinch or grunt or express his intention with his body. Instead he merely turned his cold eyes on Merriment and spoke in a flat, low tone that chilled her to the bone.

'Then I'll shut you down. I'll say you are an abortionist. My word will be held above yours.'

He didn't elaborate, but stood staring, waiting for Merriment to crumble, his grey eyes cold and hard as granite.

'You'll have to prove it,' Merriment replied, keeping her voice level. Years at sea had taught her to stand steady, aim clearly and keep her responses to a threat short.

'No, I don't.' Rochford shrugged. 'I don't have to prove anything.'

The blood drained from Merriment's face. She was cornered. At sea, she could jump overboard. On land, she was backed against a wall. Rochford looked about him, flush with victory.

'The girl's a liar,' he said. 'The slattern says she's five months gone. I've dispatched my son to the continent and I want you to cut his bastard out.'

'She's too far along.'

'Maybe for herbs, but not for surgery,' Rochford countered. 'You were a ship's surgeon. I have that on good authority. I told Margaret Leeson you'd be calling. You appear to know each other. Get rid of the child and I will reward you handsomely. Do it this evening. I will call over, see that you've done the job.'

He flung a scattering of silver onto the table. The coins rolled and tinkled, spinning on Merriment's taut nerves.

'Do nothing and you will be out on the street in a week.'

He grabbed the salve and left the anteroom swiftly, the edge of his silver-tipped cane banging against the counter as he passed. Merriment sank onto the edge of the table, covered her mouth with her hands and closed her eyes. There was only one thing she could do.

20

Rosie

The light was beginning to fade when the wind picked up, driving a bank of yellowish cloud down from the north. Solomon looked at the baleful sky and wondered if it would snow. Draped across his left forearm were the last remaining copies of the *Occurrences* with the added *Pue's News* broadsheet outlining the story of the missing pigs and furnished with quotations from the apostle Mark. Boxed off in a square to the right of the headlines were the details of the curfew, passed by a resolution in both houses that very morning. The streets were to be clear by seven.

'Read all about it,' Solomon called. 'The Black Dog to be exorcised. Dolocher drags pig corpses away with him. Will the Dolocher return? Curfew at seven.'

He'd been running all day. Early in the morning he'd dashed to the meeting run by the bicameral houses set with the task of protecting the city; then he rushed off the broadsheet, coerced the printer to speed print his *Pue's News* and sent Corker over to the Northside to sell the paper while he covered the Southside of the city. He'd been so busy that he'd had no time to think about Merriment. It was only when the sun was getting low in the late afternoon sky that he realised he hadn't eaten. He stood at the top of Winetavern Street, the tips of his fingers blue from the cold, and called out the headlines.

'Banished to hell. Pigs vanish. Read all about it. Has the Dolocher been slain?'

He stamped his feet and was about to return to the office to pick up his bag and go in search of an inn for the night when he noticed a solemn procession rounding the corner from Castle Street and coming towards him. Led by a tall man draped in a black cloak and carrying a wooden cross, the crowd came quietly forward. The darkly clad people moved like a slow, approaching tide, their feet softly scuffing the pavement, their breath coming in white puffs, their heads bowed, hands clasped, eyes filled with a bright, terrified light.

'Do you renounce the devil?' the tall man bellowed loudly.

The crowd responded, 'I do.'

'Do you reject Satan and all his works?'

'I do,' they chorused.

'Do you reject Satan and all his empty promises?'

'I do.'

The tall man stared dead ahead, his ashen face framed by a grey powdered wig, his gloved hands tightly gripping the crucifix draped with rosary beads and decorated with scapulars. As he passed Solomon, he asked loudly, 'Do you believe in God, the Father Almighty, creator of heaven and earth?'

The crowd responded, 'I do.'

Solomon pressed himself against the wall, watching the sea of endless faces pass, their expressions haunted and uncertain and filled with intense concentration. Stray passers-by joined the procession. Solomon's heart jolted. Merriment was there, holding Janey Mack by the hand. She was wrapped in a green cloak, her hair loose and softly flowing down her back, her head held high, looking straight ahead. She moved slowly, her pale face pinched and worried, her mouth firmly closed, resolutely not praying. Solomon wanted to call her name. He wanted to reach in, take her hand and bring her aside. He wanted to say, 'Don't be afraid.'

He bit the inside of his lower lip, watching her glide past, the back of her head moving away, moving with the crowd, which followed the priest as he turned down Saint John's Lane and led the congregation into the Augustinian friary. He wondered, had the fright of the Dolocher at her back door converted her? Driven her into religious submission? Made her overthrow everything? Solomon thought of his own transformation after his encounter with the demon. If a desire to reform could animate him to alter, why not Merriment? But there was something about this idea that did not sit well with him. Something of her resisted, her gaze, her refusal to join in the prayers. He was confused, and was mulling over what she could be doing in such a pious congregation when a short woman with watery eyes asked, 'Ye selling that?'

She pointed at the papers folded over Solomon's forearm. Solomon nodded.

'Yes, with a broadsheet containing more information, all for eight pence.'

He sold the last of the *Occurrences* and walked to the corner of Saint John's Lane, blowing into his freezing hands and glancing furtively at the scattering of people gathered outside the Augustinian gates. He thought of mingling with the congregation, of seeking Merriment out. Perhaps she was inside the old friary. He thought of slipping into the seat beside her, of whispering to her, his lips close to her ear, his breath warming her neck. He imagined saying, 'I can come back,' and dreamed of her tentatively reaching for his fingers, her hand sliding into his, her eyes silently gazing straight ahead as she nodded. Stung by the absurd romanticism of such a thought, Solomon rounded on his heels and marched through the network of narrow alleys and lanes at the back of the church, blind with self-recrimination and seething with the burning desire to escape. He was lost in his own thoughts when someone reached for his shoulder and hauled him back, flattening him against a wall.

'Hey.' Solomon pushed, instinctively kicking, then seeing a neat row of teeth smile at him, his heart sank.

Pearly had him in a stranglehold, his large fist squeezing his collar tight, heaving all his weight into Solomon's gullet as he held a knife to his throat.

'So,' Pearly grinned, 'Mister Fish, I am here on account of Billy Knox and an outstanding game fee.' Then, suddenly dropping Solomon and slipping the blade up his sleeve, he stepped back and brushed down his pale blue nipped jacket, his fingers tentatively touching the pristine white ruff of lace bubbling down over his breastbone.

'I take it ye have some shekels in yer pocket from yer broadsheet sales.' His eyes flicked to Solomon's pocket.

'I . . .' Solomon clamped his teeth together, organising his thoughts. 'I can pay in instalments,' he ventured, 'come to an agreement with Mister Knox, a weekly stipend.'

Pearly shrugged, 'If ye like. But there'll be interest charged because of the massive inconvenience.'

Solomon sighed, watching Pearly pull out his notebook and scribbling Solomon's name.

'Yer landlady,' Pearly cocked his head to one side, 'does good business. Couldn't get into her place yesterday.'

'You sick?' Solomon's eyes narrowed suspiciously.

'Nah,' Pearly grinned. 'Knoxy likes to know what businesses are thrivin'. Good trade in tea and chronic nerve problems,' he chuckled. 'Good trade in potions and herbs, who'd have thought.'

'Yeah, well, tell Knoxy—'

'Billy Knox to you,' Pearly interjected sharply, pointing his pencil at Solomon's nose.

'Tell Mister Knox,' Solomon growled, 'that if he keeps expressing an interest in Merriment O'Grady's business he will have the Sheriff's office on his back.'

Pearly was greatly amused by this threat.

'Y'er well connected.'

Solomon shook his head. 'No,' he replied bleakly. 'But Merriment O'Grady is.'

'Yeah, well,' Pearly added cryptically, 'not all fees are collected through the front door.'

'What do you mean?' Solomon frowned.

'Ah now, pretty boy.' Pearly tapped Solomon's forehead with his pencil. 'Stop asking me questions.' He scribbled in his notepad and cocked his head to one side. 'Do ye like yer landlady?' he asked, his eyes dancing with a provocative light.

'No,' Solomon snapped.

'She like you?'

Solomon shook his head. 'Let me cut you short . . .'

Pearly grinned. 'She a follower of Sappho? Not interested in yer charms. I knew it. I said so.' Sniggering, his shoulders bouncing up and down, he muttered, 'Knoxy owes me four guineas on that one.'

He snapped his head up, held out his hand, his expression suddenly hard and sharp. 'What are ye paying off then?'

Solomon handed him five shillings, wondering how he was going to square things with Chesterfield Grierson.

'Right.' Pearly counted the coins, slipped them into his pocket, closed his notebook and sauntered off, leaving Solomon bewildered by his assailant's hasty departure. There were no goodbyes, no 'see you next week, farewell', and then Solomon realised that Pearly's sudden departure was intentional. It was to keep Solomon on his toes, always ready to pay. As he watched Pearly march away, he heard him whistling, understanding clearly the unspoken message. Solomon would be followed and pounced on whenever and wherever it suited Billy Knox.

He banged the back of his head off the brick wall behind him, furious that now he would have to figure out how to repay Chesterfield. Why hadn't he told Pearly that Merriment was no longer his landlady? That information would at least have protected her. He clamped his jaws, suppressing the stinging sensation in his chest. When would he see Merriment again? Exhausted and depressed, he sighed through his teeth.

He dragged his right hand over his face, pulling on his flesh, his fingers digging into his jaw, dragging his chin, trying to wipe away the mess he was in.

'To hell with this.' Solomon launched himself forward and quickly hurried after Pearly. He followed a good twenty paces behind, ducking out of sight whenever he had to, his eyes fixed on the blue coat, watching it dip and weave through the throng of city dwellers. It was over near Cornmarket, down from New Row that Solomon squeezed into a doorway just as Pearly was met by a small man with an angular face. This was the second time that Solomon had seen Pearly meet with Hawkins.

Solomon would never forget the Keeper of the Black Dog. He recalled the brutal savageness of Hawkins' temper, the wanton glee he expressed in violently attacking Charlie, the spiteful pleasure he took in robbing Solomon, the pounding weight of his fists, the unremitting pummelling, as over and over he punched Solomon's face. Hawkins was the kind of man that revelled in violence, found a sick pleasure in beating a man half to death, delighted in dominating and crushing, seemed nourished by the crack of bones and the splatter of blood. His swagger and bluster were backed up by a deep-rooted lawlessness. He looked at Hawkins as he cheerfully greeted Pearly, his flinty eyes shifting right to left. It scalded Solomon to see the brigand who had beaten him black and blue and robbed him blind walking free and easy in the streets of Dublin, but he was intrigued that Billy Knox's right-hand man was creeping about meeting Hawkins in the shady side streets, looking shifty as he muttered something under his breath.

Solomon tried to read what was going on. It was obvious that Pearly and Hawkins had something going. A smuggling caper perhaps? Some kind of illicit racket? They were up to no good, whatever it was they were plotting. They chatted hurriedly for a moment, both of them parting quickly and heading their separate ways.

Perplexed, Solomon wondered if it would be worth looking into Hawkins more. There was something about Pearly's manner, a faint subservient bow of the head, the barest flicker of anxiety in his expression. Perhaps Hawkins had something over Pearly and if Solomon could find it out, then maybe he could find a way to extricate himself from his current debt to Billy Knox. Solomon made his way back towards Christchurch. He thought of heading down to the Cock and Hen to do a bit of asking about, see what he could find out, but something in him couldn't face Jenny. He sighed as the dusk began to turn a garish yellow, the failing light tinged with purple, his heart like lead in his chest as the unbearable weight of no longer living under Merriment's roof struck him hard. Going home had become a thing. Returning to the warm fire in the ante-room, writing at the supper table while Janey Mack and Corker chatted, sneaking glances at Merriment while she worked, had become part of his evening routine. Heartsore and miserable, he turned onto Purcell's Court and smirked when he saw a painted sign for the Boar's Den tavern. He made for the peeling black door, thinking, *This is appropriate*, and stepping into the warm, grubby interior he pulled a chair over to the blazing fire.

The tavern consisted of a grimy room with a squat roof and a mud floor strewn with straw. Scattered in odd corners was a collection of rickety tables and cobbled-together benches. Two windows criss-crossed with diamond-shaped leaded panes faced onto the street but gave little light. A make-shift snug had been constructed from salvaged wood and hammered together to make a wall. Sitting to one side of the snug, wrapped in thick brown shadows, was a large man with a massive, jowly face and hard suspicious eyes. He seemed to melt into the darkness as soon as Solomon acknowledged his presence with a nod. It took a few moments for Solomon to place the man. He knew him. It was the colossus who had emerged from the Black Dog the day that he met Maggie. His thoughts immediately drifted to his mother's old friend, to a time when things seemed simpler and easier, when life was less complicated.

Solomon shifted towards the fire, spreading his fingers wide, his hands tingling as they absorbed the scorching heat. He watched the flames dance and the flakes of thick black soot that lined the back of the chimney breast flutter like soft black wings. As his body began to thaw out, his resolve began to melt away. He felt broken and lonely.

'What'll ye have?' asked a gruff woman with two top teeth missing while she poked her index finger into her ear and twisted it, pulling out a wodge of dark, crumbling wax.

Solomon swallowed, taking a chance.

'Have you stew?'

'We do.'

And without further repartee the woman turned and limped away, her filthy skirts smeared with gravy and stinking of turnips. Solomon glanced over to the snug. The man in the shadows glowered back then hacked up noisily and spat a long, dark streak of spittle onto the sawdust floor. Solomon averted his eyes, looking back into the fire. He thought of ambling down to the docks and taking a boat to somewhere warm.

Nothing to stay for, he told himself.

He knew this inner voice very well. How often had he absconded? Just left? Ten? Twenty times? That was what he did. He wished he could drown out the voice once and for all, could make a decision and stick to it. He was sick of hearing himself think.

He sat in the gloomy tavern, staring at the floorboards, breathing in the faint stench of urine mingled with the stale smell of sweat and chewed tobacco. Consumed by the half-light, in this dark pit, he searched the depths of his bones, trying to drag up the will to stay. If it killed him, he thought, scratching his jaw, he would force himself to try. He recalled the jagged dark hairs bristling from the Dolocher's fleshy skull peering down

337

at him from a height. He remembered the Dolocher hunched over him like a grotesque living gargoyle and the image sent a flood of liquid fear coursing through his chest. His heart began to shiver and palpitate. The devil was after him. In an effort to bite away the fear he clamped his jaws tight and shut his eyes, straining to block out the Dolocher's fearsome visage.

I will change, he told himself. *I will change.*

He would remain in this friendless city, working at a writing job, hawking newspapers and keeping his head low. This was where he was going to start. He thought of Corker and Chesterfield Grierson, of Eliza May and Sally Loftus, and at the edge of his consciousness, on the distant horizon of his thoughts, was the faint hope that perhaps, some days, when he walked to the office or walked by her shop, he would catch a glimpse of Merriment and her assessment of him would improve and maybe . . .

He snapped the idea in half, relinquishing his longing, and looked around the bleak interior.

'Here.' The limping woman handed him a bowl of grey, oily stew and a wooden spoon. 'Anythin' else?' She sucked her upper lip noisily through the gap in her teeth. Solomon recoiled from the odour of the meal before him.

'Do you have any beer?'

The question made the limping woman snort.

'We're a public house, aren't we? Course we've beer.'

'A tankard please.'

The woman shuffled away grumbling, while Solomon picked at the slop in the bowl and stared at the fatty globs of gristle floating in a pool of sloppy potato and greenish-coloured parsnips. Outside the sun was setting and the clouds were heaping up over the rooftops. The limping woman lit a candle and placed it on a stray table. She coughed into her tea towel, wiping the filthy rag across her mouth before flinging it over her shoulder. She brought Solomon his beer, slamming it down onto the mantelpiece. The drink was flat and faintly sour. Solomon didn't care.

He was fishing for an edible sliver of onion in his mystery stew when he heard footsteps trot across the room behind him. Glancing up, he saw a little man with leathery skin wearing a patchy jacket and tattered boots and immediately recognised him as the one who had barged into him that day outside the Black Dog, knocking his bag to the ground. The little man scurried into the snug and addressed the lumpy man sitting in the shadows.

'There ye are, Jessop. It's freezing brass monkeys out there.' The little man's high-pitched voice chimed through the gloom.

Jessop leaned forward and grunted. 'Y'er late, Fred.'

Fred plunged his fingers under his threadbare wig and scratched his bald pate.

'Am I?'

Fred didn't care. He spun round and greeted Solomon with a blank, toothy grin, before sliding into his seat and pulling out a cube of tobacco.

'Here, Ethel,' he called, his voice rising an octave, 'bring us a candle to warm me fingers – I can't hold me penknife I'm that cold – and a bowl of stew and a nip of whiskey.'

Ethel pointed at the candle over on the empty table.

'What's wrong with that?' she scowled, pouring a shot of whiskey into a smeared glass.

'Nothin'.' Fred grinned, hopping off his stool and fetching the candle, the sole of his right boot flapping as he walked.

'Well?' he asked Jessop, sliding his knees back under the table and lowering his voice. Solomon picked up the word 'merchandise' and remembered the cartload of barrels and sacks being hefted into the prison cellar. Fred and Jessop obviously ran some business over in the Black Dog, and Solomon's interest was piqued since all roads seemed to lead back to the prison. He strained to listen to what they were discussing.

Jessop pulled his huge shoulders forward and smirked. 'I have it sold.' His eyes darted around the room, the candlelight washing over his wide, unshaven face, falling into the creases of his jowls and highlighting the folds of skin bulging above and below his eyelids. Solomon stared into his bowl, looking preoccupied with his food.

Fred stopped peeling his tobacco and paused as Ethel handed him his whiskey and grey stew, his black fingernails reaching for the bowl and spoon.

'Have ye been out there?' he hissed at Jessop, his wizened profile exaggerated by the candlelight. 'The town criers are bawling about a curfew.'

'We'll be grand.' Jessop shrugged.

Fred wasn't so sure. He clacked his wet tongue, his false teeth moving independently as he spoke.

'Will we now?' he queried, shoving a spoonful of stew into his wide mouth. 'How will we be grand with a rake of soldiers patrolling the streets?'

Jessop winked, his jowls wobbling slightly.

'It's organised,' he said. 'Let's just say the boss has it under control.'

Fred sat up and poked his lips out, his teeth shooting oddly forward.

'Right. Good.'

He dug into his food and ate noisily, making strange sucking sounds as he masticated.

The Boar's Den began to fill up with labourers from the docks and the tannery, all of them grabbing a quick drink before the curfew. Solomon sipped on his sour beer and handed Ethel back his bowl.

'What was wrong with it?' Ethel wanted to know, staring down at the remaining stew. 'Ye hardly touched it.'

Solomon shrugged. 'Nothing,' he lied.

340

'You're still getting charged for it,' Ethel warned him as she walked away muttering.

She upended the contents of the bowl onto the floor, letting a skinny, three-legged dog lap it up. Solomon gazed out at the fading light. He knew he should find somewhere to stay for the night. For a time he toyed with the idea of going back to Merriment's and begging her to reconsider. He just wanted to be near her. Was it her body? He imagined her naked beneath him. Yes. It was her body, her breath, her eyes, the way she moved, the way she paused, the slender gap in her front teeth, the thread-like scar above her upper lip, her long hair, her fingers, those legs, those breeches, the pistol by her side. Solomon sank back in his chair and sipped, his whole being aching when he recalled the little anchor tattooed into the base of Merriment's neck.

He wanted to touch all those years at sea, to explore all the nuances and changing tides that had turned Merriment into the woman she was. He saw her in his mind's eye, working in the anteroom, moving around him as he wrote, adjusting the retorts, pouring and sifting, moving with an easeful grace that hinted at a profound sensuality. He imagined the glide of her fingers on his skin and smiled bitterly. For the first time ever he was trapped, stuck in the sticky web of longing and desire. For the first time ever he wanted a woman that did not want him and he was consumed by a kind of sweet agony. He understood that he was not staying to improve his character or right past wrongs. He was staying to seduce the one woman who had resisted his face and his charm. The devil could chase him and drag him to hell; at that moment, all he wanted was Merriment O'Grady wrapped in his arms, flush with passion.

*

Merriment stared at the neat lacework of stone decorating the gothic architraves spanning the side aisles, unable to take in a word of the book she had brought with her. She waited, worried that everything was taking so long. She calculated that it would take her twenty-five minutes to walk over to Henrietta Street, longer if she took Janey Mack with her. Maybe if she could find Corker, he might mind Janey. She dismissed that idea immediately and gazed up at the darkening rays of the setting sun softly penetrating the stained glass trapped in the rose window above the altar. She'd have to bring Janey Mack with her.

Across the way, a cluster of shabbily dressed people kneeled praying, while around them lines of slender tapers burned in thin brass troughs with finely wrought legs. The tapers balanced in sand, all slowly dipping to one side. The sea of tiny flames glittered off the polished vases that decorated the alcoves and niches, sending a golden hue up the pale walls. Merriment was tired. The events of the day had taken their toll. She stared blankly at her surroundings, sinking into a daze, waiting while Janey Mack confessed. The air about her was thick with whispered conversation. The lull of the vaulted atmosphere burnished by red terracotta tiles and quivering with the golden hue of reflected candlelight somehow eased her into a mild torpor and for a while she thought of nothing.

She jumped a little when a low, soft voice whispered, 'Hello.'

Merriment looked up, surprised to find Stella standing over her.

'Stella.'

'Merriment, how are you? This is unexpected.'

'Yes. Janey . . .' Merriment flicked her hand towards the confessional by way of explanation. 'She needs comfort.'

Then, seizing the opportunity, Merriment clasped Stella's hand and drew her down into the seat beside her. 'I need you to do me a huge favour.'

Stella was stunned; her long, pale face glanced at the row of plaster niches carved into the side wall.

'A favour,' she repeated, her frown producing a Y-shaped indent above the bridge of her nose.

'Only for an hour,' Merriment promised. 'I need you to take Janey back to the shop.'

Merriment pulled a large brown key from her pocket, while Stella blinked nervously, her thin lips open a fraction, ready to decline Merriment's request.

'I have to go somewhere urgently. I won't be long, and we'll both walk you home when I get back.'

Stella's dark curls shivered beneath her bonnet as she looked down at the key between Merriment's fingers. In the candle-light her nose looked larger and her pale face appeared more washed out.

'I don't think . . .' she began.

'I wouldn't ask you,' Merriment pleaded, 'only I'm stuck. Please, Stella.'

'But my father . . .'

Janey Mack emerged from the confessional box, her eyes lowered, her head bowed. She made her way to the altar rail and knelt piously before it, muttering her penance.

'She'll be no trouble.' Merriment flung her book into her bag, snapped the catch shut and stood up.

'I just can't, Merriment,' Stella whispered frantically.

Merriment checked the rose window: a purplish darkness pressed against the stained glass.

'Please. I will be back shortly.'

And before Stella could protest further, Merriment slipped out a side door and into the cool, twilit evening. She passed knotty groups gathered by the fountain, all of them chatting quietly. Nobody wanted to linger long. There was a cold nip in the air. A robin chirruped in the gloom and three horses tethered to a post snorted and whickered, their shod feet clip-ping noisily on the slippery cobbles. Merriment brushed past them. Turning quickly off Saint John's Lane she made her way towards the quays, taking large, brisk strides as she navigated through the network of narrow, deserted streets.

Town was emptying out early; the hawkers had packed up and shopkeepers had called it a day. Anyone she passed hurried by. Everyone was eager to get home before the light faded. Merriment ran a little, keen to get out of the dreary side streets and over to Sackville Mall. She emerged near Smock Alley. To her left, the river glowed darkly. The boats tethered to the bank bobbed softly on the rising tide. Behind her the red sun descended in a haze of dramatic clouds and seemed momentarily poised on top of a steeple. Merriment could feel her chest constricting, she wanted to stop, take a breath. She hadn't time. Holding her bag tight, and skirting a pair of sedan chairs, she forced herself to keep striding, feeling the comforting bulge of Damascus steel fastened into the holster at her waist. To the east the sky was dark, in the west a streak of red-gold bled into the thickening clouds. The day had slipped hopelessly away from her. Now as the sun set and the last rays of daylight disappeared, she could feel her fear mounting. With the approaching darkness a fresh wave of uncertainty flooded through her. The images in the *Malleus Maleficarium* worked on her mind, pulling it towards a primal terror. The very air was somehow unfamiliar as it oscillated with the bristling possibility of ghosts and demons. What if the Dolocher had been looking for Solomon? For Janey? She stopped and clutched her side a moment, sorry now that she had left Janey and Stella alone. Desperate to quell her panic, she kept walking.

The theatre near the Lying-In Hospital was closed. A huge poster pasted over the door read, *All Shows Cancelled Due to Olocher's Demon.* Management advised that all theatre-goers take strict precautions and remain indoors after dark until further notice.

Furious that she had so little time, Merriment paced by Yarn Hall, cursing Lord Rochford and his whoremongering son.

She rounded onto Henrietta Street, out of breath, faintly panicked and roasting hot, and came to a shuddering halt, faltering at the unexpected sight of rows of lantern-lit carriages disgorging noisy party-goers. The top end of the street was teeming with revellers all sumptuously dressed, most of them wearing pig masks and laughing raucously. Coachmen jockeyed for prime positions, angling their carriages as close as they could to the pavement. Pairs of horses, draped in silver-trimmed tackle, became skittish. People poured noisily into any clear space available, while the night watch grumbled past and a town crier reminded everyone that there was a curfew at seven. When he'd finished the crowd cheered loudly, applauding the announcement. Merriment stared at the giddy multitude, holding the stitch in her side, her breath rasping in her throat, and tried to decide what to do.

She heard one woman cry, 'A jewelled snout. Isn't that wonderful?'

A sea of ostrich feathers and silk gloves gleamed in the twilight. Men sporting brocaded jackets and carved tusks smeared with splashes of red paint jibed and poked at each other, the younger bucks shoving their friends into ladies as they passed. Merriment's heart sank as she watched the crowds file into the brightly lit Number 17. Margaret Leeson was hosting a Dolocher party and it looked like half of Dublin society thought it was a splendid idea.

It can't be more than half five, Merriment thought, confounded by the idea that the aristocracy would come out dressed to the nines long before ten in the evening. *It's the curfew. Peg's convinced them to break it.*

Furious with the obstacle in front of her, Merriment trailed the crowd moving indoors, squeezed into the tightly packed hall and pushed her way into the dining room. The house was uncomfortably crowded. People gathered in thick groups on the stairs, poured into every room; every door was open, the whole house bulged at the seams, the atmosphere was cloyingly hot, the air thick with perfume and cologne. Chandeliers and mirrored candles blazed, adding to the suffocating heat and conversations were so loud that it was impossible to be heard without shouting.

Merriment ploughed through the tight squeeze, past dressers and tables festooned with sugared sweets fashioned into the entrails of pig. There was sweet black pudding, cherry-glazed hooves, sugar-spun curly tails, cream snouts and piglets moulded in jelly. Sickened by the macabre festivity, and worried about what she had to do, Merriment searched the masked faces, hoping that she might see Beresford. She was keen to discuss the bizarre charges that Mister Shelbourne was levelling at her. Beresford carried weight, he could press countercharges of wrongful accusation, make the anachronistic allegation of witchcraft disappear. He had connections. He had power. She scanned the crowd desperate to find him, anxious to evade Lord Rochford; at the same time, she had to find Peg Leeson and warn her of what was happening. Had Beresford received her note and brushed it aside to come to this party? Frustrated at the thought, Merriment reasoned that half the attendees were politically connected: if he had chosen this event over her, it was a strategic move to advance his own career and inveigle his way into the inner circles of power. While she could logically understand why he would be here, the decision to dismiss her note needled her, to the point that she wondered if she did run into him would she be happy or disappointed? *Forget it,* she chided herself. She stood by the table in the main dining room, scrutinising the revellers, hardly noticing the full roast pig complete with a miniature Christ Church Cathedral clamped in its jaws, sprawled on a bed of decorative lettuces with a pair of satanic horns protruding from its skull. What if she ran into Rochford now? This moment? Would he stand over her, make sure she carried out the operation?

She had to hurry. Sliding past the group of musicians playing loudly in one corner she made for a door leading out onto the landing, not caring as she shoved into cavorting couples half dancing, half flinging themselves about, grabbing fresh drinks from the rows of waiters who carried trays of claret and Bordeaux around the room for the guests to enjoy. Furious at the delay and the wild frenzy, feeling time running out, Merriment grabbed a waiter and shouted, 'Margaret Leeson? Where is she?'

The waiter shrugged and offered her a glass of wine.

Perched on a marble fireplace was a white-faced clock with a painted ceramic shepherdesses sitting above it. It was only a quarter to six, but already outside the windows an ominous darkness hung over the rooftops.

'Exciting,' she heard one woman gush. 'Very exciting to break the law.'

Merriment pushed her way upstairs, threading through the crush of bodies. The whole crowd heaved, moving through doorways in a surge, giddy with the idea of being out during a curfew. A frisson of anarchic lawlessness coupled with the humour of turning the Dolocher into a fancy-dress spectacle unleashed a high-spirited abandon through the crowd. The usual codes of behaviour disintegrated, drink flowed freely, and the plague toast of 'Eat, drink and be merry, for tomorrow we may die' was raucously shouted by men and women alike. Older men started to bet younger men that they couldn't pass down Sackville Street after seven o'clock without being arrested. Money began to fly as wagers were taken on. Upstairs was equally crowded. Beds had been disassembled, furniture pushed aside and card tables set up. A gypsy fortune teller was ensconced in a window seat, dispensing prognostications, and in another room a disgraced politician was holding court. The house was stifling hot and Merriment was thinking about removing her cloak when a man grabbed her and kissed her, his tongue darting quickly between her lips. She pushed him away roughly and forged on, gritting her teeth as she doggedly ploughed her way up another level. She stopped a young maid carrying a tray full of fine bone china and asked again where Peg was.

'Upstairs,' the girl said, passing out a row of teacups.

Merriment sighed, frustrated. The effort of finding Peg was weakening her determination.

Setting up shop was a mistake, she thought. *Leaving the sea was a mistake.*

Feeling diminished and uncertain, Merriment pushed past all the finer rooms and climbed up to the emptier servants' passages. The steep, narrow staircase that cut up into the roof was lit by a single candle balanced on a tiny table sitting at the top of the stairs. Merriment gripped the slender banister and began to mount the bare steps, her cloak brushing against the creamy walls, her mind swirling with a list of remonstrations.

I shouldn't have come. I had no choice. I should have told Solomon to stay. I had no choice. What if the Dolocher is after Janey Mack? She's a little girl. I'm becoming hysterical. What if Rochford is already here? On and on the voice in her head provoked and rebuffed.

The noise of the party began to recede, muted by the empty upper passages.

'Hello,' Merriment called. Looking down a long corridor, her heart felt a sudden pang. Something about the leaning walls, the narrow space and the faint smell of teak oil reminded her of being onboard ship. At the far end a door was ajar; light poured from the slender opening and she could hear voices. Conscious of the time, Merriment strode down and rapped on the wooden door frame.

'Hello.'

There was a quick scurry and a young girl with flushed cheeks and an enormous wig pulled the door back.

'Yes?' Her eyes glittered drunkenly.

'I need to speak to Margaret Leeson,' Merriment said firmly. 'It's urgent.'

Peg's sublime face popped out from behind the door. She was dressed in silken undergarments and had no wig or make-up on. Still she looked beautiful, her eyes wide open with genuine surprise.

'Merriment.'

'There's trouble,' Merriment said quickly. 'The girl, pregnant by Lord Rochford's son, you have to send her away. He expects me to do a termination; the risks are too great. Get her out of your house. Rochford is coming over this evening.'

There was a gasping cry from behind the door and a flutter of 'ohs' and 'ahs'.

'Wait.' Peg pulled Merriment into the small, chokingly hot bedroom where a young girl sat weeping, surrounded by a host of pretty girls all fabulously dressed and squashed into the hot interior, fussing and whispering and wondering what to do.

'Everyone out,' Peg ordered. 'Downstairs quickly. Sarah, I want you to fetch me the veneer ivory box from my room. Hurry.'

Peg flicked her small, slender fingers and the girls vanished. The weeping girl looked forlornly up at Merriment and her huge green eyes blinked helplessly as she clutched her stomach. She couldn't have been more than fifteen.

'Ye'll not do it, will ye, miss? Ye wouldn't cut the child out of me.'

Merriment shook her head, feeling utterly exhausted, ready to bolt now she'd informed Peg. The tiny attic room contained a single cot bed and was flanked by two chairs. A bowl of marzipan strawberries was balanced on the mantelpiece, along with a decanter of wine and a row of empty glasses.

'You'll have to tell him she ran away,' Merriment explained to Peg.

'Yes,' Peg simpered, standing by the tiny dormer window twiddling the pink ribbon that fastened the neck of her powder-blue dressing gown. 'Yes, of course.'

Merriment looked from one to the other, agitated by the lack of movement.

'What are you waiting for?' she asked the young girl.

'We love each other,' the young girl began to protest. 'Me and Desmond. We're to elope, three days from now, get a boat to England.'

The girl didn't know. Merriment had to tell her.

'Rochford has already sent his son to the continent,' she said softly. 'Desmond is gone.'

For a moment, the young girl was overcome by a shaking fear and confusion. Her mouth began to form a question before she stopped and turned to Peg, frowning, her dark brows betraying an underlying insolence.

'Someone told his father,' she gasped. 'How else would Lord Rochford get wind of our plans?'

'Of course someone told him.' Peg clacked her tongue and crossed her arms.

The young girl stared a moment, reading Peg's silent glare.

'Well, it weren't me,' the young girl exclaimed, jumping to her feet. 'And it weren't Desmond. And I only told the others this evening.'

The young girl froze, her bee-stung lips hanging open, mute with horror.

'You,' she bellowed, the two dark ringlets framing her face bouncing as her whole body juddered with rage. 'You told him,' she wailed. 'You bitch.'

'It was never going to happen, Rosie.'

Peg's flushed face became hard and unpleasant as she squared her body, turning on the young girl, ready to fight. Merriment swept her hand through her hair.

'Listen—' she began, but Peg cut over her.

350

'It was never going to happen.'

'How could it happen with you blocking my every hope?' Rosie shouted. 'You told Lord Rochford, for what? For money? To have him owe you a favour? Of course you did,' Rosie howled. 'You wanted him in your back pocket.'

Suddenly Rosie dived on Peg, screaming madly. She clawed at Peg's face and snatched a huge fistful of hair with vicious force, savagely dragging Peg to the ground. Quickly Merriment plunged between them.

'Stop,' she bellowed, prising their rigid arms apart. 'Stop.'

The two women collapsed away from each other, whimpering.

'You destroyed me,' Rosie wailed. Looking frantically about her, her eyes feral with spite, she yelled, 'I put a curse on you, you evil bitch. All this' – she waved to the rafters, her plump lips glistening, her voice wracked and full of vitriol – 'all of this will come tumbling down on your head, you pox-ridden whore. I hope the Dolocher finds you and rips your rotten heart from your miserable chest, you conniving, back-stabbing bitch.'

Peg sank onto a chair and smirked, her fingers spread across her heart, her breath coming in shallow, low gasps, her eyes sparkling with profound resilience.

'Delightful,' she grinned. 'What would Desmond think of your tongue now?'

'Fuck you.' Rosie's lower lip quivered.

Merriment swept her hand along her moist forehead. She was roasting and completely baffled by the turn her visit had taken. She dug her fingers into her thick hair and shook her head calmly.

'I have to go,' she said. 'You tell Lord Rochford that Rosie ran away. Say I came to carry out his wishes.'

'Why?' Peg asked sharply, her perfectly shaped eyebrows rising quizzically. Merriment's heart pattered. Was Peg really going to defy her?

'What do you mean?' Merriment snapped harshly, completely unsure of Peg's mood.

'Why should I do anything you say?' Peg's bright eyes blazed with defiance.

Merriment stared out at the black night, appalled by the twist the evening had taken. She had completely wasted her time and now it was pitch black out. Not only would she have to walk home in the dark, but Rochford would pull her livelihood away from her. She had become entangled in nets of intrigue and deception and was submerged under a weight of cultural ritual she didn't understand.

'Look,' Merriment responded, determined to conceal her anxiety. 'I don't care what kind of house you run, Peggy. I am merely trying to save a young girl's life.'

'Very noble.' Peg was in a combustible humour.

'Rochford said he'd shut me down,' Merriment found herself pleading.

'She doesn't care,' Rosie yelled. 'All she cares about is what use someone is to her. You don't matter. I don't matter.' Rosie poised herself on her toes and, leaning forward, she pointed. 'She'll use you and betray you. She's a spiteful dog in heat, that one. A horrible, ugly woman with no friends and no one to love her.' Rosie crumbled, collapsing onto the floor sobbing miserably. 'I only wanted a little bit of what you have,' she blubbered, looking up at Peg. 'Just a little taste of the fine things, but you were too selfish and jealous to let me be.'

Peg sat upright, her face hard and implacable.

'Rosie, you are gormless, you bought all that twaddle Desmond spouted. It never once landed in that thick noggin of yours that Lord Rochford would never stomach his youngest son marrying a prostitute.'

'If the deed had been done, he'd have no choice in the matter. Three days, that's all I was asking. In three days, we could have been married.'

352

'I have to go.' Merriment tried to leave. 'I have a child waiting at home.'

Rosie scrambled to her feet and brushed the tears from her face. 'I'm going with you.'

Merriment's jaw dropped. 'You're not,' she gasped, but Rosie didn't listen. She ran to the door, opening it as Sarah barged in carrying a neatly carved veneer box.

'I have only one wish for you.' Rosie swung round and bitterly snarled, all the venom and disappointment in her heart exploding with one last shot. 'I hope that you, Margaret Leeson, die a barren, poverty-stricken, sick old maid. That you are tortured by agonies of regret.' And, faint with blinding temper and inconsolable loss, Rosie gripped the door frame and blubbered, 'I hate you,' before running to her room to pack her small chest and grab her paltry belongings.

Sarah stood gobsmacked, her head turning left and right, staring at Peg, then at the empty door.

'What did you do to her?' she asked, flummoxed.

Peg bounded from the chair and grabbed the veneer box.

'Give me that,' she fumbled, 'and make sure she takes a decent cloak with her, not that useless cape Desmond gave her.' She pushed Sarah forward. 'Get out, go on.' Then, slamming the door, she blocked Merriment's way, popped open a secret drawer in the box and drew out five pounds.

'Bring her to the Brazen Head.' She stuffed the wad of money into Merriment's hand. 'She can hole up there for tonight. I have a friend in London. She can get a boat over tomorrow.'

'You're helping her?' Merriment felt befuddled. 'But . . .'

Peg tugged a pencil from the box and scribbled an address on a small scrap of notepaper.

'She's one of my girls,' she explained hurriedly. 'A conniving little wench, but still, one of my girls.'

She shoved the address into Merriment's hand and lunged through the door, glancing quickly back.

353

'You can't lumber me with this,' Merriment insisted.

Peg coolly patted her sore scalp.

'You're involved whether you like it or not, Merriment. Now, I have to go. When Rochford comes I'll tell him Rosie fled. And for pity's sake, don't believe everything Rosie tells you.'

'Wait,' Merriment called, 'is Lord Beresford—?' but Peg was gone. She disappeared down the stairs and rushed into her dressing room, leaving Merriment staring at the crumpled money clutched in her hands.

She met Rosie on the stairs dragging a battered chest and wearing a short velvet cape.

'You won't be warm enough,' Merriment told her.

Rosie sniffed and shrugged.

'I'm on my own now, aren't I? I can wear what I like.'

She dragged her chest noisily down a few steps.

'We can't go through the party,' Merriment sighed, swooping down to help her. She lifted the rope handle of the pine wood chest and pointed to the service door. 'Go that way. Take us out back.'

Rosie slammed her shoulder into the door that led to the servants' passageway and brought them down a dank stairwell into a cold, dark hall where a single lantern burned feebly on an iron hook.

'Will ye take me to your house?' Rosie asked, taking the lantern and pushing into a cold room where pheasants and wild game hung from ceiling hooks, their meat tenderising in the cool air.

'Yes,' Merriment told her. She had already decided not to risk the longer trip to the Brazen Head at this late hour, and she was also anxious to get back to Janey. 'You'll be safe there. Tomorrow you can go to England.'

Rosie nodded forlornly as she looked back at Merriment, her face painfully young. She was only a few years older than Janey Mack.

354

They plunged out into the backyard, through a steel door, the freezing night air slicing into their skin as they stepped into the shadowy darkness. Rosie knew where she was going. Merriment could discern a high back wall and the rooftops of the carriage house and adjoining stables. When she glanced back, every room was illuminated. Through the elegant windows she could see crowds of party-goers chatting and laughing, drink glistening in their glasses, the sound of music and chatter seeping through the thick walls and drifting up into the clouds. For a moment she thought she saw Beresford and her heart jolted. She wanted to talk to him, but she couldn't go back, there was no time. She looked away, tugged her cloak tighter and tried walking abreast of Rosie, both of them moving cautiously across the cobbles, Rosie's neat heels clicking on the dry ground. The air smelled of wood smoke and burning coal. She could hear the sound of horses whickering and coachmen coughing and spitting. In the distance, echoing over the chimneys, came the familiar heavy rattle and jaunty clipping of a coach and four.

'There's a gate here somewhere,' Rosie whispered, holding the lantern aloft and peering into the darkness. Merriment gazed at the soft grey tones shifting in the blackness before her. She could distinguish the outline of nearby trees. There was a pillar.

'Straight ahead,' she said, and Rosie started to whimper and shiver.

'I'm cast out into the street,' she snivelled. 'I hate the dark. And the Dolocher is out here. The heartless bitch, sending us to die.'

The lantern glistened off the bars of a thick iron gate. Rosie unlocked it and Merriment followed her through into a narrow alleyway littered with dead leaves. She could see Rosie's breath issuing in swift white waves from her lips. But beyond Rosie's face she could see nothing. A wall of darkness lay dead ahead.

To the right and left of her, high up, lone candles burned in occasional windows. And all she could hear as she walked was Rosie's thin heels clicking and her own boots pattering with every footfall.

'We've to cross the river.' The darkness forced Merriment to whisper.

'But the Dolocher is over there,' Rosie moaned.

'It's where I live.' Before Rosie could protest, Merriment continued. 'I don't think it's curfew yet. Can you bring us out of this alley onto a street?'

'I don't mind being arrested. I'll feel safer being arrested than going near the Dolocher's patch.'

Rosie stifled a sob, pausing a moment to gaze into the gloom, holding the lantern high.

'If you're arrested, Rochford will catch you,' Merriment whispered. Rosie's face crumpled.

'Peggy's flung us out to die,' she wept, appalled. 'And me with child and all.'

Merriment grabbed the lantern and inspected the prickling darkness. A stray snowflake tumbled slowly before her, followed by another and another. Somewhere in the distance she heard a commanding shout and the trot of several horses.

'Damn,' she cursed. 'Curfew might be about to start. Come on.'

They moved through the alley, following its twisting course as it snaked past the back walls of fine mansions. Merriment pinched her lips tight; she wanted her gun. Rosie cried uselessly, stumbling forward, complaining.

'Be quiet,' Merriment told her, 'and carry this.'

She gave Rosie back the lantern, unholstered her pistol and walked with the hammer snapped back and poised above the flashpan, ready, should she need to let off a shot. The slightest sound made her jump. A cat slinking under the ivy, a rat skidding through a hole, a pebble loosely rattling. The darkness was thick and seething, the air quivering with dense shadows confused by intermittent snow showers. Why did she ever? How could she? The thoughts came quickly and half formed. The images of goat-headed demons fused with the blurred recollection of what she had seen the night before swam before her eyes. Her whole body seemed to empty out, she began to feel weightless, light and incorporeal, moving like a mist through the shifting blackness, her feet barely touching the ground, as though she was flying. The woodcut of witches sitting on brooms flashed in her mind. Merriment stopped, taking a second to catch her breath.

'What is it?' Rosie panicked, halting. 'Did ye see something?'

'Where are we?' Merriment asked.

'I think we go straight on. We should come out by the river,' Rosie muttered, her voice snagging on darts of terror.

Merriment dragged on the chest, pulling Rosie forward as she peered through the soft blur of snow, only able to see two feet ahead of her.

'It's snowing,' Rosie sobbed, then muttering more to herself than to Merriment she repeated over and over, like a doleful prayer, 'I'll never get into heaven. I'll never get into heaven.'

They picked their way through the detritus and the darkness and came surprisingly and suddenly out of the alley onto a wide footpath and an empty road, lit by intermittent braziers that made the adjacent river gleam like dark pewter. The snow eased into a faint powdery haze and because there was a light dusting of white on the roads and along the quayside walls the route to Fishamble Street was partially lit by the sparkling ground.

'This way.' Merriment pointed to Essex Bridge. The bells of Christ Church Cathedral rang out mournfully, seven long chimes, and Rosie muffled a terrified whelp, pulling the edge of her decorative cape to her mouth.

'Come on.' Merriment glanced behind her, searching the

357

roads that spanned towards the river for mounted guards or pairs of foot soldiers. The city was eerily deserted. Nothing moved. All was quiet. Seeing that the coast was clear, and relieved to be out of the confines of the alleyway, Merriment strode along Bachelors Walk and headed down the river towards Ormond Quay.

She rushed them both across Essex Bridge, calculating the best way home. She couldn't go the main streets that were well lit and patrolled by soldiers and she couldn't go by the darkest alleyways. It was like threading a needle. Merriment tugged the chest to one side, dragging Rosie left at Smock Alley away from the wide comforting expanse of the quays, back into a constricted street that felt oppressively narrow in the pallid light. Empty buildings swooped up either side of them but the smattering of snow helped. A meagre brazier pierced the gloom, casting out a greyish-yellow circle before them.

'Not far now,' Merriment whispered, trotting a little. She was five minutes away from opening the shop door.

Christ, she thought. *Stella.*

Merriment was beside the edge of a building, its brickwork slatted with snow. She saw a lump of rubbish poking up from the gutter, frosted and glistening. The darkness moved, thickened. Burst open. Merriment reeled backwards. Rosie shrieked. He surged from the shadows, his snout dripping. Billows of white stinking breath puffed out from his spiked teeth. His black cloak fluttered wide, exposing a balding cape of bluish-grey decomposing flesh pitted with black hairs. He lurched at Merriment, slamming into her, heavy as a work horse, knocking the wind out of her, flattening her to the ground. She couldn't scream. He straddled her, pushing his knees into her pelvis, crushing her beneath him.

She couldn't breathe. She couldn't breathe.

The Dolocher's hands wound around her neck, squeezing like a vice. The last shreds of air scraped up her throat. The

Dolocher's jaws loosely dangled; pared white teeth, lustrously sharp, glimmered from his black upper palate. His dark, oily snout dripped moisture. Wafts of stale breath issued white from his savage jaws. His remote, unforgettable eyes glistened from a depressed bony darkness, glaring out at her from deep, hollowed sockets. He grunted with exertion, pushing Merriment into the ground as she scratched at his wet, slippery flesh, feeling his skin tear away in her hands. She heaved, kicking and thrashing. He weighed on top of her like a collapsing building. Crushing her. Pushing her down into the earth. Beyond. She fought back. His long, hard nails pushed into her side and a burning rush of pain flared through her body. She scrabbled for the Answerer, fumbling with the trigger. The pan flashed; a white litmus glare illuminated the quivering snout. The sound of the musket erupted with a deafening snap. The Dolocher flinched and gave a dull moan as his iron fist came down hard and heavy on Merriment's head.

The world turned white.

21

The Wound

Merriment plunged upwards out of a deep, sore darkness and gasped for air, her eyes dancing wildly.

'It's all right. You're home.' Solomon sat on the bed beside her, his arms gently enfolding her, drawing her to him until she exhaled.

'Oh my God,' she muttered, her throat raw and sore. She folded into him, her whole being releasing into his embrace, giving in, glad to be encircled, to be held. Solomon squeezed her so tight she could feel his forearms warmly keeping her together, preventing her from breaking apart. She stayed a long time resting her head on his shoulder, her eyes closed, sinking into a soporific stillness filled with the sound of heartbeats and the gentle ebb and flow of breathing.

'The Dolocher,' she whispered at last, the words rasping up her throat, tearing at her crushed and bruised oesophagus, cutting the tender lining of her vocal chords. It hurt to speak.

'I know,' Solomon replied. 'I thought you were dead.' His lips quivered, his brow furrowing. 'When I saw you, lying in the snow, bleeding, the lantern at your head . . . I thought you were dead.'

'You found me?' Merriment was confused. She sank back into the pillows away from his arms. Solomon stroked her fingers and gazed into her face.

'I found you,' he nodded. 'Brought you back home.'

Merriment examined his features, searching for something, her mouth half open.

'I . . .' she began, meaning to thank him. Instead she tried to sit up, only to discover she was sore and sick and hurting.

'Jesus.' She grabbed her side.

'You were cut.' Solomon fetched her some more pillows and propped them behind her back. 'We cleaned the wound, put a bandage on it.'

'He cut me?' Merriment frowned. 'I didn't feel . . . I didn't know . . . I thought he'd set my side on fire, that his touch was sulphurous.'

Merriment frowned and lifted the pale eiderdown. She was still wearing her breeches. She gently folded back her shirt and saw the bloody edges of a bandage.

'It's not so deep.' Solomon sat on the edge of the bed, one hand over Merriment's covered legs. 'A flesh wound. Janey put some kind of powder on it and cobwebs to staunch the bleeding.'

'Janey?' Merriment searched the empty cushions before the fireplace.

'She's asleep in my room, with Stella.' Solomon tapped her arm reassuringly. 'She's fine. The little thing was hysterical. We had a hard time calming her down.'

Merriment stared around the room. A single candle burned on her bedside table, next to a decanter of sweet sherry and a small cut glass. The fire was lit, the flames dancing, making the light jump. The shutters were closed. She was warm, cocooned in soft light and familiar shadows.

'I – I,' she stammered, 'I didn't see him . . . It was so dark. He came at me from nowhere. Out of the walls.'

Solomon nodded, his face clouded by concern and empathy.

'And his mouth . . .' Merriment swallowed, wincing as her throat throbbed.

'I know . . .' Solomon stood up to fetch her a glass of sherry. 'I

361

mean . . .' He couldn't find the words. Merriment watched his every move. The way he drew the cork out of the decanter, the arch of his shoulders stooping as he poured honey-gold sherry into the small engraved glass, strands of his blond hair falling forward along his jaw line. He seemed broader than she remembered: his shirt was loose fitting, his waistcoat open. When he turned to look at her, his eyes were filled with a brilliance that showed his fear. He brought her the glass, sitting down close to her. A tortured expression flickered over his face and without warning he suddenly leaned in and softly kissed her. His lips gently met hers, brushing her mouth with the barest of touches, lingering sensitively, saying everything he could not find the words for. When he pulled away, he could not leave her completely; his face hovered close to hers, their breath mingling as he inhaled the scent of her skin, drinking in the subtle heat of her body. For a long time he kept his head close to hers, afraid that if he retreated she would vanish into some independent quarter of her being. He wanted her to know, wanted her to feel that she was something he could not do without.

At last he sat back, his face flushed, his eyes troubled, his brow crinkled as he tried to figure out where to start, how to begin.

It was Merriment who broke the silence.

'He followed you.'

Solomon's shoulders slumped under the weight of the accusation. He turned away, his jaw tightening, his cheeks compressing, highlighting his cheekbones so that they glimmered sharply in the candlelight. He balled his hands into fists, his sore knuckles breaking a little under the pressure. Had he truly brought this darkness to her door?

Merriment's eyes glistened, her mind hot and searching, the thoughts lashing like snapped rigging, her reason buckling under the strain of her recollection.

'He followed me.'

Her eyes shimmered, tears lensing over her irises, magnifying the sheer blue quality of their colour, making her look vulnerable.

'Solomon.' She gripped her throat, pressing her hand against it to try and ease the raw, aching pain in her gullet, and swallowing with difficulty, she said, 'The Dolocher wants . . . intends . . .'

The words hoarsely burst from her being as she desperately tried to grasp what had happened to her.

'I don't know. I kept clawing at him,' she rasped, the effort of speaking stinging her throat. 'Tried to push him away. I kept scratching at him and his dead flesh came apart in my hands.'

She gazed at her wide-spread fingers as though slivers of the Dolocher's skin might still somehow be visible beneath her nails.

'When I touched him, bits of him vanished, turned to slop in my hands, cold and wet like disintegrating flesh.'

Solomon wanted her to stop. He reached for her hand, holding it, stroking it, but Merriment retracted.

'He reeked. The stench of his corpse. I mean, I couldn't breathe.' Her eyes flitted past Solomon's shoulders, worryingly unfocused, dancing into the corners of the room. 'His tongue had been gouged out.' Merriment's breath became quick and shallow. 'His eyes were far in, way inside his head. And I saw Olocher staring out at me, living, like he was trapped, staring out at me, trying to kill me.'

'Stop,' Solomon whispered softly. 'Stop. You need to drink, Merri. You've had a dreadful shock.'

Merriment craned forward and urgently hissed, 'But what will we do?' She clutched at his fingers. 'What will we do now that demons exist?'

The flaming panic written on her face pulled on all of

Solomon's inner resolve. He did not want her to be broken, but something in her expression, the glitter of her eyes, the unsettling disturbance of her fear, filled him with dread. He gently lifted the glass to her lips and encouraged her to sip.

Merriment winced as the liquid burned, sliding in cutting waves down to her stomach. She lay back on the pillows, closing her eyes for a moment. Solomon stroked her hand and for a while thought she was sleeping.

'He was in the yard,' she spoke, her eyes still closed. 'The night they killed the pigs. He was waiting.'

Then, jolting forward, she grasped Solomon's arm,

'Where's Rosie? Did he take her?'

'No, no, no.' Solomon stroked Merriment's shoulders trying to get her to calm down. 'She's in the Lying-In Hospital. She lost the baby.'

Merriment sank back into the pillows with shock. Solomon lifted the glass and made her take a few more sips. Merriment's face began to flush, the sherry working on her anxiety, helping her nerves to steady. She smiled feebly and whispered, 'What will we do?'

Solomon stared at her.

'I'll stay with you,' he promised.

Merriment's smile was full of pity. 'It won't matter,' she replied despondently, and turned her face away to gaze at the floor.

Wounded by the remark, feeling unwanted and useless, Solomon drained the glass. For a while they listened to the flames patter in the hearth before he stood up and unhooked the shutters, pulling them back to show her the night outside.

'It's been snowing,' he told her.

'Why are you here?' Merriment searched his face.

'I thought . . .' Solomon ran his fingers through his hair. He wanted to stay. His chest contracted: was she going to ask him to leave?

'I mean,' Merriment sat up a little higher, 'how did you get here?'

Solomon stood a moment, framed by the mullions of the window, his reflection distorted in the small panes of glass. Over his shoulders, the snow came in hushed waves; the flakes picked out by the candlelight flashed mildly as they momentarily drifted by before vanishing into the darkness.

'I found you,' he repeated.

'So you said.' Merriment became curiously animated, her expression suddenly filled with familiar concentration. 'But how?' she enquired, something steady in her voice outstripping her distress.

'I was staying in the Boar's Den,' Solomon began.

He didn't want to tell her he'd got into a game. He scratched his right eyebrow, looking away as he remembered joking with Fred and Jessop. He had managed to inveigle his way into their company, bought them drink, and by careful prying, hidden beneath layers of nonsense and card tricks, he had extracted slivers of information. They had left before curfew, sniggering as they tumbled out into the street, Fred wagging his finger and whispering 'scapegallows' and Jessop vomiting against the wall.

'Look at him shooting the cat,' Fred tittered. 'There's the best of Ethel's stew.' And they crept away joking about the curfew and boasting about putting up a fight and escaping the militia.

Solomon wiped his hand over his mouth and reached for the empty glass on the table. He needed more drink.

'I heard a scream. A few of us did.' He spoke slowly, staring at the glass as he refilled it. 'We ran out. And I saw you in the snow. I couldn't believe it.' Solomon looked away. 'I carried you here, a few of us . . .' Solomon took a long glug, draining the glass. 'I thought I was laying your corpse on the table downstairs.'

He sat down on the bed. Leaning his elbows on his knees, he looked at the floor. 'Janey was hysterical. Stella had a hell of a time trying to stop her crying. It was Ethel saw you were breathing.'

'Ethel?' Merriment asked.

Solomon nodded. 'The owner of the Boar's Den. She and her husband came with us and two soldiers. The others took Rosie to the Lying-In Hospital. Once we knew you were alive, we patched you up. Janey talked to you over and over. She cleaned and bandaged your wound, kept kissing your face and stroking your hair and whispering that you were going to be all right.'

Solomon sighed, looking a moment at the swarm of spectral flakes cutting the night air with soft icy precision. The snow landed on the mullions, piling inches thick on the slender staves between the glass panes, forming a crystalline depth on the window sill, gently illuminating the houses and rooftops across the way, bringing a quietening hush to the world. He was exhausted.

'She'll be pleased as punch to see you sitting up and talking,' he said.

Merriment searched his profile, watched him looking out at the snow, watched him worry his lips between his teeth and clamp his mouth shut, his expression drawn and tired.

'And you stayed,' she said softly.

He turned, his breath caught in his chest, suspended by hope. There was something in her tone, a possibility that shimmered beneath the words. Was she glad that he had stayed? She smiled, her fingers tentatively reaching towards him. He took her hand, involuntarily sighing, her fingers winding through his, squeezing softly, reassuring him.

He could stay.

They looked deeply into one another's eyes, neither of them speaking, a tender pressure building between them, the silence filled with unspoken affection, and for a long time they just gazed, relieved, quiet, warm and together.

It was Merriment who broke the spell.

'What time is it?' she asked.

'I think it's about four in the morning.'

Merriment frowned.

'It's been snowing all night,' Solomon said. Merriment looked out at the whirling flurries, turning in the bed as she gazed at the thickening snow falling from the black sky.

'I don't believe in God,' she confessed. 'Even with the Dolocher, I don't believe in God, maybe that's why . . .'

Solomon drew nearer. 'No more now,' he said. 'Enough for tonight. Try to sleep.'

He kissed her again, her lips softly responding, kissing him back.

'No more,' he said and Merriment closed her eyes.

*

When Merriment woke up the next morning, Janey Mack's face hovered next to the bed surrounded by a halo of blinding-white light.

'There ye are,' Janey Mack whispered, her huge eyes wide with anxiety. Merriment tried to pull her thoughts coherently together. Where was Solomon? It was daytime.

Behind Janey, Merriment could see the unshuttered window and a rectangle of white sky and snowy glass.

'Janey,' she whispered, carefully sitting up.

'Ye look shockin' pale,' Janey Mack said, reaching in to help Merriment haul herself up.

'I'm fine.' Merriment winced, her whole body shuddering with a dull, pervasive ache. Janey Mack grabbed the eiderdown and pulled it aside, choking back the tears.

'Let's check yer wound, make sure it's not gone sour,' she said, fighting hard to stop her chin puckering.

Merriment inspected the wound. A scab was forming. 'That's a good sign.' She gingerly tapped the edges of the cut and said that all she needed was a little *perigynium* 'to stop septicaemia setting in'. Seeing Janey Mack's expression, Merriment took a deep breath, summoning up all her inner resolve.

'You've done a wonderful job, Janey.' She smiled painfully, touching Janey Mack's hair. 'A wonderful job.'

Janey Mack shivered with relief, tears beading her eyes.

'Y'er sure?' she blinked, too afraid to be happy. 'It looks shockin' red to me.'

'Red's a good colour with a wound like this.' Merriment covered herself up. She felt hollowed out and cold. Her bones ached to the very marrow. Her heart was deeply troubled. The world was not safe and as she gazed about the brightly lit room, she couldn't shirk off the continuous waves of terror as the memory of that first moment of her attack replayed over and over. She tried not to see the Dolocher, but flashes of his black bristling skull exploded in her mind. She relived that instant when the darkness burst open and out of the inky blackness the Dolocher surged towards her, grotesquely strong and evil. She tried to swallow down the memory, but her swollen throat served as a horrific reminder of her encounter with a demon.

Janey Mack connected with Merriment's nervous glance. She climbed onto the bed and flung her arms around Merriment's neck.

'What'll we do, miss?' the little girl blurted. 'It's shockin' awful to think he nearly had ye. Cuttin' ye like that and almost haulin' ye te hell, and if ye'd have died, I'd be beside meself with grief. How would I ever go back out to scavenging after the comfort of yer kindness and the world would be sorrowful lonely without ye and I wouldn't know what to do. Ye won't die,' she blubbered. 'I couldn't live without ye. I'd be lost. I'd be lost.'

Merriment kissed the little girl's head and rocked her gently.

'Janey,' she hoarsely rasped as she mustered up enough strength to lie. 'I'm not going to die. I promise.'

Janey Mack shivered, snuggling deep into Merriment's side and burying her head for a moment in Merriment's shoulder.

'Will we have to go to sea?' the little girl asked. 'Sail far away from Dublin and the Dolocher?'

Merriment wondered the same thing.

'Did he crack the ground open to drag ye away down into the pit of hell?' Janey Mack sat up, her huge eyes barely blinking as she held her breath waiting for the answer. Merriment recalled the Dolocher straddling her, his rank breath fanning over her face, drops of moisture dripping from his snout, his vicious energy as he squeezed on her gullet, driving the back of her skull into the cobbles.

She shook her head.

'I shot him,' she said, suddenly remembering the flashpan exploding, the musket ball cracking with a deafening rapport.

'Did ya!' Janey Mack squealed, kneeling up on the bed, too astounded to be still. 'Did he eat the bullet and run off?' She leapt to the floor, her whole body animated.

Merriment frowned, her mind searching for details.

'Mother of sweet divine intercession.' Janey Mack spun left to right. 'And what else do ye remember?'

'He let out a whelp.' The sudden recollection jumped out of Merriment's mouth, arresting her, unleashing a rapid succession of questions that scattered like tacks, piercing holes in her experience.

Could a demon be wounded? Could it be destroyed?

'Where's my pistol?' she asked.

Janey Mack hunched her shoulders and pinched her fingers together, stooping a little as she asked, 'Have ye not got it?'

Merriment pointed to her cloak draped over a chair. 'Is the holster there?'

Janey Mack held up the empty leather pouch, her mouth

369

dropping open as she gasped, 'Gone. Do ye think he ate the Answerer too?'

Merriment pulled back the blankets to get out of bed.

'No!' Janey Mack ran at her and covered her back up. 'Ye've to stay in bed. I promised Sol. He'll give me a shillin'. He's downstairs cooking breakfast for ye. Whistling like a lark and frying bacon and bits of bread and he's even going to make ye a pot of tea, and,' she added hastily, 'if the Dolocher ate yer pistol, there's no getting it back. Sure, it'd have melted in his guts on account of his innards being made of smelting fire. Ye may whistle goodbye to it.'

Merriment smiled feebly and waved Janey Mack back onto the bed, a single question buzzing beneath the sea of horrible images that repeatedly burst into her mind.

Did I injure the Dolocher?

Merriment lay back on the pillows and looked out at the white sky. Across the way she could see sloping rooftops covered in snow. Desperate to distract Janey Mack and to ease the little girl's worries, Merriment asked her to explain why she wasn't out playing snowballs.

Janey Mack shrugged.

'I haven't the heart,' she sniffed, slipping her hand around Merriment's fingers. 'Did he say anything to ye?'

'The Dolocher?'

Janey Mack nodded fearfully.

Merriment looked at the ledge of gleaming snow. A grey dove landed on the sill, its yellow beak pecking hopefully as it fluffed its plumage, sending a small scattering of icy dust down onto the street below. The Dolocher's pearlescent teeth, pared into points, cut through her thoughts. She saw the edges of the skewed lantern rolling by her head cast a garish milky glow as the flame swelled, brightening at the peculiar angle, high-lighting the dark hairs sprouting jaggedly from the Dolocher's narrow snout. His wild blue eyes, bloodshot and bulging, rolling deep in his dark craterous sockets. The bristles black and coarse, flecked with russet and grey in places. The patches of blue-grey bald spots where his exposed dead flesh shivered. Over and over Merriment struggled to supress the images. The Dolocher's wild frenzy, his ferocious strength, his horrible bristling visage kept surging through her thoughts, reminding her of the noxious putrescence of his pure undistilled evil. She shuddered and clamped her teeth together, trying to quell the rolling fear sweeping through her body.

'Did he?' Janey Mack asked again. 'Did he say anything to ye?'

'What would he say?' Merriment tried to make her voice light; instead it rasped harshly.

'I don't know. He told Solomon to change.'

'I think that was metaphorically speaking.' Merriment dragged herself together.

'Is that how demons speak? Metaphorically?' Janey Mack frowned. 'Is that the language of hell?'

'Some people think so.' Merriment forced a smile, then took a slow, long breath, pain radiating though her bruised chest. 'It means that Solomon decided to change after his encounter with the Dolocher.'

She asked Janey Mack to pour her a glass of water. She couldn't shake the black concerns that swirled at the centre of her being. She would have to change. She watched Janey Mack tip water into a glass and as the clear sparkling liquid flowed with a natural brightness, she wondered how to alter the crookedness of her own spirit. Would she have to get on her knees and pray? Where was God? What was God? Was this her punishment for sleeping with Beresford? For helping Misses Lennon drug her cruel husband? For helping Stella? Had she been measured and found wanting by some remote deity? A God she had no relationship with was calling her to account and all she could do was kick and resist the idea of an all-seeing eye. Would the Dolocher come back?

The questions tumbled hot and fast, over and over as something within her baulked at the very notion of praying. God would know she had been coerced, that terror drove her to her knees, that a note of insincerity bubbled beneath her invocations. Perhaps the universal divine being that she had manufactured as a preference over the biblical God of the Old Testament did not care for her radical views on existence.

She silently repeated the phrase *an eye for an eye*, unable to steady her disturbed mind. Janey Mack handed her a full glass. She sipped on the cold clear water. Its icy freshness stung as she swallowed, and she made a silent promise. She would change. She would do her best to be a better person.

As she sipped, the memory of the Dolocher's attack erupted in a new set of flickering images. A series of half-lit contours and staccato grunts. She remembered him recoiling a fraction, his dark skull rocked a moment, his side flinched as the musket ball went through him.

Had she wounded the demon?

Janey Mack began to chatter, her little face glowing with a mixture of anxiety and relief and as she babbled Merriment began to feel curiously restored by the little girl's natural charm.

'Corker says it's a tall tale spun by Sol. But I said Sol has changed and how do you account for that? And Corker said, "A good fright disrupts bad habits for a while, but eventually the goodness wears off and the badness comes back, strong as ever." I think he's bitter, Corker, that is. I think he's bitter on account of his mam once fell down the stairs and broke her leg and was good as gold for two months and Corker was likin' her new mood and then she went wicked again, least that's what he told me and that's made him sceptic of anyone changing for the best. He reckons it doesn't last.'

'I see.' Merriment tried to sound interested. 'Well, time will tell, won't it?'

'That's what I said. I said, "Hold yer horses, Corker, last month ye were hustlin' over in Christchurch market and now yer workin' in a fine office with a fire." But he contradicted me there and said he's freezing the skin from his bones trekkin' up and down the town, selling *Pue's News*. But I said, "A fine friendship has developed between yerself and Sol and if ye think Sol will leave ye, why bother at all?" And he says, "We poor have no choice but to depend on the kindness of others." And I said, "What of it? If kindness comes, will ye not take it?" And he says, "It's like walkin' the plank: eventually y'er going to go in the deep end." And I said, "Y'er miserable even when good fortune shines on ye." And he says I'm gullible on account of I have landed in a fairy tale with you willing to look after me. And I said, "That's not gullible," and then he smirks at me, 'cause he's a tendency to smirk, and tells me I'll be let down yet. And I smirked back at him to annoy him, and I said, "That'll never happen." And the minute Sol walks in the room, there's Corker as chipper and full of jabber, all talk of court assizes and house meetings like he's a town official and him looking with big eyes up at Sol, like Sol himself stepped off a coach and four wearin' a crown. I was that cross with him sucking up to Sol with big doe eyes, I pinched him. He gave me a dig back.'

'Did he?' Merriment was glad to be distracted by Janey Mack's prattling.

'We're thinkin' of building a snowman later, out in front of the shop. I said we could put a sign on him.'

'What would it say?' Merriment asked.

'It would say, *Feeling better*, as if he'd been to visit ye, and ye fixed him up.'

'That's very clever.' Merriment sat up higher in the bed, shifting forward and propping more pillows behind her back. 'Now, if I'm going to get up at all I need hot water to clean this wound, and the *perigynium*. It's in a jar on the second shelf over by the retorts near the back door. It has a purple seal, you can't mistake it.'

'Right-o.' Janey Mack bounded off the bed. 'But ye'll not get up today. Sol was very stern about that. He says I have to do me best with the customers and turn away anyone I can't help until y'er feeling ready to stand.'

Merriment shook her head, certain that Mister Shelbourne's visit had culled her customers. 'I don't think . . .'

But Janey Mack was ready for a busy day. 'I know what the widow Byrne has, and I know where ye keep the stuff for Stella's dad, and Misses Lennon's husband's tonic is bottled and ready, ye did that yerself. And I know what the lad with the spotty face takes, and ye've lots of the calming powder crushed and ready to go in the brown envelopes. And I'll not give anything out to anyone new on account of ye not examinin' them. It'll be just regular customers only.'

Merriment glanced over at the dying fire. She thought of all the potions she had administered with a slight dilution of ingredients: all given out under the guise of sensitive care were recipes designed to quell feverish temperaments. They were a list of subtle tinctures and powders all infused with two certain qualities – to lift depression of the spirits and to stem violent outbursts. Was she truly being punished for her work? She thought of Lord Rochford and Peggy Leeson. Was it that she treated prostitutes and did not judge licentiousness? Something at the centre of her nature reeled at the moralising possibilities that resonated beneath the existence of a demon. She sighed and forced a smile onto her face. Now that she and the very fabric of society had been rent apart by the emergence of Olocher's black spirit, would she be singled out? She thought of Mister Shelbourne's fanatical religious zeal: *You are an aberration of femininity, a deviation from all that is encased in the very term woman, with your breeches and your pistol. A blight on the face of God's will, an abhorrent distortion of true nature. A hermaphrodite suckling on the teat of a devil.* She wound her fingers together and thought of packing up.

Her thoughts drifted to Solomon. Would he come with her? she wondered.

'I don't mind working,' Janey Mack was saying. 'I've to earn me keep, same as yerself, and ye've been so kind, it's the least I could do.' She cocked her head. 'And here's Sol now coming up the stairs.' She brushed her skirts down and tapped the cross around her neck.

'There you are.' Solomon beamed at Janey Mack as he passed by carrying a tray. 'And how's the patient this morning?'

'She shot the Dolocher and he ate the gun.'

'He what?' Solomon frowned at Merriment.

'Don't forget the shillin',' Janey Mack reminded him before she bounded down the stairs. Solomon stood blinking by the door, the hot food wafting tendrils of fine steam up around his face.

'You shot him?' He frowned, placing the tray carefully across Merriment's knees.

'He winced.' Merriment looked meaningfully at Solomon. While he poured her tea she asked him, 'Did you pick up my pistol?'

He shook his head. 'I don't think I'd have even seen it, Merri. The only thing I saw was you. There was a chest, I think; the contents were everywhere.'

'Rosie's.' Merriment nodded, accepting the cup of tea. Then taking a sip, she gazed over the brim of her cup, her eyes filling with a dark light. 'Makes you reconsider Pyrrho of Elis' second question.'

Solomon sank onto the bed beside her, examining her face, her mood, her state of mind. Merriment stared at the food on her plate, unable to bear the idea of eating.

'What is the Dolocher made of?'

375

Solomon took a breath, worried that perhaps she would need more medical attention. He wondered if another apothecary could prescribe something to quell the nervous anxiety obvious in the glittering motion of Merriment's eyes.

'He's made of Olocher's dead bones and a hellish swine,' he said.

'But he groaned.' Merriment floundered, examining the detail over and back, trying to recollect that moment.

'I presume he felt the impact,' Solomon ventured. 'There may be some life in the nerve channels, some feeling.'

Merriment frowned and shrugged.

'What if . . .' she sighed, the steam from her tea fanning over the cup and saucer. 'What if we could kill him?'

Solomon nodded, trying to keep his face expressionless. He pointed gently at the plate. 'You should try and eat.'

Merriment looked out at the glistening snow. The sky was thickening with clouds. She could feel her heart sliding away from her ribs, her mind running hot and anxious.

'Only the very good can slay the very bad,' she said softly. 'And I am not very good.' She paused, her mouth hovering above the cup as she recalled the Dolocher's gruesome pointed teeth.

'None of us are.' Solomon tapped her leg reassuringly.

'I might have to go somewhere else, another country.' Merriment's eyes suddenly beaded up. For the first time Fishamble Street felt like home. She blinked back the tears, not wanting to go back to sea, not wanting to have to sail away, but afraid to stay in a city where a demon roamed.

Solomon felt the proposal like a blow to the chest. His breath stopped, his mouth hung open. Merriment didn't look at him as she continued, 'Take Janey Mack, bring her with me. I lived in a place in Spain for a year. A quiet little town.'

'Don't.' Solomon shook his head and looked away, standing up to go. 'Please,' he whispered, but he knew looking down at Merriment that it was too much to ask.

Merriment seemed fragile and defeated and something compressed in his chest. She sighed, desperate to forget the savage attack, but all she could see was the Dolocher.

'His cheeks were puckered.'

Solomon stood and listened gazing down at the street below, his eyes drifting to the horns of the statue of Lucifer in Christchurch Yard.

Merriment slowly listed all she could remember. 'He had deep, deep sockets, I could see the white glint of bone around the cavities where his flesh had decayed. He had no eyelids, and blue eyes. They were bloodshot, and his gaze, not one I will ever forget.'

'I . . .' Solomon interjected. 'I never saw his eyes. Just empty sockets. Black.'

'I've seen his eyes twice, Sol: once outside the back door, and last night . . . They have an unmistakable quality.'

She shuddered and slid upright, looking at Solomon as he turned and came to sit down beside her.

'I saw a crocodile once, when we sailed to north Africa,' she told him. 'You look in a crocodile's eyes, you see something: a glinting otherness, there's no making a pet of it. Its being is wrought from dark river currents and its sole purpose in life is to bask and eat. And when it eats, its huge jaws snap open, crunching bones and muscles and ripping flesh, sending blood spurting into the water. There's no communicating with that kind of remoteness,' she said hoarsely. 'There's nothing to reach. The crocodile expends all its vigour and strength on the vicious pleasure of self-satisfaction.' Merriment took a breath, looking down at her hands a moment. 'That is what the Dolocher is: something archaic and unfettered, an abnormality from the sewers of Olocher's fetid imagination. He took great pleasure in beating me. But . . .'

She paused, her mind extracting the details, separating her thoughts from her feelings.

'What I mean is,' Merriment continued, 'I was thinking of Pyrrho of Elis' questions. You know, what is the Dolocher made of? There was peculiar ... A crocodile is a creature without wit, its calculations are callous and perfunctory. The Dolocher, on the other hand ... there was a quality to his eyes, an element of ... I don't know. His nature is atavistic, but there was an intelligence there, something almost human.'

Solomon smothered a disbelieving laugh. 'A remnant of who he used to be,' he countered. 'Think of it, the Dolocher is a malignancy constructed from the corpse of a man and somehow fused with the cadaver of a black pig. The last shreds of who he used to be as a man are somehow trapped in this monstrous reincarnation.'

'But he groaned.' Merriment floundered, examining the detail over and back, trying to recollect that moment. 'Why would a demon feel? Why would dead flesh still feel? Is it not beyond pain?'

'I presume,' Solomon ventured, 'there may be some life in the nerve channels, some sensations.'

Merriment frowned and shrugged. 'Then logically, if there is some kind of life in the nerve channels, as you put it, you have to ask ... can we take it away? What if ...' She frowned, the steam from her tea fanning over the cup and saucer. 'What if we could kill him?'

'How?' Solomon's brows shot up incredulously. 'How do you kill the dead?'

Merriment pinched her lips between her teeth, thinking a moment, holding her breath. Then, sinking back into the pillows again, she sighed and shrugged. 'I don't know. It's like trying to unpick oakum. I keep trying to pull apart the threads. I don't want this to be true.' She swallowed back her pain. 'I don't want there to be demons.'

'I know,' Solomon said, rubbing at the creases of his brow. 'But if we take the facts ... '

'Yes, the facts.' Merriment's face darkened, her eyes filling with an innate, keen intelligence. 'Pyrrho would carefully enquire, he would discern what the Dolocher is. How are we related? What's our attitude towards him?'

Solomon shook his head. 'We've done this, Merri. The Dolocher's a demon. We're his prey and our attitude towards him is one of fear.'

'But . . .' Merriment grasped at her half-formed thoughts. 'But he has weight, structure, bones, flesh, can feel pain.'

'So?' Solomon upturned his palms, perplexed.

Merriment sat forward, her hands literally trying to hold on to what she was instinctively beginning to feel in her gut. 'There has to be a rational, a reasonable . . .'

Solomon grinned at her and shook his head. 'Despite everything . . . You meet the devil and still you gravitate towards some secular.'

'Scientific,' Merriment corrected.

'Merriment O'Grady.' Solomon caught her fingers and kissed the tips. 'You are a force of nature.'

'You can't divert me with your good humour and kisses.' Merriment smiled squeezing his hand and letting it go. 'There's something not right here.'

'Well, I've been reading Pyrrho of Elis,' Solomon teased, 'and you neglected to tell me a few things.'

Merriment frowned, tilting her head to one side. Solomon obliged her with an answer.

'Didn't Pyrrho conclude that humanity cannot know the essence of things?'

Merriment squeezed her lips together, half pleased that Solomon was inspired to explore philosophy, half disappointed because she knew what Pyrrho had postulated.

Solomon walked to the window and took in a long breath. 'Didn't he say that we humans can only know how things "appear" to be?'

Merriment nodded and, feeling faintly resigned, she added, 'That it is impossible to know anything.'

Solomon looked down on the busy shambles. The fishwives clustered in groups furtively glanced up at him while they gossiped, obviously telling each other of the latest Dolocher attack.

'So by Pyrrho's reckoning,' he continued, 'we cannot know if the Dolocher is a demon or not.' Solomon turned and, exhaling, smiled gently. 'However, it is always best to err on the side of caution, don't you think?'

Merriment didn't respond. She lay looking out the window past him, her mind not fully satisfied.

Solomon came towards her and took the tray, his blond curls falling loose over his brow. His shirt was splattered with flecks of lard from cooking the uneaten breakfast.

'You should sleep,' he said softly. 'Someone from the Sheriff's office will be over later to take a statement. Stella is still below and I'm sure Anne will drop by. I have to . . .' Solomon trailed. What did he have to do now that he was leaving? 'Go to work,' he finished acidly. The idea of Merriment leaving cut him to the quick.

'Thank you,' Merriment whispered, and Solomon nodded, masking his upset with a mournful smile.

22

The Schoolhouse

The snow crunched beneath Solomon's feet as he fastened his jacket and hauled his cloak closed, bracing himself against the sharp wintry air. Corker walked beside him, his teeth chattering.

'Where to now, Sol? Skinner's Row or over to the beadles?'

'Neither.' Solomon shook his head; he couldn't face the office. 'To Purcell's Court.'

'Right-o.'

Traffic moved slowly; very few coaches had ventured out onto the icy roads. Hawkers picked their way towards the marketplace, carefully treading so as not to capsize the wares they were carrying. Everyone was late and as the Christ Church bells rang out over the snow-covered city word spread quickly that the Dolocher had attacked two more victims, this time after curfew. Corker was quizzing Solomon about Merriment.

'Janey said the Dolocher had cloven feet.'

Solomon didn't answer.

'That Merriment saw a bit of hell down through a crack in the ground and that it was sweltering hot and full of screaming victims. Janey thinks Merriment might be a bit touched.' Corker looked anxiously up at Solomon's face. 'I know ye like her and all, Sol, but she's met the devil and she may never be right.'

'She's fine,' Solomon snapped. Then, softening a little, he frowned, recalling their conversation over the uneaten breakfast. 'She was a lot better this morning.'

Skirting the market, they passed a cow that had slipped and broken its leg. The milkmaid who had led it into town was weeping and passers-by were trying to console her while someone ran to fetch a butcher to poleaxe the poor animal and put it out of its misery.

'Jaysus, the poor cow,' Corker sniffed as they passed.

'This way,' said Solomon, resolutely. He pointed up the narrow road and strode on, his mind a-swirling as he tried to figure out what to do. Dublin would be easy to leave, his time here had been mixed. Sure, he had a job and prospects but it did not pay enough to secure a comfortable life. Yet in the back of his mind he had begun to write a new future for himself. Him as editor of *Pue's Occurrences* living with Merriment O'Grady the apothecary. Their joint existence supported by each other's wages. Their life a comfortable tangle of routine and adventure. He had been altered from the haphazard insecure ways of a gambler and for the first time wanted to put down roots. To stay with a beautiful woman in a warm house, drinking fine wine, lost in conversation, lost in love. He bit down on his lips and glared at the white hard snow, the sting of disappointment wounding him bitterly. He gazed despondently before him, his footsteps crunching, his mind preoccupied, his heart sore in his chest. He should have been over in the office writing up about the new Dolocher attack. Merriment's stabbing. Rosie's dead baby. It was all so grim and suddenly pointless. If Merriment were to leave there was no reason for him to stay. And the shimmering promise of a bright, loving future was savagely cut off by a dead man's malignant spirit. Despite the grey-pink light, Solomon felt like something vital had been sucked from the world. He was to be denied a cherished hope and his very core blistered at the idea that his new life writing and living with Merriment O'Grady was to vanish and he was once more cast into uncertainty with little or no prospects.

A small white flake fluttered gently before him, tumbling right and left, see-sawing to the ground as more flakes began to fall. The snow shower was light and curiously hypnotic.

'What's up here?' Corker looked along the narrow laneway; the cobbles were completely covered in snow, only the barest kerb of the pavement could be seen and the red-brick buildings either side of them were laced with flakes. 'Is this where Merriment was stabbed?'

'Not far from here,' Solomon replied, already plotting his own departure.

What would he do about Corker? He rolled his eyes away, infuriated that the young lad would be devastated by his leaving. He wondered about having a chat with Chesterfield Grierson about giving him some sort of employment. Corker licked his lower lip, swinging his eyes from side to side, keeping a sharp look out, his heart suddenly racing.

'Doesn't come out in the day,' Corker mumbled, more to reassure himself than to start a conversation. 'They say the daylight scalds demons.'

Solomon didn't respond. Ahead he saw the painted sign for the Boar's Den tavern swinging from its wrought-iron holder. Down from the tavern was the walled schoolhouse protected by two large gates. Solomon stopped before them and tugged at the lock.

'Right,' he said, his face perplexed. The gate had been open last night.

'What do ye want to go in there for?' Corker shuddered, gazing through the bars at the deserted building.

'I . . .' Solomon wasn't sure why. Something dropped into the conversation by Fred, a cryptic remark about the 'blackguards smuggling in the Black Dog will soon be going back to school, for there was a new master in town'. Jessop had kicked Fred under the table, but Fred's erratic nature bubbled and frothed unchecked. 'What?' he protested accusatorily. 'I'm only saying they'll have to learn their lessons,' and this too, for some reason, made him laugh uproariously. It was later, after Jessop had thrown up and Fred had danced off, shadow-boxing and kicking the air about him, that Solomon had seen Fred again, swinging from the school-house railings, grunting like a monkey and pointing, before disappearing through the gate and vanishing into the snowy black.

Earlier on in the night, over a game of cards Solomon had managed to flush from the two men that the Black Dog was a centre of vice.

'I met the Keeper,' Solomon winced as Fred smacked down a card and laughed so hard his false teeth popped forward.

'Did he fleece ya?' Fred elbowed Jessop, knowing the answer to that question full well.

'And disagreed with where my nose had been placed on my face,' Solomon grinned. 'Nearly knocked my expression permanently to the back of my head.'

Jessop's huge shoulders jigged up and down but his chuckle was silent.

'I'd keep away from him.' Fred wagged a wiry finger. 'He's like a boulder rolling down a hill, once he lands on ye he'll crush ye.' He smacked three cards down on the table and rubbed his hands together. 'I think ye lost that one.'

Jessop quietly showed his hand and took the winnings. Solomon shuffled the deck ready to start a new game, nodding to Ethel to bring them more drink. Then, sitting forward, his shoulders hunkered, looking out from beneath his brows, Solomon quietly enquired, 'What's Hawkins' game over at the Black Dog, how wide is his scope?'

Fred tilted his head and tittered wildly, 'Look at him with his pretty visage thinking he can take the Keeper.'

'I was more interested in business.' Solomon sat back, letting Ethel refresh the tankards. Fred prodded Jessop in the arm.

'The milksop wants to play with the big boys.'

Jessop grinned and toasted Solomon's stupidity.

'Ever hear of Pearly?' Solomon attempted to catch them out, thinking the name might draw a response.

Fred shrugged. 'Sure, and Billy Knox and over the river the Cut with his fancy knife. We know all the boys, me and Jessop do. The high ones, the low ones, and they're all so busy cuttin' and slicin', carvin' up the city, not knowing what's to come . . .'

'Fred.' Jessop's huge hand closed around Fred's, crushing it tight. "Nuf said,' he growled and Fred chortled gleefully to himself.

'Too true, Jessop, too true.'

Then Fred pushed himself off the bench and did a ridiculous jig, waving his cap and arms to a round of applause, making everyone laugh, his mania weirdly disturbing.

Reading between the lines, Solomon suspected that a power struggle among the nefarious gangs of the city was about to kick off, and if that was the case he knew he had leverage. Pearly's meetings with Hawkins made sense now. He was exploring all options, working both sides, and, furnished with this knowledge, Solomon concluded that he could corner Pearly and negotiate a new arrangement.

He wouldn't tell Knox about Pearly's treachery and in return Pearly could settle his account.

Glad that the evening had not been wasted, Solomon walked Fred and Jessop out, watching them leave, the snow drifting lazily down out of the grey-black sky, falling in wide gentle curves around the two drunken men. They both stumbled down the road, Jessop swaying like a listing galleon, Fred hopping and jumping, before they both swung through the schoolhouse gate and disappeared into the dark. Solomon had gone back inside to convince Ethel to let him stay, flush with the satisfaction that two petty criminals had just helped him solve the problem of his gambling debt.

This morning the schoolhouse's chained gate piqued Solomon's interest. Merriment's insistence that there was something operating in the Dolocher that required closer scrutiny somehow melded with Fred and Jessop's behaviour as they left the inn last night. A jagged, tangential line of thinking pricked his curiosity. At the centre of last night's unfolding drama was an abandoned building, an old schoolhouse. Maybe it was nothing. He didn't know for certain why; all he knew was he wanted to take a closer look. He watched Corker pull a thin piece of wire from his pocket and begin picking the lock.

'Janey said Merri shot the Dolocher.' Corker wiggled the wire then paused to carefully lift up the inner mechanism, sucking on his lower lip as he concentrated. Solomon didn't answer. 'She said the bullet went straight through him and that he was that annoyed with the pistol that he swallowed it whole.'

But Solomon's eyes were searching the pavement, remembering Rosie's high-pitched scream splitting the air.

'Dolocher!' Rosie had only had time to scream the name once, but it was enough. Solomon remembered there were three of them left drinking in the pub. Ethel had wanted a lock-in, but most of her crowd opted to be home with their families, so only the single or most determined drinkers agreed to stay and spend the night sleeping on the crooked benches so long as Ethel kept the drink coming.

When Rosie screamed, the scattered few left in the dimly lit tavern froze, trembling. Ethel and her husband, both pale and blinking, grabbed a weapon: Ethel a large butcher's knife, her husband a rusty hook.

A half-blind, lame sailor jumped to his feet and, pointing a finger, shouted, 'Bar the door. Bar the door. Keep the bastard out,' but Ethel's husband led the charge, calling everyone to arms.

'There are plenty of us.' He pointed to the kitchen. 'Get a weapon, lads, there's a maid needs our help,' and fuelled by home-made poitín they bolted out to challenge the Dolocher.

Somehow Solomon was first on the scene. Through the falling snow, he could just about make out Rosie's form: doubled over and sobbing, she clawed at the ground, crippled with pain. Ethel and her husband ran up with a lantern, waving their weapons and shouting for the night watch to come and assist them. Solomon touched Rosie's head, but then noticed when he turned that there was another woman sprawled on the ground. The lantern, cast on its side next to her, spread a gloomy yellow wash over her body. And moving away, disappearing into the snowy darkness, was the unmistakable form of the Dolocher, its grotesque shadow elongated and hideously climbing over the snow-sprinkled brickwork of the surrounding buildings. Solomon caught the barest glimpse: the oversized head, the wisp of a pointed ear, the folds of thick flesh at the base of the cranium, the breadth of shoulders and a flutter of dark cloak. He stood a moment gazing at the narrow entrance to a side street, feeling suddenly nauseous. Then his eyes pivoted towards the woman on the ground, and his chest suddenly caved when he recognised the sweep of luscious red hair. He ran, knowing in his bones it was Merriment. Sure she was dead, he fell on his knees towards her, pulling her up, hauling her into his arms, willing her to be alive. Her body fell listless against his chest and for a while he rocked her, convinced she had been murdered and all his hopes condensed into a narrow leaden weight somewhere behind his ribs.

'There ye are,' Corker said triumphantly, as he popped the lock. 'Nice and dandy.'

'Good lad.' Solomon slipped in.

The yard was covered in a carpet of snow, stainless and virgin and absolutely level and flawless. Solomon trod through the thick covering, his footprints sculpting the fine white ice. The vacant schoolhouse had a peaked roof decorated with baroque swirls of granite that were mirrored either side of the keystones above each window. A plaster plaque over the right side of the building contained the word *Girls* while a parallel plaque on the left read *Boys*. In the centre, beneath the broken lattice moulding hanging from the gutters, were the ornately carved roman numerals *MDCXCVI*, denoting the year 1696. Solomon made for the door into the boys' side of the school.

'What are we going here for?' Corker asked, as Solomon twisted the door handle and pushed his way into the slender tiled foyer, now empty and freezing. The cloakroom stank of damp mould. Nailed to the wall were redundant wooden hooks and someone had left a battered lantern on one of the windowsills.

'It's like an icebox in here.' Corker shuddered.

Solomon shook the snow from his hair and glanced at the latched door directly ahead. He pushed open the bandy door, kicking it in when it caught on the warped floor tiles.

'There's this little man, Fred,' Solomon began to explain. 'I don't know if he was cutting through the yard or . . .'

Solomon stopped dead, astounded.

'Jesus,' he whispered, his eyes scanning the wide empty classroom before him. The partition dividing the girls from the boys had been disassembled and the chairs and desks were long gone. All that remained were the grimy walls, pierced by windows.

'What the . . .?' Corker stepped into the room, his blanched face looking left and right.

The walls were streaked with blood. Brackish runnels emanated from splodges of crimson and drips ran down the tongue-and-groove trim circling the lower half of the room. Blood stained the floor, running into the grout between the tiles.

'Did they kill the children?' Corker asked, his lower lip contorted with horror.

Solomon shook his head, stepping towards a bloody handprint pressed into the wall beneath one of the windowsills. He inspected the distribution of the bloodstains, noting the level and line of the smears. 'This hasn't been a school for years.'

'But there was murder done in here.' Corker's voice trembled. 'We've to get the beadles.' He stood shaking, circling on the spot, checking the walls behind him. He tugged Solomon's sleeve. 'The smell,' he complained. 'It's rotten. Is it cadavers?'

Solomon sniffed the sharp, bittersweet scent. 'Smells like . . .' The idea came swift and clear, and with it a new possibility suddenly sprang to life. Solomon frowned, staring a moment at everything around him. Had Fred and Jessop? Did they? It made sense.

'Smells like what?' Corker squeaked.

'Offal.' Solomon stroked his chin and stood a moment, contemplating a theory. 'I think,' he finally announced, 'this is where the slaughtered pigs vanished to.'

'Is it?' Corker gasped, astounded, his eyes darting quickly to the door, convinced that he needed to escape. He rolled up onto his toes, pitching forward, ready to run. 'Is this the Dolocher's lair?' He clutched at Solomon's arm. 'We should get out of here.'

Solomon didn't respond. His mind raced. A slew of new possibilities suddenly upended his understanding. Merriment's conversation this morning reverberated through his whole being. *Could it possibly be?* he wondered. *Could her instinct be right?*

'Sol,' Corker whimpered, his brown eyes flicking wildly about him, 'we should go.'

'Yes.' Solomon rounded on his heels and marched through the dank building, leaving the interior door open. He slammed the outer door shut and made his way through the thinning flakes towards the Boar's Den, his mood suddenly shifting from despondency to determination. This changed the complexion of everything.

'Do ye think the Dolocher will know we were here?' Corker trotted by Solomon's side, glancing back at the schoolhouse covered in a pristine layer of snow.

'Nope,' Solomon said firmly.

'Ye touched the handle. He might get a whiff of ye. And I might smell, I dunno, spicy or strong, on account of me youth. What if he follows us?'

Solomon replaced the lock on the gate and snapped it shut.

'Trust me,' he said, 'that is not the Dolocher's lair. Come on.'

They left the schoolhouse and walked up the narrow lane to the Boar's Den. Solomon's heart beat rapidly in his chest, his thoughts kept shifting and reorganising, orbiting the questions that Merriment had asked this morning. And, quickened by the scene in the schoolhouse, he began to ruminate on the implications of this discovery. While his mind burned, his heart began to muster. Perhaps all was not lost. And thinking of Merriment and Pyrrho's four questions, he rapped hard on the door to the Boar's Den. From somewhere deep within a voice growled, 'We're not open yet.'

'Ethel,' Solomon called. 'It's me, Solomon Fish. Let me in.'

Corker bit at the edge of his fingernails, staring down at the schoolhouse windows, keeping watch, wondering where the Dolocher slept during the day. While they waited, Solomon leaned on the door frame, his head bowed. 'Did you ever see Merriment's pistol?' he asked.

Corker shook his head. 'The Answerer,' he said. 'Janey told me about it. Said it was fancy with ivory on it and some patterns and ciphers.'

The lock behind the door squeaked as it was dragged back.

Ethel slowly pulled it open, her long, white face peeking around the door, her hard, sharp eyes tinged with fear.

'Did she die?' she asked hoarsely, the hair above her upper lip curiously visible in the bright light.

'No,' Solomon said. 'Can I come in?'

Ethel's lopsided shoulders fell. She swept a hand through her thin brown hair and stuck her filthy cap on her head, satisfied that the woman she had helped to patch up last night was alive to fight another day. She stepped aside and Solomon and Corker walked into the warm dark interior, letting Ethel slide the lock shut behind them. The room smelled of tobacco and wood smoke and sour beer and was so dark that Solomon moved slowly, giving his eyes time to adjust to the paltry light emanating from the dying embers of the fire. Ethel lit a candle and the flame shot upright, leaving a black trail of smoke behind it before settling and becoming steady. She went behind the bar, fetched three small glasses, pulled down a bottle of whiskey and, without asking, poured three shots.

'Some night,' she said, lifting the glass. 'To sinners, may the saints protect them.'

Solomon raised his glass and Corker copied him, all of them downing the whiskey in one gulp.

'Jaysus,' Corker coughed. 'It's stinging me throat. Have ye milk, misses? Me belly is on fire.'

Ethel gave him a lump of green cheese. 'Milk hasn't come yet,' she explained, and poured Solomon a second glass.

'I need to talk to you about Fred and Jessop.'

'Oh, aye.' Ethel's faded eyebrows barely lifted. Two spots of red popped onto her lined cheeks.

'What do you know about them?' Solomon asked.

Ethel took a quick swig and leaned onto the counter, her large breasts resting on her forearms. 'They used to work on the docks together. The both of them grew up in Rialto. They fight dirty and cheat at cards. Jessop did a spell in the army, long

391

ago. Fred used to be married but the wife ran off with a tanner and then Fred took up with some widow. Sure, he'd a rake of kids, eleven, I think, he needed someone to herd them home in the evening.'

Ethel kept the drink flowing and Solomon stared bleakly while she topped up his glass. He felt sick. Corker nibbled at the green cheese, surreptitiously letting it drop to the floor to get rid of it.

'Do you know who they're working for?' Solomon asked, gingerly twisting the glass between his fingers, too nauseous to bring the whiskey to his lips.

Ethel shrugged, her drooping goitre wobbling beneath her large chin. 'Why the interest?'

'Something . . . I just wondered if you knew,' Solomon said.

'Could be anyone, they're hands for hire. They're always over at the Black Dog, or drinking in the Sot's Hole, they're fast and loose, and not much good to no one. Although . . .' She paused a moment, checking Solomon's face. Last night's experience with the Dolocher had formed a bond. 'There's a rumour . . .' She sucked through the gap where her two front teeth should have been. 'Don't know how true it is,' she began. 'There's supposed to be some new boss in town. Fred, well, you know Fred, can't keep his mouth shut, said the ol' boys are in for a fright. The new boss is crafty. Said he's clever. Smart with a blade. Then he did a dance, 'cause ye know how Fred likes to dance, and said this new lad had outwitted the lot of them.'

Solomon turned the glass on the counter. 'Is he working for Billy?'

'That's what I'm saying.' Ethel downed her drink and poured another, her eyes glittering. 'According to Fred, he's not working for the usual spice or bowman-prig; this new lad, well, he's making his mark.' She sniffed and poked her finger into her right ear. 'All I know is that they're throwing coin around like they've no need for it. World knows their filching it, but how and where they're gettin' it is a dark business. Jessop does a bit of work over in the Black Dog; mind you, Fred's that sparky, I wouldn't let him near a powder keg.'

'What does Jessop do over in the Black Dog?'

Ethel scratched her huge chin. 'A bit of wheelin' and dealin' with the Keeper and the guards. Bringin' in scraps of contraband to sell to the prisoners. Sure, ye wouldn't know what the pair of them are at.'

'By any chance' – Solomon gripped the edge of the counter – 'do you know if they slaughtered any pigs the night the swine were killed?'

'Slaughtered!' Ethel's voice pitched and she flung her head back. 'Sure, didn't they organise the damn thing. They sat over there and smacked their hands together and Fred hopped up on a table, he's that short, and let out a whistle to get the attention of everyone in the inn saying, "Now, boys, there's only one way to catch the Dolocher and that's to slice his throat. And since he looks like a pig and hides among the swine, we'll kill every pig in the city, and as sure as the devil put him here, he'll die among the herd." And then he says, "Who's with me, boys? We'll catch the bastard, give him a taste of Dublin medicine. We'll get the devil by the tail and fling him back to hell." And sure the cheer that went up was mighty, particularly when he told them all that the drinks were on him.'

Ethel sniffed and dragged her huge hand beneath her drooping nose before wiping it on her apron.

'We did great business that night. The place was hoppin', burstin' at the seams. Sure the cellars were drank dry. The lads were armed with every kind of knife and sword and dagger; most of them were seven sheets to the wind, falling out of the door into the mist to kill any stray pig that crossed their path. Misses Higgins flung herself in front of her Daisy, but they hauled her away and killed the pig before her and she weeping and sobbing like a member of her family had been murdered. Bless the poor thing, she loved that pig.'

Ethel waited, expecting Solomon to ask her more questions. Corker looked around him, wondering if his mother ever came into this tavern to take a sup.

'Right.' Solomon nodded, satisfied. 'Don't let on that I was asking questions about them, Ethel.'

Ethel nodded briskly, corking up the whiskey and giving the counter a useless wipe with her filthy cloth.

'I take their orders, that's all, and listen to their blather. I keep me talk to a minimum. The less I know the better.' Ethel smiled, her breath sour and stinking as it passed through her rotten gums and teeth.

'Ye look pale,' she said to Solomon. 'I couldn't sleep a wink after. I kept seein' that little baby dead in the snow and his poor mother wailin' and mad with grief.' She scratched the back of her neck. 'But yer landlady is all right?'

Solomon nodded. 'She's hardy,' he said. 'She'll recover.'

Ethel nodded and, making a quick sign of the cross, she flicked her thumb over her shoulder. 'Himself is in bed, snoring his head off. He only fell asleep when the sun came up.'

'I left my belongings here.' Solomon pointed to the kitchen. 'Can I get them later?'

'Course ye can.'

'Will you get some rest before you open up?' Solomon asked kindly.

'Chance would be a fine thing.' Ethel rubbed her tired face. 'I've to put the stew on and do last night's dishes, wash the tankards and check the cellars. And that lump up in the bed will be kicked out of it soon. People are comin' in early for a drink and headin' on before the curfew. The damn curfew is wicked hard on business, but sure, the lock-ins keeps things tickin' over.'

Ethel walked them to the door and Solomon and Corker

squinted, the blinding light of the white world stinging their eyes as they stepped out onto the street. They said their goodbyes and for a while Solomon stood looking down at the deserted schoolhouse, his face locked in thoughtful determination. As he assembled the facts, he thought of Merriment and, inspired by the notion of a scientific approach, he knew where to go next.

'Will you go back to the office, Corker, and start drawing Rosie losing her baby. If Chesterfield asks, tell him I'm working on something. I'll be in the office later today.'

Corker nodded, shoving his hands into his pockets. 'Right ye are.'

'See you around two-ish,' Solomon said.

Corker set off towards Skinner's Row while Solomon turned down towards the Black Dog, passing a small crowd huddled around some stalls buying up stocks of bread and cheese, forecasting more snow to come and whispering about the awful attack over near Purcell's Court.

Solomon's brows pinched together as he mulled over this strange new discovery. The pigs had been secreted in the schoolhouse. It had been a culling carried out by a Dublin gang who had efficiently brought the carcasses to the abandoned building and let the city think that the Dolocher had dragged the corpses to hell. Piqued by the implications, he made his way to the Black Dog and, slipping into a side street, he waited.

He leaned against the teetering wall of the collapsing building perched on the corner and watched who was coming and going through the prison gate. A throng of ne'er-do-wells and grubby merchants passed back and forth. He saw tired-looking wenches carrying pitchers of white ale, a cobbler in a tattered jacket bent double under an enormous basket of wooden clogs. Wives and children called in to visit, some even bringing pet dogs and birds with them. He saw at least three Ordinaries come and go, and two undertakers, one leading an ass and cart carrying a selection of coffins. There were bread sellers carrying trays of loaves and fishwives with baskets of silvery stinking fish. A young chandler pulled a barrow of tallow candles behind him and limped his way into the yard. He saw Jessop loping his way out through the gate, this time without Fred following. Jessop veered up the street and disappeared through the crowd, heading for market, and behind him, wearing a new woollen jacket trimmed with beaver, was Hawkins the Keeper.

Solomon arched forward, peering round the brickwork watching Hawkins saunter away, a ring of heavy keys jangling against his thigh with every step. Emboldened by Hawkins' departure Solomon crossed the street and passed under the prison gate, swallowing as he climbed the steps, and pushed open the reception room door. Scattered over the benches and across the floor were groups of noisy visitors mingling with merchants, smoking tobacco and haggling over wares. The guards were relaxed and dishevelled, accepting mugs of sour ale and joking with the painted bawds who were leaving, and greeting the fresh supply of women who were coming in. The reception room was so crammed that Solomon didn't have to explain himself to anyone. He slipped into the green corridor, surprised to find that it was bustling as well, choked with visitors and a line of tourists who'd come to see where Olocher had killed himself. Solomon was astonished to find his broadsheets tacked to the door frames of some of the cells, and amused and perplexed by the general sense of freedom permeating the gaol. A mottled old guard with a lazy eye rang a bell and called for silence. 'Down this way here now,' he hollered, pointing a brackish-coloured index finger. 'This is where the Dolocher crept up.' And he led a straggling group of sightseers down towards the nunnery, leaving behind a handful of hawkers and the resigned inmates to finish up their business. Solomon made for Charlie's cell and was surprised to find a grizzled group of men playing cards over an upturned coffin.

'What?' a man with buck teeth snarled, his eyes flashing above the fan of cards in his hands. At his elbow was a beautiful cut glass filled generously to the brim with deep red Burgundy and in a crate by the corner were a dusty stack of at least twelve more bottles.

'Charlie?' Solomon wavered on the threshold.

'We diced him,' the man with the buck teeth chuckled, his brown eyes slanting with vicious delight, 'and we put his bits and pieces in here.' He walloped the coffin so hard with his palm that the glass bounced and teetered, splashing over the cards.

'Aye, here.' The kerfuffle sent chairs knocking back, and there were a couple of punches thrown and a lot of yelling. Solomon slipped away, looking in all the rooms as he passed, catching snatches of prisoners chatting. In one room a corpulent man wearing a dazzling necklace dictated his autobiography to one of the Ordinaries. There were prisoners buying soap, getting drunk, weeping, swiving, praying. Instead of heading for the nunnery, Solomon made his way upstairs and was surprised to find the upper floor eerily quiet.

A lone lantern hung on a hook, its feeble light mingling with the paltry daylight that slipped through the tiny Diocletian window high up at the far end of the corridor. All the doors into the various rooms were closed. The silence made Solomon's skin bristle. He tiptoed past several rooms, listening for the softest of moans, for whispers, for snoring, for any sign of life. He tested a door handle and held his breath as the door slipped quietly open. Inside was a deranged-looking old man tied to the bed, his clothes torn, his face cross-hatched with fresh scars.

'You've not come back,' the old man whispered confusedly, the whites of his wide eyes flecked with burst vessels.

'I'm looking for Charlie,' Solomon ventured.

'Yes, yes,' the old man agreed and Solomon quietly shut the door and tried the others. In each room he found anaemic-looking inmates, all terrified, all injured, all cowering. One man offered him money; he unfurled his palm and exposed the corpse of a mouse. 'A guinea, sir, the charge for my freedom.'

Solomon took to tapping on the doors and whispering into the doorjambs, 'Charlie.'

Finally someone whispered back breathlessly, 'Yes?'

Solomon turned the handle, the door creaked open and there, sitting on a tattered cot, wearing a shirt and wrapped in a blanket, was Charlie. His young face was white with terror; his fine blue eyes sparkled with confused horror. Solomon crept in and quickly latched the door behind him.

'Please, don't hurt me,' Charlie whimpered.

'Charlie, it's me.'

'You sent the lady with the pistol,' Charlie said, dropping the blanket and revealing his arm splint. 'She told Hawkins she'd be back to see me, and if he so much as touched a hair on my head she'd tell Beresford and Beresford would sack him. You should have seen Hawkins spewing lies and smiling and trying to be courteous. He went to touch her and she pulled the pistol on him. Showed him she was no doxy. Hawkins went puce trying to be contrite, saying how she got the wrong end of the stick and that he never meant to insult her womanliness and then . . .'

Solomon cocked an eyebrow, interested to hear that Merriment had defied Hawkins. *Could that be why . . .?* he wondered, a theory coalescing as he considered all the facts.

Charlie trailed off mid-sentence, his face frozen, his eyes still.

'What was that?' he whispered. 'Did ye hear that?'

Solomon shook his head.

'I wanted to ask you a few questions.' Solomon lowered his voice, afraid he would soon be found out. He leaned forward, but instead of interrogating Charlie, he furrowed his brow and whispered, 'You do know the door is open.'

Charlie nodded. He was about twenty years old, and now

that he was sober his manner betrayed a hint of aristocratic breeding. His room contained a Chinese locker and a painted commode, and to one side of his bed was a sturdy chest, open and filled to the brim with books. Leaning against one of the leather-bound volumes was a statue of Mercury carved from black onyx, holding a gold caduceus.

'You can escape,' Solomon told him.

'All the doors are open,' Charlie whispered, his long mouth twisting with revulsion. 'The curse of Tantalus,' he hissed. 'They do it on purpose. Tempt us to risk bolting. Say that our freedom is a whisker's breadth away, that we can dare to try and leave. But the minute we are caught, and they swear we will be caught, they will flay us alive. They beat one man to death for having the gall to try to escape. None of us will contradict them. Hawkins is omnipotent. He has a lackey in every nook and cranny in the city.'

'Does he?' Solomon's eyes narrowed.

Charlie shrugged his shoulders. 'We are damned.'

Solomon got straight to what was on his mind.

'Did Hawkins kill Olocher?'

The question made Charlie frown. 'Why are you here?' he asked.

'Just investigating something,' Solomon whispered. When he stepped forward to sit on the bed, Charlie flinched and withdrew into the corner. Solomon put up his hand, showing his palm.

'Shh,' he whispered. 'I found Boxty, the first night the Dolocher appeared.'

Charlie swallowed and nodded at this piece of information, his sleek black hair falling down over his eyes, his pale fingers clutching at the grey blanket that encircled him.

Solomon asked, 'The night Olocher committed suicide, was Hawkins here?'

Charlie shook his head emphatically.

'No, that night Martin Coffey was on instead. He said Olocher slit his own throat. He was mad with rage. He and Hawkins had a right set-to. Hawkins went to hammer him and Martin kicked him so hard in the crotch that Hawkins fell over and wept for his mammy. I heard the whole thing. The Dolocher taking Martin was the Dolocher finding one of his own. Martin was a bad man.'

'Was he?' Solomon sat on the hard edge of the bed and stared at the straw strewn over the flagstone floor. 'Do you think Hawkins killed Martin after the beating?'

Charlie sucked on his upper lip, thinking this over. 'The Dolocher got Martin.' Then he breathlessly added, 'I saw him.' Charlie stared earnestly into Solomon's face, letting his last statement land.

'You saw him?' Solomon whispered. 'The Dolocher? You saw the Dolocher take Martin?'

Charlie tentatively touched the fingers of his left hand; they poked out from the hard wood splint wrapped in a creamy bandage.

'I saw the Dolocher, before Martin went missing and after Boxty had a stroke. He was laughing. I was drunk out on the corridor, weeping at my predicament, and when I looked up, there he was leaning down over me, laughing. I saw his tusks, his rotting flesh. He told me to get up. "Charlie," he said, "you're a blackguard and a wastrel," and he dragged me by the hair and flung me back into my cell.'

Charlie blinked and a stray tear trickled down the side of his face.

'This place is wicked. I'm wicked. I shall roll in the fires of hell, for I'm lost to this world.'

Somewhere in the far distance they heard a door slam. Charlie gave a little whimper and hid his face with the blanket. Footsteps receded and a second door shut, followed by a protracted silence.

'He spoke.' Solomon contemplated this new piece of information, his eyes narrowing as he collated everything he had heard. The Dolocher could speak, had blue eyes and knew the prisoners by name. The demon's preternatural qualities began to diminish, straining under the weight of new information. 'He knew your name?' he said, tugging the blanket away from Charlie's gaunt face.

'The devil knows the black secrets of the heart. Why wouldn't he know my name?'

Solomon's expression darkened. He sat for a moment considering.

'What are you in for, Charlie?' he asked.

Charlie's blue eyes searched the air vaguely, like he couldn't remember why he had been imprisoned. 'Seditious pamphleteering,' he said finally. 'And I've managed to extend my sentence by not paying Hawkins enough for my lodging. The man says I owe him two hundred pounds.' Charlie's pale face blushed. He began to shiver involuntarily. 'I'll never see daylight again.'

Solomon sighed and stood up to leave.

'Have you no family?'

Charlie swallowed back a chunk of tight tears. 'I am dead to them. My incarceration brought great shame to my parents. They packed up and went back to London, left me to my politics, left me to rot here, never spoke one kind word or offered one kind gesture.'

Solomon knew it was by stealth and sheer good fortune that he had managed to avoid being flung into debtors' prison, and looking down at Charlie trembling in a knot on a miserable prison bed, he saw how forlorn and desperate a situation could be compounded by the harsh cruelty of others.

'When the Dolocher comes,' Charlie said, staring bleakly at the floor, 'and he will come, because he knows my name, I will take his hand and walk with him. He can rip me limb from limb and then this will be over.'

Solomon wanted to touch Charlie's shoulder, wanted to say something to give him a shred of hope.

'I will see what I can do,' he whispered hoarsely.

Charlie turned his face away, hiding his upset.

'Don't,' he mumbled. 'Leave me alone.'

And Solomon slowly and carefully opened the door, crept out into the corridor and snuck quietly down the stairs. The tour was now squashed into a condemned man's cell, with a further twenty or so voyeurs crammed in the corridor, all trying to hear the man's last words now that he had only hours to walk the earth.

'Tomorrow I'll swing. Tonight I'll dine with the Dolocher. I'll give him yer best. Tell him to shove yer righteous faces right up his gaping arse.'

'Have ye no remorse?' one woman ventured.

'Only sorry I didn't take my women two at a time.'

There was an uproarious cheer and the condemned man burst into a bawdy song, roaring the chorus, while the tourists laughed and joined in. Solomon pressed his way through the reception room and out into the wintry afternoon.

The bells of Christ Church pealed through the intermittent snow. Twelve rings. Midday. Solomon fastened his cloak collar and made his way to Ormond Street, his brain organising and rearranging the titbits of information he had gleaned last night from Fred and Jessop and this morning from Ethel and now Charlie. Merriment's words rang in his ears: 'But he has weight, structure, bones, flesh, can feel pain.' Emboldened by a growing conviction, he marched through the city.

The snow thinned to fine powdery flakes as he turned down New Row onto Cutpurse Lane and then onto High Street, his heart pattering unexpectedly. Even in daylight he couldn't help but feel his chest tighten as he remembered the Dolocher leering down over him, a living macabre gargoyle suspended above him in the darkness. He carefully examined the tall buildings to his right and left, and noticed, sandwiched between the high wall and the weavers' meeting place, a singular building, an old Dutch Billy house. It was four stories high, with a distinctive cornice of Portland stone carved into elegant baroque swirls that framed two dormer windows. The front door was to one side and painted cavalry blue. It was humble and without a fanlight. The second-storey windows had no ledge but those on the third and fourth floor did, and Solomon stared, recalling the backlight of buttery yellow that had illuminated the Dolocher's head.

It dawned on him that the miraculous and unexpected emergence of the Dolocher through a wall, floating high above him, could well have been the demon lifting a sash window to look out at the street below. And the terrestrial nature of the explanation filled him with a curious excitement. Everything began to make sense. He needed to tell Merriment.

He let out a long sigh and hurried across the road to survey the house, the preternatural qualities of the Dolocher evaporating, while a sinister theory exploded fully formed in Solomon's mind. He wrote down the address and headed away, slipping his notebook and pencil into his pocket.

It stopped snowing, but the sky was thickening with fat yellow-tinged clouds. Blue smoke trailed from the chimneys and the world looked beautiful; every imperfection, every squalid setting, the rooftops, the roads, the trees, all were covered with white. Children ran about screaming, flinging snowballs and sliding down Lazer's Hill in makeshift sledges. Small birds puffed up their breasts and pecked wildly at any stray speck on the ground. And hanging in the butcher shop windows on Ormond Street were sides and hinds of pork, with severed pigs' heads decorating the sills and large signs jokingly advertising *Try a Bit of Dolocher, Makes a Fine Supper!* Solomon paused, looking at the prices, before stepping into one shop and joining the long queue.

403

He bought a side of ribs for half the usual cost and heard a cluster of women talking about how the Dolocher had cut out an unborn child and taken it away.

'Happened down near Smock Alley last night,' one woman said, shifting the toddler in her arms to her other hip. 'She was with her lover, rushing home before the curfew when the Dolocher attacked.'

As his meat was being parcelled up in brown paper, Solomon listened to the chatter, amused that Merriment had been mistaken for a man, no doubt because of her breeches and her pistol.

'Dolly Shelbourne's husband says the apothecary is a witch, brought the Dolocher with her back from sea.'

Solomon was intrigued by the circuitous ramblings the imagination could take once an idea took hold. It was a plump woman with wild red hair who set the queue straight.

'Dolly Shelbourne's husband's as pious a missionary that would bore the ears off yer head with his constant quoting. How his mother didn't throttle him in the cradle for his pontificating ways is a wonder to all and sundry and she the greatest hell-cat ever to walk the streets of Dublin. How a Bible-thumping pious Joe like that should emerge from such a jilt is a riddle the devil himself can't figure, and as for Misses O'Grady's misfortune, I am only delighted she didn't perish on account of her havin' reinvigorated my Ned.'

'Jaysus, poor Ned,' someone piped up. 'He'd want the strength of ten horses to cope with you, Molly Jenkins,' and everyone laughed.

'We'll send you out, Molly. Ye can lash the Dolocher with that tongue of yours, flay him to death, ye termagant.'

Far from being insulted, Molly regaled the crowd with quips on how she'd brace the Dolocher between her thighs and smother him with her breasts. And the assault on Merriment and Rosie deteriorated into a comedy about how all the

Dolocher wanted was a fine Dublin woman with a bit of go in her to sort him out.

Solomon took the ribs and hurried out into the snow, racing to Skinner's Row, keen to finish up his business early. The office was hot as an oven. Corker was asleep before a blazing fire, and sprawled over the desk was an ink sketch of Rosie giving birth in the snow with the Dolocher crouched over her.

'Corker.' Solomon flicked the young boy's ear. 'Uppity-up-up.'

'Sol?' Corker squinted. 'I must have dozed off.' He ran his hand through his tousled hair. 'Where to now, Sol? The court assizes? The beadles' office? The garrison on duty last night?'

Solomon pinched his nose and glanced out the office window. 'We don't go to print until Tuesday night.' He slipped his hands into his pockets. 'I want to look into a few things.'

Across the way, two pigeons cooed and pecked along a length of guttering. Solomon slapped the side of ribs he had left on the table. 'Do you know how to cook pork?'

Corker shrugged. 'That's women's work.'

'Listen to me,' Solomon instructed, 'I want you to go to Ethel's first and fetch my stuff.' He flung him a shilling. 'This should pay for a chair, saves you lugging things through the snow. Go back to Merriment's and put the griddle on the fire. Oil this, salt it and sprinkle it with rosemary. Don't ask Janey to do it, she's busy.' He wagged his finger. 'When the griddle is scorching hot put the ribs on it. Make sure they sizzle. It has to sizzle,' Solomon insisted. 'It'll take well over an hour to cook. I'll be back by then.'

'But what about the schoolhouse?' Corker squeezed his lips together, sulking at the idea of doing a girl's job.

'I still have a bit more investigating to do. Meanwhile, we'll have delicious crackling for supper.' Solomon tweaked Corker's cheek and ruffled his hair, curiously feeling in better humour. 'Now, run along.'

*

405

Merriment was sitting up in bed surrounded by books. She had been visited by Anne and Stella and, despite Mister Shelbourne's accusations, the shop was busier than usual, most of the customers crowding in to hear Janey Mack's account of what had taken place the night before.

'Misses O'Grady was helpin' Rosie, who wasn't well' – Janey Mack was standing on the counter and pointing up at the ceiling – 'when down out of the sky in a whirl of snow came the Dolocher, with the ends of his cloak blazing, the hem still burning from the fires of hell and he screaming like a banshee as he tumbled down out of the rooftops. The Dolocher rushed at her meaning to gore her with his tusk, but she had her pistol made of fine Damascus steel and didn't she point it and shoot him square between the eyes.'

The room gasped, enthralled by Janey Mack's eye for detail.

'Like she did her lover,' a tall woman with thick black eyebrows told the room. 'Song says she shot him straight between the eyes when she caught him walking along with his lady gay.'

'That wasn't true.' Janey Mack clacked her tongue. 'The song got it wrong. Johnny Barden became an ostler, settled in Liverpool with a wife and three children.'

'But she'd a brace of pistols.'

'She didn't,' Janey Mack sniffed. 'She'd a single pistol decorated with ivory and rifled to make it shoot better, but that didn't knock a whit out of the Dolocher. All he did when the musket ball ripped through him was whelp like he'd been stung by a bee, for that's what the musket ball was to him, nothing more than an irritation.'

Janey Mack satisfied her audience with choice details. 'His hands had long black nails pared to points and his feet were cloven. Large boils burst across his chest and there were gaps in his ribs where his rotten flesh had fallen through and bits of bubblin' intestine could be seen glistenin' between the bone.'

She told them that the Dolocher took Rosie's baby and almost got away with it only Solomon Fish arrived with the militia. When Corker popped his head in and tried to get Janey Mack to cook the pork, he was roundly chided and sent into the anteroom.

'I'm workin',' Janey Mack hissed down at him. Then, turning back to the crowded shop, she said, 'Now, everyone, ye've to purchase something to assist the patient upstairs. We've powders for to calm the nerves, drops to stop the tremors and drive away the terrors, we've tea to cool the mind and honeyed wine to help ye sleep.' Janey Mack nodded at Anne, who had volunteered to stay and work. 'Ye tell me what yer ailment is and I'll do me best and ye give Anne the payment over there.'

Meanwhile Stella was upstairs feeding Merriment fish stew and telling her over and over again that she would have to leave early.

'My father was in a state when I got home, thought I was surely dead. And to think . . .' Stella pressed a hanky to her mouth; her long face looked drawn, her eyes marked by dark circles. 'Ye were almost killed by it.'

Merriment nodded mournfully. 'Thank you for staying.'

Her neck was badly bruised. Large blue patches spread around her gullet and up towards her ears. She accepted the flowery shawl that Janey Mack had given her and wrapped it about her throat to hide the discolouration.

'Used to be me ma's,' Janey Mack had said softly and Merriment patted her cheek and smiled.

Stella slipped away, leaving Merriment alone. She lay back on the pillows, looking out at the sky, and wondered if Solomon would come home early. She wanted to talk to him, wanted to see him. She had relived last night's attack over and over, and with each recollection she became more certain that something wasn't right. She gingerly held her side as she settled further in the bed, longing to see Solomon's face. She wanted

407

to hear his voice, to tell him she had no intention of leaving Dublin, not now, to ask him to come back, to have him put his arms around her. She closed her eyes, remembering Solomon's spontaneous kiss, and imagined him kissing her again, only to have the Dolocher's malignant face intrude unexpectedly. And as she tried to sleep, snatches of last night's attack erupted violently into her mind: the pared white teeth, the oily snout, the roar and grunt, the eyes glaring, the hollowed sockets, the weight, the pressure. She jolted, her arms thrashing until she realised she was in her bedroom. Sinking back, she blinked at the dimming light, amazed that somehow she had slept. She listened to the fishwives in the shambles packing up their stalls and, smoothing her fingers over the bedclothes, she drew in a long deep breath.

'Up,' she instructed herself, keen for distraction while she waited for Solomon to come home. She pushed aside the covers and climbed out of bed.

*

Over at *Pue's Occurrences*, Solomon tapped on Chesterfield Grierson's office door.

'Come in,' Chesterfield called. 'Ah, Solomon.' He smiled sombrely, lowering his glass and leaving it to be contemplated upon later. 'Dreadful news about your landlady. Corker says you found her.'

'Yes.' Solomon inspected the map of Dublin pinned to the old cabinet and surveyed the red dots sprinkled across it.

'I've added last night's encounter.' Chesterfield pointed to a red dot carefully coloured at the beginning of Smock Alley. 'There has been a meeting of bishops and talk of carrying out an exorcism. We should write an editorial. We should mention Prudentius.'

Chesterfield offered Solomon a glass of port. Solomon shook his head.

'You don't happen to collect recent crime reports?' he asked. 'Do you have anyone who collates complaints? Or do I need to visit the beadles myself?'

'We wouldn't be an instrument of up-to-date information if we did not collect the most recent travesties of the law. What do you think they are there for?'

Chesterfield Grierson waved at the mountain of files piled onto the table nearest the fire.

'Excellent.' Solomon began rooting through the folders much to Chesterfield's chagrin.

'Please, please,' Chesterfield winced. 'Philmont is meticulous. Allow me. Don't mess with his excellent filing system. What are you looking for exactly?'

Solomon pointed at the map. 'I want any information on robberies carried out near Corn Market House.'

Chesterfield nodded. His long fingers skated up the stack, drew out one and pulled a sheaf of loose paper from a folder marked with purple string.

'See, it's organised according to quadrants on the map. He's colour-coded the districts,' Chesterfield explained.

'Thank you,' Solomon said, immediately scanning the reports from the Thomas Street beadles' office, while Chesterfield amused himself quoting Prudentius.

'"'Tis said that baleful spirits roam abroad beneath the dark's vast dome; but, when the cock crows, take their flight sudden dispersed in sore affright."'

Chesterfield looked bleakly at the glass of port warmly reflecting the fire's glow. His quote fell on deaf ears. For a while he stood watching Solomon read.

'Did you know that the word *hell* relates to the word *hole*?' Chesterfield said at last. 'It's derived from the Anglo-Saxon word *helan*, meaning "to hide".'

'Is it?' Solomon was only half listening. Chesterfield was in a gloomy mood. He had overdone it at Margaret Leeson's

Dolocher party and now was wracked with guilt for merely having imagined what it would be like to roll with Margaret on a soft bed. Because of his sinful imaginings, he indulged in remembered fragments of scripture and oddly gathered facts relating to the devil.

'The word *devil* derives from the Old English *deofol*, which means "a nuisance" and is related to the Greek *disbolos*, "an accuser" or "slanderer".'

No reaction from Solomon. Chesterfield gazed into the flames flickering over the logs in the fire.

'In ancient texts, demons were considered to be mischievous or malignant entities with unnatural abilities,' he said. 'Normally they didn't appear in a religious context, it was only later that the belief emerged that demons could possess people. Then they were held responsible for causing disease, even splits in the personality, and in that context the word *demon* evolved from the Greek *daimon*, emanating from the verb "to divide".'

Solomon nodded absently and slid his finger along a list of names, noting the dates of court applications, and quickly read one plaintiff's testimony in particular. *I had two fine candleholders made of beaten silver and a porcelain vase given to me by my mother-in-law. I had four knives and forks and twelve silver teaspoons and a clock that came from Italy and chimed on the hour. Three hairpins were taken, one carved from ivory and inlaid with mother-of-pearl, one with a gold filigree border and the other shaped from gold and silver intertwined. All my lace mantles were taken and . . .*

'Ulrich Molitor was a professor of law at the German University of Konstanz.' Chesterfield gave in and sipped at the glass of port. 'Responsible for the publication of *De Lamiis et Pythonicis Mulieribus*. Anyway, in it Molitor says that the devil can shape shift into any form he wants. Like our Dolocher taking on the form of a pig. Of course, for a long time pigs have been associated with demons, and the goat; actually the goat is

410

probably more commonly considered a satanic creature.'

Chesterfield Grierson looked out the window. 'And women,' he added forlornly. 'They are long affiliated with demonic forces.' Chesterfield moved across the room and sat in a fine embroidered chair, crossed his legs and recalled the bacchanalian delights of the previous evening. 'Some women are so pretty,' he sighed. 'And they move . . .' He waved his hand. 'They have limbs that seem to glide and sometimes they allow their fingertips to linger, and I swear to God the fire they stoke with their pert lips and silky tongues, like delicious succubi . . .' Chesterfield closed his eyes a moment, wishing he had never seen Margaret Leeson and her den of iniquity. His head hurt and his heart was filled with shame. He was so preoccupied with the ailing condition of his dilapidated soul, and promising to never, ever again allow a sinful thought to take full form in his mind, that he did not notice Solomon grab an armful of files and maps until it was too late.

'Where are you going with all of that?' Chesterfield half rose from his chair.

'I need to study these,' was all Solomon said. 'I'll be back for more.'

'I don't think . . .' Chesterfield protested mildly, but Solomon was already down the stairs and out in the street hailing a sedan chair.

'Wait here,' he told the carriers. 'I've more to fetch.'

He was rushing out of the office when Philmont beckoned him and quietly asked, 'Mister Fish, I've been calculating the takings and there is a matter of five shillings outstanding.'

Solomon's stomach lurched; he tried to hide his fluster as he recalled handing over the five shillings to Pearly at knifepoint in the alleyway.

'Yes, yes, I know about that.' Solomon turned and promised, 'That'll be sorted.'

He loaded up the chair and instructed the carriers to walk with him under Skinner's Row Gate out onto Cork Hill and over to Fishamble Street, his brain buzzing, trying to figure out how quickly he could replace the money he'd taken to pay off Knox. He ruminated over possible solutions, leaving the carriers to grumble all the while that the snow was bad for business.

'Bloody Aldermen refusing to throw down hay or sand or boards at least, useless bastards.'

When he pushed open the door into the apothecary, it was empty. The bell that announced customers tinkled cheerfully, the notes bouncing over the glass cases, but no one appeared. He went back outside, his breath coming in white billowing pillows from his mouth. Overhead the sky was dimming, the clouds scattering, and a handful of bright stars glittered yellow-gold above the rooftops. The fishwives were packing up and the market traders were making their way home early, cautiously navigating the cobbled streets. The snow had already begun to harden and crunch underfoot. The chair carriers were sharing a nip of brandy when Solomon scooped up an armful of files from the velvety interior and asked them to give him a hand bringing in the remainder. He was stacking the scrolls over the countertop when Janey Mack stuck her head out of the anteroom.

'Sol!' she beamed, then calling back over her shoulder she chirruped, 'Sol's here.' She jumped out into the shop, grinning, and announced, 'We're dividing the pork,' her eyes wide with appreciation as she watched Solomon pay the chair carriers handsomely for their trouble.

'What's all that for?' She pointed at the papers, but Anne emerged from the anteroom, rushing past and calling 'wait' to the rheumatic men, who were lifting the chair ready to park for the night and head home. 'Can ye take me to Hanbury Lane?'

'But the pork?' Janey Mack wailed.

'More for you,' Anne grinned, pinching the little girl's cheek as she dived into the chair and snapped the oak half-door closed.

Janey Mack waved her off and locked up, turning the sign in the window to read *Closed*.

Across the way, a man swinging a silver-topped cane, dressed in a thick worsted jacket and wearing a beaver-trimmed hat, idly occupied himself by pushing the snow off the edge of the path onto the road with the tip of his boot, his eyes occasionally shifting over to the shop. On seeing the sign flipped, he drew out his pipe and lit it, watching two drays pulling a wagon full of freshly barrelled porter manufactured at the brewery on James Gate as they sloped past.

Solomon found Merriment standing at the table dividing out the darkly coloured ribs, while Corker's eyes bulged with disbelief and Janey Mack stared at the meat being portioned as though if she looked away it might disappear.

'Jaysus, me mouth is watering that much, there's no point in swallowing, just gushes back up again.' Corker could barely breathe with anticipation. 'Doesn't it smell that fine? Must be how King George eats every evening.'

Janey Mack picked a little grit off the griddle and popped it into her mouth.

'Hey!' Corker jolted her, then looked for his own piece of grit to steal.

Merriment smiled at Solomon and said, 'Thank you for supper,' but there was something about his expression that made her pause. He stood at the threshold, his sombre face lit by the lantern near the door, his expression intense and curiously anxious, and without coming in he indicated that he wanted to see her in the shop, away from the children.

Merriment responded to his signal and handed the little girl a fork. 'You divide out the potatoes, Janey.'

The shop was filled with brooding shadows. The countertop was obliterated by wads of bound manuscripts and scrolls, and Solomon looked agitated and uncertain as he stepped close to her, taking her arm and quietly clicking the door shut.

'Are you fit and well enough to be up?' he asked.

'Yes,' Merriment nodded.

413

'You're sure?' he checked again, his expression full of concern.

'Yes,' Merriment reassured him.

He reached for the shawl about her neck and slowly drew it back, wincing at the purple bruises spreading in a dark fan up towards her ears.

'They look bad.' He swallowed.

Merriment nodded, her fingertips reaching for his hand.

'I . . .' She needed to say something, but all she could remember was the brush of his lips on her mouth. Solomon's expression darkened.

'Merri,' he said softly. 'Something's happened.'

Merriment stepped away and covered her neck up again. A creeping fear seeped through her skin as the daylight dimmed and night approached. She glanced nervously towards the window. A man with a cane looked over from across the street. She closed up the shutters and doubled checked the door was locked. As she stooped over another candle and lit it, she tried to reassure Solomon.

'I feel better,' she told him. Then, noticing the agitated light in his eyes, her brow crinkled and her head tilted to one side. 'What has happened?' she asked.

'Somehow,' Solomon began, 'a criminal gang is using the Dolocher to cover their operations.'

Merriment drew her brows together and looked to the scrolls Solomon was pointing at, listening as he outlined the details he had discovered.

'Yes,' she nodded, gleaming with satisfaction as she encouraged Solomon to show her the files. 'I knew it.'

*

Janey Mack and Corker sat furtively in the anteroom, picking at their feast and wondering what Merriment and Solomon were whispering about.

'Do ye think he's leaving?' Corker ventured, his huge eyes bulging with terror.

Janey Mack shook her head. She pushed a potato around her plate, licking the last of the ribs.

'The papers are from Chesterfield's office. Do ye think Sol's been sacked?'

Janey Mack clacked her tongue, affronted. 'I don't know why they said we've to stay in here. What's to be spoken about that we can't listen to?'

Jumping off her chair and creeping towards the door, she put her index finger to her lips, warning Corker to be quiet. She pressed her ear against the dark wood, the candle throwing a soft pallid light over her face. All she heard was mumbling.

Solomon and Merriment worked under the glare of five candles and spread a map of Dublin over the counter. Merriment fetched a bottle of green ink and a quill and as Solomon called out addresses she began to draw green x's all over the map.

'You're well enough to do this?' Solomon checked again, his eyes full of concern.

Merriment smiled. 'I'm made of sterner stuff, Sol. And you have done a fine evening's work here.' She pointed the quill at the map. 'Now, carry on.'

Warmed by the fact that Merriment had used the shortened version of his name, Solomon felt a flicker of hope. Full of admiration for her fighting spirit, he paused over an open file, his eyes lingering a moment on her face.

'Go on,' Merriment encouraged him. 'What else?'

'This is dated the night I saw the Dolocher, from 4 New Row, the Dutch Billy house. Among the items taken were two candleholders made of beaten silver and a porcelain vase.'

Merriment marked a green x on the map, then she stood back.

'Look.' She shook her head, incredulous. 'There are three here. All in close proximity to sightings of the Dolocher. All in Thomas Street.'

Solomon stood near her, his arm pressing gently against hers.

Merriment gazed at the map, her eyes following the tendrils of alleyways drawn in spidery ink, edged by rectangles shaded grey, all representing homesteads. The network of backstreets near Copper Alley and on over to Cornmarket were scored by red dots and green crosses.

'This is extraordinary,' she said, examining the evidence, animated by the facts spread before her. 'How are they doing it? How do they know when the Dolocher will strike? Do they know his lair? Is he under their control in some way?'

Solomon shook his head, 'I don't know. That's where I hoped you would apply your reasoning.'

Merriment laughed a little, then sucked a short sharp breath through her teeth, quickly holding her side to decrease the darting pain. 'My reasoning, I see.'

Solomon leaned towards her, pleased to see a return of Merriment's spirit, longing to draw her body nearer. 'Well, it was you who brought about this revelation.' He slipped his arm around her waist.

Merriment stepped closer. 'Is that so?'

'This morning, your conversation got me thinking, made me see things differently.'

'Did it?'

A sharp, urgent rap came to the shop door, rattling the hinges. Merriment jolted and stepped back. Solomon blinked and caught his breath.

'I'll go.' Solomon stroked her arm.

'Wait.' They both stood frozen, the blaze of white candles flickered as a second rap came to the door, making Janey Mack peek fearfully out from the kitchen.

'Is it the man come to take ye away?' she asked, her little face floating pale over her dark shoulders.

Solomon's features compressed, darkening. He glanced at Merriment's pinched face, his fingers finding her hand and squeezing lightly as his heart pounded in his chest.

'O'Grady,' a confident voice called in, 'it's me.'

Merriment let out a sigh, rallied and grabbed a candle, shooing Janey Mack back into the kitchen before unlocking the shop door. Ashenhurst Beresford swept in on a cool Arctic breeze, wearing a dark naval cloak over a jacket trimmed with gleaming brass buttons.

'Is it true?' he asked, his hand falling protectively on Merriment's shoulder.

Merriment nodded, latching the door. 'You got my note.'

'What note?'

She looked perplexed. 'I sent it by messenger yesterday.'

'I got nothing.' Beresford gazed down at her, his sharp profile handsome and full of power. 'Is it true you were attacked?' He undid the shawl at her neck and, seeing the bruises, drew her into his arms. 'My God,' he muttered. 'My God.'

Merriment shifted uncomfortably.

'Sorry, you're hurt.' Beresford kept his hands on her upper arms. However, it was not only the wound in her side that made her flinch; rather she was piqued by Beresford's gush of affection. He thought he still had a claim on her, a claim beyond friendship, and perhaps three months ago she would have enjoyed that distinction, but now . . . Now there was Solomon.

Solomon looked on, his mind reeling. Merriment had called for Beresford; it was him she needed comfort from, him she turned to, him she wanted. Devastated, Solomon turned away, feeling suddenly like an intruder. He began to gather up the files and scrolls, but Merriment drew Beresford over to the counter.

She pointed at the map scattered with red dots and green crosses. 'Solomon has uncovered something extremely bizarre.'

'Not just me,' Solomon interjected. Then, catching Beresford's hawkish gaze, he muttered softly, 'Merri.'

As they explained, Beresford listened, his hawkish eye examining the statements from the court assizes and carefully inspecting the maps. 'How are they doing it?'

Solomon's brows raised. 'That's the question.'

'Unless . . .' Merriment pressed her bandaged wound, her face darkening. 'What if the Dolocher is controlling them?' She waved her hand over the map, two flecks of red popping into her cheeks as she excitedly theorised, 'It's human.'

The reduction of the Dolocher to the position of crime lord threw a unifying light over the map and files as they excitedly assembled the information.

Beresford inspected the map one more time and, snapping up straight, said, 'Well, here at least we have some way to start. There must be eight gangs in the city.' Beresford stroked his jaw. 'We should strike while the iron's hot, give them no time to scarper. Maybe with the curfew things are quieter, but a raid on the most notorious dens might kick up something. I'll get on to the Sheriff.'

'A force to accompany us would be nice,' Solomon admitted, his face vibrant with purpose. 'But there's only one place we need to go. One man we need to question.'

23

Torched

A new moon hung over the spire of Christ Church Cathedral. The empty streets were eerily lit by the freezing snow, which cast a bluish hue that vanished down long, desolate alleyways. The cold night air was strangely silent as the citizens of Dublin barred their doors and windows half an hour before curfew, calling in their hounds and fixing traps with large iron teeth at the thresholds, keeping rapiers and blades, pistols and tacks and every kind of makeshift weapon close to hand. Over doorways they hung crosses and scapulars and clutching their Bibles and prayer books gathered in one room, everyone fearfully listening to the slightest creak, petrified that creeping down the stairs or up from the cellar was the Dolocher.

On the slope down past Saint Audoen's Church, the cool blue glare of the snow-shrouded steps was lit by three flickering lamps, beneath which a tight group of heavily armed military escorted Solomon, Merriment and Beresford. They walked past Cornmarket and turned down Cooke Street. The soldiers moved swiftly, their boots crunching in the frozen snow, their eyes brightly alert as they made their way to the Black Dog Prison. Beresford had quickly galvanised the patrol, using his military connections and meeting up with an army captain he had once fought with aboard his ship, the *Livid*. Amused to find two children in Merriment's back room, Beresford arranged for an armed guard to stay at her shop, while she insisted on the satisfaction of finding out where the Dolocher was emerging from. Now, caped and armed, keeping close to Solomon and tightly surrounded by a party of twelve soldiers and Captain Willis, who according to Beresford could shoot the eye out of a snail, she felt a mixture of tingling excitement, undercut by waves of anxious anticipation. Glad to be surrounded by armed guards. Glad to be close to Solomon. She kept step with him, occasionally glancing up at his pale face lit by the cool blue reflection of the snow. He looked ghostly. Handsome. He tapped her hand reassuringly and she slipped her fingers around his for a moment and squeezed, communicating her relief that he was there. She gripped a borrowed pistol in her other hand, starting at every noise, attentive to every crunch and rattle, her eyes gliding up, up at the towering houses past the snowy gables at the hard dark sky where remote constellations glittered. The snow snapped icily under foot, the cobbled streets stretched eerily white far into the distance and this extended vision of a pallid, frozen world filled Merriment with an uncanny sensation, like she was walking in another land filled with a brittle silence and the possibility of another encounter with an interloping malevolent being. Should they meet the Dolocher now . . . She swallowed back her nervousness, quickly looking at Solomon. He gave a reassuring smile, his fingers gently tapping the base of her back as they made their way, curiously quiet, past the high wall of the Black Dog Prison.

The gaol's snow-capped walls were heavy and imposing beneath the sickle moon. The braziers at the entrance made the steps glisten silver and orange. As they crowded into the reception room, a stunned coterie of rough-looking turnkeys sitting around a table playing cards froze mid-game. All of the players were too surprised to swipe away the brimming tankards or the three bottles of Burgundy wine, too shocked to close their mouths and scrabble to hide the winnings or knock away the box of imported snuff and grab their weapons and pretend to be working.

'Would be about right.' Willis winked and Beresford unsheathed his rapier and let the blade glint before snapping out, 'Hawkins?'

An ancient guard with a pronounced lower lip pointed slowly at the large green door that led to the cells. He gawped, astounded at the cluster of soldiers, the long-haired woman carrying a pistol and the blond-haired man in oxblood boots, who he thought he recognised.

'Stay put,' Willis ordered two of his men, 'and make sure none of them move.'

The soldiers cocked their weapons at the turnkeys, who grumbled that a spot of card playing on a winter's evening to while away the long hours was hardly an offence.

'Is if the wine's stolen,' one of the soldiers grinned.

'A gift, from Jimmy the Squire, before they hung him,' the fat-lipped guard countered.

Solomon flung open the door into the dark corridor expecting a burst of noise and clamour, but all that greeted him was the dank gloom and the muffled sounds of some inmates quietly conferring. On Willis' command the guards meticulously entered every room, upending furniture and quizzing the prisoners.

Solomon climbed to the upper storey, pushing open door after door, meeting one miserable inmate after another, some pathetically asking if they had been pardoned, others so petrified that they whimpered into a corner and cried. Merriment stayed close to him, her eyes flitting down the passageways as she watched Solomon's back, the pistol Beresford had given her primed and ready to cock should she need it.

'The doors are open,' she whispered, perplexed, as Solomon pulled a torch from the brazier and climbed a further set of stairs.

'I know.' Then, pausing a moment, he told her, 'I haven't been this far,' pushing open a warped old door with iron-riveted

421

hinges and a circular handle. The door creaked into a narrow sloping passageway filled with clutter and dust and broken furniture.

'Just storage,' Solomon whispered, drinking in Merriment's proximity as she leaned against him and peered over his shoulder into the musty gloom, her breath warm against his neck.

'Stacked to one side,' Merriment remarked, her eyes adjusting to the poor light. 'Like a path. Is that a door?' She pointed the glossy black barrel of the pistol to the far distance.

'He's not here.' Solomon turned, his face suddenly close to hers, their mouths almost meeting. For a second they were suspended on each other's breath, their bodies compressed by the confined space, their lips magnetically close. Solomon wanted to kiss her; instead their attention was drawn away by the torch flame searing a large drooping cobweb, making it glow, like gold filigree suspended from the dusty rafters.

Merriment slipped by and, taking the torch, she crept past the stacks of broken chairs and tables, past old frames, crates and barrels; her eye curiously drawn to the almost imperceptible gleam of the door handle, polished by use rather than attention. She observed the lack of cobwebs over the door frame and was drawn by the tantalising position of the door itself. The feeble rays of the torch fumbled in the gloom, as Merriment crept along the clear path, Solomon close behind, their heads bowed to avoid the sloping rafters. The musty air was suffocating, the dust curiously scented with coal and a bitter overnote that Merriment thought might be cheap brandy. She swallowed back, her heart pounding, her eyes wide, her brain reeling. *What if he's here?* she asked herself and recalling the Dolocher's bristling head she jolted to a halt.

'What is it?' Solomon asked.

Merriment shook her head. 'Nothing,' she whispered, steeling herself. She reached for the handle and turned it. The narrow door opened and an overpowering admixture of squalid smells, brine, chopped liver, brandy and coal slack, issued from the gap.

'There's a room,' she whispered, her voice catching on the rancid atmosphere. She peered into the dark windowless interior. 'It's empty.'

They both entered and moved towards a small four-poster bed hung with lush purple curtains. Merriment's eyes were instantly drawn to the line of strange objects dangling from the carved bedhead. A withered dead bird hung with one eye popped out of its socket, the lustrous iris glittering like a circular gem on the black feathered neck. A bleached sheep's skull gleamed dully, its bone eerily white against the dark carved post. Below it was a talon tethered by blackened sinew and beneath that a strange appendage that looked curiously like a digit.

'I think this is a finger,' Merriment whispered, leaning in and instantly recognising a knuckle joint and finger nail. 'It is,' she grimaced, retracting her head, her eyes flicking over the dishevelled and filthy bedclothes, where, scattered among the folds, were odd accoutrements: a saddle, a candlestick and a ticking clock. 'Is it a prisoner's room?' she wondered, her eyes landing on a fine lace collar discarded on the mantle next to a small basket of expensive candles. Solomon flicked open the lid of an ornate gold box.

'A brooch,' he said, stepping off the fender and knocking over a large pair of worn boots that leaned against the carved legs of a fine armchair.

The grim room had been painted a gloomy ochre and appeared to have been only recently vacated. Solomon was examining a torn scabbard when Merriment turned to say something to him. Staggering slightly, she whimpered, her words catching in her throat. He looked up at her and when he did she was frozen in terror, her eyes fixed over his shoulder, her face blanched. She opened her mouth but her voice was dry, soundless.

There was something behind him.

Merriment stumbled backwards, the gun trembling in her hand. Solomon spun around so quickly that the torch made a low muffled *whoosh* and sent a shower of sparks erupting through the pungent air. He cried out, his body jolting involuntarily, his pupils dilating as the flames flickered over the awful shape lurking in the corner. There was a sudden explosion, a sharp phosphorescent flash accompanied by a loud rupturing bang, sending such a deep vibration through his bones that Solomon was momentarily deafened; his ears rang with a high-pitched squeal, his whole body rippling with the shock of the gun going off. And swaying in the browny gloom was the Dolocher, his pale skin glistening, his tusks a dull white, his body gliding side to side, moving like an otherworldly being, his empty eyes filled with the hollow darkness of the grave.

Petrified that Merriment's bullet had done no damage, Solomon yelled and charging forward shoved the torch into the Dolocher's mouth with such force that the flames momentarily spat from the eyes and singed the fine hairs on its scalp so that black vaporous trails issued from the ears. Solomon pushed with all his might, sending the Dolocher back into the stinking shadows. The fizzle of burning hair and the hiss of charred flesh crackled as the Dolocher resisted, his flaming jaws spitting fire as his teeth bit down on the torch and his whole head began to swivel, turning unnaturally so that Solomon lost his footing and plunged into the wall. He pivoted to face the creature, vaguely aware of the thump of feet climbing in the distance, his mind reeling with confusion. The Dolocher swung violently, turning right to left in a juddering semi-circle, the partially extinguished torch sizzling in his mouth, the black bristles on his jowls bursting into quick-burning flames. But the Dolocher did not lunge at him, giving Solomon time to realise that the beast's drooping shoulders were draped over an open sternum that showed the empty cavernous hollow of lined ribs. For a fraction of a second he feared the Dolocher had burst from the split belly and slithered away up the chimney, but the gleaming S hook shining from the rafters told a different story.

Solomon and Merriment looked at one another and in an instant they understood, and that understanding came in an ominous surge, rolling in from all sides. What had been centred on one dark principle, the fulcrum upon which the unspeakable evil of the Dolocher pivoted, now dissolved in this tiny hidey-hole in the Black Dog Prison. The macabre and gruesome idea of a demon melted from the dehumanising capacities of man's imagination. The preternatural disintegrated into the natural. Heaven and hell collapsed into the grotesque nature of the criminal mind and the gothic terror that had gripped the city dispelled in the chilling, cold light of revelation.

The Dolocher was a demonic disguise. Nothing more than a hollowed-out carcass worn as a hideous mask.

Stunned, Solomon blinked incredulously at the grisly revelation before him.

The shot had raised the alarm, but when Beresford and some of the militia burst into the room they were greeted by Merriment waving her hand and telling them to stand down. She pointed at Solomon, who was prising the torch from the Dolocher's jaws. One of the guards cried out with fright.

'It's a carcass,' Merriment reassured him. 'Hanging from a butcher's hook. Look.' She directed their gaze, her face luminous with a mixture of incredulity and relief. 'We have all been tricked.'

Captain Willis inspected the disembowelled corpse.

'It's magnificently fearsome.' He shook his head. 'Taken out of *situ*, I mean. If we saw it in the butcher's shop, we wouldn't bat an eyelid. But here . . .'

He paused, curiously relishing the unusual sight before him,

425

on some level admiring the dark ingenuity that had come up with the plan.

'And by your reckoning, Solomon, we have the man who used it as an engine to terrify us all. Clever really, if it wasn't so distasteful. Hiding out here, in his own prison. He had us all fooled.'

Merriment tugged at the dishevelled pile at the foot of the bed. Some objects fell onto the floor with a thud. She saw a glimpse of ornate ivory and recognised the polished Damascus steel of the Answerer. She drew it up between her forefinger and thumb, shaking her head.

'I knew. It was his eyes . . .' she muttered, but all around her was busy.

'We need to move quickly and stealthily,' Beresford insisted. 'Make sure Hawkins doesn't get wind of the fact that we are onto him. He's not in the gaol.' He quickly scanned the room, noticing the chest of stolen objects beneath a pile of robbed clothes, and snapped into action, asking Captain Willis to send two of the guards back to the barracks to get more men.

'We need to search the town for Hawkins. He has to be somewhere local. And two should remain here and make an inventory of the stolen items' – Beresford pointed to a pair of guards gawping at the dead pig swinging from the ceiling – 'then bring them to the beadles' office on Thomas Street.'

Captain Willis took a pinch of snuff and waved to the soldiers singled out by Beresford. 'You heard the man. Gather the items, make a note, no filchin' mind, put them in some-thing.' Snapping the snuffbox shut, he tossed it to Beresford and winked. 'There's no more men over in the Royal,' he informed his friend. 'This is it.'

Merriment was about to stuff the Answerer into her waist-band when one of the soldiers held out his hand and said, 'Sorry, miss, evidence and all.'

She looked forlornly at her pistol, not wanting to give it up. 'But I only found it.'

'Ye'll get it back.'

She passed her weapon over and stepped out of the way, watching the guards rip down the bed curtains and empty armfuls of stolen objects into the thick velvety material, whispering to one another about hiring a cart to get all the stuff transported.

She approached the swinging carcass, her fingers reaching out to touch the cold, silky pigskin. It slid beneath her fingertips.

'What the dark imagination can produce,' she said quietly and Solomon stroked her arm reassuringly.

'Hawkins will swing for it.'

A hue and cry came up from below. Everyone was swift to react, rushing down the stairs. Hawkins had emerged from the nunnery, where he had been so engrossed in the occupation of roundly beating an inmate that he had heard nothing of the military search over the wails and cries of the prisoner he was torturing. He was confounded to be greeted by two armed guards who insisted he call out his name. What identified the Keeper was a fearful prisoner who peeped through the food slot and hissed, 'Hawkins, y'er for it now.' The alarm raised, Solomon and Merriment were last down the stairs to see Hawkins, red-faced and panting, his knuckles raw from his night's work, crudely shaping up to the circle of soldiers around him.

'What's this?' Hawkins rasped, astounded to be cornered in his own gaol.

'We have you now, you reprobate,' Beresford snarled.

'What?' Hawkins jolted backwards. 'The blackguard needed chastising. How else will he reform?' he spluttered, pointing back down to the nunnery.

'Don't deny it,' Beresford growled as Captain Willis ordered his men to make the arrest. Hawkins retreated towards the wall, his eyes exploding with fury, a spray of spittle drenching his chin.

'Arrest me!' he howled. 'For what? For doing me job? The inmates have to be cajoled, otherwise there would be no control. They would be lawless, left to their own devices, robbing the eye out of each other's head, not paying their way. It'd be mayhem.'

'Strap him in irons.'

'Wait, wait.' Hawkins flattened himself against the wall. 'What are the charges? You can't believe what any of them says.' He pointed at the cells. 'They're all born liars.' Then Hawkins' jaw dropped, his eyes rolling upwards as he caught sight of Solomon. He recognised his face.

'Him,' he roared, pointing a bloodstained finger. 'That pretty boy has a bone to pick with me. He's a liar. Whatever he told you. He's a liar.'

'Get the manacles,' Beresford shouted.

'I asked yez, what are the charges?' Hawkins bellowed. 'I only ever did me job. This is a stitch-up. Do ye hear me? A stitch-up.'

'You're arrested on two counts of murder, including the killing of an unborn child.' Beresford stuck his blade under Hawkins' pointy chin. Hawkins' eyes bulged huge in his head, his mouth dropping open, his tongue wagging black and bulbous in his mouth.

'Murder,' he sneered.

'And for robbery and for posing as the Dolocher and terrifying—'

'I never,' Hawkins roared, his face puce with a mixture of fury and incomprehension. 'Are ye out of yer minds? The Dolocher is the devil's charge.'

'Your room is being dismantled as we speak and the evidence of your malfeasance is being collated for your trial.' Beresford stepped back to allow the young guard to handcuff the reluctant keeper. Hawkins put up a vicious fight, taking on five of them, his fists flying, his legs kicking. They had to pin him to the floor and kneel on his back to get his hands chained.

'I don't have a room upstairs,' he kept whimpering as he was flung into one of the empty cells and left with two armed guards outside his door. 'I'm not the Dolocher. It's not me. Let me out. Let me out. The Dolocher is a demon. If I were him, would I not defy these chains and drag yez all to hell? It's not me. Are yez mad? Let me out.'

Hawkins roared and bawled and thumped on the door, kicking at the panels and flinging anything he could against the walls.

'He's enough strength anyway.' Beresford scowled, leading the others back into the reception room where the speechless turnkeys who had heard the racket sat gawping at one another, swallowing with disbelief.

'Well now,' Beresford grumbled, slumping into a fine leather chair and swinging his legs up onto the table, 'isn't this a sorry shop. The House of the Sheriff and Commons will tidy this cesspool up, and you' – he stabbed a finger at the turnkeys in their crumpled uniforms – 'you degenerates better cough up all you know if you don't want to march to Gallows Green with the Keeper there.'

The turnkeys groused and shifted while Captain Willis ordered the two soldiers guarding them to wait for the Ordinaries.

'When they come, get them to take statements.'

Then, reassuring one spotty young soldier that the streets were now safe since the Dolocher was nothing more than a dead meat mask, he ordered the young lad to rush to the Sheriff's office at the Castle and ask to speak to a Mister Ward. 'He'll send us a bunch of Ordinaries to mop up this lot's lies.' He smiled broadly when Beresford bellowed, 'They'll swing from the gibbet if an untruth passes their measly lips.'

Beresford jumped to his feet and circled the table. 'You leave nothing out,' he warned. 'I want everything you have on Hawkins, his methods of extortion, his smuggling . . .' He picked up the unlabelled bottle of wine and sniffed the dark rich aroma of cherries flush with spicy notes. 'Damn me, only the best for you rogues,' he snarled. Then, pulling fresh bottles from the cask under the table, he handed one to Solomon and Merriment and nodded to Captain Willis, indicating he should look after himself.

'Come on,' Beresford said to Merriment, 'I'll escort you home.'

*

Solomon looked at his half-full glass. The wine glowed a rich ruby colour and tasted very expensive. He stretched his legs out in front of the warm fire and waited, the drink easing into his being, helping him to unwind. In the distance, he heard the night watch announce it was ten o'clock and all was well. Somehow it felt a lot later. He let his head hang back and listened. Merriment and Beresford were at the shop door saying goodbye. It had taken half an hour to get Janey Mack to bed even though Corker was sick of telling her that Sol and Merri had solved the mystery.

'It's not that,' the little girl had protested, wondering who the man with the eyepatch was. 'It's . . . I'm in the habit now, of being frightened.'

Solomon put Janey Mack into Merriment's bed and told Corker to set up on the cushions before the fire.

'Your mother'll be worried,' he remarked, but Corker shrugged.

'She'll not even notice.'

While Solomon told Janey Mack the story of finding the carcass one more time, because the little girl wanted to catalogue all the minutia of the grisly revelation, Beresford stood next to Merriment in the anteroom and accepted the glass of wine she offered him.

'Thank you.' He unfastened his cloak and cast it over the arm of a chair. 'How are you feeling?' he asked.

'Astonished.' Merriment stood next to him, warming the backs of her legs. 'I mean, last night, at first, I genuinely thought I had been attacked by a demon. I can't tell you how relieved I am that my gut instinct . . . I just knew something didn't feel right.'

'You're so level-headed,' Beresford interrupted, resting his glass on the mantelpiece. 'I've always admired your capacity to be measured, stay calm under pressure.' He slipped his fingers onto her outer hip and turned her towards him. 'Merri,' he whispered, lowering his mouth towards hers, but before he could kiss her, Merriment stepped away. She let out a short sigh and smiled a little nervously.

'I . . .' she began, not quite knowing where to start. 'I am not for you, am I, Ashenhurst? You have your wife, and Peggy Leeson; you have no room for another.'

Beresford's eye danced with an amused light. Shifting uncomfortably, he nodded and patted her shoulder.

'You want me to choose? That is no problem.'

'No.' Merriment raised her hand, stopping him. 'It's not that. It's . . .' She paused, looking at the gap in the door that led out to the shop and upstairs to the man putting Janey Mack to bed.

'*I've* chosen,' she said firmly; and the words unchained her, freed her from all her previous romantic tragedies, liberated her from her past. She was in love, it was reciprocated, and all she needed to do was honour the truth of her own desire and stake her claim. She wanted Solomon and no other would do.

Beresford paused, frozen, searching her face. He heard Solomon walk the floorboards above and fully understood who Merriment referred to. Aware that the woman he had taken for granted for so long was no longer to be called upon when it suited him, Beresford nodded stoically and took in a deep breath.

'I see,' he said quietly. 'He's a lucky man.'

431

'So were you.' Merriment's eyebrows rose playfully; then, adding what she sincerely hoped would be true, she said, 'We won't let romance get in the way of good friendship, will we?'

Beresford studied her face and with deep affection said, 'We most certainly will not.'

When Solomon returned down to the kitchen Merriment and Beresford were drinking wine. They poured him a glass.

'To a good night's work,' Beresford toasted. Then, standing by the fire, he looked into the flames and shook his head. 'You can't fathom that kind of distorted thinking,' he said and Solomon watched Merriment sink into her chair, her glass balanced on her thigh.

'You have to admit it was a macabrely ingenious way to clear the streets,' she agreed. 'Fooled us all. Ask Solomon, he'll tell you, last night, I thought I had looked into the devil's eyes.'

Beresford shrugged and drained his glass. 'How do you know you didn't?' he asked, cocking his head to one side.

'Because the carcass hanging in the Black Dog would assert otherwise,' Merriment countered.

'No.' Beresford sucked on his bottom lip. 'You being a woman of philosophy, if you push your rationale a little further. Think of it: in a way, a devil did attack you. I don't know, maybe Olocher poisoned his mind, although . . .' He paused. 'I can't help suspecting that Hawkins was born bad. I'm sure if you dig deep enough you'll find he's killed prisoners.' Beresford left his glass on the mantelpiece. 'Well, there'll be an investigation and no doubt you'll be given the keys to the city.' He grinned at Solomon. He grabbed his cloak and bowed swiftly. 'You did a good job, sir, a very good job.' Beresford's words rang with a note of loss. Solomon had done more than a good job solving the mystery, he had managed to capture the heart of a fine woman, and as Beresford held Merriment's gaze, he communicated the full impact of his sorrow. The look was a lingering one of 'goodbye' to an old romance.

432

Solomon misunderstood it completely and felt cut to the quick. He bowed his head and looked away, embarrassed to be present at such an intimate moment, when it was obvious that they wanted to be alone.

'I should go.' Solomon shifted.

'Finish your drink.' Beresford swept towards the door. 'My night's work is not over. I'll report to the Sheriff, but I'll see you soon,' he said pointedly to Merriment, and Solomon's heart jolted, disappointed and confused that he had misread all of Merriment's tender looks.

Beresford grinned mischievously. 'That matter with Mister Shelbourne will be easily resolved.'

'Excellent.' Merriment grabbed a candle to walk him out.

'Although' – Beresford's hand gently touched the hollow of her back, leading her towards the door – 'you're sure you're not a witch, with your potions and enchantments?'

'Very amusing,' Merriment smirked.

Solomon smarted as he observed the casual familiarity between them. He dropped down into his chair and sipped his wine, his eyes drifting sadly over the anteroom, memorising the details. The polished copper retorts, the peculiar glass pelicans used to distil oils, the dark glass bottles of tinctures, the jars of pickled roots and paper bags of dried seeds, the boy in the oval frame. He would miss everything. The warmth, the fire, the furniture, Merriment. He settled his glass on the arm of the chair and smiled dejectedly when Merriment returned and sat down opposite him.

'I can't believe it.' She shook her head, her eyes shining brilliantly. 'Such a bizarre thing to do, don't you think?'

Solomon nodded.

The snow began to fall outside; a gentle wind drove the flakes into swirling eddies.

'At least we can return to normal.' Merriment could feel her heart lightening. 'For a time there . . .' She pinched her lower lip between her teeth, almost embarrassed by her belief that her only hope of protecting herself from the Dolocher was to flee to another country and to take to praying. 'I thought I might have to become a nun,' she chuckled.

Solomon smiled gloomily.

'Now that all this is over,' he said and looked into the fire, turning the stem of the glass in his hand, 'I thought I might go to London.'

'But, what about your job?' Merriment craned forward. 'What about Corker?'

She looked suddenly stricken. Solomon thought of Beresford embracing her and answered sombrely.

'I can get editorial work elsewhere. I'll sort Corker out before I go.' He stood up to leave, unable to bear the weight of having to let everything go.

'Don't,' Merriment whispered.

Solomon stared down at her. She gazed back up at him, her breath coming soft and shallow, her eggshell skin glowing delicately, the candle flame highlighting the earnest expression in her blue eyes as she rose out of the chair and stood near him.

'Please,' she said.

And Solomon swept his arm around her back and drew her towards him.

24

Actus Reus

The morning light poured through the unshuttered window infusing the room with a mellow glow. Merriment awoke warm in the bed and lay looking up at the ceiling. Solomon wrapped an arm around her and drew her in.

'Morning,' he whispered. 'You look serious.'

Merriment curled towards him. 'Just hard to believe.' She cast her eyes to the window where the sky over the rooftops dramatically unfurled in orange and yellow streaks and a line of pink clouds began to dissolve into thin white feathery cirrus. 'He seemed such a little man,' she remarked.

'Hawkins' – Solomon kissed her face – 'had fists like hammers. You saw what he did to me.'

'I keep seeing the Dolocher floating in the corner behind you. Every time I shut my eyes there's his ghastly form emerging from the shadows.'

Solomon pulled her tight and stroked her hair. 'It's over,' he said soothingly.

'God knows when I'll get the Answerer back.'

'Are you planning on shooting somebody?' Solomon laughed.

Merriment swept her arm over his chest and for a while they lay silent, listening to the distant gulls complaining and the sound of the traders beginning to negotiate the snowy streets as they made their way into the city.

'I really contemplated,' Merriment said at last, 'after what happened to me. I really did begin to think that perhaps there were such things as demons and angels.' She drew herself away to look in Solomon's face. 'The idea of another world infiltrating this one, sending evil . . .'

'Are you disappointed to find that it was Hawkins all along?' Solomon leaned up on his elbow and brushed his tousled hair away from his eyes.

Merriment's expression darkened. 'No, not at all,' she said firmly. 'But,' she kissed the tips of Solomon's fingers, 'this whole experience has upended my thinking completely. Now we have to move to the refined realm of intention. Was Hawkins poisoned by demonic thoughts?'

'I'm poisoned by demonic thoughts.' Solomon grinned and teased her seriousness, rolling over her. 'I'll let you go when you've kissed me. We should move to the refined realm of my intention,' he announced, his hand gliding along the outer edge of her thigh.

'You've had enough,' Merriment laughed. Playfully pushing him away, she warned him, 'You know what they say, too much of a good thing . . .'

'I think you'll find the expression is: you can't have too much of a good thing. And you . . .' He paused, looking down at her, his face suddenly serious. 'You are that rarest of all things.'

Merriment's eyebrows raised. 'God almighty,' she smiled. 'You're very poetic in the mornings.'

Solomon grinned and rolled over. 'That's not all I am in the mornings.'

Merriment dived forward, trying to jump up, but Solomon hauled her back and tickled her, making her laugh.

'What's for breakfast?' he said, and Merriment playfully pinched him.

'There'll be no mollycoddling in this union,' she scolded him light-heartedly.

They laughed and chatted, wrapped in a haze of love and comfort while the sun rose up over the city and the noise of the morning traders filled the air. The bells of Christ Church Cathedral chimed over the dark waters of the Liffey.

When Merriment arrived down into the kitchen she was surprised to find Janey Mack and Corker cooking up sausages, drop scones and griddle bread and making tea.

'He wouldn't let me rap on the door,' Janey Mack complained of Corker, 'even though I could hear yez jabbering away. I kept tellin' him yez weren't asleep.'

Merriment leaned over the griddle and inhaled the aroma rising from the pan. 'I'm here now.' She smiled and ruffled Janey Mack's hair. 'And we're having tea,' she remarked, looking at the unlocked chest.

'There's a pinch left,' Janey Mack told her, warning Corker to look after the drop scones and telling him to hurry up and slice the bread.

'Boys are shockin' single-minded about tasks. They do them in a line instead of all together.'

'I'll help Corker,' Solomon said, coming into the kitchen and grabbing a knife, cutting up yesterday's half-loaf. 'It's a bit stale,' he told them.

Janey Mack beamed. 'We'll fry it, make it tasty.'

Breakfast was cheerful. They all sat around the table laughing and talking, eating heartily. Corker sipped his first cup of tea and Janey Mack added sugar chunks, the two of them agreeing that sugar made all the difference. They discussed Hawkins, and Janey Mack sat riveted in her chair, her huge eyes blinking incredulously as Solomon described in great detail the discovery of the hanging carcass swinging in the squalid bedchamber high up in the roof of the Black Dog Prison.

'But isn't it shockin' wicked,' she said over and over, and as Solomon went through the night's events the gaiety of the morning slipped into a more sombre mood.

'We do have quite a bit of work to do.' Solomon glanced over at Merriment. 'I've to pen an editorial and Corker will have to draw.'

'That's right,' Corker chirruped, jumping off his stool and mopping up the last of the oil from the griddle pan with a crust of bread.

'Of course. Me and Janey will have a busy day ahead as well,' said Merriment.

Janey Mack nodded. 'It was black yesterday. There must be ten pounds in the till. At least, I saw a lot of money.'

'Good.' Merriment smiled. 'We should start preparing infusions of balm and citrus because as soon as the snow begins to thaw there will be a spate of coughs and colds.'

In unison they stood and put away their dishes. Solomon ran upstairs to grab his bag and jacket. Merriment unfastened the shop shutters and counted out yesterday's earnings, surprised that there was really was almost ten whole pounds in takings stuffed into the wooden box. Corker and Janey Mack ran out into the snow and pelted each other with chunks of icy snowballs, oblivious to the city traffic trundling by, unaware of the man with a silver-tipped cane peeping from the alleyway that led to the backyards of the buildings.

Solomon emerged from the landing, wrapped in his cloak, his face bright with the satisfaction that comes from requited love. He looked his most handsome and exuded a new-found confidence. He swept his arms around Merriment and stole a kiss.

'You make things better.' He grinned, and with a wink he let her go and jauntily said, 'See you later.'

She pulled him back, stopping him in his tracks, and forced him to pause and return her gaze. The moment was full enough for him to expect some kind of declaration: instead a mischievous light filled Merriment's eyes and she quipped, 'You are ridiculously pretty.' Then, teasing his vanity, she added, 'Try not to trip over yourself on the way out.'

*

Solomon Fish and Corker waded through the snow to the office, full of chatter and plans.

'Another *Pue's News*, I think. This time I'll do some small sketches in squares down the side of the pamphlet, a big square at the top with the Dolocher in it swinging from a hook. What are you thinking of for the heading?' Corker asked.

Solomon played with titles, his mind dancing light, full of an overwhelming sense of his luck having finally turned.

'I was thinking "The Demonic Dolocher Uncovered" or "The Dolocher Unskinned", with a subtitle, something like "The Keeper of the Black Dog's Dark Secret".'

They passed lines of workers and traders, charwomen and young servants, chair carriers, footmen on their day off, worshippers heading to Saint Werburgh's, and as they turned down Castle Street, they joined a throng of clerks all heading to their offices. Already people were beginning to break into knotty groups of twos and threes spreading the word that the Dolocher had been apprehended. A stranger chatting to a well-heeled group of four gentlemen hailed Solomon.

'Mister Fish, from the *Occurrences*, is it true?'

And Solomon told them brightly, 'By God, not only is it true, it is a remarkable tale. Now, gentlemen, it's urgent that I get to the office and write up an editorial, but the revelation of who and what the Dolocher is will astound you all. Be sure to buy a copy of *Pue's News*, it will be available by eleven this morning. Will we send a few copies to your offices, gentlemen?'

And Solomon took an order for thirty copies, one of the clerks

439

saying that the accounts office employed fifty people alone. Flush with a new-found sense of place, Solomon bounded up the stairs into his office two steps at a time, followed closely by Corker.

'Mister Fish,' Chesterfield Grierson called to him.

'Yes?' Solomon stuck his head around the door grinning. Chesterfield Grierson peered over the files on his desk, a warm coffee steaming in a cup beside a fresh plate of pastries.

'I have heard your news,' he announced. 'Could you make this stretch over two editions?'

Solomon winked, 'Brevity may be your talent, Grierson. Mine is quite the opposite,' and he patted the door frame as he left, for the first time in his life feeling he was in the right place at the right time.

Chesterfield's surprised brows lifted a fraction as he mournfully sipped, muttering to himself, 'Why does that sound like a jibe referring to my virility?'

Time was of the essence, and although Solomon found it hard to sit still, his delight in Merriment constantly distracting him, he managed to hurry off a piece revealing the details of the night before and informing readers that there was so much more to come, tempting them with snippets, including 'Olocher's Whispering Evil' – an outline of the way Olocher inspired Hawkins to come up with the idea of the Dolocher; 'Hawkins' Criminal History' – an in-depth analysis of the nefarious criminal fraternity headed by the Keeper of the Black Dog; 'The Devil Finds His Own' – on how evil is transmitted, including interviews with prisoners who each had a tale to tell about Hawkins.

'I'm on fire.' He grinned at Corker. 'How are the sketches coming?'

Corker proudly showed him his drawings and Solomon finished his tantalising snippets with a reminder that readers should purchase a copy of *Pue's Occurrences* to follow the extraordinary trial in the court of Oyer and Terminer due to take place. Solomon sat with Chesterfield Grierson, sipping coffee and chatting, as Corker rushed about getting himself ready to go to the printers with the article and the illustrations.

'Just get *Pue's News* printed,' Solomon called and Chesterfield shifted uncomfortably in his chair.

'I intend to turn a profit in my business,' he grumbled, 'not make myself bankrupt.'

'Ten thousand copies,' Solomon added, and Corker bolted past Philmont and out into Skinner's Row.

'The laws of supply and demand,' Solomon said, stirring sugar into his coffee. 'We'll sell ten thousand sheets, mark my words, a lot quicker than three thousand broadsheets.'

And satisfied with Solomon's logic, Chesterfield Grierson relaxed, took a line of snuff and listened as Solomon outlined how they were going to extend interest in the Dolocher over several editions. They were still chatting when Corker ran back up the stairs red-faced and panting and burst into the office announcing that the Black Dog had been swarmed.

'There's mayhem. They want him tried this afternoon. The butchers are swinging hooks, insisting that Hawkins has damaged their reputation. The army are trying to hold everyone back.'

Solomon jumped to his feet and laughed. 'This story just keeps giving.' He tapped Corker's shoulder. 'Come on. When will the printer have the sheet ready?'

'Twelve. He's put other work on hold. I saw him call four lads to set up the frames. He couldn't believe it when he read your piece, said his wife had collected all our work.' Corker caught his breath.

'No time to rest.' Solomon ruffled Corker's hair. 'To the Black Dog.'

*

The swell of people crushing through the prison gates was too thick to penetrate.

'Round the back.' Solomon pushed past the pressing crowd. The back entrance was guarded by four armed soldiers.

'Solomon.' One of them recognised him from last night's search. He waved Solomon and Corker through. 'Judge Coveny was in reception having a barney with one of the clerks waiting for Beresford to show up with the Sheriff. Some problem with the statements.'

Judge Coveny was ensconced in a high-backed chair behind the desk, surrounded by several members of the Board and armed guards. He was an elderly man with folds of skin looping his face and an expression that Corker likened to 'a disgruntled bulldog sucking a wasp'. He wore a powdered wig and blackened his eyebrows, a fashion he had adopted when he was a young man and had never quite abandoned. He hunched over the desk, nursing a stiff brandy, and banged hard on the table.

'Damn it to hell, the law will not be rushed, fiend or no fiend. There must be a suitable garnering of information. A lawyer needs time to collate all the facts relating to the crimes.' He pointed a fat hairy finger at the door. 'That is a lynch mob out there and I will not be chastised by the ignorant masses.' He coughed and spluttered. 'No matter how right they are.'

Beresford had arrived and stood next to a bewildered-looking sheriff. He glared at the brandy glass in the judge's hand, a nerve dancing in his clenched jaw.

'Your honour, the evidence has been compiled swiftly since this is a matter of urgency. Three Ordinaries took the statements. The city is naturally reeling. The citizens want justice to be served promptly.'

'Bah!' Judge Coveny swatted away Beresford's remark. 'That's the new way, isn't it? Speediness matched by sloppiness. Everything is feeling now, feeling and sentiment, no place for logic and rational deliberation. I will not rush a trial to please that lot out there. You succumb to the rabble and you rue the day. They are always at it, always trying to inveigle their way into the nooks and crannies of your sympathy, and before you know it, the law will be undone and the land will be usurped. Mark my words, as soon as you run with the crowd civilisation crumbles to dust. Think of Rome. Think of Rome.'

Beresford rolled his eye to heaven and spun round to hide his face from the judge. Satisfied, Judge Coveny downed another shot of brandy, leaned back on his chair, folded his hands over his rotund belly and waited for someone else to step forward and counter him.

'Your Honour,' Solomon began, the few law lectures that he had attended suddenly serving him, 'we have enough evidence to prove *actus reus* and *mens rea*, and plenty of witnesses, myself included, to attest to the Keeper's character. As you know, under the current laws regarding retribution, those citizens out there' – Solomon pointed to the large door holding the mob at bay – 'they obey the law and Hawkins has contravened it. By the related theory that includes the "righting of balance", he ought to suffer since he has not only inflicted unfair detriment upon others, but he has fully and wilfully intended harm.' Solomon could feel his heart beating furiously as Judge Coveny's penetrating eyes bored into his face. 'As you well know,' Solomon concluded, 'one who murders must be executed himself.'

Judge Coveny snorted. 'It is not his guilt that bothers me, it is the haste with which a case can be built and a jury convened. That lot would hang the blackguard today, and hang he must, but I detest hurrying through the proper channels. Mark my words' – he waved his fat finger in the air and sat forward – 'conduct a trial in haste and repent at leisure.'

Judge Coveny hauled himself upright and tugged on his fur-lined cloak.

'Find me twelve good men, collect your witness statements

and every last shred of evidence, and bring them to my court-room in two days' time.'

He pushed past the guards, allowing his own entourage to lead the way, and grumpily barked his farewell as he flattened a tricorn hat on his round head and limped off. Once the door closed, the whole room seemed to sigh.

'If that old codger had his way the trial would take half a year.' Beresford shook Solomon's hand. 'You seem to have lit a fire under him.'

'Just quoted the procedures of the law. Still doesn't seem happy, mind.'

'The man's a consummate humbug.' Beresford signalled to a clerk. 'Let the crowd know there'll be a trial in a couple of days and send them packing.' He smacked Solomon's back. 'How's Merriment?'

Corker interjected, 'She's pink and dandy. Rosy with—'

'She's fine.' Solomon prodded Corker forward. 'I'm going to stay working, interview some of the prisoners while they still have a tale to tell.' He bowed a prompt goodbye, and he slipped into the prison corridor winking down at Corker. 'Come on, you do some quick sketches.'

*

They moved from cell to cell, asking the prisoners questions; Corker sketched while Solomon took quick notes.

'I saw a cloaked man going up the stairs,' one inmate said, his eyes bulging, his fingers draped over his knees like long pallid stalks.

A fat man wearing a reverend's collar and a woman's skirt sat fanning himself on the edge of his bed and whispered coquettishly, 'Once in the dead of night I heard laughin' and mutterin' coming out of that room and I was that scared I ran into me bed and locked the door after meself. I'm sure it was Hawkins, he was rollin' with the devil. He used to slip into

Olocher's cell, didn't beat Olocher, no, no, no, used to treat him to cherry brandy and listen to Olocher's filthy talk. They were birds of a feather.'

All afternoon, one testimony after another outlined how Hawkins ran a roaring trade in contraband, had a tap-room that served watered-down gin and cheap cherry brandy, had a side business pimping tired old bawds for general usage and mollies for the sodomites. He beat prisoners for the exercise, had a strange fascination with torturing women, extorted money as a matter of course, robbed indiscriminately, took advantage of daughters and wives and had the manners of a pig. His snout was always in the trough, grubbily taking what was not his. Everyone owed him money.

Solomon closed the door on a pair of prisoners and was about to tell Corker that they should pack it in for the day when an old man with a faltering voice called his name.

'Mister Fish.'

At the end of the gloomy corridor, shrouded in green-grey shadows and leaning on a gnarled walking stick, was a white-haired man wearing a dark worsted jacket and grubby breeches.

'Mister Fish,' he drawled hoarsely, waving a hanky for fear that somehow Solomon might not see him.

'Yes?' Solomon moved cautiously forward.

'Over here, Mister Fish.'

Corker cocked his head and winked, 'I think that aul' fella wants you.'

'Funny.'

Solomon glanced behind. The sun was captured in the Diocletian window; the clear bright sky was burnished a coppery red and cast a pale gold shadow on the upper reaches of the dreary walls. It was later than he had expected. He'd had a busy day. Solomon walked towards the old man and it was only as he drew nearer that he recognised something in the features, around the eyes.

445

'Boxty.' Solomon reached out to shake his hand.

Boxty trembled, his head constantly bobbing.

'Heard ye were here,' he said, coughing up a wedge of phlegm and quickly spitting it out. 'Shockin' what the bastard did.'

Boxty pointed to the reception room, which was empty now that the crowd had dispersed. Someone had lit another two candles in the niche and placed three lanterns on the desk.

'I won't sit in this place in the dark.'

'You're working here?' Solomon was genuinely shocked.

'They're paying me double for the next few days. Figure I won't let anyone in or out to assist Hawkins in his deviousness. And by Jesus, I won't either.'

Boxty blessed himself, his blasted frame shaking and malfunctioning.

'Look what he did to me.'

He tapped the numb side of his face, his features distorted in a downward slump. 'Had me praying on me knees, shivering with the fear. He took me job, me livelihood, dressing up like a devil and lunging at me out of the dark. I'll tell ye' – his eyes filled with a chilling glee – 'it'll lift me heart to see the bastard swing.'

Boxty eased his skinny frame down into the large reception chair and turned his worried eyes to Solomon's face. The old man was completely altered. His hair was white, one side of his face still hung half-dead and he had a stoop. Boxty seemed smaller and more fragile then when Solomon first met him.

'Hawkins.' Boxty clacked his tongue, his large Adam's apple running up his gullet as he swallowed, his head bobbing involuntarily. 'To think he did this to me and we sharing drink and dividing out any excess that came our way.' Boxty sniffed and pulled a large musket that leaned against the wall over onto the table. 'He was always a black bastard,' he snarled. 'Look at what he did to Martin, the pair of them thick as thieves till they fell out.'

'What did they fall out over?' Solomon asked.

'What do that kind ever fall out over?' Boxty pressed his hanky to his nose and, his hand trembling with a palsy, he blew. 'Money.' He licked one side of his mouth and looked furtively at the door to his left. 'Martin owed Hawkins well over twenty pounds. Some smuggling caper that went wrong.' He sighed and tutted. 'Martin owed everyone. The poor sod's paid his debts in full now.'

A young guard with a rash over his nose wandered in and took up his sentry, nodding at Solomon and looking at Corker's sketch.

'Has ye down to a T, Boxty,' he said.

Solomon and Corker left Boxty sitting in the bright reception room telling his tale of woe to the young guard with the rash.

'Well then.' Solomon looked up at the twilit sky, his breath leaving his mouth like a fine mist. He looked at the blue smoke trailing in perfect straight lines out of the chimneys. The hush of the frozen city crept into his heart. The crystalline night, exquisitely beautiful, seemed to mirror the expansion he felt behind his ribs. He was about to head home. The unspeakable pleasure of having a regularity to his existence, along with the immeasurable sense of life suddenly having meaning now that he had Merriment to return to at the end of the day, made him breathe in a long, slow, deep breath.

'Freeze the balls off a brass monkey.' Corker blew into his hands. 'Are we away? Or are ye keen to view the rooftops a bit longer?'

'We're away,' Solomon laughed, 'you'll have a bit of supper with us, and here' – he handed Corker two shillings – 'buy a bit of grub for your siblings.'

Corker whistled. 'Much use it is now, when the hawkers

have gone home. But there's always a few pies at the Swan, I might get something there. I can't join ye for supper, Sol, much and all as I'd like te. It's not for me ma's sake I'm heading back, it's just Effie. She'll be walking the streets with worry.'

'Fair enough.' Solomon pinched Corker's cheek.

Despite the weather, when they glanced down one of the side streets they saw a queue for the Italian Opera.

'Word's out the streets are safe,' Corker chirruped. Then: 'Were ye thinking of marrying her?'

Solomon ruffled the young lad's hair. 'Pack it in.'

'She keeps a grand and tidy house. Nice warm fires. But I likes to see the boobies meself, neatly displayed like pies on a tray, and Merri tends to cover hers with men's shirts and waistcoats.'

Solomon grinned to himself as he crunched through the snow. Corker continued.

'And I like skirts; they swish and you can lift them and see a dandy ankle. Merri likes to keep her legs well covered, but she's nice.' Corker faltered. 'Me own ma wouldn't give ye the steam off her chamber pot. Merri's the gait of a man and the habits of a man, talks straight and doesn't flutter her lashes. Ye mustn't like frippery, if ye've cast yer hat at Merriment O'Grady, and she could do much worse than yerself.'

Solomon beamed. 'I'll tell you, lad, I've never felt more lucky.'

'I'll stop ye there, Sol.' Corker grinned. 'Can't bear to hear a man talk poetry about his bird, tends to turn me stomach.'

Solomon smacked Corker's back and laughed heartily. 'I wouldn't want to be responsible for giving you indigestion.'

They parted at the back of Skinner's Row.

'I'm cutting up this way, Sol. See ye tomorrow.' He ran to the mouth of an alleyway, waving goodbye and calling, 'Don't wear her out, Sol!' He pitched his head back and laughed before vanishing into the snowy darkness.

Solomon cut into Burris Court and was heading for Saint Michan's Lane when an arm reached from the shadows and snatched him into an old doorway. Solomon instinctively pushed and was knocked against the snowy bricks for his trouble, his spine and ribs ringing from the collision.

'There now.' Solomon saw a dazzling row of teeth. 'Knoxy wants another instalment.'

Solomon groaned, realising that the only leverage he had with Pearly was now locked up in the Black Dog, but being in fighting mood, he tried to negotiate a new deal. Wriggling free from Pearly's grip, Solomon tugged his jacket down and rearranged the collar of his cloak.

'Pearly,' he coughed, his eyes flicking into the vanishing dusk, the distant snow winding through the cobbled alleyway gleaming with a purple light, 'you know that Hawkins has been confessing to the Ordinaries.'

'All birds sing.' Pearly grinned, his dimple curiously pronounced in the twilight.

'There's three clerks writing down in detail his various business ventures.' Solomon's eyes sparked with a steely light, hoping the veiled threat would hit the mark. 'He seems particularly keen to name his associates.'

Pearly nodded, his hand briefly sweeping up to his temple before snapping out and lightly punching Solomon on his nose, making him reel back in pain.

'Ow, for Christ's sake.' Solomon's eyes smarted, his nose particularly sensitive after being reset. 'What the hell?'

Pearly chuckled and slid a blade out from his gold-trimmed sleeve.

'Sorry, I must have given ye the impression I wanted to parley. You want to prattle about the Keeper and I have work to do. Give over yer money.'

Solomon grumbled as he fidgeted in his pocket and drew out three shillings.

'I saw you with Hawkins.' Solomon's voice crackled with nervous bravado. Pearly smiled, cocking his head to one side. Drawing up the blade in his hand, he pressed it to his cheek, letting it dully rest against his beaming smile.

'I could cut you a fresh pair of dimples,' he chuckled, 'or carve off the tip of yer nose, take the old sniffer in instalments.'

'He's named you as a partner in some smuggling racket,' Solomon blustered, quickly holding out his money.

'Well now,' Pearly chortled, 'nose it is.'

He grabbed Solomon in a headlock, brought the blade to his cheek and sharply cut. Solomon yelled 'no' and flinched away. Miraculously he managed to heave Pearly against the wall and scramble away, running and slipping onto Saint Michan's Lane, followed by Pearly's throaty laugh. A razor-thin line of blood bubbled beneath Solomon's left eye. He mopped it with the edge of his cloak and clacked his tongue: getting away from Billy Knox and his debt collector was proving to be just as difficult as he had first supposed.

The sun was setting and the first stars were glittering as the lamplighter and his assistant began lighting the three oil lamps newly erected outside Christ Church Cathedral. Solomon turned down Saint John's Lane and emerged onto Fishamble Street, chastened. How was he going to escape Billy Knox's clutches and pay back the money he now owed Chesterfield? He thought of Merriment and hated that her bright face should flash behind his eyes. Could he ask her? He bit the inside of his cheek, snapping the idea in half, frustrated that his old weak habits still lurked just beneath the surface of his new-found strength.

God damn it, I will fix this myself.

He was so preoccupied with this thought that he was uncon-scious of the two men opposite Merriment's shop, one with a cane, the other hopping with a jittery energy from the kerb to the road and back again. As Solomon approached wondering if selling his law books would raise the money he needed, both men wandered off, melting into the pedestrian traffic. He paused a moment, looking across at the dark shuttered windows of Merriment's shop.

'Damn this,' he hissed, striding over the hard snow and putting his key in the lock. 'I'll work something out,' and taking in a breath, he heaved open the door to the sound of Janey Mack singing at the top of her voice a ballad about a girl who dressed herself up like a sailor.

25

The Slow Swing

Two days later the slush prevented Solomon from taking long, light strides to the High Court, but nothing could quell his buoyant mood. He breathed in the crisp chill air, passing dripping sills and drainpipes and checking and rechecking with Corker whether they had included all the prisoners' statements in their submission to the judge.

'I dropped everything over like ye asked me to. His clerk took it.'

'And there's still no sign of Fred and Jessop?'

'They've hightailed it. What are ye worried about, Sol?'

'Nothing.' Solomon smiled. 'Absolutely nothing.'

The courtyard of the Tholsel heaved with excitement. Someone had hauled the gallows down from Stephen's Green and parked it right by the entrance so that as Hawkins was led from his boarded-up carriage the first thing he would see was the hanging platform.

'That'll sober him up,' one man said, tapping the large wooden wheel of the portable scaffold; the crowd around him laughed. Someone called out Solomon's name as he pushed his way through the crowd and up the steps.

'Sol, Corker, over here.'

Gloria waved frantically from behind her stall and ran out to hug Solomon and kiss him on the mouth.

'Who scratched ye?' She glanced at his wound.

'His new mot likes a bit of rough and tumble,' Corker

chimed in and Solomon chuckled as they teased him about Merriment.

'Well' – Gloria mopped up her fake tears – 'can't say as I'm not surprised, you were bound to be snapped up in a flash. But I'm heartbroken ye didn't try a bit of my delights.' Jiggling her enormous breasts, she grabbed Solomon by the arm and pulled him towards her makeshift pie stand. 'Here he is,' she announced loudly, 'the man that saved us all. This is the lad that found Hawkins out.'

And before he could pull himself away, a crowd fought to shake his hand and kiss his cheek and tell him what a man he was. While Solomon basked in his new-found fame and Corker asked Gloria for two pies, the court beadle arrived and there was a crush for the door.

'I've to get inside.' Solomon tore himself away from the appreciative crowd and pushed his way up the steps and through a side door with Corker screaming after him, 'Wait for me.'

The courtroom was packed to the seams. Every lord and lady interested in the case had reserved seats in the gallery or bribed their way into prime locations down on the floor. Solomon met Chesterfield and Beresford by the prosecuting bench.

'Damn scuffle,' Chesterfield complained. 'Are you ready?'

Solomon nodded, catching his breath. The air was thick with tobacco smoke and perfumed with cologne and the underlying musk of stale sweat. He looked about the courtroom, having only once peeked into it when he was a student. It was grander than he remembered. The imposing dais holding the judge's chair was constructed from polished oak and set beneath a huge domed ceiling decorated with ornate coffers painted gold. The witness stand was to the right of the dais and spread in a semicircle before it were rows of carved benches, arranged to accommodate the teams of lawyers, assistants, clerks and sundry officials. To the left of the raised platform was the stand where the accused was placed and directly behind and above it was the gallery already full to capacity with eager observers keen to get the best view.

The hum and chatter in the courtroom rose to a fever pitch as the crowd became agitated and the beadles tried to stem the tide of bodies squeezing their way into any free space. Everything was delayed as more and more members of the public insisted that, if there was standing room, they had a right to stand and see the scoundrel that had terrorised them.

Solomon flattened down his jacket, smoothing the lace ruffs of his best shirt beneath his waistcoat, and in his mind quickly went over the events leading to his suspicion of Hawkins in the first place.

'Did you sign in?' Chesterfield Grierson queried.

Solomon shook his head. 'Where?'

Chesterfield pointed to a stout man with a drooping moustache. The beadle hammered the mace on the floor with three loud resounding thuds and ceremoniously cried, 'All rise.' Solomon pushed his way forward and quickly hissed his name to the clerk who would call the witnesses. The jury stood in two neat rows of six men, all dressed in bright silks, all coiffed and powdered and ranging in age from twenty-three to ninety.

Judge Coveny looked like thunder. He marched into the courtroom, his cape fluttering, his powdered wig leaving a faint chalky trail behind him, and sat down, scowling at the thick portfolios stacked on the bench before him.

'Call in the accused,' he grumbled, pouring himself a generous glass of claret.

The nudging and whispering stopped. A thick, expectant silence descended. No one breathed. Everyone inched higher in their seats or stood on the tips of their toes, straining to catch that first glimpse, their hearts trembling with a mixture of anticipation and morbid fascination, everyone's nerves teetering on the edge. The sound of a large door slowly creaking open

454

cut through the air like a gothic prelude to a cautionary tale. Women corseted and decked in lace craned forward. Men perched straight-backed and tall, their eyes fixed in the direction of the creaking door. Even Judge Coveny froze, poised over his drink and his notes. Solomon could see Corker across the way quickly sketching, his eyes flicking towards the door, his pencil hovering as four armed guards marched in, the sounds of their boots stomping on the tiled floor blotting out the shuffle of Hawkins' feet.

Hawkins swallowed back the gush of saliva that rushed into his mouth, his head darting right and left, his feral eyes jumping from the judge to the crowd to the ceiling. He had tied back his hair in a scrawny ponytail and buttoned up his battered jacket in a desperate attempt to improve his appearance. The crowd drank in his wiry form, his rattish face and jerking movements. No one breathed as he climbed the steps into the stand and placed his manacled hands on the polished oak enclosure. No one whispered when his lips curled into a defiant snarl. Then, cutting through the silence, tearing at the air with abrupt unexpected defiance, Hawkins opened his mouth wide and howled at the top of his lungs, 'I am innocent.'

The courtroom erupted. A burst of hissing and booing shook the rafters. The floodgates opened and the crowd rose to its feet and hurled abuse, insults, whistles and catcalls.

'Rapist!'

'Murderer!'

'Beast!'

'Devil!'

Despite Judge Coveny hammering his gavel furiously and bellowing for everyone to stop at once, it took a full five minutes to quell the crowd.

'You shall all be held in contempt,' he sputtered, turning beetroot, pointing his gavel round the room. 'Every last one of you.' He drew in a long, rasping breath and warned them all to contain themselves. 'Or the trial will be conducted in secret and you will be denied access to this most sacred process.'

The crowd settled, baited to silence by the prospect of being excluded from hearing all the salacious information. While the list of Hawkins' deeds was being read, Solomon sat perched on the edge of his seat, his heart racing in his chest, unconsciously squeezing his knuckles. The prosecuting lawyer was a tall, myopic man who wore thick spectacles that enlarged his eyes so that they looked too big for his face. He had the peculiar habit of constantly sucking on his gums and poking his tongue under his lips. Despite his idiosyncrasies, Mister Freedman had a flair for theatre. He called on Jedediah Sorrel to take the stand.

Solomon watched as Boxty, using a walking cane, slowly climbed the steps and placed his hand shakily on the Bible, his head bobbing in constant affirmatives with every word he spoke.

'I swear to tell the whole truth and nothing but the truth.'

'Mister Sorrel,' Freedman boomed, 'I will address you by your sobriquet Boxty, if you don't mind, sir?'

Boxty nodded.

'Tell me about the night Olocher died.'

'I were waiting for Martin Coffey to relieve me of me duty.' Boxty's stricken face blushed on one side. 'It were a cold, lonely night and Olocher was muttering to the devil and I was fearful.'

The courtroom nodded in sympathy; women clutched their hankies over their hearts imagining the grim, dripping interior of Olocher's last confinement. Mister Freedman let a pause hang beneath the domed ceiling, understanding that silence was a useful tool when wielding the precision of the law.

'Martin Coffey arrived and then what happened?'

'We talked for a moment. I said how Olocher was peculiar, sitting quiet mostly, sometimes muttering, and to comfort me Martin offered me a bit of peach and then there was this sound.'

At first, I thought Olocher had fallen, but . . . he'd cut his own throat.'

'Remember, you are in a court of law.' Mister Freedman wagged his finger. 'You have sworn an oath.'

'On me life, on my wife's life. Olocher sliced his own throat.'

'And where was the Keeper when this calamity occurred?'

Boxty's head bobbed. 'In his office.'

Mister Freedman rolled his tongue over his lower row of teeth and stood waiting with his lower lip bulging out.

'Doing what?' he finally asked.

Boxty's right shoulder rose higher. 'Doing some young one who wanted to get her father out of trouble.'

Hawkins shook his head and bellowed, 'That's a lie.'

Mister Freedman spun round and snarled over Hawkins' protestations. 'I have here in my hand the witness statement of one "Miss M", who shall remain nameless on account of the shame you have heaped upon her.'

Hawkins grinned and fervently shook his head.

'She's a lyin' cow.'

The courtroom hissed.

Mister Freedman waved a sheaf of yellow pages at the gallery. 'And several other accounts of distressed females all saying that they were violated by you.'

The men and women jumped to their feet, waving hankies and pipes, outraged. Hawkins coloured, his large forehead jutting forward, his eyes hard as steel.

'They're lyin' bitches,' he complained. 'They're whores and queans. You can't take their word for it.'

Judge Coveny downed his glass of claret in one gulp and let the room shout down Hawkins' remarks, before hammering his gavel and telling Hawkins to desist from such profanities.

'The Board,' Mister Freedman archly announced, 'of the Black Dog gaol share the burden of responsibility to these women, for it was by their council that this reprobate standing

457

in the accused's stand before you was set in his position of Keeper.'

Beresford shifted uncomfortably at Mister Freedman's chastisement, the edges of his pale face burning with repressed rage as he felt his political aspirations diminish greatly.

'So,' Mister Freedman continued, 'while Hawkins was satisfying his lust, Olocher was bleeding to death.' Freedman turned to Hawkins and sneered sarcastically. 'What a pretty house you kept, sir. Moving on, it was you, Boxty, who alerted Hawkins to the situation in the nunnery. What happened then?'

Boxty nodded, his crooked mouth snarling. 'Then there was a right set-to. Him and Martin Coffey went at loggerheads. Hawkins said that Martin Coffey killed Olocher.'

'Why would Hawkins think that Martin Coffey had killed Olocher?'

'On account of Martin hated Olocher. Ye got to understand, Olocher had a way of getting under yer skin. But Martin never did it, as true as I'm standing here. I saw it with me own eyes, Olocher did himself in, but Hawkins was havin' none of it. He roared and shouted that this would bring the roof down on us. Hawkins knew there would be terrible trouble so he let fly at Martin and it turned to fisticuffs.'

'Hawkins beat one of his own employees?'

'Aye.' Boxty's head bounced and a thin line of spittle drooled from the sloping edge of his mouth. 'That'd be him. He's a shockin' temper.'

'Go on.' Mister Freedman poked his tongue up under his upper lip and waited, his huge magnified eyes blinking as Boxty spoke.

'He came out the worst in that set-to. Martin gave more than he got and Hawkins curled up on the floor shielding his head and I had to pull Martin away on account of it had all got out of hand.'

'So Hawkins was furious.'

'Oh aye. And he bided his time too before he exacted his revenge. God rest me colleague Martin, ended up gutted like a fish by him there.'

Boxty pointed a jumping finger at Hawkins, who above a sea of catcalls and hisses yelled, 'Yer honour, yer honour, I never killed Martin Coffey.'

'Oh, you killed Martin Coffey.' Mister Freedman lurched forward dramatically, his arm waving accusingly at the prisoner. 'You killed him and disembowelled him. Just as surely as you murdered poor Gertrude Baker and Margaret Fines. Is this your knife, sir?'

Mister Freedman drew a bone-handled knife with a six-inch blade from beneath a sheaf of papers on his desk and held it above his head for the court to see. He then handed the weapon to the jury to examine. Hawkins glowered at Mister Freedman, his ugly scar livid, his features distorted in aggressive revulsion.

'What of it?' Hawkins spluttered. 'I'm holed up with vagabonds and criminals. A man's a right to protect himself.'

'I put it to you that this is the knife that eviscerated Martin Coffey.'

'No, it's not,' Hawkins shouted.

'You,' Mister Freedman roared, 'you, Mister Hawkins, concocted the idea of the Dolocher as a means to exact revenge. You saw a way of deflecting the Board's inquiry into Olocher's suicide by manufacturing a demon from your own polluted imagination. You attacked your employees. That man there' – Mister Freedman pointed at Boxty leaning sideways, his head constantly bobbing, one eye drooping while he mopped his drooling mouth with a hanky – 'you affrighted that man so much that he took an apoplexy. And do you feel remorse? No.'

Hawkins said nothing.

Satisfied that his case was sound, Mister Freedman returned to his seat.

The crowd turned to the defence lawyer, examining his face

and frame, disapproving of the very fact that Hawkins should have the gall to muster up any defence at all. Jeremy Lightfoot had been in Solomon's class. He had been a bumbling boy of eighteen the last time Solomon had seen him and now he was a bumbling man of twenty-eight, with sweaty hands and oily skin.

'Mister Sorrell . . .' Jeremy stumbled, aware of the crushing atmosphere emanating from the crowd, pressuring him to sit down. 'Isn't it true that you and Martin Coffey disliked Mister Hawkins?'

Boxty shook his head. 'I never minded him much. Hawkins could be difficult. But then he did this to me and I'll never forgive him.'

'Isn't it true that Martin Coffey beat the prisoners?' Jeremy glided over Boxty's last remark.

'Only to keep them quiet when they got rowdy.' Boxty's eyes darted to the floor.

'Didn't Mister Coffey have a temper?'

'What of it?' Boxty snorted. 'The poor man's dead.'

Mister Freedman jumped to his feet and objected. 'Your Honour, I appreciate that the defence is trying to discredit my witness. However, it beggars belief that he is also trying to insinuate that a dead man brought about his own demise.'

'I'm trying to establish that my client acted in self-defence,' Jeremy Lightfoot feebly countered.

The courtroom laughed.

Jeremy did his best to disentangle Hawkins from his predicament, but the truth was Hawkins was an unlikable man with savage tendencies and a penchant for exaggerated self-interest and nothing Jeremy Lightfoot could do or say could dilute the overwhelming evidence laid out by the prosecuting council.

The stout clerk with the drooping moustache called Solomon to the witness stand. Solomon stood tall and confident as he recited the oath and the gathered ladies nudged one another

460

with approval, glad to have a handsome man to admire, his blond hair and proportional features adding to the glamour of the day.

'This mopsy,' Hawkins muttered, his manacles clinking as they knocked against the witness stand. 'Yer Honour,' Hawkins pleaded to Judge Coveny, 'this man is a broadsheet writer. Every word out of his mouth is a gilded lie.'

'Is that right?' Judge Coveny scribbled something and sipped on a fresh glass of claret.

'It is, Yer Honour.' Hawkins tugged at his collar button. 'His profession is to twist the truth. He dissembles. He's not to be trusted.'

Mister Freedman guffawed. 'The audacity,' he bellowed, pointing at the accused. 'The audacity. This man, as you can see, has a skewed sense of honesty.'

The courtroom laughed while Hawkins nearly burst a blood vessel in his forehead.

Solomon settled himself and waited while the prosecution lawyer licked his top and bottom gums and read a short statement.

'"Hawkins robbed me of my monies when I happened to call into the Black Dog to investigate the disappearance of Martin Coffey."' The tall lawyer curled his tongue behind his upper teeth and paused with his mouth open. 'This was your first encounter with the Keeper of the Black Dog Prison, Mister Fish?'

'Yes, sir,' Solomon nodded.

'From the statement of one Mister Charles Bartle,' Mister Freedman continued, the low timbre of his voice now punching through the air with tremendous gravitas. '"Hawkins beat me regularly to within an inch of my life. Broke my arm. Took money from me. From all the inmates."' Then turning to Solomon, Mister Freedman asked, 'You witnessed this beating, Mister Fish?'

461

Solomon nodded. 'And was beaten myself trying to save Charlie.'

'Would you consider Mister Hawkins a strong man?'

'Extremely.'

'Despite his slight stature?'

'Yes.'

Mister Freedman pulled a printed advertisement from one of his portfolios showing a pair of boxers dancing bare-chested and bare-knuckled. It read *Bulldog MacCabe Takes on the Firebrand*.

'Here, ladies and gentlemen, is an announcement that informed the general public of a fight that took place on Stephen's Green some ten years ago. You, Mister Hawkins, are none other than the Firebrand illustrated in this advertisement. A pugilist of some renown back then. A skill you have kept well-oiled by exercising yourself with the prisoners of the Black Dog.'

Hawkins now stood subdued, his face turning pale, his features locked in grim subordination, submitting to his fate. Turning to Solomon, Mister Freedman tapped his spectacles.

'Then you discovered that Mister Hawkins ran an efficient black-market operation, not only in the Black Dog but on the Southside of the city?'

Solomon nodded. 'I overheard two associates of the plaintive talking about shifting merchandise. Their names are Fred and Jessop, I don't have surnames. I believe they are Mister Hawkins' henchmen. They reported to him, called him "the boss", and acted on his behalf. They organised the slaughtering of the pigs.'

Solomon outlined his investigation of the schoolhouse, his mapping of the robberies and sightings of the Dolocher.

'Initially,' Solomon continued, 'I suspected them of nothing more than using the Dolocher's attacks as some kind of screen to shield their nefarious criminal activities. I realised that the attacks coincided with robberies and the one place my mind kept going back to was the Black Dog.'

'How fortuitous for us that your instincts were correct.' Mister Freedman stood next to the jury. 'You informed a board member and then what happened?'

'I and Lord Beresford went to the prison to question Mister Hawkins but we couldn't find him. As we searched, I happened upon a secret room and that's when I found his disguise.'

'And here we get to the crux of the matter,' Mister Freedman hopped in. 'You found a carcass, hidden away in an upstairs room. You found the Dolocher's den. A grisly discovery.'

'And I knew then and there for certain that the Dolocher was not a demon but a man.'

The silence of the courtroom was ruptured, filling with gasps and whispers, everyone conferring, satisfied with the abundance of evidence. Hawkins jolted in defiance, his manacled hands punching the air, a spray of spittle issuing over his contempt.

'Y'er twisting the facts to suit yer tale,' he shouted. 'Twistin' the facts.'

Mister Freedman paced to the middle of the courtroom. He stood directly beneath the oval window in the centre of the dome, taking full advantage of the shaft of light shining directly down on him, illuminating him like a messenger bathed with divine sanction.

'Mister Hawkins' ingenuity knows no bounds.' Freedman raised his voice and arms, revelling in the energy of being centre stage. 'The depths of his hideous personality knows no end. His character is so barbaric, so lawless and godless, so bereft of the barest shreds of human decency that he maliciously and wickedly invented the Dolocher from the blackened recesses of his disfigured nature. Out of his malignant soul, he looked on a dead pig and saw an opportunity. Only when he had ruined Boxty's health and murdered a fellow guard did he recognise the full potential of the Dolocher. How quickly

463

he saw the Dolocher as a mechanism for satisfying his own dark leanings. How quickly he saw the Dolocher as a way of furnishing himself with macabre opportunities to enhance his own wealth. And then, when the basest of instincts took him over, how malevolently and deviously did he prowl on the women of this city attempting to have his way with them. Think of Florence Wells, think of Ester Murphy, think of poor Gertrude Baker, a sixteen–year–old girl horribly raped before being brutally murdered.'

The courtroom exploded in seething fury. The crowd stood and heckled, the women hissed, the men roared for vengeance. Hawkins' narrowed eyes scanned the room, his knuckles white as he clutched the edge of the stand.

'The devil take the lot of ye,' he bellowed.

The crowd shouted him down. Solomon watched as Judge Coveny blustered, whacking his gavel off the bench furiously.

'There isn't enough money on this earth to recompense a man for being a keeper,' Hawkins roared.

Enraged, the crowd took this to be a complete confession of guilt. And suddenly, like a tide, the front rows of the courtroom surged forward, overrunning the guards, pushing Mister Freedman to one side and dragging Hawkins kicking and screaming from the accused's stand, while Judge Coveny hammered and bellowed and screamed at the guards to hold them back.

But the crowd was feral and unanimous. The men pulled at Hawkins, shunting him forward, kicking him, lifting him overhead and ferrying him towards the entrance. Solomon leapt from the witness box and pushed his way through the melee, past ladies wailing, crushed by the frenzied squeeze. Men climbed over the knocked benches and slammed forward, roaring at the top of their lungs, 'Hang him. Hang him.' And the regiment sent to oversee the trial fractured, dispersing into knotty groups, discharging muskets into the air to no avail.

The execution was speedy and cruel. Clumps of Hawkins' hair were ripped from his scalp, his face was bloody and his coat was shredded. He was hastily noosed, the rope fastened to a horse, and without pause or ceremony he was suspended from the gallows, kicking and choking while the crowd cheered and laughed and flung stones at his thrashing body.

Solomon reeled from the shock of the sudden execution. At the same time he couldn't help but feel a certain satisfaction that justice was being served. Hawkins squirmed and jolted, and Solomon thought of Maggie Fines being lowered into her grave, of Gertie violated and cut open, of Merriment lying wounded in the snow. Hawkins was paying the highest price for his deviance and, disgusting as his last moments were, his life was a fair exchange for all the horror that he had initiated.

A stream of urine dribbled from Hawkins' legs, his last gasps drowned out by the chanting crowd. Solomon stared as Hawkins' body jigged and reeled, suspended high up on the portable gallows, framed by the sky. As Solomon watched Hawkins fight for breath, he thought of the pig carcass swaying from the butcher's hook in the secret room in the Black Dog. He recalled the gloomy lair, the covert den where Hawkins had hidden his stolen items; he thought of the crumpled bed, the fireplace. And slowly, like the ground crumbling away from beneath him, a creeping, unsettling doubt began to gnaw at the edges of Solomon's satisfaction. Something – he couldn't put his finger on it, couldn't quite pick it out – something wasn't right, but for the life of him Solomon couldn't define what was wrong.

'Die, Dolocher, die,' the crowd chanted, and Solomon stared at Hawkins' tiny feet as they kicked furiously. Something in his mind started to twitch, and then Hawkins stopped moving and at last swung limp on the end of the rope. The mob had had their justice and the corpse now turned slowly in the air, but Solomon was still staring, his eyes fixed on the size of Hawkins' feet, this singular detail pricking him with curiosity. The crowd hummed with satisfaction, but Solomon's thoughts reeled with doubt.

He frowned, looking on with disgust as the crowd tugged and ripped at Hawkins' remains, pulling tokens from his strangled corpse. Solomon stared at the Keeper's swollen tongue and distorted face and then pushed his way towards the main gate, away from the clawing fray and chattering women. He stared down at the dark waters of the Liffey, a half-formed observation undulating like a serpent at the back of his mind. He was trying to remember something, but it just wouldn't come to the surface.

As Solomon was leaning against the quayside wall, Corker plunged through the gate and ran over to him.

'Hell of a way to go. Someone's cut one of his fingers off.'

Solomon thought of the token on the bedstead in the garret room of the Black Dog Prison and shuddered. Across the way he saw Billy Knox with a group of cohorts laughing. Billy's head suddenly turned: his glittering eyes bored into Solomon's face, picking him out and holding him to the spot. Unnerved, Solomon patted Corker's back and swallowed.

'Have you enough sketches?' he asked.

'Plenty.'

26

Kill-Grief

The execution of the Keeper of the Black Dog and the trajectory of Hawkins' crimes, culminating in the Dolocher attacks, were covered in microscopic detail by *Pue's Occurrences*. The paper sold out on the first day of publication and Chesterfield Grierson made the optimistic decision to quadruple the print run of further copies, much to the satisfaction of the Board, who were delighted to see at the quarterly meeting that the quadrupled order had also sold out. It was put to a vote that Solomon's wages should be increased and the motion was passed uncontested.

It was while he was researching for a special edition of *Pue's Occurrences*, called 'The Dolocher Unmasked', that Solomon hit a snag. He was cross-referencing Florence Wells' sighting of the Dolocher with Hawkins' file when he stumbled across a statement from a woman claiming to have been violated by the Keeper on the same night. When Florence Wells saw the Dolocher, 'Miss S' was trying to reduce her brother's misery by bargaining with Hawkins, letting the Keeper do whatever he wanted to her.

Solomon stared at the dates and the times and the doubt that had been niggling at the back of his mind suddenly reappeared.

'What do you think?' he asked Merriment.

'Well,' Merriment said, resting her head against Solomon's shoulder as they lay on the bed. '"Miss S" must have got the date wrong. These things can happen.'

Satisfied, Solomon wrote his editorial and all the other articles in the special Dolocher edition and drank a port with Chesterfield Grierson on the afternoon the third print run sold out.

Dublin emerged from the stranglehold of the Dolocher's reign of terror by announcing a new season right before Christmas. All the theatres opened late. The Italian Opera ran matinees, and the streets, until recently cleared by half past six, were still busy after midnight with revellers and brawlers and every sort of traveller, all intoxicated by the liberating knowledge that the devil did not own Dublin town.

The city had been emancipated from the preternatural grip of demonic forces and for a few days its citizens were high-spirited and relieved. The rituals of locking up at night became less manic. The frenzy of praying and the renunciation of fun was abandoned to be replaced by good-humoured pranks and celebrations. There were tea parties held among the genteel, and visiting, no longer limited to sober afternoons, increased enormously. Now, people lingered at twilight and admired the sunset and did not shiver at the approaching dark. For that first week after Hawkins' execution, a kind of feverish release took hold of the city; everyone it seemed was in a wonderful mood.

Business at the shop thrived. As Merriment had predicted, the melting snow had presaged an epidemic of coughs and colds and sniffles, and her reputation as an apothecary grew. She carried bottles of citrus balm into the crowded shop and announced that anyone with intermittent fever should firstly change their bed linen. 'Before any of you take any balm you must wash thoroughly with warm soapy water and wear only clean clothes.'

The customers laughed and groaned respectively, while Janey Mack sprang to Merriment's defence.

'Hoppy John lost his leg because he didn't wash his knees.'

468

A corpulent man guffawed so hard, he choked into his hanky.

'I'm telling ye.' Janey Mack's huge eyes scanned the room. 'Maggots took up residence in the dirt of his wound and invited in flies and spiders and between the lot of them they turned his leg black and gave him ulcers on top of ulcers.'

'Ah, now listen,' one woman protested, 'I didn't come in here to feel more sick.'

'Then wash yer knees,' one man piped up.

The room chuckled and people split into chatty groups, waiting their turn to list their ailments and purchase a suitable cure. Over near the glass case containing silver and enamelled snuffboxes, a dark-complexioned man with vicious eyes calculated the worth of the merchandise and licked his tongue across his teeth when he spotted Merriment's trousered legs. He rubbed his thumb over the top of his silver-headed cane and slipped quietly out into the street as a tall, narrow-faced man lobbed three rocks through the shop window. The glass shattered with a loud splintered ringing, and the room surged away from the tumbling glass and cracking mullions, everyone crying out, the rocks hitting different customers. Over the tumult someone hollered, 'Witch,' and Merriment rushed through the crowd, flinging the door open in time to see three men dashing towards the quays.

*

At the same time as three men thundered down Fishamble Street, Chesterfield Grierson ordered a juicy chop for lunch and Corker bought twelve pies from Gloria to bring home to his starving siblings.

'Not much news since the Dolocher.' He grinned broadly, showing all his crooked teeth. 'Sol's let me off early and given me me wages and here I am givin' me earnings to you.'

'For the best pies in Dublin,' Gloria chuckled. 'Here,' she tossed in some extra pies, ''cause we go way back.'

469

'You're a cracker, Gloria, with the best kettledrums this side of the Liffey.'

'Cheeky,' Gloria laughed, and she wrapped Corker's pies in brown paper.

Down the road, Philmont tapped on the door to Solomon's office and in a low tone began, 'There's a . . .' He paused, his brows dipping as he searched for the words. 'There's a gentleman here to see you. Says he has a story you might be interested in.'

Solomon put down his quill, flung a log onto the fire and blandly said, 'Show him in.'

He heard Philmont coolly announce, 'Mister Fish will see you now,' and turned to greet his visitor. His heart sank instantly as the edges of a blue nipped jacket filled the door frame. Pearly was grinning broadly.

'Mister Fish,' he smirked, jumping theatrically into the chair opposite Solomon's desk. He drew out the blade from his sleeve and began spinning it on the desk before Solomon.

'I'm here with a message from Billy Knox.'

*

When Solomon returned home he found the windows boarded up and Beresford sitting in the anteroom drinking wine and laughing.

'You've missed an exciting day,' Beresford grinned, rising from his chair and leaving his empty glass on the table. 'Merriment's been arresting zealots.'

Beresford grabbed his cloak and flung a whole pound note down near his empty glass.

'For the windows,' he explained.

'Don't be ridiculous,' Merriment objected. 'They won't cost the colour of that.'

'Oh, I think you'll find craftsmen expensive and if your reputation as a witch continues you might discover you've to

470

pay to have yourself exorcised before the glaziers will replace the panes.'

'Very droll.' Merriment pinched back a smile and Solomon watched her fold the bank note and pass it back to Beresford. 'I owe you enough already,' she smiled.

Beresford took the money and Solomon watched him slip it into his waistcoat pocket, wondering at how for some people money was just paper to be flicked away or crumpled up. Some had so much currency that their word alone could purchase buildings, while for others, he mused, thinking mostly of himself, money was as difficult to catch as a moonbeam on water.

While Merriment let Beresford out, Solomon rattled the coal in the fire and sent a flurry of sparks up the chimney. He stood gazing down at the flames thinking about Hawkins' execution. It had satiated the populace: most were very satis-fied that the Dolocher had been annihilated. Although the criminal fraternity had slinked into the shadows and were keeping a low profile, they still went about their business unperturbed. The bicameral House of Aldermen and House of the Sheriff and Commons had mustered up enough force to keep the Dublin gangs visibly off the streets, but there were not enough resources, not enough room in the gaols to arrest every thief and murderer in the city. So Billy Knox and the Cut ate in polite coffee houses, sending their henchmen out at twilight, giving them enough gin and coin to bribe the night watch, and their respective gangs curtailed their crimes to low-key extortion and the quiet subterfuge of moonlight smuggling. Pearly had very politely managed to rob Solomon of ten more shillings. Solomon knew there was nothing for it. He was going to have to pay Billy Knox, somehow.

Merriment paused at the threshold. 'You look despondent.'

Solomon reached for his bag and pinched it open.

471

'Thought you might like this,' he smiled, handing her an object wrapped in cloth.

Merriment immediately recognised the weight and beamed. 'The Answerer. Ah, my old friend.' She turned the pistol over in her hand.

'Merri.' Solomon swept a strand of hair away from his face. 'I've got myself into a bit of trouble.'

*

Solomon slipped into the Cock and Hen, his heart pounding in his chest as he scanned the tables and benches looking for Billy Knox and Pearly. The air was thick with pipe smoke and the choking fumes of turf that billowed from the smoking chimney. Jenny was draped over the bar chatting to two sailors and some builders were kicking cement off their boots and grinding it into the straw strewn over the floor. There was no music tonight, no high jinks or festivities. Merriment squeezed Solomon's hand and whispered, 'Is he here?'

Solomon shook his head and nodded to Badger, who was drunk and waving from a far corner.

'Here, Solomon Fish, Harry wants to lighten yer pockets. Bring the half-wench with ye.'

And Solomon made his way over to the card table, casting Jenny a quick glance as he passed.

'Did ye ever see Bombay?' Harry grinned at Merriment.

'I did,' she said, wrapping her wet cloak tight and nodding to the barmaid to get her attention.

Solomon swept a hand over his damp brow. 'Where's Billy tonight?' He looked across at the corner where Billy Knox usually sat.

'Eating crumpets with the strumpets,' Badger chortled, flinging a handful of coins onto the table. He grinned up at Solomon. 'Now, are ye in or out?'

It took a pitcher of gin for Badger to reveal that Billy Knox would be holding court in the Cock and Hen on Friday after nine o'clock. Once they got that information Merriment and Solomon stood up to go.

'Ah, here,' Badger slurred, but he was too drunk to object and in the process of complaining became distracted by Harry, who was making up some rhyme about Badger's lack of manhood.

Jenny sneered a goodbye as they were leaving. Merriment paused at the door when she spotted one of her customers, a portly woman with gout, weeping in the corner and being comforted by a thin woman with an inflamed boil above her left eyebrow.

'Misses Jessop?' Merriment ventured over. 'Everything all right?'

The thin woman glared at Merriment's breeches and spied the pistol strapped to her side.

'It's our husbands,' the thin woman sniffed. 'She likes hers.' Then taking a swig of gin, she bawled over to Jenny, 'Jen, another round of kill-grief, if ye please.'

Solomon gently placed his hand on Merriment's lower back, letting her know he was with her.

'Is your husband sick?' Merriment asked Misses Jessop.

'He's missing,' the thin woman sniffed. 'And my Fred's gone gallivantin' too.'

Misses Jessop paused between her tears to knock back a finger of gin before resuming weeping again. 'I'm that distressed,' she blurted.

'She's that distressed,' the thin woman continued, her boil glowing in the candlelight. 'It's the new boss. Everyone's mad to have Hawkins back. Someone wanted to snick him in the jugular to see if that'd revive him from the hanging. I ask ye. I've seen toddlers fighting over a rattle with more brains.'

'My Jessop.' Misses Jessop's fleshy face folded towards her nose as she squeezed out her tears.

'Her Jessop's quiet.' The thin woman clacked her tongue.

'But my Fred, he dances that much ye could put him in a barrel of grapes and he'd make wine.' Then, hailing Jenny for more drink, she patted her fat friend's large knee and said, 'Come on, Assumpta, Jessop will fetch home with a story, and sad to say my Fred will turn up and all, worse luck.'

Merriment nodded and said she was sorry for Misses Jessop's trouble and gave Jenny a shilling to buy the two women another round.

'Used to work for Hawkins,' Solomon whispered close to her ear, drinking in the scent of her skin as he squeezed her hand. 'Hightailed it as soon as we arrested the man. They're lying low.'

They stepped out into the blustering night. It was lashing rain and the wind was gusting from the south-west, pushing fierce squalls before it. Torrents spilled from the oppressively dark sky, making the pitch in the torch at the end of the lane spit and smoke. Merriment and Solomon ran laughing as the heavens washed down over them. They piled into a doorway desperate for shelter and Solomon wrapped his arms under Merriment's cloak and pulled her towards him, both of them soaked, their eyelashes and hair jewelled with raindrops, their breath warm and fragrant as they kissed.

The wind whistled down along eaves, rattling old doorways and sending an abandoned bottle rolling and clinking over the cobbles. Water gushed along the gutters, dragging all kinds of litter with it. On the river the tethered ships bobbed. The rigging snapped against the masts like whips and the bells chimed, sending a flurry of notes tinkling over the choppy waters. Loose slates whistled out of the sky and smashed on the street below, while theatre-goers bolted from their reveries into awaiting carriages and chair carriers grumbled as they heaved into the wind and rain, their cloaks blowing open useless in such bad weather.

Once the squall had passed and the rain was pushed

northwards a chink in the tattered clouds revealed a half moon. It hung in the stormy sky washing the wet city with an eerie blue light. Torn clouds scudded in wraiths before it. Merriment looked up at the chimney stacks illuminated in bright relief, able to distinguish the ochre colour of the clay chimney pots. Her eyes followed the line of gleaming roofs washed with pools of pale moonlight. She shivered a little at the empty windows, filled with a sombre and foreboding darkness, and felt grateful to be in Solomon's arms. For the first time in many years she was glad not to be at sea.

Solomon kissed Merriment's cheek. 'Billy Knox will want protection money,' he told her. 'No matter how much we pay him off.'

Merriment looked at his handsome face, admiring his features picked out in the pallid light, his good looks chiselled by shadows and bright planes, his eyes vivid blue and full of intelligence.

'We'll threaten him with Beresford. Anyway there's talk that the two houses are to be joined and formed into a new cooperation. The guilds are demanding that the city be cleaned up. All these felons are bad for business.'

'You're bad for business.' Solomon squeezed her tight.

'What does that even mean?' Merriment asked, but they were too happy to care about making sense.

27

The Pits

On the Thursday evening following the hanging Janey Mack sat at the table in the anteroom learning her letters, while Merriment mixed up recipes.

'This is a C, Janey.' Solomon dipped his quill and carefully drew the letter C for Janey Mack to copy.

'It's shockin' hard to make ciphers.' Janey Mack wiped her face with a tea towel and squeezed and stretched her fingers. 'Ye do have to pinch the feather tight and ye have to be very quick or the ink will run off on ye.'

'But you're very good.' Solomon patted her shoulder reassuringly and glanced up at Merriment as she spooned seeds into a mortar and began to grind out the unguent oils locked inside the flecked shell. She smiled back at him, her heart full of the new delight of being in love and having a family. Lost in the soft perfection of the moment, they were all startled to hear an urgent rapping on the front door. Solomon heard his name being called.

'It's Corker!' He dashed for the door.

'Sol.' Corker fell into the shop breathless and wet. 'Ye have to come.' He grabbed Solomon's arm. 'Get a lantern and yer notebook.'

'What is it?' Janey Mack squeezed her hand.

'There's murder, over in the tannery.'

*

The tannery on Tannery Lane was a dark, unremarkable building fronted by a wide forecourt and surrounded by a high wall. The gates were open and the yard was buzzing with activity. Three horses and carts had pulled up near the archway that led into the back courtyard where the pits were. Clumps of cloaked men swinging lanterns stood in sundry groups talking and laughing and waiting for someone official to crack an order. Solomon and Corker made their way through the spitting rain past the sundry groups and cut into the archway, unhindered by questions from the beadles or the night watch. The air was so thick and noxious that Solomon was forced to cover his nose and mouth with his cloak. He held his lantern before him, the candlelight throwing faint shadows up along the glistening walls and over the wet ground as he stepped into the back courtyard.

Before him were four large, foul-smelling pits, all filled with urine and excrement mixed with water, and soaking in the repugnant pools, floating like strange lotus flowers, were various cow hides. Solomon's eyes smarted as the offensive blast of the pits' odour assaulted his system.

'Jesus,' he hissed, burying his nose deep in the folds of his dark worsted cloak. Corker covered his face with a scarf and pointed at three men across the way who were peering into one pit in particular, their lanterns glittering on the poisonous liquid, picking out swirls of floating turds and mottled hides. They stared into the dark pool, where, bobbing face down among the excrement and skins, was a man.

Solomon skirted the pits, making his way forward just as one of the men slapped a grappling hook into the toxic water and hauled the body to the side. The other two heaved the bloated corpse up, letting the dead man flop onto his back and gaze at the cloudy night.

Solomon stooped in beside them and stared down at the dead man's face. The left side of his skull had been hammered in and the corrosive agencies in the pit water had already begun to eat away at the dead man's scalp. But despite the condition of the corpse, Solomon immediately recognised the dead man's face.

'It's Jessop,' he said, his heart racing in his chest.

The three men with him were astounded. 'Ye know him? I never seen him before. Who's he to ye?'

The night watch was called over.

'This fella knows the deceased.'

The night watch was a crotchety octogenarian with poor hearing. He carried an elaborate horn and held it to his ear.

'In all me years,' he moaned, 'I never seen the like. A young lad fell in the pit once. We got him out in a flash but he died of the fumes and foul water. Me job is to lock the gates and make sure no one steals the tans. The better skins are locked in there.'

He pointed to a large bolted shed secured by an enormous lock.

'I have worked here nigh on forty years and never had no trouble.' The night watch waved his enormous conch-like hearing implement at the sky. Used to being deaf, he took full advantage of his ailment and kept talking, regardless of the others.

'I came out to piss into the pit when what do I see but a floating bulge. At first I thought it was a sack of meal, can't say why, just came to me that that was what it was, and then I sees the neck and ear and I thinks to meself, well, Cyril, I thinks, this is trouble and I ran and fetched the beadles.'

The night watch looked down at Jessop's dead features and shook his head.

'Never seen him before. He never worked here. Never called into the yard.'

'This fellow knows him,' said the man who had fetched the grappling hook.

'Do ye?' The night watch stuck the horn into his ear.

478

Solomon shouted into the hearing implement, aware of the faintly comic absurdity of standing in the rain besmirched with splashes of excrement and choking in the overpowering air.

'He was a consort of Mister Hawkins,' Solomon roared, thinking of Jessop's fat wife weeping into her gin in the Cock and Hen. She had been right to be worried.

'Fine death for him, so,' the night watch declared, removing his hearing aid to take full charge of the conversation again. 'Ye don't think,' he said, scowling, his thick bushy brows rushing to meet the bridge of his nose, 'it couldn't be that the Dolocher is back, could it? If something jumped from Olocher to Hawkins on the night he died, couldn't something jump from Hawkins to someone else?'

'The Dolocher wasn't a demon,' Solomon said, but the night watch was developing his own theory.

Solomon glanced at Jessop's foul corpse, took a few notes then surreptitiously cocked his head at Corker and they both slipped away to the edge of the pit while a few men drifted into the courtyard to take a look at Jessop lying dead in the rain.

'Let's take a look around,' he whispered. Corker managed to filch a lantern and followed him up a narrow flight of stairs into a long musty corridor. Most of the doors were locked; those that were open led into pokey offices and cluttered storerooms.

'What are ye lookin' for?' Corker asked, following Solomon back down into the yard and over to a ramshackle cluster of makeshift sheds.

'I don't know.' Solomon pushed in one door, swung the lantern high and stopped in his tracks, the blood draining from his face, his hands shaking. He gasped as he recognised the ornate sleeves and nipped waist of a blue jacket. He stood gazing at Pearly, who seemed to float out of the musty gloom, the lantern light picking out odd details, little flashes of yellow glittering on the sleeves, the buttons, the tips of his shoes. Pearly's body dangled gruesomely inches off the floor. He had been strung up so that the ground was tantalisingly close to his feet. His face was swollen and purple and contorted into a bizarre expression as his lips curled away from his perfect smile, exposing his neat white row of teeth. His eyes were bloodshot and bulged out over his grotesque grin. Someone had slashed his belly, so that as he swung he bled; his breeches and boots were saturated in blood, and chits and receipts and torn pages from his notebook floated in the crimson pool that oozed thickly over the dirt floor.

'Christ.' Corker staggered back and catching hold of Solomon's arm held himself upright as his knees buckled.

Solomon swallowed and reached up to gingerly touch Pearly's swollen face, wincing with disgust that his first thought was that perhaps now he would be free of his debts.

'Still warm,' he muttered.

Corker pointed back out into the tannery yard. 'Did the lad in the pit string this fella up?' he wondered, the curiosity of touching a corpse getting the better of him as he glanced his fingertips over the dead man's knuckles. 'Look,' he whispered, pointing at down at a floating page, 'that says Merriment's shop, doesn't it?'

Solomon stared at the line of figures and quickly understood that Pearly had been watching Merriment's shop, totting up guessed earnings.

'He meant to rob her,' Solomon whispered.

'Did he?' Corker gasped as Solomon took the lantern and moved deeper into the partitioned shed. Corker whispered fearfully, 'Where are you going?' Solomon didn't answer, he just moved forward, holding the lantern high and examining all around him. The shed was crammed with pallets and old tools and was partitioned by haphazard oddments, nailed-together doors, old packing boxes and barrels stacked high, torn skins, mottled and patchy and of little or no value. The atmosphere was rank, thick with dust and foul smells. The interior was pitch dark, the lantern's feeble light barely penetrating six feet around.

A long sheet of tarpaulin hung like a screen from one of the rafters. Hidden behind it was a tiny stove with a pot still bubbling on the dying embers. To one side of the stove was a tattered mattress covered with filthy blankets, and stuffed into a set of broken shelves was a bag.

'Someone was hiding out here.' Corker peeked into the cooking pot and saw potatoes split and boiled to mush. 'Someone was cookin' their dinner.' Solomon tugged out the bag and rifled through it. He drew out a small shirt and a crumpled cap and immediately thought of Fred's wizened face.

'Fred and Jessop were holed up here.' Solomon sat on the edge of the makeshift bed.

'D'ye think so?' Corker paused.

Solomon looked at the hat in his hand and sucked a moment on his lower lip.

'The man in the blue jacket hanging from the rafters was a bully who worked for Billy Knox. Did you ever hear of him?'

Corker nodded mutely, tugging a moment at his cowlick and swallowing back his anxiety.

'How do you know them?' he asked, but Solomon didn't answer. He sat frowning, his heart thumping in his chest, all his thoughts converging on one point: anyone who had worked for Hawkins and who may have double-crossed or plotted against Billy Knox was being murdered.

Solomon shoved the hat back into the bag. 'I think there is a new boss in town.'

He stood up and sighed, looking at the filthy mattress. A dark thought pierced his mind, luminescent, sudden and half formed, as the memory of Hawkins lurching forward in the dock screaming 'I am innocent' cut through Solomon's certainty and left him feeling utterly doubtful. What if Billy Knox had known Hawkins had been using his men? What if Hawkins had been telling the truth? What if he had been stitched up? The clashing times in the witness statements now rang with an accusatory clarity. A cold chill rushed through Solomon's body, a tight pressure squeezed around his heart. What if Billy Knox had manufactured the Dolocher? Solomon's thoughts spun, recalling the curiously vacant glint and hardened cruelty of Billy Knox's stare. He thought of the chits of paper floating in Pearly's blood. He thought of Merriment's face.

'Do ye think this Fred fella is dead somewhere here?' Corker asked him, as he prised open the lid of a battered tin he'd found stuffed under the mattress.

'Could be.' Solomon licked his dry lips anxiously. 'Listen, we have to go.'

Corker looked into the tin and almost keeled over backwards. A sheaf of curled pound notes had been stuffed into the faded tea canister.

'Mother of God,' he howled. 'There must be twenty pounds here.'

Solomon counted the money.

'There's no way anyone would leave this behind.' He frowned, looking up at the rafters, his heart stopping in his throat. There, floating, suspended in the gloom, was a face. A narrow, wizened face, unshaven and twitching, washed over by shadows and barely discernible in the paltry candlelight. A creamy smear of angles with flashing eyes that jolted as soon as Solomon looked up. The face desperately scrambled backwards, trying to conceal itself in the shadows. Dust and specks of earth and plaster crumbled to the floor.

'What is it?' Corker reached for a lump of wood and watched, shocked, as Solomon dropped the money, fetched a broom handle and bellowed up into the roof, poking at the rafters, 'Get down, Fred. I've seen you, for Christ's sake.'

Fred squealed and fell to the ground with a thud, rolling up onto his feet and crouching with his arms extended and a pistol in one hand.

'He's here.' He trembled, his voice screeching pitifully, his eyes popping wildly as he spun searching the shadows. 'Gone mad. He's taken to it, all the killing, all the killing. Ye have to help me.'

'Who's here?' Solomon demanded, grabbing a stray bar that had been leaning on a broken chair. He glanced behind him, terrified that Billy Knox was crouching in the gloom.

Fred spun in a frantic circle, his body jerking with spasmodic shocks, his eyes darting.

'Please,' Fred hissed. 'He's going to kill me.' He froze. 'Did ye hear that?'

Corker receded. The tarpaulin lifted. Fred squealed, rushing away, knocking over a barrel, quenching the lantern. He staggered, reeled round and fired his pistol. The crack of the discharge snapped loud and hard.

Corker flinched and wailed, falling backwards. Solomon lurched forward, scrabbling in the gloom, calling Corker's name. The cinders from the fire cast the barest orange glow. A huge form crept out of the shadows. A black swine's snout glimmered a moment. Fred howled, thrashing frantically, desperate to escape. Solomon's ears thrummed, his heart pounded. He saw the blackness move. The outline of a large pig's skull. He heard a visceral squelch. Fred's voice suddenly vanished. There was a dull thud. A crash. Fred had been asphyxiated.

Silence.

Solomon searched the darkness.

Nothing.

'Corker?' he hissed urgently, stumbling in the direction he had seen Corker fall.

Outside he could hear a hue and cry, the thunder of feet rushing across the tannery yard. Five men with hooks and blades and lanterns rushed into the shed, shouting and hollering, wanting to know what was going on, one of them screaming, 'There's a corpse hanging here.'

'In here,' Solomon shouted. A man with a lantern dragged back the tarpaulin and the light fell on Corker's shaking body.

'Jesus Christ,' Solomon cried, diving towards him, his eyes falling on the boy's bloodstained shirt. 'You're going to be all right, lad.' He trembled, his hand pressing on the bubbling wound.

Corker coughed, his face washed white and spectral, his brown eyes filled with terror.

'Sol,' he whispered, his fingers reaching for Solomon. 'It hurts.'

Solomon's lower lip puckered. Desperate to do something, anything, he scooped his arms under Corker's knees and shoulders. 'I'll take you to Merri's,' he blubbered.

'Wait,' Corker whispered, his body contorting in agony. 'I . . .' He struggled for breath, his fingers winding softly around Solomon's hand.

Solomon lowered him gently down onto the floor, holding him in his arms.

'You're going to be all right,' he whispered.

Corker groaned. A short hiss emanated from his mouth. His body suddenly stilled. His expression softened. His fingers fell loose. Something in his eyes vanished as he stared blankly up at nothing in particular.

*

Janey Mack cried inconsolably as Corker's body was laid on the table. Solomon was deathly pale, his blue eyes burned red raw from crying. Merriment trembled as she fetched a basin of scented water and slowly and stiffly began preparing poor Corker's body for the grave.

'I should have sent him home,' Solomon whispered and Janey Mack sobbed, her little heart broken.

484

'He was me best friend,' she wept. 'And shockin' good to his brothers and sisters and his mam, even though his mam'd drink. Why would anyone want to kill him?'

'A bad man did it,' Solomon said and he buried his face in his hands and wept, his whole body shaking with inconsolable grief. 'The poor little lad,' he gulped. 'God help him. The poor little lad.'

Merriment paused, covering her mouth.

Solomon went to Merriment and, gently taking the cloth from her hand, said, 'Let me.'

He carefully washed Corker's frail bare chest and face and arms. They dressed him in a fresh shirt belonging to Solomon, and Janey Mack combed his hair and kissed his face and whispered to him all the places he had once told her he would visit.

'I'll go to Glendalough on yer behalf, Corker, and put a flower in Saint Kevin's Church for ye there. And I'll take a ship to London when I'm older and put a flower on Tower Bridge in memory of ye. And I'll go to Queenstown and fling a rose into the sea to honour ye and I'll never forget ye, I promise. Never.'

Janey Mack's whispering broke Solomon's heart. He crumpled in the chair and cried, shaking his head with grief and disbelief. Merriment wrapped her arms around him and stroked his hair, fighting back the tears, desperate to be strong for Solomon's sake.

Janey Mack lit two corpse candles and placed them by Corker's head. She found a small Bible and folded his hands over it, entwining rosary beads around his fingers.

'He kept his family goin',' Janey Mack sniffed. 'Ye looked after him, Sol. Gave him a chance and he was doin' fine and dandy, workin' in a grand office, drinking port with yer man Chesterfield and ordering that lad at the office about.'

Solomon's heart stung listening to Janey Mack repeat the tall tales Corker had told her about his own advancement.

'He loved you, Sol.' Janey Mack's lower lip quivered. 'Ye gave him a chance.'

Solomon blinked and turned his face away.

'Say some prayers, Janey,' Merriment quickly interjected, desperate to ease Solomon's grief. She took Solomon's hand and squeezed it. Solomon bit back the tears. 'Merri,' he whispered. 'There's something you need to know.'

He glanced over at Janey Mack as he slipped out into the shop, and waited for Merriment to join him. 'The Dolocher. It wasn't Hawkins. He's still out there, somewhere.'

He rolled his eyes as a realisation suddenly dawned on him. 'The boots,' he muttered. 'Of course.'

'What boots?' Merriment asked.

'That day on the gallows, as Hawkins was swinging, I noticed his feet. He had small feet and the boots by the fender the night we found the Dolocher's lair, those boots were large. Damn it to hell.' He brushed back a wedge of blond hair, frustrated and distraught. 'I have to find him.'

Merriment's face was pasty white, her eyes wide with sorrow. 'You have the militia searching for him.'

She gently pressed her hand to his distressed face and wiped her thumb over his cheek. 'Sol, this is a terrible business.' She searched his eyes. 'There was nothing you could have done.'

But he couldn't hear her, couldn't bear the words.

'That little lad' – he pointed into the anteroom, his lips shaking – 'what had he to do with any of them?' He was trembling with rage, barely able to breathe, when a knock came on the shop door.

'Mister Fish,' someone called in and Solomon wiped his face and drew back the lock.

Two militia with flaming torches stood before him.

28

The Cock and Hen

Solomon stood beside Merriment outside the front of the shop bleakly listening to the soldiers who had been among the patrol that had searched the tannery outbuildings high and low.

'Vanished,' one said, 'into thin air.'

Solomon groaned and shook his head. 'He's not a demon,' he hissed in despair. 'His name is Billy Knox and he is the Dolocher.'

The soldiers looked pale and tired; it was after one o'clock in the morning. The city was deathly quiet. A red baleful moon hung low on the horizon, casting an eerie light over the silent streets. In the anteroom Janey Mack was sitting at Corker's side, holding his hand, saying countless prayers over his clean and sweet-smelling corpse.

'We've searched the Black Dog, the docks, the safe houses, all the places you told us. There's no sign of him,' one of the soldiers sniffed, scratching his nose.

'He's escaped somehow. Call up more soldiers, look harder, leave no stone unturned.'

'We're doing our best, Mister Fish. The boats are being searched as we speak, in case he has decided to stow away. He must know we're on to him.'

Merriment squeezed Solomon's arm. 'Come on, Sol, come inside.'

Solomon leaned against the shop front and dragged his hands over his face as the soldiers strode away in the direction of Dublin Castle.

'I can't.' He bit down on his lower lip, unable to go back inside and see poor Corker's dead corpse laid out on the table. He took Merriment's pistol from its holster.

Merriment reached for him. 'Sol, what are you doing?'

'I'm going to find Billy Knox,' he growled, storming off up the road.

She rushed after him. 'Wait,' she pleaded. 'You can't go alone. Where are you even going? What do you think you're going to do?'

'He's a man, Merri. A pernicious, nasty, evil man, not some demon with supernatural powers. A man in a pig's skin. He's flesh and bone and I'm going to kill him with your pistol. Now, go back to the shop.'

'You can't.' Merriment could feel herself getting frantic. She glanced back at the partially open door. Janey Mack's wan face peeked out.

'Get back inside,' she called, then turned back to Solomon, who was charging off. 'But where do you think he is?' she called forlornly, only able to pick out Solomon's blond hair and the tops of his shoulders washed in pallid moonlight. He vanished silently into the shadows.

'Damn.' She gritted her teeth.

'Where's he going?' Janey Mack whispered.

'Come on.' Merriment shooed her back inside and they both stepped into the anteroom to hold vigil over Corker's frail body. Merriment glanced anxiously at the door, swallowing back her fears. *Solomon will be all right,* she reasoned. *Billy Knox will be hiding out, gone to ground. He won't be long.*

And convinced that Solomon would be home shortly, she sat by the fire, watching Janey Mack walk in circles around

Corker, touching the young boy's white face and fingers and fussing over his cowlick, trying to smooth down his hair.

*

Fearless with grief and boiling with a need to avenge, Solomon strode towards Christchurch market, his face locked in grim determination. The red moon hung low beneath the steeple, casting a malevolent ruby light. The statue of the devil that at one time had overlooked his stall emerged ominously out of the gloom, the black motionless figure of Lucifer baleful in the garnet moonlight. Solomon rushed past, hurrying towards the vague grey gateway that cut behind the ancient cathedral walls, the Answerer in his hand, the image of Corker's dead face propelling him along the dreary, narrow passageway of Hell. Blind with rage he marched fearlessly through the dark alley, his footsteps echoing on the cold, still air. He cut onto Winetavern Street and down along Cooke Street. The city seemed deserted. Silent. Tense. Solomon moved quickly, coming to the gloomy, locked-up premises of the Cock and Hen.

'Jenny,' he hollered at the top of his lungs, hammering the door. His voice was frantic, raw. 'Jenny, it's me. Solomon Fish.'

He listened, his breath quick and anxious.

He thought he heard a pattering of steps.

He hammered the door again.

'Jenny.'

The latch swung back. The door flung open.

'Oh, Sol.'

Jenny was dishevelled, her face blotched raw from crying. She looked frantically about her and pulled him through the door. The tavern was ablaze with candles. The light was blinding.

'Sol,' she whimpered, terrified, her fingers curled as she pressed her fist against her anguished lips.

'What is it?' Solomon clutched her arm.

'I have to go.' Jenny twitched. 'I have to get out of here.

Bring me to a boat. My bag's upstairs, Sol, I'll only be a minute.'

She turned to dash upstairs, her body pitching forward. Solomon grabbed her, hauled her back, his eyes snapping to a corner. Divided by the wall jutting from a snug, he could see the shoulder of a man sitting with his back to him.

'Jenny,' he hissed, keeping his voice low, his eyes fixed on the man. 'Where's Billy Knox? Where's his safe house?'

'Oh Sol, it was awful. I hid in the cellar. I couldn't come up. If you'd have heard his voice. If you'd have heard it.'

Jenny began crying, her mouth opening in a raw, terrified, silent bawl. She shuddered, her whole body wracked with fear.

'Jenny.' Solomon bit down on her name, his jaw hard and determined.

'Look what he did,' Jenny snivelled, pointing a jagged finger at the man sitting across the way. Solomon dropped her arm and, raising the Answerer, he cautiously approached the sitting man, his breath coming in quick shallow drafts.

'You,' he called, expecting the man to turn.

The shoulder stayed motionless. Solomon saw the jaw, the profile. He marched in front of the man and staggered to a halt, his head recoiling with disbelief, his breath catching, as he jolted backwards, confused.

Billy Knox stared back at him with wide horrified eyes. His throat had been slit, the wound a dark jagged gap. The exposed gullet glistened purple and a white sliver of spine was visible as Billy Knox's head leaned back against the wainscoting, his hands splayed on the table, his right index finger missing at the lower knuckle.

'Jesus,' Solomon gasped, raking his hand incredulously through his hair. Jenny clutched his arm, her eyes pathetically jerking around the room.

'He didn't know I was below,' she stammered. 'He tortured Billy Knox, asking Billy if he could see hell.' Jenny swallowed and clutched her heart. 'He said this was his town.'

'Who said?' Solomon gripped her shoulder.

Jenny shook her head.

'His voice, Sol, he kept whispering. I heard Billy fight him. I hid. I crouched behind barrels. Made myself small. Snuffed the candle. "This is for pointing with," he kept saying. I think it was Billy's finger he was talking about, I don't know. All I could hear was Billy gasping. Jesus, Sol, the sounds.'

Jenny's eyes darted towards the cellar door.

'I think he sat before Billy watching him die, talking to him. Whispering at something, saying, "I am, I am. Listen to me, I am."'

'Who was it, Jenny?' Solomon squeezed her arm tight. 'Who did this to Billy?'

Jenny swallowed, shaking her head, her mouth contorting with fear. 'I think it was the devil, Sol.'

Solomon dragged her to the bar, opened a jar of whiskey and poured her a dram.

'Drink it,' he hissed. He gulped down a shot himself and glared over at the corpse of Billy Knox leaning back against the snug wall and dragged the back of his hand over his mouth. Who the hell was the Dolocher?

'The Cut,' Solomon hissed.

'Dead.' Jenny knocked back another glass, her face tight with fear. 'Found three hours ago: that's why Billy came here. Hiding out. He was alone. He was afraid, Sol. He knew something was after him. Said he was away to London on the morrow. Said . . .' Jenny couldn't stop the tears. She shook her head, petrified, wringing her hands.

'The devil kept whispering, "The only one who knows is the witch." Kept saying he was going to take her money. Give her what for. I thought he meant me, Sol.' Jenny's face crumpled. 'I thought he knew I could hear him and that he was going to do away with me. But then he said, "She knows me. Saw me in the backyard. Saw me with those witch eyes. I can't have that. Can't have that." I could only make out bits and pieces, Sol. Sometimes he laughed, then one time he shouted, "Witch will want to make a pet of me. Witch and demon. Demon and witch," and he sounded that angry, I tried to creep further away and I almost knocked a barrel over, and me heart, Sol, me heart.' Jenny gulped down another drink. 'He didn't come down the stairs. I held me breath, sure he was going to creep down and do away with me. Sure I was to be cut up.' Jenny swallowed. 'He left. I heard him rustling. Hissing and whispering and then I heard the door close and I waited and I'm going, Sol, I'm leavin' here.'

Solomon's heart stuttered in his chest. He jolted, the blazing candlelight searing white, bleaching the room as the recollection of Merriment's words drove him forward: 'I've seen his eyes twice, Sol: once outside the back door, and last night.'

'Sol,' Jenny wailed as he bolted away from her, throwing open the door and running into the ghastly moonlit night.

*

Janey Mack had laid her head on her folded elbows and fallen asleep whispering to Corker. Merriment had dozed off in her chair when the handle to the front door turned slowly and pushed open. Merriment shifted, opening her eyes, the sound of the bells tinkling somewhere at the back of her consciousness, half heard. The candles had burned to a stub and quenched. She fumbled in the darkness, raking the embers to expose the red coals smothered beneath a layer of ash. She fetched a candle and bowed before the fire to light it but looked up when she heard a soft click, bemused as the door handle slowly turned.

'Sol?' she whispered hoarsely.

Janey Mack blearily raised her head. The door creaked slowly open. A tall shape slid noiselessly into the room.

The Dolocher's demonic skull, dark and unearthly, cast a grotesque macabre shadow up the length of the wall. His black bristling face revolved as Janey Mack screamed and sprang to her feet. Merriment teetered backwards, emitting a muffled groan. The Dolocher came slowly forward, his dark snout moist, his tusks glowing dimly, his broad cloak sweeping over the floor. In one hand he held a severed digit between his forefinger and thumb, like he was dowsing, and he pointed it towards her.

'Stop,' Merriment whispered, her eyes falling to his other hand where a blade gleamed dully.

'There she is, the witch.' The Dolocher waved the severed finger, his voice a coarse faraway whisper coming from deep inside the black pig's skull. Janey Mack screamed at the top of her lungs, pulling Merriment back, tugging at her to run. The door behind the Dolocher was kicked wide. Solomon lunged in. The Dolocher spun round, the blade in his hand glancing high as he swiped for Solomon's arm, knocking the gun out of his grasp and pushing him back. Merriment pulled at the Dolocher's cloak; it slipped loose, exposing the dark bristled flesh of a black pig carcass.

The pistol shot cracked loud and sharp, the room blazed blue, the atmosphere scorched a moment by an icy phosphorescent light as the walls seemed to oscillate. The Dolocher stood a moment, the amputated finger drooping, before his legs buckled. He thudded to the floor, his head noisily clattering as his large pig jaw cracked on impact and a pool of dark blood spread across the flags.

Solomon hunched, clutching his bleeding arm, blinking through the gunsmoke as Merriment spun round to find Janey clutching the Answerer, her gaunt face frozen in an expression of terrified resolution, her huge eyes wide with shock.

'I killed him,' she stammered and, dropping the pistol, rushed into Merriment's arms, burying her face as she bawled. 'I killed him.'

'Good girl, Janey.' Merriment squeezed her tight. 'Good girl.'

Solomon staggered forward, checking that Merriment was not hurt.

'You all right?' he asked hurriedly.

Merriment nodded. It was all over.

Solomon wiped his hand over his brow, stepping over the corpse on the floor. He pulled away the rancid pig's skull and the cape of pig skin that hung around the Dolocher's shoulders and looked down at the contorted features of the corpse. The dead man had a large jaw and blue eyes, and his lips were pulled away from his teeth. His gums were speckled with the telltale signs of gum disease.

'You know him?' Merriment asked, touching Solomon's shoulder.

Solomon shook his head.

'No,' he whispered. 'I never saw him before.'

Epilogue

They buried Corker two days later.

The church was packed, which surprised Chesterfield Grierson more than it did Solomon. Corker may only have been fourteen years old, but his personality was such that he had inveigled his way into so many situations with such ragamuffin charm that he was well known and well liked. All of the stall-holders at the Christchurch market turned up for the funeral; even Jody Maguire made an appearance. Effie and Janey Mack wept the loudest and all his sisters sang a heartbreaking hymn while his mother stared stony-faced as the coffin was lowered down.

'Will the rain get inside his coffin?' Janey Mack asked, her large eyes beaded with tears. Merriment squeezed Janey Mack's hands.

Janey Mack looked over the gravestones as she walked out with Merriment, fastening her shawl with her free hand.

'I once had a notion, that maybe when we were older, we were thinking, I don't know how it came up, but he told me about it.' Janey Mack looked guiltily at Merriment. 'Before I was sure of me place with you, ye understand.'

Merriment nodded.

'We were thinking of joinin' the East India Company and goin' to take a look at some hot countries.' Janey Mack shook her head. 'I don't think we'd've done it, though. Not when push came to shove. He said he'd go to India on account of wanting to see a tiger with his own eyes.' Janey Mack bit the inside of her cheek, her chin puckering. 'I can't go to India to put a flower there to remember him by. I'm not sure how I'm goin' to get to London to do it.'

'We'll plant him a rose bush,' Merriment suggested. 'In a pot, outside the back door, to pretty up the yard. And if we ever move we can take Corker's rose bush with us.'

'That'd be nice,' Janey Mack agreed, watching Corker's sisters miserably filing through the church gate, their poor tired bones wrapped in threadbare rags. 'We're not going to move though, are we, miss?'

Merriment shook her head.

Anne and Stella gave Janey Mack a bag of fudge to take home by way of some small comfort.

'We bought them between us,' Stella said. 'We know what good friends ye were.'

Solomon collected donations and paid Ethel over in the Boar's Den three guineas to put on a good spread for Corker. The funeral party lasted well into the night, with Corker's mother toasting her beloved eldest son with a tankard of gin.

*

The Dolocher's corpse was laid out in the largest lecture theatre in the College of Surgeons and the public were invited to call in to see if they recognised the man who had shocked the city for so long. The pig's skull he had worn on his last attack was pickled in an enormous jar and morbidly displayed next to the corpse, while a queue of eager onlookers filed past and shook their heads.

Chesterfield Grierson pressed a scented hanky to his nose and glared at the passing crowd.

'It's decomposing,' he complained. 'This fellow will have to be autopsied soon. If we leave it any longer he'll fill with gas and, I don't know, erupt.'

'It's been two days,' Solomon sighed, 'and no one knows who the hell he is. Someone had to know him.'

He stared at the corpse covered with little more than a sheet: the edges of the Dolocher's dead flesh was slowly beginning to tinge with patches of blue and yellow, his abdomen had begun swelling as the juices in his intestines fermented and expanded. Solomon watched one woman laugh and nudge her friend, while two men seemed to be betting one another about the amount of teeth in the Dolocher's head.

The people coming to view the Dolocher's corpse ranged from the simplest and the poorest to the most elevated and refined. Even Judge Coveny dropped in and took a moment to chat to Solomon and clack his tongue.

'Oddest damn thing I ever heard of. Mind you, if you'd met Olocher, now there was a man linked to the devil if ever I met one. Had the most sinister eyes and a kind of electricity about him, charged the air with a peculiar sort of prickling discomfort. Unnerving scoundrel, so he was. And there's his demon.' Coveny waved his silver-tipped walking cane at the discolouring cadaver and sniffed. 'The malfeasance carried out by that rogue there was inspired by a very special kind of blackness, if you ask me. Damned Dolocher. Let's hope this is the end of it.'

Judge Coveny had brought his young nephew to inspect the corpse and took the opportunity to lecture those near him about the corrosive vices that an unschooled imagination can manifest.

'Temperance and rational thinking, that's what we must encourage. Idleness and ignorance generate this sort of stuff. You should all read more books.'

Someone added, 'And go to church.'

This remark made Judge Coveny cough and splutter.

'Nonsense,' he growled. 'Blithering nonsense.'

Solomon sat on one of the student benches of the lecture hall, looking down on the trailing queue, scribbling notes into his notebook and wondering when Chesterfield Grierson would be back with his mutton pie when he spotted a shock of white hair in the crowd. He jumped to his feet and tripped down the steep steps, weaving through the queue until he stood before the shaking man and extended his hand.

'Boxty.' Solomon smiled.

'Mister Fish.' Boxty's numb face grimaced. 'I only heard today of yer encounter and me misses brought me here to see if I might know who it was did this to me; we were away.'

Boxty's wife smiled; most of her teeth were missing.

'You can skip the queue.' Solomon took his elbow. 'Come with me.'

He waved at a soldier standing guard and hurried Boxty as quickly as the lame man could move towards the cadaver laid on the cold, hard autopsy table.

Boxty's uneven eyes glared down at the corpse, his twisted mouth curling up at one side as he gasped in disbelief.

'Christ almighty,' he hissed. 'It's Martin. Martin Coffey from the Black Dog.'

*

When Solomon got home that afternoon and told Merriment, she couldn't believe it.

'It's sinister,' she whispered incredulously.

'I know,' Solomon agreed. 'It seems he came up with the idea to pay off some of his debts. Martin Coffey owed quite a bit of money and he wanted Hawkins off his back. Dreamed up the Dolocher and started robbing people. He organised the pig slaughter and it was at that point, I think, that he intended to get rid of all opposition, and stitched Hawkins up.' Solomon paused and shook his head. 'Then something, I don't know. He got a liking for it. Some other aspect.'

He tried to frame the unprecedented quality of Martin Coffey's sadistic cruelty. 'He seems to have identified with the demonic qualities of the Dolocher and just taken to killing, as Fred said.'

Merriment nodded and sighed, 'Which brings us back to Olocher and his predilections. It does make you wonder if something was whispering to both of them, if they came in contact with something otherworldly, or, were they naturally evil?'

'Exactly.' Solomon shivered as he paced the anteroom, agitated with excitement. 'That's the subject of my next article. I was thinking of opening like this: "In the dark recesses of a subterranean cell a condemned murderer whispered to his degenerate guard and a demonic notion sprang to life, as Martin Coffey with unparalleled cunning and unequalled ingenuity plotted to carry out a reign of terror that would scandalise and horrify an unsuspecting city . . . "'

Merriment raised her eyebrows, kissing Solomon as he passed.

'Sounds like the opening to a novel,' she said.

Solomon stood back and cocked his head to one side.

'Do you think I should write a book?'

Merriment raised her brows and shrugged. 'Why not?'

Janey Mack ran into the anteroom grinning.

'Hiya, Sol,' she chirruped. 'What's happening?'

'He's going to write a book,' Merriment announced.

Janey Mack gasped, her eyes opening wide. 'Are ye, Sol?' She ran towards him, letting him scoop her up in his arms.

'I am.'

'Will I be in it?'

'Of course you will,' Solomon replied, and Janey Mack

squealed and hugged him tight, delighted by the notion of being immortalised in print.

'Oh, that's dandy,' she cried. 'That's the dandiest thing I ever heard,' and she squeezed his neck tight, holding her hand back to touch Merriment's head.

'We'll all be in it,' she sighed contentedly. 'Even Corker.'